TOR BOOKS BY KEN MACLEOD

THE FALL REVOLUTION

The Star Fraction
The Stone Canal
The Cassini Division
The Sky Road

THE ENGINES OF LIGHT

Cosmonaut Keep
Dark Light
Engine City

DARK LIGHT

KEN MACLEOD

A TOM DOHERTY ASSOCIATES BOOK
NEW YORK

This is a work of fiction. All the characters and events portrayed in this book are either products of the author's imagination or are used fictitiously.

DARK LIGHT

Copyright © 2002 by Ken MacLeod

Edited by Patrick Nielsen Hayden

A Tor Book
Published by Tom Doherty Associates, LLC
175 Fifth Avenue
New York, NY 10010

www.tor.com

Tor® is a registered trademark of Tom Doherty Associates, LLC.

ISBN: 0-765-34496-3

First edition: January 2002
First mass market edition: January 2003

Printed in the United States of America

0 9 8 7 6 5 4 3 2 1

To Andrew and Lesley

ACKNOWLEDGMENTS

Thanks to Carol, Sharon, and Michael, for more than usual.

Thanks to Farah Mendlesohn for reading and commenting on the draft and for historical information about Rawliston (any mistakes are mine); to Catherine Crockett for details about the sky people; to Rachael Lininger for help with the folk song; and to Mic Cheetham and Tim Holman for holding out for an ending.

Don't fear that philosophy's an impious way
—superstition's more likely to lead folk astray.

—Lucretius, *De rerum natura*, Book One
   paraphrased by Joanna Taine

Contents

1

Urbi et Orbi

RAWLISTON SPRAWLS; from space it's a grubby smudge, staining the glassy clarity of the atmosphere along fifty kilometers of coastline. Biggest city on the planet, home to a million or so human and other beings. Seven centuries old and ever renewed; two centuries on from the biggest jolt it ever got; hours away from another. It's coming like an earthquake, coming like a runaway train, coming like a lightspeed ship.

Stone froze in a cold sky. Around him, the glider's struts creaked and its cables sang. Hundreds of meters below his feet, the valley crawled. The Great Vale stretched fifty or so kilometers before him and the same distance behind him, its fields and towns, rivers and screes filling his sight. Through the imperfect glass disks of his goggles he couldn't quite see the mighty rockfalls at either end that had, thousands of years ago, isolated the valley, but he could just make out the distant gleam of the lake formed by Big River against the natural dam at the eastern end. The midmorning sun glimmered on a series of meanders in the river's fat, lazy length along the valley's broad floor. *The word for world is "valley,"* he thought, *and the word we use for ourselves is the "flying people," and the word the savages use for themselves is "people." Oh, but aren't we a sophisticated and self-conscious Stone Age civilization!*

He hung in a leather harness; the handles he gripped were made from the paired humeri of an eagle; the fabric of the wing above him was of hand-woven silk doped with alcohol-thinned pine resin; the craft's singing structural members were tensed bamboo, its cables vine and its stitching gut. Flint blades and bone needles and wooden shuttles had been worn smooth in its manufacture; no metal tool had touched it. No man, either; the whole process, from harvesting the raw materials through building it to this, its test flight, was women's work. It would be bad luck for a man to touch it until it had been brought safely back from its maiden flight and formally turned over. Stone wryly reflected on the canny custom that assigned the rougher and riskier parts of glider production—finding the eagle's carcass, tapping the resin, testing the craft—to women like him. He enjoyed the excitement and the solitude of these tasks, though they would not have been so welcome without the background of days he spent in the secure and companionable society of other women, working in long, airy sheds with the needle or the loom, the glass saw or the stone knife.

He banked into an updraught and followed its upward spiral, almost to a level with the mountain range on the western side of the valley. Below him, a pair of wing-lizards skimmed the corries. Two black flecks, their wingspans almost a third that of the glider. He kept a cautious eye on the upper slopes as he drifted past them; sneaking across the skyline was the preferred approach route for savage scouts and even raiding parties, and firearms were one product of the metalworking peoples whose use none of the stoneworking peoples—including his own—dared to disdain.

From his high vantage he could see the other aerial traffic of the valley: a few hot-air balloon-trains lofting to cross the eastern barrier on the way to Rawliston, dozens of other gliders patrolling the slopes or carrying urgent messages and light freight from one town to another. A quick upward turn of his head caught him a glimpse of a high, fast glint as one of the snake people's gravity skiffs, on some incomprehensibly urgent mission of its own, flashed across the sky like a shooting star. The skiffs were a common sight, starships rarer. Every few weeks a ship would follow the line of the Great Vale in a slow, sloping descent to Rawliston; it'd be at an altitude of two kilometers when it passed above the western end of the valley, down to a thousand meters by the time it reached the other.

Swinging out of the updraught, he set the machine on the long descending westward glide that would take him back to the launching-and-landing slope of the airfield above his native town, Long Bridge. He was following the course of Big River at a few hundred meters—an altitude quite low enough for him to smell the smoke from the kilns and see and hear children pointing and yelling at him from each village he passed over—when he heard a screaming from the sky to the north and west. Stone looked up.

Something huge and black hurtled in a second from the zenith to behind the hills, just ahead of him and to the left. Reflexively he closed his eyes, flinching in expectation of a crash and an explosion.

None came.

He sent a quick and self-consciously futile prayer of thanks to the indifferent gods and opened his eyes. What he saw made him almost shut them again. Behind the brow of the mountain range a vast, ramshackle contraption was rising like a malignant moon. Evidently the object seen falling, it moved forward, almost scraping

the summit. Lurching and yawing, it careened to above
the middle of the valley. Then it stopped, hanging in the
air half a kilometer away, right in front of him. It turned
around.

The air crackled; Stone could feel every hair on his
body prickle. He was still rushing forward, on a collision
course that in seconds would splatter him and the glider
across the front of the thing like a fly on goggles. He
swung his upper body forward and his legs up, and
tipped the the bone levers to tilt the glider into a dive.
Down and down, he aimed for Big River, in the slim
hope that if he couldn't pull out in time he might just
survive a crash into water.

The shadow of the unidentified flying object passed
over him. Something, not the air and not his own efforts,
slowed his descent, at the same time buffeting him as
though with invisible fists. He felt, incredulously, that
he was actually being lifted. Then the shadow and the
strange lightness passed, and he began to plummet again,
but now he was able to pull back. At fifty meters above
the river he was in level flight, at a speed that a small
and cautious upward flex on the controls turned into a
shallow climb.

The long bridge that had given the town its name
whipped beneath his feet like—so it seemed—a just-
missed trip wire. He banked leftward above the rooftops
of tile and thatch, slowing and spilling air as the field
came into view, closer and closer, he could see the
blades of grass, and then he was down with a thump that
jarred every cartilage from his ankle joints to the top of
his spine and running, running faster than he'd ever run
before, sprinting up the slope as fast as a man running
full pelt down it to take off, the glider still flying at
shoulder height and no weight at all, and then he could
slow and finally stop.

He stood for a moment, unbuckling the harness and
lifting the wing, then stepped out from under it and let
it sag to the grass behind him. His breath came in deep

sighing gusts; he could not control it. His legs shook; he could control them, and he walked stiffly away from the glider toward the sheds at the top of the field. Later he would ache. For now, he just felt an immense surge of exhilaration carrying him along.

Slow Leg, the pilot for whom Stone had been testing the new craft, waited for him under the eaves of the glider shed. In his twenties, a few years older than Stone, lounging elaborately against a log pillar, Slow Leg was clad in nothing but a short pleated skirt and a pose that showed off his chest, arm, and leg muscles to advantage.

His calm cracked to a wide grin as Stone approached.

"That was magnificent," he said. "That's a well-tested wing."

Stone grinned back, in unabashed gratitude for the laconic praise.

"It is yours," he said, controlling his breath as best he could. He took off his goggles and wiped sweat from his forehead, then removed the feather helmet.

Slow Leg nodded and walked past him and picked up the glider and carried it reverently to the shed, where he lifted it into an overhead rack and returned to the post and the pose.

"Thank you."

Stone dipped his head, then, formalities over, looked up and asked the question at the forefront of his mind: "What *was* that thing?"

"A ship."

Stone laughed. "That was never a ship. Unless the sea people have taken to crossing space in *rafts*."

"It did look like something lashed together from a bedstead and barrels," Slow Leg admitted, "but I don't think the sea people made it."

He had the look of someone waiting to tell a joke.

"The sea people don't *make* their ships," Stone said, teasing him with precision.

"All right," Slow Leg said. "It was not made by the

snake people for the sea people, like every other ship we have seen."

Stone stepped behind the straw-mat screen where he'd left his clothes and began unpicking the fastenings of his down-quilted jacket and trousers. Most pilots flew in nothing but a breechclout, but modesty and frailty were allowed for in test flying. Only men had to be tough enough to bare their skin to the high-altitude winds.

"So how do you know that, Slow Leg? Did the gods make it, and tell you in a dream?"

"I saw it with . . . my own vision!"

Slow Leg guffawed at his own joke; Stone laughed politely. He untied his long fair hair and shook it out, ducked into his knee-length blue silk tunic and stepped into the matching trousers, strapped on the sloping compressed-bark wedges of his sandals, and emerged from behind the screen. When he met Slow Leg's eyes again he noticed, as he had so often in the past, the subtle, swift shuttering—something as quick and involuntary as the nictitating membrane flicking across the eyes of one of the snake people—that signaled the sudden shift in the basis of their conversation. Slow Leg's literal stance shifted: He stopped leaning against the log and took a step back, and hooked his thumbs in his belt.

"Vision," he said, tapping beside his eye. "There was a name written on the side of the ship, and I read it."

Phenomenal visual acuity was normal among pilots; literacy was not. Slow Leg had some justification for the lazy self-satisfaction in his tone.

Stone let his eyes widen. "What was it?" His voice had taken, quite without artifice, a slightly higher pitch and lighter note.

Slow Leg sucked in his lips and gave a small shrug. "There were several words, or names," he said, "some of which had been painted over, but there were two words that were quite clear, in the Christian language and lettering . . ."

He paused again, playing a smile.

Stone spread his hands. "Please."

"Bright Star."

Stone mentally translated from the Christian.

"Bright Star?" He felt the pitch of his voice rise out of control, to an undignified squeak.

"That was what it said." Slow Leg shrugged. "Whether it was indeed that ship, I don't know."

He turned and gazed down the valley, as if he could still see it. "But it looked as one would expect that ship to look, and as for its piloting . . ." He chuckled.

"If that was flown by one of the sea people, they are in a bad way indeed. No, I think that was flown by a— you know the Christian word, a *human*."

"Or by one of the snake people?" Stone suggested. "A very experienced skiff pilot?"

Slow Leg passed a hand over his eyes. "Or a very inexperienced one!"

Stone smiled slyly. "It takes a very experienced pilot to dive down to ground level and then pull out. . . ."

Slow Leg shook his head in self-reproof, slapped Stone's shoulder, then let his arm drop awkwardly.

"Of course, of course," he said. "I forget myself. I must pour you a drink, Stone."

They walked along the front of the glider shed, mostly empty at this time of day, Slow Leg padding barefoot on the grass, with the almost imperceptible drag on the left foot that had inflicted his name, Stone stepping carefully in the short-paced gait imposed by the built-up heels of his sandals. Against the far end of the shed was an unattended table with a skin flask of beer propped in a wicker frame and a few pottery cups. Slow Leg ignored the beer, ducked under the table, and fished out a glass bottle of corn-mash spirit.

"Ah," said Stone. A smuggler.

Slow Leg smiled and winked as he filled two cups with the rough liquor, then hid the bottle again. He leaned an elbow on the table and raised his cup, then noticed Stone wasn't leaning on the grubby, sticky table.

He waved for a pause and hurried to drag up a stool.

"Thank you," said Stone, taking the seat.

Slow Leg resumed the toast. "High flights!"

"Safe landings," Stone said, heartfelt. The reaction was already getting to him, his body belatedly assimilating the reality of his narrow escape and beginning to tremble. He gulped, steadying himself, blinked as his eyes stung.

"Wooh!"

"Good stuff," said Slow Leg. He licked it off his lips, looked away, took another sip. He seemed to remember something.

"If that ship really was the *Bright Star,*" he said slowly, "then many things will change. Others will have recognized it too. It will be the talk of the valley within hours."

"You're right there," Stone said. His mind was still racing through the implications. They unfolded as though before his eyes, with the slow-motion inevitability of a glider crash. The *Bright Star*'s arrival, over two centuries ago at a world that he vaguely thought of as five years' journey away, was so fundamental to the sky people's whole existence that it was part of their religion. A late part, of course, but already seamlessly incorporated in legends that went back through countless generations to the Cold Lands, to what the Christians called Earth. The gods had brought that ship to the New Worlds, with its message of deliverance. Without it, the sky people's religion would in all likelihood no longer exist, and the sky people themselves would be miserable wretches.

If it had now arrived at Croatan, it could only be a portent.

"You realize," Stone went on, "that what happened today will be remembered in the stories of our people?"

"Of course," said Slow Leg. "It will be called something like, let me see, 'The Story of How Stone Fell from the Sky.' "

Stone laughed. "That sounds about right. Or 'How Slow Leg Almost Lost His Wing.' "

"That's how the women will tell it, yes," Slow Leg said wryly. "Oh, well, I suppose we will know the truth about the ship soon enough, and the consequences will be what they will be."

Stone nodded agreement with this profound but entirely uninformative remark. Slow Leg made a small chopping motion with his hand, to indicate that as far as he was concerned they'd said all there was to say on the subject. Stone waited politely for the man to introduce the next.

But Slow Leg hesitated, drank a little more, stared moodily into the distance for a minute before turning and saying abruptly: "You really are a very good pilot. That was truly amazing."

Stone looked down, as though modestly, thinking *here we go again*. He raised a hand and let it flap down from the wrist.

"I was lucky," he said. "The ship's spirit, its *field* "— he used the Christian word—"pulled me out of the dive."

"Even so. It took great skill and presence of mind. You are as good as a man."

There it was, the usual clumsy, well-meant but unwanted compliment. At least it was done. He smiled and, again as usual, fluttered his eyelashes. Slow Leg put down his cup and gave Stone a hard, steady look.

"I would be happy to have you flying with me."

"What is this?" Stone said. "A marriage proposal?"

That would have flustered him less than the kind of partnership that Slow Leg was, ever so deniably, suggesting: to join him in his smuggling.

Slow Leg laughed and threw a pulled punch in the direction of Stone's shoulder.

"One wife is enough! More than enough, to tell you the truth. No, seriously, Stone. Let me ask you, then: Would you be interested in flying with me?"

"That is not possible."

"Yes, it is. If we are careful."

Stone sipped the liquor and held up the cup. "I take it you already do some very careful flying."

Slow Leg nodded. "There are things we have that the councils of the Christians disapprove of, and they have things—such as this—that our elders frown upon. There is profit in the trade, if you are careful. But not enough profit—almost all our traders will stuff a few such items into each trip. I have been thinking. There must be some Christian things that the women want and that the elders and the councils forbid. Simple and light things, easily carried." He shrugged. "I would not know what they are. But you might."

"I can think of plenty," Stone said. "Steel needles, small sharp blades, scissors, eyeglasses . . ."

There were already a few such treasures in some of the women's hands, discreetly used and jealously hoarded; he knew of them only from glimpses and grumbles. The thought of joining in Slow Leg's scheme expanded as warmly in his mind as the drink did in his belly. To fly regularly, and to see the city, and to be the prestigious source of such valuable tools . . .

"Yes," he said. "I would like to do that."

"Very good," said Slow Leg. As though emboldened by this agreement, he leaned forward and continued, intently: "You're a natural flyer. With practice, you could be a great one. Instead you let your ability run to waste as a woman and fritter your days in weaving and stitching and gossip. Why don't you turn your back on all that petty stuff and become a man while you still can?"

Stone was unsure as to what would be an appropriate response. He compressed his lips, took a deep breath, smoothed the lap of his tunic. Reactions to his status ranged from good-natured joshing to fascinated admiration, with most of that range occupied by a matter- of-fact acceptance. An active attempt to persuade him out of it was unheard of: Neither tradition nor what he could recall of the books of anthropology afforded a precedent.

But he had just seen one event without precedent; he wondered if Slow Leg's boldness was somehow incited by the feeling that had gripped them both of great changes to come. So instead of taking offense, or laughing it away, he took it seriously and calmly.

"There is some truth in what you say, Slow Leg," he replied. "I love flying, and I wish I could do more. But I also love the women's work and the women's company, which is not as petty as you imagine. But besides all that, the fact remains that I chose it for a reason, which you well know. I may be good at flying, but I couldn't be good at fighting."

He spread his hands.

Slow Leg had listened with an expression of growing frustration and now burst into eager, urgent speech.

"I could train you!" he said. "Fighting is just a skill. To tell you the truth, a woman could do it, if she practiced enough and didn't mind the pain—and I've seen birth, pain I couldn't imagine. Women have their own pain, so don't tell me they couldn't endure some blows and cuts. Don't tell me *you* couldn't. We could practice, somewhere quiet, until you were ready for the challenge."

Stone winced inwardly at the mention of the challenge but kept his expression carefully bright.

"Ah, that's just the trouble, you see," he said. "Nature, the spirits, the gods—call the power what you will—has given mothers the strength to give birth, and fighters the strength to fight, and to me and my like neither. I accept that, and I'm happy to be as I am."

Slow Leg still fixed him with a stern gaze.

"I knew you when you ran and fought and hunted with the other boys," he said. "You had the makings of a man, and you still do. You're no coward." He frowned for a moment. "If it's that you"—he made a quick vulgar gesture with his fingers—"to tell you the truth, some of the men, the hunters and warriors, they too . . . with each other, and nobody thinks any the less of them."

"I know that," Stone said with a sigh of exasperation. "That's not the difficulty."

"So what is?"

"It's as I said."

Stone wished he could have said more, but what he felt was so chaotic, and threatened so much to make him weep, and so difficult to put in words either in Speech or in Christian, that he left it at that.

"All right," said Slow Leg. "I am sorry I raised the matter."

"It is forgotten," said Stone. "But I will fly with you, as we agreed."

They finished their drinks. As Stone left, Slow Leg called after him, "See you soon!"

Stone glanced back over his shoulder and gave him a sly smile and a friendly wave. The path from the glider shed to the road was paved with flat, irregular stones, leavings from the paving of the road, and therefore equally ancient. He walked down its left-hand side, on the outside of the pair of ruts left by centuries of identically spaced cartwheels. The roofs of Long Bridge's streets of stone houses and long wooden industrial sheds looked like broad steps in a jumbled collection of giant stairways descending the hillside to the river.

That was itself a detail of the pattern of much larger steps, the terracing of the fields, which earthworking in turn was laid over the succession of the raised beaches that appeared at various points along the sides of the valley. The airfield had been formed in the slope between two of them; after the next downward slope, the field was on a level with the roofs of the uppermost street, and on that field's trampled grass the town's boys and young men practiced their sports and the arts of war. As he walked past he was recognized by some of his former companions, one of whom shouted a suggestion after him. Stone waggled his hips defiantly.

"I wouldn't have you fuck me," he shouted, looking back, "if you were the last man in the world!"

Matt Cairns peers at the city through a window frosted with micrometeoroid impacts, troubled by the sense of height induced by looking at it from space but not from orbit, and by the feeling that *none of this has happened yet.* Some clock or calendar at the back of his mind is still tidal locked to Earth's distant turning; for him *the present* will always be 2049 plus however many years he lives, and most of that time up until now has been lived in *the future,* piled on top of an already dizzying stack of light-years.

So here he is, uncounted thousands of years and light-years away from *now* and *home,* standing in the drive's local gravity on a ship built for free fall and looking at a city that hangs improbably in front of his face and grows larger by the second. He turns away.

The ship's control room, the subject of several iterations of retrofitting and hacking, is about two meters high by three deep and ten across. At the other end of its long, low window stand a young man and a young woman, as intent as Matt had been on the planet's looming surface. Gregor Cairns resembles Matt in his swept-back black hair, narrow nose, and thin mouth—and the set of his shoulders, which is that of a man ready for trouble. Elizabeth Harkness, her left hand straying like a persistent-minded small animal on Gregor's back, stands a little taller and noticeably bigger in build; her black hair tumbles thick to a sharp, impatient-looking cutoff at the level of her chin. The ship's pilot, perched on a high stool between Matt and the couple, is himself intent on the surface of what looks like a tilted lab bench, to which various pieces of apparatus are strapped, lashed, or wired. His arms are elbow-deep in the cluttered array.

Matt gets the uneasy impression that the pilot is deliberately ignoring the proximity of the globe filling the window.

"Is this the right way to come in?" he asks. He can hear faint overspill of the planet's radio traffic from a speaker, vaguely wonders why such transmissions had never shown up on the Solar System's most sensitive radio telescopes in their most meticulous SETI sweeps, and remembers, again, that *this hasn't happened yet* ... quite possibly in 2049 the lightspeed ships carrying the very first human specimens from Earth's deepest antiquity had still not reached their destination.

"No," the pilot replies, not looking up from the jury-rigged controls. "It decidedly is not. We must swing around and approach by the normal flight path. Please, everyone, hold on to something while I adjust—"

The direction of the field sways sickeningly for a moment, then stabilizes. The apparent size of the planet stops increasing.

"Okay," says the pilot, standing up and turning around and dusting his palms. "We are now in a stable position. It may take some time to plot the approach."

"You mean you don't know?"

Matt stares at the pilot, caught by another mental glitch: Just as the present sometimes seems to be the future, so he can't help seeing the pilot as an alien. Salasso isn't an alien—saurs and humans have a common terrestrial ancestor, an undistinguished vertebrate somewhere back of the Triassic—but he has an eerie, almost comical resemblance to the image of the alien that was iconic in Matt's ancient youth. Long familiarity with the saurs hasn't entirely erased that early imprinting. It can still make the hairs on his nape and forearms prickle. Not even the image of the truly alien, the garden of the gods that still glows in his mind after two centuries, can displace the sinister semblance: the hairless head with huge eyes and tiny mouth above a scrawny body, the long arms and long four-digited hands are species markers of the classic mythical alien, the Gray.

Matt has long harbored a dour suspicion that this is far from a coincidence. The saurs' disk-shaped gravity skiffs lend some weight to the notion.

And the fear and anger, still there like trace elements of a poisonous heavy metal, or an isotope with a long half-life, not yet nearly spent . . . he's ashamed of it, he fights it and tries to hide it, from others if not from himself.

"We know in principle," Salasso says stiffly. "From here on in it's partly skill, which . . . I am learning, and partly calculation—ah, Gregor?'

The young man moves away from the window and the woman, and joins Salasso in a huddle over a monitor and keyboard on the table. After a minute of watching them scribble, mutter cryptically, check readings, and punch data, Matt reckons this is not going to be quick. He walks past them and stands by Elizabeth. She doesn't look away from the view.

"It's wonderful," she says. "I can hardly believe I'm seeing this. Croatan, wow!"

Her finger traces in the air the outline of the eastern coast of Croatan's western continent, New Virginia, on which Rawliston stands out like a blemish on a cheek. West and north and south of its smoke haze spreads a patchwork—from this height, more a stitchery—of green and gold and black; beyond that, a deeper green of forests and then the gray slopes and white tops of a mountain range that roughly parallel the coastline at a distance of between one and two hundred kilometers. Clouds are piled up along the range, like surf. East of the town, the ocean shines blue.

"It is beautiful," Matt agrees.

She turns, her black hair swinging, her black brows lifting.

"Did you ever see Earth—like this?"

Matt sighs. "Yeah, for a few seconds, just as I was leaving it. In real life, that is. Lots of times on screen, of course. Live pictures, VR, wallpaper . . ."

She wouldn't have known quite what he meant, but she looks at him sympathetically.

"You miss it."

He scratches his chin with a thumbnail. As usual after spending time in space, he feels he needs a shave. He doesn't: This journey has been that short. "Yeah, I miss it. I've had some time to get over it."

As though reminded that she herself has more pressing reasons for homesickness, Elizabeth looks quickly down, then back at the new world below. After some minutes the view begins to slide to the right, as the ship moves west. In a moment they're looking straight down at the mountains.

"Please take your seats," says Salasso. "We're about to attempt a controlled vertical descent."

"I bloody *wish*," says Matt, heading for the seats, "that we'd brought that skiff. I'd rather risk a Roswell crash than a fucking *Tunguska Event*."

The others know better than to ask him what he means by that. They don't have a skiff. They'd hired one, back on Mingulay, to use as a shuttle while they renovated the *Bright Star*, but it had been too expensive to take with them and anyway would have been missing the point, which is to set up a human-controlled spacefaring capability. They've left most of the fabs and labs behind, in the same old orbit, along with most of the ship. What they have now are modules of the life support and living quarters, some modules with carefully selected scientific equipment from the labs, a vast corpus of knowledge downloaded to an assortment of still-functioning computers, a cargo hold stuffed with Mingulayan manufactures, and the lightspeed drive.

A drive that, throttled back to some infinitesimal fraction of its capacity, can be used for gravity work—in-system space and air travel. Your standard strange light in the sky.

Matt straps in alongside the others, in cannibalized, bolted-down seats that were originally designed for minor jolts and unscheduled burns in free-fall maneuvering. The belt looks as though some small animal has taken bites out of it, leaving crescents of acidic spittle to fringe the bites with interesting burn marks—just a couple hundred years of slow-motion, vaccuum-resistant bacterial rot, but leaving the belt something he wouldn't have wanted to rely on in a car.

Salasso eases what looks worryingly like a rheostat a millimeter or two forward, and the zoom effect begins again. A brightening glow and rising screech indicate that they've hit stratosphere. There is no shudder; the field surrounds the ship like an elongated bubble, which is just as well because otherwise they'd be shaken apart like an oil drum raft in rapids. The mountain range expands rapidly from a rendered contour map to a papier-mâché model to the real thing, a planetary surface about to come through the window. Matt glances sideways at Elizabeth and Gregor. They stare straight ahead, rapt but untroubled. Their only experience of air travel is in airships and gravity skiffs. Matt's is a little wider, and his grip on the armrests is hurting his hands.

He opens his eyes as the howl of the air stops. The view ahead is filled with tough tussocky grass and boulders gray and yellow with lichen. The ship's gravity and that of the ground a few meters below are perfectly perpendicular to each other. He looks away queasily. Salasso rotates his big black eyes and eases back the control. The ground pulls away again—Matt can see rabbits scattering—and sky suddenly swings down and fills the screen. Most of the screen. The lower quarter shows a rugged ridge. They lurch upward then forward—Matt's toes curl, waiting for the scrape—and then they're hovering above a big, wide valley between that ridge and the next. Salasso pokes a long finger into something, and the ship swivels, looking straight down the valley. Matt glimpses a great river meandering along its floor, green and black fields in a landscape dotted with white towns.

And straight ahead, coming at them like a fly at a

windshield, a black shape like a gigantic bird or medium-sized pterosaur. Salasso takes the ship a few tens of meters up as the object plunges into a dive. As it flashes past below, Matt can see it's a wing, without a tail and with some kind of struts and lots of colorful decoration.

"What the fuck was that?" he yells.

"Hang glider," says Salasso imperturbably. "No doubt its pilot is asking the same question."

Through the angled inward slope of the lower part of the window Matt can now make out more of what they're passing over. The valley stretches for at least fifty fast-diminishing kilometers before them. Its breadth varies from two to five kilometers, densely inhabited; fields and cultivated woodlands extend from the fertile floor to the terraced lower slopes, with contours that he guesses are raised beaches; watermills where the current flows fast in the loop of meanders; a circuit board tracery of irrigation and drainage ditches, with the white blocks of low buildings its capicitors and switches. Thin, wavering columns of rising smoke. Beasts in the fields that flock like cattle but seem far too big. Boats and barges and—

"Watch out!" Matt yells. Salasso shoots him a pained look and lifts the ship yet farther, above the path of a drifting . . . blimp, Matt thinks at first, then realizes it's half a dozen linked balloons from which a single long gondola hangs swaying.

"Shit," says Gregor, jumping from his seat and peering forward through the glass. "There're dozens of them, balloons and gliders. We're in somebody's *airspace*."

"I'm more concerned about being hit from behind," says Salasso. "If we stray into the regular starship approach path."

"Not very likely," says Elizabeth.

At the eastern end of the valley, the river broadens into a lake behind a natural-looking rockfall dam, over whose rim it cascades. After that the valley floor drops sharply, and far on the horizon they see the blue gleam of the sea and the yellow-gray haze of Rawliston. They cross above rough country which, as the mountains dribble to densely forested foothills, opens out to a wide floodplain, farmed and fertile, across which the river fattens and snakes. Swift as a descending airliner, silent as a balloon, they drift forward until the city fills their sight.

"Like L.A." Matt says.

"What?"

"City on Earth, ages ago." He waves a hand. "Forget it."

He's too busy staring at Rawliston to talk about it. Elizabeth too falls silent; like Gregor, she's never seen a city of this size—a human city, anyway—from above. The primate brain is hardwired to respond to complexity with fascination, as Matt knows too well. The asteroid habitat of the aliens still haunts dreams from which he wakes bereft. A city from the air is but a crude outline of that and still the most complex object of human devising you can grasp in a single gaze.

First the suburbs: shanties with allotments, on the outermost fringe where they merge with the poorer farmland close to the city; then the shacks are replaced by more substantial dwellings, and all the roads, not just the main throughfares, are visibly paved, gleaming black rather than dusty brown. Water tanks on stilts like marching Martians, instead of rain butts and culverts; decorative floral gardens and lawns, instead of tiny, frantic fields. The traffic too has changed—out on the fringe it was human or animal, interspersed with great laboring machines farting smoke, and small overladen contraptions buzzing among them, and lots of bicycles; closer in, the vehicles shine, the large trucks and haulage vehicles gleaming with vivid colors and polished metal piping, the small ones carapaced in enamel, their shapes like oval, painted fingernails. Bridges, large and small,

unite the two sides of the broadening river that divides
the city.

The average height of buildings rises, as does their
mass. Built of stone rather than concrete, brick or wood
or corrugated iron, just before the seafront they rise like
a stone wave, this crest breaking to a lower, less salu-
brious splash of industrial and commercial buildings,
docks and quays on either side of the river mouth and
around the curve of the bay.

Beyond that the harbor, crowded with ships; and beyond these ships, out in the roads, two kilometers out to
sea, the starship berth is flagged by buoys. Three starships lie there, floating more in air than in water.

"The de Tenebre ship," Salasso remarks, bringing
them in alongside one of them. Matt has always felt that
identifying a starship by the merchant family who travel
in it makes about as much sense as naming an ocean-
going vessel after some lineage among its complement
of rats. The starships—or motherships, as he sometimes
can't help calling them, in another mental glitch—are,
well, as he thinks now, *big* mothers: hundreds of meters
long, bigger than any other machine he's seen apart from
oil tankers and heavy-lift boosters. Close up, the de Tenebre starship looks even bigger, reducing their own
fifty-meter-long lash-up of modules and walk tubes to a
raft bobbing alongside.

As the drive powers down to the minimum required
to keep them afloat, or aloft—they can see the waves
break against the invisible screen of the field—a babble
of radio voices breaks through, along with a lot of hissing and howling as Salasso, slightly rattled, twiddles the
dial. He finds the channel he seeks.

". . . yourselves please," says a voice with a twangy
accent. "Ship in the roads, identify yourselves please."

Matt leans forward as Salasso hesitates.

"Tell him," he says, "that the *Cairns* ship has come
in."

2

There Dwelt a Lass in Rawley's Toun

Gail Frethorne's grip on the spanner slipped as Joshua's yell startled her, and her hand grazed a raw flange. She saw the red blood on the black oil for a moment as her hand went to her mouth. Sucking her barked knuckles, she slid the low-wheeled platform she was lying on smoothly out from under the car and wound back a load of curses to hurl at Joshua.

He stood in the garage workshop yard a couple of meters away, gazing up openmouthed. From her low vantage, the apprentice looked like an allegorical statue of Astonishment. On her back, conveniently placed to look at the sky, she tracked the direction of his gaze.

"Holy fucking shit," she said, her ready-primed profanities sliding into reverence. The thing that floated by a hundred meters overhead was too big for an airship, too small for a starship, and surely the wrong shape for either. Christ, there were *holes* in it! You could see the sky through them.

She scrambled to her feet, not looking away from the

thing. It was coming down, sinking in the sky as it headed east across the city. Joshua shot her a reluctant glance.

"Some kinda new airplane?"

She could tell from his tone that he grudged consulting her on the question.

"No," she said, trying not to sound scornful. "Not the right shape for a lifting body, too fast to be an airship. If it had jets or rockets we could see them and hear them. I think."

"You don't reckon," said Joshua, watching it out of sight, "it could be something new the heathens have lashed up, out of, I dunno, gliders and balloons or something?"

"The heathens don't go much for *new*," Gail said. "No more nor the saurs or the krakens. Nah, that's a fucking ship or maybe skiff all right, man, and it's a kind we've never seen before. Nor heard of, neither."

"Hey!" Josh put his knuckles to his brow and waggled his forefingers. "Aliens!"

Gail laughed. Joshua's sole evidence of literacy was his painfully slow but persistent reading of sensational pulp comics.

"There ain't no aliens, 'cept the Powers Above."

"We don't *know* that," Joshua said stubbornly.

"Yes we do," Gail said absently, still gazing at the sky. Then she turned sharply to him, a big grin stretching her face. "And you know what that leaves?"

God, he was slow.

"People!" she said, clasping her hands above her head. "Our people! It's the ship from home! They've come here!"

Joshua frowned. He looked over at the big blaring radio, balanced precariously amid engine parts, jars of hazardous liquids, and tins of nuts and bolts on the shelf by the garage doorway.

"No need to *speculate* about it," he said, surprising her. "If it's anything special it'll be on the news, right?"

"Oh, yeah." Gail reached for the tuning knob and twiddled it through howls to the news band. After a minute of the usual midday prattle about crimes and traffic, the announcer's voice changed. You could hear the rustle of paper and the clunk of telephone switches.

"News just in," she said. "A starship has a few moments ago berthed off Rawliston and has identified itself as the *Bright Star*. We're sending out an urgent message to Chris, our eye in the sky, to give them a buzz, and meanwhile we'll keep you informed."

Some crackly exchanges followed with the man in the light aircraft whose job it was to keep an updating eye on the city's endlessly snarling traffic flow, and some old geezer from the university was roused from a siesta by the sound of it to talk incoherently about how marvelous and historic all this was, and with a defiant look Joshua wrenched the dial back to music.

"That's it, then," he said. "You were right. It's the cosmonauts."

He sounded disappointed. Gail gazed at his sullen face, pondering what depths of stupidity and disproportionality might lie beneath that expression. What daft dreams of aliens had been dashed by the discovery that the pilots of this unprecedented craft were merely, gloriously, human? To her it seemed the best and biggest news of her life.

"It's a big deal," she said. "You'll see."

Joshua shrugged and wandered back to disappear under the raised hood of the car on which he'd been working, halfway across the yard. The other two mechanics were in the dim interior of the machine shop, still welding—she blinked away the floating afterimages of her quick glance—and seemed not to have seen the ship or heard the news on their radio. The boss, scowling over dockets behind the window of the office that jutted from the yard's other corner, was equally oblivious.

She turned away quickly, before he could look up and catch her idle, and licked the still-welling blood from her knuckles. With one part of her mind she considered how to shift that recalcitrant nut. To play a flame on it was tempting but far too dangerous. Several sprays of penetrating oil seemed not to have penetrated at all. She ambled over to the cupboard where they kept the tea break stuff and nipped a twenty-centimeter strip from the coil of plastic heating element, about the amount they usually took from it to boil a liter can of water.

Back under the car, she wrapped the purloined strip around the nut and flicked it hard with her thumbnail. After a few seconds it glowed yellow, then orange. After it had burnt itself out she blew away the crumbling ash and applied the spanner again, and managed to loosen the nut just before the heat crept up the spanner and made it too hot to hold.

She abandoned the task until everything had cooled down a bit and hauled herself out again just as David yelled from the machine shop, "Abigail! I thought I saw you making some tea. Where is it?"

"Coming *right* up," she shouted back. "Davy!" she added, a variant of his name he detested as much as she did the one he'd used of hers. Making the tea was part of Joshua's job, but Gail felt obscurely obligated to the apprentice for her uncharitable thought that had marked him down as dimmer than he actually was.

She wiped her oily hands on her oily overall, hurried to the cupboard and the tap, and repeated the trick with a length of the disposable heating element. The boss had once wasted an hour or two laboriously proving to his own satisfaction that this saur product was cheaper than electricity. As she waited for the tin kettle to boil, Gail wondered idly why it wasn't more widely used and turned over vague notions about economies of scale and so forth, but eventually (as she threw a handful of tea leaves into a blackened earthenware pot, poured on the boiling water, and let it stand) concluded that it was just another example of the odd criteria the saurs had about what they would and wouldn't trade. They'd sell their leaf-thin solar panels and plastic tubing from the genetically engineered jungles that they aptly called the manufacturing plant, and they were downright helpful about petroleum extraction. But they left most human industry to muddle through on its own. They wouldn't sell skiffs and grudged even to rent them out. They were considerate and conscientious in selling restorative surgery, and swift to limit the spread of diseases introduced by interstellar trade, but they certainly weren't about to share the secret of their own long lives.

She poured the tea, and David, Mike, Joshua, and the boss gathered around for their half-past-ten break. The garage yard's usual din was replaced by the tinny tone of the radio, the creak of metal and glass and wood differentially expanding in the rising heat, and the low murmur of conversation and laughter. The three older guys were a lot less sanguine than Joshua about the arrival of the ship. As they talked, one aircraft after another buzzed over, heading from the airfields on the edge of town toward the sea. Eventually, Gail could stand it no longer.

"Uh, Mr. Reece," she said to the boss, "do you mind if I knock off for the day? The engine mount job is coming along fine, and, well, I'd like to get out to the runway."

She could almost see the calculations clicking away behind Reece's narrow eyes. It was a rare request on her part, she normally worked longer than necessary anyway, the job was ahead of schedule and the car's owner couldn't pick it up earlier than arranged . . .

"Yeah, okay," he said. "Just so long as you're in early tomorrow."

She grinned at him and at the lads, put down her mug unfinished, and set off for the washroom at a run.

An hour or so later, just before noon, she racked her bicycle in the club shed and walked out on to the grass, feeling that she needed another wash, this time to remove not oil but sweat and dust. The garage was on the fracture zone between the suburbs and the shanties, and most of the westward roads beyond it were rutted and rough. The green open space of the airfield was like cold water after all that.

Its perimeter was about five hundred meters by two hundred, its fences marking off an area of rough grass on relict riverbank soil too pebbly and gravelly to farm. Hangers, huts, a wind sock, a token mooring mast— most airships docked much farther in toward the center of town, or down at the quays—the circular concrete blockhouse containing the kerosene tanks, and a row of fabric-and-bamboo monoplanes and biplanes. The club had a dozen aircraft, all but three of which were at present in the air, no doubt buzzing the newly arrived starship.

Away off in one corner was a wide patch of grass— trampled by landings, blackened by liftoffs—where the heathens arrived and departed in their hot-air balloon trains. Around it was a wider area, torn and tire-rutted, where the much rarer gliders landed and from where they were relaunched by towing them—the pilot standing on a slatted wooden platform with six bicycle wheels until he'd built up enough speed to take off, and for a minute or so afterward was towed through the air as he soared, until he let go of the handle and the rope snaked back down to earth behind the club's car.

It was that car, at this moment parked neatly behind the clubhouse, that had given Gail her way in a couple of years earlier, when she was sixteen and just hanging around on the edges, unregarded, watching the aircraft take off and land, or herself circling the perimeter of conversations among the pilots and mechanics, catching snatches of information and jargon, assumed to somebody's kid sister.

She'd seen, a hundred meters away, the tall half-naked heathen heft his curious contraption, step lightly on the undercarriage, and shout and wave. The car had coughed into life, revved up, roared forward. The heathen stood braced between the wing above him and the wood at his heels, bouncing across the grass. And then the car had stalled, and the line slackened, and he'd tumbled forward, caught himself, and run for a little before going all of a heap, the glider tipped and sticking up above him at an angle.

She'd run up. The heathen was on the ground, clutching his knee, whey-faced but tight-lipped. The glider appeared undamaged. People were ignoring him, standing around the raised hood of the car and shaking their heads. As she'd elbowed her way in she'd realized that none of them had a clue: Their expertise with aeroengines didn't extend to those of cars.

Hers, as she rapidly demonstrated, did, and that was it. She'd fixed the distributor cap that was the source of the problem, and an hour later the heathen—who'd done something nasty to his left knee but was studiously, stoically ignoring it—was up and away. From then on Gail was in with the lads, just like at the garage; she had credibility, she had a regular role here, maintaining the old car. She'd done more than maintain it; she'd tuned and tweaked the engine until it ran reliably and smoothly every time.

The heathen pilot had not forgotten her. Two weeks after his accident, he had returned, startling her with a silent approach as she worked on the car. The proposition he put to her had startled her even more, but in the time since then, it had resulted in a welcome addition to her income, albeit one that occasionally nagged at either her conscience or her fear of being found out.

She strolled past the clubhouse and spotted Paul Loudon flight checking the Kondrakov-LeBrun 3B, a twoseater high-winged monoplane. Paul owned the small engineering company that had built it, under license from its Mingulayan designers. In his midtwenties he was already independently wealthier than most of his landowning family, and looked it: tall, with sharp dark eyes, fine cheekbones, a proud nose. He never gave the slightest indication that he noticed her sex, or her class, for that matter; Gail wasn't sure whether the reasons for this were good or bad, but she counted the result entirely to his credit.

"Oh, hi, Frethorne." He slid shut a tiny hatch above a fuel valve in the side of the fuselage and wiped his fingers on a white handkerchief, then raked them absently through his swept-back brown hair. "Just caught the fuss by chance on a radio at work. Probably missed most of the fun. Bloody nuisance."

"What sort of fun? You can still go up and have a look."

"Oh, to be sure, that's just what I'm about to do. But all the other chaps have no doubt got reporters and photographers along for the ride and are raking in fees by the fistful."

She knew it wasn't the money that mattered to him; it was missing the cachet of having been among the first to witness and record a little bit of history that was pinching his brow and mouth.

"Well," she said, "that means none of them are taking pictures for the club. . . ."

"Aha!" He slapped his thigh. "Good point!" He looked somewhere above her, then below. "Ah, I don't suppose, you wouldn't mind awfully much coming along and shooting a spool or two?"

"No," she said, keeping her face straight. "I wouldn't mind that at all."

She'd been hoping he'd let her spin the propeller.

Lydia de Tenebre knew exactly what the black rectangular structure was, even before its dangerously low passage, skimming the rooftops of Rawliston, had brought it close enough for her to glimpse through the haze its crudely painted name. She had hoped to see it someday but had never quite believed that she would, and certainly not so soon, after a mere three months of her life. Trying not to run, she hurried down the crowded waterfront street. The low-slung, carbon-coughing vehicles lurched and paused, lurched and paused, in a typical downtown morning traffic jam. People mostly made way for her: The extremes of beauty, like those of ugliness, could part crowds, and Lydia used her beauty like a scythe. Only the occasional gigant or pithkie grudged her passage and stepped aside with a grunt or a flash of bright, sharp teeth.

The walls of the warehouses and offices cut off any view of the starship's landing. When she arrived at the street that opened to the quays, the coppice of masts in the harbor blocked any sight of the sea. She paused in a convenient shopfront doorway and pulled her radio from the hip pocket of her dress. She flicked it on, wincing at the babble and howl—the frequencies were more crowded in Rawliston than anywhere else in the Second Sphere, more even than in Nova Babylonia itself, where strict regulation kept the numerous channels well distinct. Here, it needed all the fine discrimination built into the set to find the correct wavelength.

"Lydia on shore to the ship," she said.

"Come in." The operator sounded distracted.

"Has the other ship landed safely?"

"If you can call it a ship," replied the operator. "Yes."

"Praise the gods," said Lydia. "Signing off."

She looked up and down the long shorefront street. A recent rainfall had left it gleaming and puddled; cars and buses and trucks threw curls of water from their wheels as they passed, splashing the sidewalks. The traffic flowed faster than on the side streets; along here the street was a continuation of the broad boulevard that bordered the more residential and commercial, less industrial and mercantile, segment of the seafront and retained its sweep though not its trees, umbrellas, and cafés.

She waited for one of the inexplicable halts in traffic that happened at random every few minutes and dodged across the road. A quick jump over a low chain fence took her onto the tarry timbers of the pier, from which long quays fingered out. She dodged among bollards and barrels, carts and trucks, dockers and hauliers, the crowd less dense but its components faster and heavier. She stayed nimble and alert until she'd crossed the swing-down customs barrier that restricted entrance and exit to the landing stage that had been set aside for boats to and from the starship berth. Then she relaxed with a long, shuddering exhalation and strolled its hundred-meter length to the end. She was in her own territory now.

An inflatable dinghy rocked on the water at the bottom of one of the stairs. She called down to the crewman, a distant cousin, snoozing in the stern. "Hi, Johannes! Can you take me out?"

Johannes started awake and waved up at her. "Yes, come on in."

She descended and sat down facing Johannes on a seat made, like most of the rest of the boat, from thin plastic that had once been transparent and had by now been scratched and stained to a watery translucence. Johannes cast off, shoved clear of the barnacled stanchion, and fired up the outboard motor.

As the dinghy puttered out through narrow gulfs between the hulls of wood and steel, Johannes grinned at her and said, "What's the rush? Didn't expect you back before evening."

"You didn't see it?"

"See what?"

"The Mingulayan ship coming in? You know, the cosmonauts' ship?"

Johannes scratched the back of his head. "Hells, no, I missed that. Good gods, they actually did it?"

"Yes," said Lydia. "They navigated here themselves." She shook her head. "I never expected Gregor to crack it . . . so soon. I'm impressed."

Her cousin was looking at her with sly amusement. "I bet your father will be even more impressed. Changes things a bit for you, eh?"

"That's for me to decide."

She smiled, just to show that the firmness of her tone didn't indicate a reproof, and turned away to look forward, beyond the dinghy's rounded prow. As they emerged into clear water they could see both starships far ahead. The Mingulayan ship was a dark, flat shape, barely discernible beside the circular aspect of the de Tenebre starship's cylindrical length seen end-on. As the dinghy bounded across the waves, Lydia began to make out a line of light between the small ship and the sea; it wasn't even big enough to make a significant depression in the water. She found herself wondering idly what exchanges might be going on, between the *Bright Star* and her family's ship, and between either of them and the Port Authority, and then realized that her speculation need not be idle.

She pulled out the radio again and thumbed the switch and turned the tuning knob very slowly through a small part of the dial.

". . . in your ship," a voice was saying. "I repeat, remain in your ship. A Port Authority vessel is on its way."

"Acknowledged," returned another voice, which she didn't recognize. She looked astern and saw another, much larger inflatable boat powering out from the harbor, far behind in their wake.

"Can you make this go faster?"

Johannes nodded. "Sure. We'll get a bit wet. . . ."

"Do it, please."

The crewman leaned on the tiller, and the engine's note deepened. The boat surged forward; salt spray began splashing in. Lydia raised the radio again.

"Calling the *Bright Star,* come in, please."

After a few crackling noises the reply came back: *"Lydia?"*

Her heart jumped like the boat; her eyes filled with water like the spray.

"Yes, it's me! Gregor?"

"Hi, Lydia. Good to hear you." His voice sounded more level this time. "Where are you?"

She told him.

"That's great," he said. "But let's keep off air for the moment, we don't want a swarm of—"

The hum of an aircraft engine drowned out his words; a seaplane flashed by about fifty meters above her head. She stared after the rickety craft and saw it slice the sea with its floats and rock to a stop beside the ships. Within moments a converging flock of small airplanes was circling the starship berth. From somewhere behind the harbor mole a blimp wallowed in the same direction. She rolled the dial to the data-transfer channel: It was buzzing; fuzzy photographic reproductions were obviously being transmitted to Rawliston's newspaper offices. The radio news channels, too, were busy, with no news she didn't already know.

"Damn!" she shouted above the sound of the outboard and the growing racket overhead.

"What did you expect?" Her cousin's amused look had returned. "That ship is legendary! This is historic!"

"I know," Lydia said. Her notion of a quick, quiet reunion with Gregor now seemed naive. "I just didn't expect the locals to catch on so *fast*."

But that too was naive, she realized as soon as the words were out of her mouth. She grimaced and turned again to face forward.

It had been less than a quarter of a year ago, in her own life, that she'd heard of the *Bright Star*'s first arrival—not at Croatan but in polar orbit around its daughter colony, Mingulay, five light-years distant. In that time Croatan had made about two hundred circuits of its sun, two hundred years that had been radically affected by the event. The buzzing aircraft themselves were one of its consequences, as was much of the surrounding industrial landscape. Not that Croatan hadn't been industrializing quite effectively on its own, but interstellar trade with the rest of the Second Sphere and even the limited technology trade with the vastly more ancient and advanced saurs just couldn't hold a carbon-arc lightbulb to the effect of a shipload of downloads from the Earth and Solar System of 2049, which had begun to arrive in the seasonally adjusted Year of Our Lord 2057. The current approximate anno Domini was 2270-something, according to Croatan's calendar, which quite sensibly discounted the countless millennia lost in lightspeed transit. Elsewhere in the Second Sphere, Nova Terra's year was standard, and its zero date was the founding of the city now called Nova Babylonia, which had recently celebrated its tenth millennium. Lydia felt some patriotic pride in that, though she well knew that to the older hominid species, let alone to the saurs or the krakens, this was all very novel, and to the gods it was as yesterday in their sight. She herself was, like everyone on the merchant ships, a one-way time traveler, skipping into the future with every subjectively instantaneous lightspeed jump; in her two score years she'd left her date of birth centuries in the past, and in that sense she was older than Rawliston. The town had changed faster than anything else she'd seen in her travels: *My, how she's grown!*

The dinghy dodges around the seaplane's floats and into the gap between it and the *Bright Star*. Matt and Elizabeth crowd behind Gregor, who stands in the opened hatch of what was once an internal doorway. Their own dinghy, deflated and folded around its gas cylinder, is stashed alongside that hatch in another piece of botchy retrofitting. The whole ship is scarily unsuitable for space flight: only one airlock, in a very awkward corner; ESA-issue EVA suits that haven't been tested or used for centuries; life-support hydroponics incorporating decades of unedited mutation, which occasionally give off rank swampy whiffs. The humid air from the outside feels fresh by comparison. The saurs have kept the *Bright Star* maintained and ticking over, mothballed in

Mingulayan orbit, but they've done the work by the
numbers, painstakingly following instructions they've
recovered from files: Whatever life-support engineering
skills they ever possessed has atrophied over the millions
of years in which they've never had to spend more than
a few hours at a time in actual hard vacuum. The digit
they're missing is the human's green thumb.

Over Gregor's shoulder Matt sees the woman
crouched in the dinghy's prow, straining forward.
Through the side of his arm he feels Elizabeth, peering
over Gregor's other shoulder, tense. Wavy black hair
blown in the wind, light brown skin, a really quite beautiful face; Matt understands some of the reasons for Elizabeth's tension at the sight of Lydia and on an impulse
gives her shoulders a brief, fortifying squeeze.

She glances sideways at him for a moment and blinks.

The dinghy heaves to. Gregor catches a flung rope and
steps back into the control room, scattering his companions behind him. After a moment of puzzlement he
lashes the rope to the fixed stanchion of one of the seats.
By the time he's turned back Lydia has climbed in, followed by the lad who has steered the boat. Lydia's dark
blue dress is cut in pleats and concertina folds; its skirt
flares, and when she shakes the salt spray from her hair
the drops slide off the fabric leaving no track.

Lydia embraces Gregor for a long moment, then steps
back, her hands on his.

"You did it!" she says. "You made it! Oh, I'm so
proud of you! I'm amazed."

Gregor shrugs modestly. "It wasn't all my own
work. . . ." Then he grins broadly. "But mostly it was!
Thank you."

Lydia spins away and grabs Elizabeth, who gives her
a very uncertain hug in return, then shakes hands with
Salasso and introduces her cousin and crewmate, Johannes.

"And this is Matt Cairns," Gregor says, "my ancestor."

Her awestruck look as she grasps his hand is strangely gratifying, after a protracted lifetime of secrecy on that very point.

"Hello, Lydia," he says. "Very pleased to meet you. I've heard a lot about you."

"Likewise," she replies, smiling.

"Oh?"

"Your friend Grigory Volkov speaks well of you."

"I'm sure he does," Matt says, as smoothly as he can manage. "I look forward to meeting him."

"Of course," says Lydia, dropping his hand with a final flare-up of her smile and turning to Gregor.

"We don't have much time," she says. "The news people and the Port Authority will be all over you in minutes. I just want to say that you're all welcome on our ship and that my father is eager to meet you and has much to discuss."

"As do we," Elizabeth says pointedly.

The two women look at each other, and Gregor looks, rather helplessly Matt thinks, from the one to the other.

"Excuse me," says Salasso. "However personally fraught this situation may be, the matter of the Port Authority is considerably more urgent. What can we expect from them?"

Lydia frowns. "Shouldn't be a problem."

Gail had cadged a few flights before, but only as a passenger. There had always been the feeling of being indulged. This was different. In the borrowed leather helmet and the navigator's goggles, with the strap of the heavy camera tugging at the back of her neck, she was part of the crew of the KL-3B. She had a job to do. She'd written her name in the club's logbook in block capitals and signed it, just below Paul's, and beside it he'd scrawled, *photographer*.

She had to crouch a little to keep her face behind the plastic windshield and out of the slipstream. Paul, though as tall as she, didn't have to. She guessed he had a lower seat. Her fingers, cold in far-from-windproof gloves of silk with rubber fingertips, fumbled a little as she adjusted the few knobs and levers of the camera that hadn't been previously set up for her by Paul.

"Just slot it on the bracket," he'd said. "Point and shoot."

Easy for him to say. The bracket was clamped to the lip of the rear cockpit. You couldn't mount the camera on it before takeoff—too much risk of its being sheared off by the bumping. She heaved it up from her quivering knees and levered it out on her elbow-propped forearms, twisting around awkwardly to do so. By the time she'd got it slotted into place, Rawliston had passed beneath them in a jerky series of glimpses like blurred snapshots, and they were banking into a long swing around the starship berth.

Paul waved and yelled something over his shoulder to her, his words whipped away by the wind. She guessed he meant it was time to get busy and folded out the periscopic apparatus of the viewfinder so that she could look through it right in front of her, then with her other hand found the shutter button. Looking through the tiny viewfinder with goggles on was just about impossible; she slipped them up to her forehead, shielded her eyes with one hand, closed one eye, and screwed up the other.

The view juddered constantly. The larger starship made a complete diagonal: *click*. Another aircraft skimmed dangerously close; sky and wheels filled the view for a moment: *click*. Down now, so that only the *Bright Star* and a seaplane and some little dinghy were in the scope: *click*. Curving around it, back for a low pass. A much larger boat cut a white V toward the berth. Gail recognized the stylized turret-on-shield of the Port Authority ensign, snapping sharply in the boat's own slipstream. By the time Paul had pulled back and returned, that boat had hove to, and three or four dark figures were moving up its deck toward some opening in the *Bright Star*'s side: *click*.

Down again, so low that the highest, lightest droplets of spray from the wave tops salted the breath, and the seaplane rocked as they roared past it. Gail pulled on a lever that angled the camera upward, for a straight sideways shot of two men entering the starship: *click*.

Their rifles showed clear and sharp.

Gail almost yelled. An armed boarding of a ship was rare—of a starship, unprecedented. She could hardly believe it.

The two remaining on the deck had rifles too, and they brandished them at the KL-3B and the other buzzing aircraft: *click*. When Paul ignored, or failed to notice this and made another low run over, the two dark-uniformed men dropped to one knee and brought their rifles to their shoulders, the muzzles swinging around as they followed the airplane's swift, low flight.

At that point Paul got the message and veered off and headed for home—but not before Gail had got the picture: *click*.

3

Customs

MATT HOLDS HIS hands well clear of his dinosaur-hide jacket's weapons-laden side pockets and glares at the boarders. Each has a rifle slung on one shoulder, and he has no idea how fast their reflexes might be, or how twitchy their mood. More reassuringly, they are both middle-aged men, with weathered, outdoor complexions, their build burly rather than tough. One of them is tall and clean-shaven, the other short and bristly. Their uniforms look more suitable for pirates than for customs officers: cravats and loose shirts with broadcloth jackets and lots of braid and frogging and general macaroni, worn with blue jeans under open orange waterproofs blazoned with the Port Authority name and flash.

"Who's in charge of this ship?" the taller of the men demands.

Gregor twitches.

Matt steps forward. "Who wants to know?" he asks.

With an air of practiced weariness, the big guy fingers a folded sheet of printed paper from a vest pocket.

" 'Rawliston Port Authority, Customs Division, under International Commerce Regulation 453C of the local common year 2234, requests and requires in the name of the sovereign people, et cetera et cetera, full access to all information respecting but not limited to cargo crew master owner provenance origin destination of all ships entering the harbor."

"That doesn't apply to starships," says Lydia, "as well you know."

The officer gives her a grudgingly respectful glance, looks back at his paper, and runs a fingernail along a footnote, apparently in small print to judge by his labored delivery: " 'For the purposes of this regulation 'ship' shall be construed as any vessel whether surface or otherwise on or above the surface of the harbor waters as defined above subparagraph 86E and owned or operated by members of the Adamic races.' "

He looks at Matt, then flicks his gaze over Gregor and Elizabeth. "That means you, you, and you." A smile at Lydia, a nod at Johannes, a carefully blank blink at Salasso. "Not you, you, or you."

Matt reckons he's sussed that Lydia is from the de Tenebre ship—probably by her dress—and her companion by his crew fatigues, and that he has assumed the same of Salasso, or has wisely decided that his authority doesn't extend to saurs, no matter what ship they rode in on. The thought of claiming that the undoubtedly non-Adamic Salasso is the *Bright Star*'s owner tempts Matt for only a moment. He nods at Gregor, who takes the cue.

"I'm in charge here," Gregor tells the customs man. "On behalf of the Cosmonaut Families of Mingulay. Now, what do you wish to know?"

"Uh, that's still to be decided. We have to ask you to accompany us to the Authority office on shore, where you'll no doubt have to fill in a manifest and provide a bill of lading and other documentation, which we'll check when you unload, or before that by inspecting the ship in your presence."

"Couldn't we just get that over right now?"

The officer shakes his head. "No, because what comes after the check is a tariff, and that has to be determined on shore, not by us out here. To prevent corrupt arrangements, you understand."

Or to reserve them for a higher level of officialdom.

"All right," says Gregor. "We'll come along. But I want you to note that we do so under protest, and that we don't accept that human-crewed starships are covered by your regulation—"

"When it was written," the other officer breaks in, sounding apologetic, "there weren't any human-crewed starships."

"That's as may be," says the first officer. "But right now it does cover them, and if the assemblies meant anything different, it's them who're going to have to change it."

Gregor reiterates his objection, and with that point made they rummage up the ship's scant documentation and follow the officers onto the big inflatable boat. Salasso, Lydia, and Johannes remain on the ship.

Dark Water was sawing through a bundle of bamboo with a gut rope on which ground glass had been glued. The rope was wound around an arrangement of wheels and pulleys, powered by a foot pedal. She looked up, keeping the saw humming, as Stone walked carefully past her.

"Ha!" she said. "You've been drinking spirits. If Slow Leg comes home with that stuff on his breath I'll beat the shit out of him."

Stone steadied himself with a surreptitious hand on the bench behind him and faced her glare with a grin.

"Come on," he said. "It was only a mug to celebrate my successful flight."

"A mug of beer's one thing," Dark Water said, bending again to her task. "Whiskey is something else."

Inwardly Stone had to acknowledge the truth of this. His senses of sight and balance seemed affected—things went out of focus very easily and swayed a little all the time. But he couldn't help defending his friend.

"Slow Leg will be all right," he said. "He'll be busy with the wing all afternoon, anyway. The wing, remember?"

But nobody was talking about the wing. All along the the shed the talk was only of the ship. Women's voices floated up and down, swooping around the hum of pulleys and rasp of saws, the clatter of shuttles and the hiss of spinning wheels, the slap of wet clay and the roar of kilns. The scent of their sweat mingled with that of fresh sawdust and wood shavings, of burning logs, of vegetable and animal oils and hot glue, and of the fragrant breeze off the hillside fields and meadows that kept the air in the long shed breathable.

Ignoring the giggles and barbed comments that his carefully steady progress provoked, Stone made his way to the area where he usually worked. Children scooted and scampered and screamed around and between the benches and looms.

He looked down at the scored surface of his workbench, at the small stack of seasoned wood and the rack of flint tools with which he had to turn the wood into the complex, interlocking shapes of a glider harness attachment. The thought of getting hold of good steel blades was a lot more attractive than the task before him.

Outside, the sound of drumming began. Stone looked up and saw in the glaring sunlight a shaman's apprentice bashing the taut skin circle with evil-spirit-scaring enthusiasm, as the shaman himself ducked into a smoke-filled tent to consult the spirits of the ancestors, which were contained in the sacred book whose title Stone had once heard whispered: Christopher Dawson's *Autochthonous Hill Tribes of New Virgina: A Preliminary Anthropological Survey.*

*   *   *

The small boats that approached the starship berth have by now turned tail; the small aircraft have either departed or are circling at a much safer distance. Wet from spray and splash, sweating in the muggy heat, Matt huddles morosely between Gregor and Elizabeth on one of the boat's seats and tries to look as interested and surprised as they are by the endemic features of Croatan's native life.

This isn't his first visit to the planet, but he isn't about to tell his companions that, not just yet. He had, one long evening, given them a long and rambling account of the vicissitudes that had brought him and others with the *Bright Star* to Mingulay: his early life on Earth in the mid-twenty-first century, his journey to the asteroid research station, and his initiation into its real discoveries: the alien life within the asteroid, and the gods' revelation and specification—Greek gift or Trojan Horse—of the lightspeed drive and antigravity craft. He has told them little of his long, clandestine life on Mingulay, and nothing of his life off it.

So he stares and points and looks wide-eyed with the rest of them. Here, small pterosaurs fill the niche occupied by seabats back home on Mingulay; their narrow, angled wings, harsh cries, and vertical dives sending up high fountaining plumes remind Matt poignantly of gannets. The boat passes close by a swift-leaping group of sea animals, known locally as "seals" and homologous to porpoises or ichthyosaurs; Elizabeth excitedly points out the long, yellow serrated beaks and the tail-equivalent fused webbed feet that mark them out as birds, though with aquatic adaptations far more extensive than those of the penguins from which they're descended.

Another difference between Croatan and Mingulay becomes apparent as they get closer to the shore. The haze that hangs over Rawliston isn't fog—as, Matt guesses, his companions have assumed—but smog. Coal smoke and petrol-engine exhaust; the smell brings on some nostalgia, as well as a roughness in the back of the throat.

Elizabeth wrinkles her nose and looks at the bearded customs officer sitting across from her. "How do you *breathe* this stuff?"

"What stuff?"

Then he cracks a smile, relenting. "Yeah, I know. But it's part of the terraforming—greenhouse effect, yeah? The saurs say it's helping to hold off an ice age."

"Didn't think this planet *needed* terraforming," Gregor says.

"Call it fine tuning," says the officer.

"What's intriguing me," says Elizabeth, "is where the fossil fuels came from in the first place. When were the coal measures laid down? How long has this planet had Earth life on it?"

The Authority man shrugs, turning away to look over the prow. "You'd have to ask the saurs, and they don't know or ain't telling."

Well, you could do more than ask the saurs, Matt doesn't say. *You could ask the gods.*

He's still brooding on that thought when they've hove to, climbed up the quayside ladder, and walked into the Port Authority offices by the back entrance, avoiding the baying crowd of reporters and photographers around at the front.

The office has a row of orange plastic chairs along one wall, by the door, and a heavy hardwood desk opposite them across a couple of meters of frayed gray-green carpet. A wide window overlooks the harbor sound, but the minuscule crack by which it's opened does little to refresh the air of the room. A case of thick leatherbound books stands against the rear wall. The big comfortable-looking swivel chair behind the desk is, for the present, unoccupied, and on top of the desk lies nothing but an ornamental inkwell and long dip pen, a leather-bordered blotter, a telephone, a broken-handled old mug containing a clutch of dip pens and a single ballpoint, and a globe of Croatan.

"Looks like we've been left to our own devices," Matt says, after they've sat waiting for no more than a minute. The damp patches on his clothes are beginning to dry out, as well as to chafe. He stands up and strolls over to half sit on the desk and idly spin the globe, ignoring the disapproving looks from Gregor and Elizabeth. In their short and relatively privileged lives they've never encountered any authority that wasn't light-handed and legitimate, and Matt's pretty sure they don't know how to behave when they encounter the other kind. For himself, he'll try disrespect first, and if that doesn't work, and resistance isn't an option, he'll grovel. The important thing is not to pretend that voluntary consent is involved, either way. Matt studies the globe and waits for the door to open.

New Virginia, the continent they're on, is in roughly the position of North America and roughly the size of Australia. Croatan has seven other island continents, none of them particularly close to each other. Only the indentations of their coastlines indicate that they'd ever been joined; local scientists have wryly dubbed that past supercontinent New Gondwana. Nobody's yet measured continental drift, instrumentation—and funding—not having yet caught up with the theories that the *Bright Star*'s files downloaded long ago. But the indications are that the continents are still dispersing across the globe; tens of millions of years in the future, some of them may collide, throwing up, perhaps, New Alps and New Himalayas, but for now they inch apart, hurrying away from each other like the galaxies after the big bang: Nova Europa, Elizabetha, New Hindostan, Arctica (joined to New Virginia by the polar ice), St Paul's Land, Discovery, Havenbless.

The coast, and much of the interior, of New Virginia has been well mapped; the outlines of the other continents look more artistic than scientific, and large areas of their interiors are, on close inspection, essentially blank. All of them, however, have human inhabitants, descendants of at least two episodes of involuntary human arrival: the more recent one that founded Rawliston in historical times, the other, or others, prehistoric, and the origin of the various pockets of heathen savages, as they're called here. In a time before even prehistory, in some epoch reachable only by palaeontology, the other hominidae and the large mammals were brought; and still earlier, drilling down into geological time now, the saurs and the kraken and the megatheria and marine birds, the pterosaurs that rule the skies, the insects and insectivores and all the rest of the ecosystem made their varied ways to this world.

Whatever the origin of the planetary body itself—and Matt has his suspicions about that, given the paucity of Earth-like worlds and orbits in the Solar System's vicinity, and their abundance in the Second Sphere—it's long ago been established that its whole biota bespoke a created world, on which the transplanted products of an original evolution have themselves evolved further: distant descendants of Earth's stolen and unknown children. Matt tends to think of this pattern, prevalent throughout the habitable planets of the suns of the Second Sphere, as a *backup file*. What catastrophic losses of data this backup was intended to forestall, the gods only know, but Matt has every intention of finding out.

The door opens, and a man comes in, with a file.

Lydia turned away from watching the customs boat's disappearing wake through the open hatchway and found herself looking at Salasso, who returned her gaze with an expression unreadable even by saur standards. She tugged her radio from her pocket and raised her eyebrows.

"Please," said Salasso.

She tuned the dial to her ship's channel, switched on

the scrambler, and raised the Traders' House.

"Lydia on the *Bright Star,* to the house."

"Hi there, Lydia," Esias de Tenebre said, in the accented English he staunchly stuck to when on Croatan. "Good positioning, my number-seven daughter! Consider your back clapped. Any idea what the hell's going on?"

She recounted the Port Authority's arrival and departure.

"That sounds heavy-handed," her father remarked. His sigh was a white noise in her ear. "It seems not long ago when such travelers would have been welcomed royally, not bureaucratically!"

"I remember," Lydia said soothingly. "I miss the dear old king, myself."

She was anxious to deflect Esias's standard canned rant against democracy, a political system that Rawliston had recently and violently adopted. As a member of the Electorate of the Republic of Nova Babylonia, the senior de Tenebre took a dim view of universal franchise.

"However," she went on, "I think this is more than just a case of local officialdom overstepping its mark. The news channels and the populace seem pretty excited and enthusiastic about it, and I can't imagine what the Port Authority thinks it's trying to accomplish by delaying our friends' making contact with them."

"You've put your finger on it," her father said. "Delay is exactly what they're accomplishing. And if some jumped-up winner of the administrative lottery decides to embargo the ship while his minions crawl around it . . ."

Again the white noise, from spluttering this time. Lydia held the earpiece away until her father's voice resumed, in a calmer tone: "Could be some onshore agents of our competitors behind all this—some loose-lipped third cousin or lazy servant has no doubt been bragging in a bar about how we've been expecting the cosmonauts' ship to turn up any day now."

"I certainly wasn't expecting it," Lydia said.

"But you were hoping," her father said wryly. "Weren't you?"

"Yes," she said. She paused for a moment, to indicate that she wanted to change the subject. "What would you like me to do now?"

"Oh, stay on the ship," Esias said hastily. "If they'll allow you."

Lydia raised her eyebrows at Salasso, who would have overheard every nuance of both sides of the conversation, inaudible though the faint sound from the earpiece would have been to Johannes, only a meter or two away. The saur nodded firmly.

"Salasso's happy with that."

"Salasso, by the gods! He's there too? Well, let him know we'll send someone out to see him."

"I will," Lydia promised unnecessarily—Salasso's usually impassive face was indicating bright delight already. "Signing off for now."

"Signing off," Esias said. "Take care."

Salasso looked at her. "Thank you," he said. "I shall look forward to that meeting."

"Well," said Lydia, with an awkward, light laugh, "I don't suppose you could show us around your ship, while we're waiting?"

"Certainly," said Salasso. "Except for the cargo itself, which is commercially confidential."

"Of course." Lydia wondered if Salasso could read her small smirk at the presumption of thinking that competition from the *Bright Star*'s cargo was likely to worry the de Tenebre family business; probably he could. His nostrils widened fractionally, the corners of his lips extended sideways a little: a smile.

He glanced at Johannes, who still stood, almost at attention, by the exit hatch.

"Both of you?" he asked.

"Uh, no," Lydia said. "Johannes, would you mind just . . . keeping an eye on the door?"

"Not at all," said her cousin, in a tone that indicated he minded a bit, but not enough to make a big deal of it. She'd have to make it up to him, afterward with a detailed description over drinks.

"Let us begin where we are," said Salasso. "This is the control room. The controls themselves are mounted on this table, and are undeniably crude. However, as we have demonstrated, they work."

Lydia had not expected that the clutter of data-input devices, tangles of cable, and cannibalized electrical apparatus on the tilted table could be the controls. She'd assumed it was some bits of legacy junk and had vaguely imagined a shining console with wraparound screens in the bowels of the ship. But then, she had never actually seen the controls of a starship—for all she knew, the kraken might play their tentacles over something equally uneasy on the eye. Though not, she guessed, with such shoddy insulation.

She ducked after Salasso through an oval hatch that led to a strip-lit tubular corridor with free-fall handgrips along the sides and retrofitted planking along the bottom. After a few paces the saur pointed sideways at a doorway.

"Fabrication unit," he said as he passed it. Hurrying to keep up, Lydia caught a glimpse of a module dominated by a floor-mounted cluster of glittery, spidery machinery that looked sinister and alien and that she suspected—but it could have been a trick of the light—was in tremulous motion.

"What do you plan to do with it?"

Salasso glanced back, pausing at another doorway. "It may have industrial applications," he said. "But that is for the long future. We took it in case we needed to make repairs."

He led her quickly on, pointing out habitation units, cargo bays, labs, and finally, as they turned a corner at an intersection and stopped before something huge and bolted to the corridor floor, the drive.

She stood looking over the saur's shoulder, struck silent by the sight. Smooth, as though cast in one impenetrable piece, its flowing curves and fluted flanges and flared, funnelled ends were those of a jet engine designed by gods. It stood on a pedestal, and by moving about she could take in its approximate dimensions: two meters high, one across, and four long. From any angle, it looked as though streamlined to move in that direction. The beauty of its form was fused with its fitness for some incomprehensible function, making it irresistable and at the same time uncomfortable to look at.

"It plays tricks with the eye," said Salasso. "It makes the head hurt."

"Yours too?" she asked.

"No," said Salasso, turning away. "You have never seen one before?"

Lydia closed her eyes and put her fingers to her temples and turned her back on the drive. She could still see it, in her mind.

"No," she said. "The krakens don't give us tours." She laughed weakly. "Just as well."

"I have not seen one on a ship," said Salasso. "Only newly built ones, in the manufacturing plant."

Lydia gazed, unseeing, at the far end of the corridor. "I still can't believe Gregor actually figured out how to control that thing." She gave the saur a shrewd sidelong glance. "It wasn't you, was it?"

"No indeed!" Salasso sounded slightly indignant. "I could not, even if I would. No, Gregor's work was the culmination of generations of hand calculation by members of the Cosmonaut Families. It was implemented on this ship's remaining functional computers after Gregor had independently achieved the key insight."

"Oh," she said. "And what was that?"

The saur's large black eyes regarded her, his expression verging on something like humor.

"Octopodia."

There was a feeling in her back as though she were being watched.

"Take me somewhere else," she said.

"I think you have seen all you need to see," said Salasso. She followed him as he headed back to the control room by a different route. On the way she glanced into a lab module through a glass pane in its doorway.

She stopped. "What's that?"

Again, it was something she couldn't look away from, more alien by far than the complex fabrication tool kit or even the drive itself. Like an enormous model of a snowflake rendered in fine sheet metal, partly folded and partly crumpled, it almost filled the room.

Salasso turned and looked back at her, impassively.

"That is the device that the crew of the original ship— when it was a research station on the surface of a god— used to communicate with that god."

"Oh," said Lydia. She shivered, as though the snow-flake sculpture were making her cold. "It seems a strange item to bring with you."

"It might have been necessary," Salasso said, "in an emergency, if Gregor's navigation calculations had been mistaken."

"I see," said Lydia. "Like you brought the fabrication unit."

"Yes," said Sallaso. "Like that."

Lydia followed him to the control room without further interruption and stepped through its hatchway with a sense of relief. She had found the tour fascinating but disturbing; all her life she had traveled in a ship piloted by giant squids; a ship built, crewed and serviced by saurs, and whose original design, she knew, had come from the gods themselves. That remote and limited interaction with those distant and indifferent divinities had been mediated by the two known species of greater intelligence and antiquity than the human. Now she was standing in a ship built by human beings that had touched the very face of a god, and she now knew that at least two men of her acquaintance, Matt and Volkov, might have had even closer communion with it than that.

No wonder, then, that these two old cosmonauts seemed ageless. Perhaps it wasn't, as Volkov had claimed, some advanced medical treatment received long ago in the Solar System that had bestowed this gift, unexpected as it had been. Perhaps some cold fire from the icy mind of the god had entered their nerves. As always when she thought of Volkov, a hot fire entered her own.

As soon as she'd cleared the hatchway she saw that Johannes was no longer alone in the control room. A saur stood in the external doorway, behind which an extending ladder sloped back and up to the just-visible underside of a hovering gravity skiff.

"Bishlayan!" Salasso said. The two saurs met in the middle of the floor and held each other by the shoulders for a moment. Keeping his hand on her shoulder, Salasso escorted her to one of the battered seats and almost lifted her into it, then swung back and up into another.

"It is good to see you," Bishlayan said.

"Likewise," said Salasso. The two saurs, politeness satisfied, dropped out of Trade Latin and into their own language, of which, like most humans—even her father—Lydia knew little more than a few everyday phrases and the odd technical word. Their body language of mutual affection, subtle but intense, she found almost embarrassingly understandable.

It suddenly ocurred to Lydia that the de Tenebre ship's last-but-one visit to Mingulay had been less than a year ago in Bishlayan's life, and in Lydia's, but more than four hundred years in Salasso's if he'd spent all that time on the same planet. A long time for lovers to be parted, even though the saurs saw love from the different perspective provided by their millennia-long lives.

The thought of parted lovers, and of long lives, brought a pang. Gregor Cairns and Grigory Volkov, the one young and bright, the other old and sly, might between them provide the solution to both problems . . .

though the two of them presented her with a different problem and the prospect of a difficult choice. Lydia looked away from the saurs' sibilant, sinuous conversation and ambled idly about the control room, looking out of the forward window—and it was a window, not a viewscreen—at the shipping, looking over the shoulder of Johannes, who'd slumped in one of the chairs behind Salasso's back and was carefully inspecting, and carefully not touching, the control system.

Like black rocks perturbing a smooth current, the names "Volkov" and "Cairns" suddenly cropped up in Salasso's speech. Johannes, not as attuned as Lydia to the language or to the names, and still tracing wires with his gaze, didn't seem to have noticed. Lydia moved around to get an inconspicuous sidelong view of the saurs. They were both leaning forward. Salasso's long fingers were gripping his knees. Bishlayan's hands were held in front of her, quivering. Both spoke more quietly than before, and sometimes—almost unthinkably for their kind—at the same time, interrupting each other. The cosmonauts' names came up again and again, each time more harshly dissonant than before.

Then Bishlayan leaned back slightly—in a human, it would have been a violent recoil. Her hands—open, palms down in front of her—moved sharply apart: *cut*. She grasped the arms of the seat and slid out of it, stalked across the floor to the exit, and ascended the ladder. In a moment the steps slid back into the craft, and its shadow passed across the forward window as it flitted away.

Salasso sat bowed over, with his elbows on his knees and his head in his hands.

Matt takes his time about shifting his buttock from the desk, as the official strides over, nods with a passing frown, and arranges himself in the chair. His sallow-skinned face projects above the high collar of a uniform too big for his short and skinny frame: knee breeches to midcalf, epaulettes that almost reach his ears, the blue, brass-buttoned coat's sleeves turned back at the wrists to reveal a square foot or two of greasy silk lining. He shuffles the papers he carried in and adjusts the blotter, looking sternly downward as Matt eases himself back to an orange seat.

Then his sharp, dark eyes look up.

"Good afternoon," he says. "Citizen Obadiah Randolph, secretary of customs, at your service."

They return greetings in an awkward chorus.

Randolph smiles. "Well," he says, "I suppose I had better welcome you to the city, and the planet, and I do, but I shall spare you any disquisitions on the historic significance of your arrival. The chatterboxes will no doubt stuff your ears with plenty of that before the day is out. It's their job. Mine is to ensure that you are not carrying any prohibited products, to apply any applicable tariffs, and to make arrangements for currency conversion. May I see your bill of lading, please?"

Matt fiddles with the flimsy sheets for a moment.

"What we would like to query," he says, "is whether this whole procedure is applicable to arrivals by starship, given that the established interstellar merchants don't have to go through any such clearance. In short, and with all due respect, we question whether your authority extends to our ship."

"Ah!" Randolph leans forward, steepling his long fingers. "I'm afraid it does. The great merchant families"—he waves a hand vaguely at the window—"such as the de Tenebres are, as you say, established. Tariffs, by immemorial custom, are not applied. As for quarantine regulations—well! The ships in which the established merchants travel are owned and crewed by beings whose experience in this regard can, I think, be safely reckoned to be vastly greater than ours." He smiles again, not so warmly. "And in *my* experience, the krakens and the saurs are our mental and moral superiors, and the difference in both knowledge of consequence and sense of responsibility is . . . noticeable."

"I'll give you that," Matt says dryly. "It just seems odd that you'd be ready for something that's never happened before. I mean, come on. An independent starship arrives—and not just any starship, at that—and the first thing you think of is to drag it through *customs*?"

Obadiah Randolph's lips narrow. He spreads his hands. "It's true, we've only recently realized that such an event might be possible, and made . . . contingency plans. A thousand apologies if it seems burdensome, but if it does, would it not be better to get it over with?"

Contingency plans, huh? Matt has a good idea how the Port Authority just happened to have them worked out recently.

"Fine," he says, rising and passing the papers across the desk. "Let's get it over with."

Randolph shows no signs of hurry to get it over with, as for the next hour or so he queries every line in the manifest, hauling book after book down from the shelf and looking up obscure precedents and arcane definitions, all for tediously innocuous items of Mingulayan manufacture—high-value stuff, jewelery and precision intruments and so forth, as the economics of the trade dictate, but nothing of obvious malign use or biological origin. Matt kicks his heels, stares out of the window, wishes for a drink or smoke; Gregor and Elizabeth talk quietly and, in the end, desultorily.

The telephone buzzes once. Matt notes that the apparatus isn't cabled; still using radio, then. Citizen Randolph listens intently, murmurs briefly, returns the handset to its cradle and his attention to a musty volume. About ten minutes later he replaces it on the shelf, brushes its dust from his fingertips, and slumps back in his chair. Then he reaches into a desk drawer, produces a tinned inkpad and a large rubber stamp, and thumps an imprint onto each sheet of the cargo manifest with an air of a job well done.

He slides the papers back across the desk.

"That's it," he says. "All in order, as far as I can see. No embargoed products, and nothing in your cargo appears on the schedule of imports on which tariff is liable. A small fee of five hundred talers is due for my services, of course, but as long as it's paid at my office downstairs before your departure—"

Gregor raises a hand. "Excuse me." He pulls a bundle of Croatan currency from his pocket, peers at it, peels off five, and slaps them on the desk with ill grace. "There."

"Thank you," says Randolph, vanishing the cash.

Matt picks up the documents, smiling for a moment at the blurry curlicues of red ink.

"Thank *you*," he says. Out of the corner of his eye he sees that Gregor shares his looming, forward-leaning stance and seizes the moment of psychological advantage. "Now, citizen, could you please enlighten us on what the point of this whole rigmarole has been?"

Randolph leans back and blinks. "I beg your pardon?"

Matt gestures out of the window. "I've watched a dozen surface ships come in this past hour, all heavy-laden merchantmen, and by their rig and flags I guess they must have have come from at least four different distant shores, and you have the time to personally inspect our documents in the most pernickety detail?"

"I doubt that any of their cargoes are as significant as yours. If human starship traffic is possible—and you have shown it is—it will be repeated and extended. The cargoes of our surface shipping will change and multiply. We'll have both the need and the ability to map and explore our own planet much more intensively then before." He waves a hand at the globe on his desk. "No more of that 'here be dragons' nonsense. Besides"—he leans farther back—"the cargo is the least important part of what you have on your ship. The past hour has given us time to initiate an independent inspection of the rest, for ecological, biological, chemical, or other hazards. I have just heard that the boarding has been successful."

Matt has a strong impulse to tip the chair right back and send the man sprawling, and an equally strong conviction that this won't do them any long-term good.

The loud-hailed warning from outside jolted Salasso out of his hitherto unshakeable gloomy trance. He walked slowly to the exit hatch and leaned out, then stepped back.

"It's an inspection," he said.

The man who came through the hatchway was younger and slimmer than his predecessors and more elaborately dressed, with tall boots and a plumed hat, which he doffed with a bow to Lydia.

"Citizen Charles Cargill," he said. "Your servant. Customs, excise, and public safety."

They introduced themselves. Cargill turned to Salasso. His black hair hung in a pigtail down the back of his green coat.

"You are in charge here?"

"For the present," said Salasso.

The inspector pulled a radio from his pocket and spoke into briefly, too quickly and quietly for Lydia to catch. He clicked it shut and put it away.

"You'll be glad to know," he said, "that your documentation is in order. Your declared cargo is cleared for landing, pending inspection."

"You are welcome to inspect it," said Salasso.

"Thank you," said Cargill. "But that is not my purpose. You are free to leave the cargo sealed for the moment. It will of course be checked on landing. My duty is to inspect the ship for possible public hazards."

Lydia had a brief surge of the feeling she associated with the gravity's being switched off.

Cargill looked about, frowning, and pointed at the table in the center of the deck. "Perhaps you would care to start by explaining *that*?"

"Certainly," said Salasso. "This is the control panel."

Cargill studied the apparatus warily, noting the dodgy insulation with pursed lips and a shake of the head.

Salasso stood by the door to the ship's interior. "I will now show you around the ship," he said.

Lydia thought she could detect a strained note in his voice. He stepped over the bulkhead, beckoning Cargill after him.

They reappeared some twenty minutes later.

Cargill made his way to the nearest chair and sat down in it, visibly mustering his composure. His clamped hands stopped the quivering of his knees, but one of his heels, apparently without his awareness, kept tapping on the floor.

"This ship . . ." he said. His tongue flicked along his lips. "This ship is impounded."

4

The First Man on Venus

T HE STEPS INSIDE the Port Authority building are of worn concrete; those outside, spilling down to the street from the double swinging doors, are of chipped but clean marble. The sunlight is harsh against the white stone as Matt emerges blinking, Gregor and Elizabeth at his heels. At the bottom of the ten or so wide, shallow steps are a couple of dozen people, holding up heavy cameras or holding out thick black microphones. Many of them are clutching radios to one ear and talking, and scribbling on pads of paper. Behind them in the broad street huge trucks and small cars are alike trundling by in low gear. Drivers and pedestrians loiter and stare. The din of voices and vehicles is distracting. A few brown-uniformed men sweating under polished steel helmets and clutching two-meter staves are urging people to move on, but beyond preventing a complete standstill they're not accomplishing much.

There's no surge up the steps, though, so Matt ambles down to face the thicket of microphones. A woman holding one of them shoves a big flapping sheet of paper into his hands. The paper is warm, and the black lettering smudges under his thumbs. A bold masthead in antique font announces it's **The Hourly Electrostat** over a blocky headline screaming **STARSHIP SEIZED**. The rest of the top half of the page is a grainy but perfectly distinct photograph, obviously taken from a low-flying aircraft, of the two customs men boarding the *Bright Star* and two others pointing rifles at the camera. Matt is impressed: The event happened less than two hours ago. Maybe the masthead's boast is justified.

Matt has no time to read any more of it. A microphone is thrust in front of him.

"Mr. Cairns, do you have anything to say about what the Port Authority's doing?"

Other reporters crowd around, shouting questions about why and how the *Bright Star* has made the light-speed jump. Matt turns to Gregor, who is after all in charge of the ship. Gregor shrugs and mouths silently. Elizabeth shakes her head. Matt realizes with some irritation that the other two have decided that he has to speak for them.

He smiles at the woman who gave him the paper and says, "No, I have no comment at all on what the Port Authority has done."

"Don't you think it's—?"

But he's already turned to answer someone else.

"We're here on a trading mission," he says. "And to test the ship. That's all. Navigator Gregor Cairns here has solved the problem of navigating the jump between Mingulay and Croatan. We're of course relieved that it works"—he pauses, smiling for a camera until someone smiles back—"and we're delighted to be here."

The woman from the *Electrostat* fixes on him again and swings her microphone dangerously.

"Why have you come? You personally, all of you?"

He nudges Gregor to take this one. The younger man shrugs and scratches his head as though this is some deep question. Typical scientist. The dead air stretches for twenty seconds.

"I'm here," Gregor says, "because I did the navigation, and I would not ask anyone else to bet his or her life on my calculations and stay behind myself. My, uh, relative Matt is here because he had some expertise on the working of the ship itself. He has, ah, made a special study of it. And Elizabeth, uh . . ."

"I'm here," Elizabeth says firmly, "because I'm a scientist. A marine biologist. I'm here representing the university, not the Cosmonaut Families."

"Isn't there anyone back home you'll be missing?" the reporter asks her, with a sly smile.

"Of all the people I know, Gregor is the only one I could not bear to be away from for ten years." That raises a laugh and some whoops.

Another microphone pushes in front of Matt's face. "Is it true that the saurs are helping you?"

"A few are," Matt says.

He turns away sharply from that mike and answers some more questions fulsomely but evasively and makes sure to clasp his arms around the shoulders of his companions, partly for the cameras and partly because he can see both of them beginning to look a little dissociated. He knows the feeling: It's culture shock, combined with the even bigger shock to the human animal brain of finding itself on a different planet, with the gravity ever so slightly off so that your heels come down a bit wrong and you thump things and the air carries unfamiliar smells in a slightly different mix of gases that your brain can't quite make sense of but that you notice in every cell.

And all the while he is wondering how they are going to get away from all this and where they can go when they do, when suddenly he sees a delightfully familiar and welcome sight, a real taste of home: A flying saucer slides above the rooftops of the high buildings opposite and begins to descend, reflecting the entire scene in a wondrously distorted image in its perfect-mirrored lenticular surface as it settles slowly on the street. Vehicles and people shift out of its way, in a cacophony of squealing brakes, crunching fenders, tinkling glass, engines revving and people shouting. Its three legs telescope out and its entrance hatch opens like a liquid eye, and a dull-gray stairladder extends to the foot of the Port Authority steps.

The de Tenebre girl, Lydia, takes a few steps down the ladder and glares around at the crowd, then grins down.

"Come on in," she says. "We can take you to the Star Traders' House."

Matt sways on the spot as first Gregor, then Elizabeth ascend. It's as if his leg muscles have locked. Then, with a shake of his head and an effort of will, he follows them up into the skiff. The hatch seals soundlessly behind him. Inside, it's exactly like every other flying saucer he's ever been in, with a wraparound screen showing the outside clearer than a window, and a sort of angled soft shelf all the way around the bottom of that, with a small arc of it recessed to the control panel before which the saur pilot sits. Another touch of home.

Salasso is already on board. Matt smiles at him and sits down beside Lydia on the circular bench whose comfortably padded back wraps around the central faring over the craft's engine. The floor is cluttered with suitcases, among which he recognizes his own.

The pilot looks back over his shoulder. "Everybody ready?"

"Yes," says Lydia. "Take us away, Voronar, if you please."

There's no sense of motion, but the view in the screen tips and slides down. For a moment Matt looks down at the crowd of reporters, some of them still holding their microphones skyward, or more rationally their cameras, and then the view swings up again and there's nothing but hazy sky ahead.

"So what happened out there?" Matt asks.

Salasso exhales a long, hissing sigh and gestures at Lydia as though he is beyond speech, which he may be.

Lydia is herself furious. "That *fop*, that *bureaucrat* Cargill marched all over the ship and impounded it as a hazard! We just managed to get your stuff off. None of you are allowed back on except Salasso, and that's just because he persuaded Cargill that the drive needs regular attention or it'll be a *bigger* hazard. They have two armed patrol boats moored alongside now. You can unload your cargo, but that's all."

Gregor frowns and leans forward awkwardly around the curve of the bench. "Do you think Cargill really was genuinely frightened by the sight of the drive and the other bits of advanced kit?"

Lydia laughs, and when she speaks the spitting rage has gone out of her voice. "I know it scared him—and it scared me! But that's not a rational reason to embargo the ship. No, it's a pretext."

"So what's the real reason?"

"We'll discuss that at the house," Lydia says. "My father knows something of the matter."

She stands up and looks out of the viewscreen. The air is clear outside, the sky bright blue. The skiff has sped beyond the city's edge to fly low along a coast road. Between the road and the long white beaches, large villas and mansions are set in broad gardens. Toward one of the largest of them, it dips, then yaws and sideslips like a falling leaf into a paved, palm-lined courtyard where fountains play with rainbows. Its legs and ladder, extending, neatly straddle the central bathing pool.

"Here we are," she says. "Welcome to the Star Traders' House."

Lydia led them to a table under the courtyard's interior colonnade. A couple of distant cousins had run up for the baggage, and the skiff lifted off over the roof to immediately descend again, this time on the long lawn of long grass between the house and the beach.

Her father, Esias, and his third wife, Phoebe, rose to greet the new arrivals. Esias, evidently relaxed, wore an informal loose toga, Phoebe a similarly Nova Babylonian light robe of green cloth flecked with silver threads. Much handshaking and backslapping ensued; Matt was the only one who needed an introduction. Phoebe started filling glasses from a large, ice-clinking jug and signaling to some cousins across the courtyard for more drinks at about the same time as Voronar strolled in through the open passageway from the front and joined Salasso as they all sat down.

Lydia found herself on Gregor's right; his left arm was around Elizabeth, who had no attention for anything but the tall glass that had just appeared in front of her.

"You once asked me where we lived, between journeys," Lydia murmured. "This is where we live when we're here."

"It's wonderful," Gregor said, craning his neck and gazing around. "How do you keep it, between visits?"

"We don't," Lydia said. "It's rented to any merchant family that happens along, and betweentimes, I imagine, to local rich folk who want some time out of the city." She leaned back and looked around, noticing as if for the first time the weathering of the slates and the flagstones, the lichen and the creeper on the walls. "It's changed a lot, in the last few months, I mean centuries . . ."

Gregor looked at her wryly. "Yeah, I'll bet. Are there any other families staying here?"

"No, no, just us. Four wings, three stories—it's just about big enough for all of us. Sixty-odd humans, thirty or so saurs—that's a fairly typical trader clan and crew, and the others in at the moment have other villas up and down the coast."

"Better than the Keep, do you think?"

Lydia smiled, recalling the vast prehuman castle that

the Cosmonaut Families maintained outside Kyohvic, Gregor's native town on Mingulay.

"More comfortable, perhaps, but not as interesting, with no one staying here to give us hospitality. No dinosaur heads on the walls, and no clifftop walks, either."

Gregor smiled momentarily over the shared memory, then reached for his drink. Matt Cairns and Esias were already talking quietly and intently; the two saurs were passing a pipe of hemp back and forth between them, puffing fragrant smoke rings from their narrow mouths, and Phoebe was drawing out Elizabeth with some sympathetic small talk across the table, a conversation to which Gregor turned his attention.

Lydia didn't need to ask whether Gregor and Elizabeth were still in love with each other—Elizabeth's presence here was earnest enough of that—but she had no idea whether this passion excluded her. She suspected it did. Mingulayan custom was sexually tolerant but emotionally constrained, holding up mutual physical attraction combined with friendship as the only worthy basis of marriage, and disdaining romantic love as a dangerous but transitory disorder of the mind, a flimsy foundation for any protracted partnership. The predictable result was that infatuation flourished in a furtive manner, its stems not tall and flowering but creeping along the ground, pallid and twisted and entangling. She couldn't help but regard her own culture as much healthier and more natural, giving fleeting romantic attachment an honorable but ornamental place alongside the more businesslike affair of marriage.

At that moment, her father's second wife, Lydia's mother Faustina, walked in from the passageway accompanied by Grigory Volkov, both of them naked and dripping from the beach, chatting and toweling and teasing each other, and Lydia almost cried out with the hot fury of her jealousy. There was nothing to it, nothing; of course there was not; Volkov could swim with anyone he liked, and he did. Right now he was grinning straight at her, his white teeth gleaming against his new tan, his blond hair palmed casually back in inch-long damp spikes. He knotted the towel around his waist as he noticed the new guests, and his smile subtly changed as he greeted them and swung around the table to drag up a chair at the corner beside Lydia, while Faustina snuggled damply up to Esias opposite.

"So you made it," Volkov said, to Matt rather than Gregor. His soft baritone and the indefinably cultured accent of his English gave Lydia, as always, a sensation like that of stroking a cat's back. Or, she fancied, of being a cat and having its back stroked.

"We made it," Matt said firmly. A cousin had wheeled up a rattling trolley of bottles and was slowly orbitting the table. Matt glanced away from Volkov long enough to make a selection, then fixed him again with his gaze as he absently tipped several fingers of clear vodka into his fruit juice.

"Good to see you all," Volkov said, flashing his smile around. "I could hardly believe it when I heard it on the radio." He chuckled. "So I went swimming. Ah, large vodka. Thanks, Arianne." He smiled up at the cousin serving and raised quick eyebrows to Esias. "Have you got to business yet?"

Esias shook his head, frowning a little. "I thought that could wait until after dinner. Our guests need to relax."

"Naturally," said Volkov. He fingered water from his ear and looked around again, head tilted, as though shyly. "I'll be going in the pool and the fountains to wash the salt off, and I'm sure Faustina will do the same. Would any of you like to join us?"

"What an excellent idea," said Esias. He shed his toga and, wearing nothing but his immense dignity, picked up his second wife and walked to the pool, threw her in, and jumped after her.

Volkov looked sidelong at the startled expressions of Gregor and Elizabeth.

"But we have nothing to—" Elizabeth began.

" 'When in Rome . . .' " said Volkov, and after a little more persuasion, they did as the Nova Babylonians had done.

Esias is a broad-beamed, sturdy man in his midforties, with springy, gingery hair and a spray of freckles across his flat nose. From the head of the table, flanked by his first and second wives, he chairs the after-dinner conversation with nothing more obtrusive than a narrowed eye or a cocked ear. With intent that might be mischievous or tactful, he has seated Volkov between Faustina and Lydia—his seventh but, for this occasion, most-favored daughter—and Matt directly opposite Volkov, between Claudia and Phoebe. Gregor, then Elizabeth, are to Lydia's left; Salasso, Bishlayan, and Voronar to Phoebe's right. Farther on down the long table are other senior clan and crew members, saur or human; as seems customary, various junior relatives have done the serving, and the rest of the shop's complement are scattered among other tables, on this outer verandah or on the tussocky seaside grass in the house's long shadow that, with the sea breeze, makes this a cool and pleasant location for an early evening meal. Harp music from nearby merges with the tinkling of the fountains from down the passageway in the courtyard behind them, to provide a similarly soothing and cooling effect on the mind.

Matt has found conversation with the two ladies on either side of him interesting but something of a strain. Like the rest of the de Tenebres they know of his—and Volkov's—untoward longevity and are intrigued by his recollections of Earth. Matt has had little experience of recounting them to people who hadn't been there themselves, and there's a fine line between mystifying them with too little explanation and making their eyes glaze over with too much. Volkov, he notices, has no such difficulty, chatting easily to both Lydia and her mother, calling across to other people whose acquaintance he's obviously cultivated during the past quarter, and always making a point of thanking the younger folk on waiting duty rather than taking their attentions for granted like their relatives do.

Matt dourly reflects that Volkov was always good at winning people over. It's entirely possible that his genuine competence as a cosmonaut, and the authentic if scientifically worthless heroism that took him to and from the hellish surface of Venus, were themselves effects as well as causes of his political ascent through the bureaucracies of the European Space Agency and the Communist Party of the European Union. In the past couple of centuries these achievements have been entirely moot, but he's had several business careers since then under different identities, and each one has usually left a nice little nest egg for its successor to hatch for the benefit of the reappearing Volkov, billed as a long-lost son or other legitimate inheritor. Unlike Matt, whose typical transition from one incarnation to the next has involved arson, major insurance fraud, and faking his own death to escape angry creditors. Avoiding any reference to these serial suicides, self-embezzlements, and so forth has been not the least exacting part of his small talk with Claudia and Phoebe.

Gregor, too, is having an awkward time, talking mostly to Elizabeth and almost cold-shouldering Lydia, though she's hanging so much on Volkov's conversation that she may not have noticed. At least Gregor and Elizabeth look like they've got over their planet shock, though Matt expects them—and himself—to crash down to an early night. The three saurs at Matt's right are silent, torpid from their hearty eating—each has a plate in front of him or her piled with the bones of the main dish, small pterosaurs that taste like chicken—and whacked out of their heads by a recently shared pipe of hemp. Matt absently accepts a joint from Claudia and finds his gaze drawn away from the table to where the harpist is sitting, her back half turned, leaving her cheekbone, jawline, and pensive mouth as visible and as fascinating as the straight blond hair that hangs to the waistline of her leather trousers.

Matt is shaken out of the resulting erotic reverie by the sound of Esias elbowing the table and clearing his throat, so he leans past the vacant black eyes of the nodding saurs to pass the joint to starboard and settles back and looks to the head of the table.

Esias makes a big deal of lighting up a fat cigar with a fancy new device he's just imported from Mingulay, which Matt does not doubt he is inordinately pleased with and has high hopes of franchising elsewhere. The lid of the knockoff Zippo clicks shut and Esias puffs smoke to clear the petroleum whiff.

He coughs again, just to make sure. It's discreet but as emphatic a signal as the rap of a gavel to the few who hear it. The only person other than those around the head of the table who responds is the harpist, who stops playing and turns around (another moment of distraction, as Matt catches sight of her lean, pale features). Esias plays air harp for a moment, urging her to resume playing. She does. Salasso, Bishlayan, and Voronar jolt out of their trance. Esias leans forward on his elbows and speaks quietly.

"Before we've all had too much to drink—which, I expect, we will—we have some business to attend to. Everybody here is guest or family, so we needn't worry about being overheard, and doubtless everything I say will get around, but we have a moment of not-too-obvious semiprivacy, so let's use it by getting the, ah, more delicate matters out of the way first. . . ."

He closes his eyes momentarily, and sighs, and combs greasy fingers through his shock of hair. Lydia suddenly blushes and looks, desperately, as though she doesn't know where to look and settles on staring fixedly across at Matt. Baffled, he returns her what he hopes is a friendly and reassuring smile.

"As some of you know," Esias goes on, "I promised

Lydia's hand to Gregor here, a few months ago back on Mingulay, if he could meet us in his own ship. He has done that. I also repeated that promise, on different terms, at another time. Lydia's consent was"—he smiles at her, briefly—"evident at both times. We consider ourselves bound to it. Gregor, the decision is in your hands. You need not make it now, but it would be . . . convenient if you did."

Matt is shaken. He knows there's some tension between Gregor and Elizabeth over Lydia but has assumed it no more than the normal jealousy over an ex not over an outstanding arrangement. Are the interstellar master traders really as primitive and patriarchal as *that*? Brideprice? Christ, by 2049 we'd stamped that out in fucking *Afghanistan*. . . . He realizes that this is the first time in years that he's thought *we* and meant the European Union.

Gregor and Elizabeth have clasped hands firmly above the table. Esias takes this in but speaks to Gregor only. "Your relationship with Elizabeth is not an obstacle to your accepting the offer, as far as we are concerned."

Gregor, floundering until now, seizes on this like a thrown line. "It is, as far as I am concerned," he says. "I appreciate what you're saying, and I thank you for it, but we—on Mingulay we have a different way of looking at these things."

"Indeed you do," says Esais wryly. "But I must ask you formally: Do you release Lydia from my promise?"

"I release her," says Gregor, then surprises Matt by turning to Lydia with a big grin and adding, "but, you know, no offense . . ."

Even Elizabeth joins in the laughter at that; even Lydia, though she's blinking a little rapidly and at the same time looking released and relieved.

"Thank you," Lydia says. "I'm sure I'll live down this rejection."

"It's not a—" Gregor begins hotly, rather blowing the wit and tact he'd a shown a moment ago.

Lydia puts a hand over his mouth. "I'm such a tease," she says.

Too much of a one, Elizabeth's dark glance agrees, but the whole strain of the situation has been collapsed by Gregor's apparently artless compliment. Matt is sure that no one else but Elizabeth has noticed that beneath his light tone was a note of regret.

"Very good," says Esias. He looks around his wives, who all seem as cheered as he is by the settlement of that particular item on the agenda. "Let's, um, move on. About the ship and its impounding. Since our last visit here this city has adopted a new political system: legislation by assemblies of the entire populace, with almost all public offices filled by citizens chosen by lot. Out-and-out democracy, if you ask me." He shakes his head sadly. "Well, they'll learn. That kind of straightforward tyranny of the majority has many disadvantages, one of which is that it makes officeholders difficult to bribe, beyond the most routine grease and graft, and makes it even more difficult to place sympathetic people in useful positions."

Matt laughs, then realizes from the surrounding silence that the merchant is being quite serious.

"Nevertheless," Esias continues, "it does seem to me that more is involved here than some petty bureaucratic enforcement of a regulation in an area to which it was never intended to be applied. Not that they *have* a bureaucracy, as such. Just those gods-damned jumped-up lottery-picked citizens. The only exceptions are the Port Authority itself—which, as it happens, *is* a bureaucracy, albeit a notionally private corporation—and posts requiring specialized knowledge: the military cadre, and public health and safety officers such as our friend Citizen Cargill. He might have provided the entering wedge."

"I got the impression from Citizen Randolph that the regulation has recently been taken down from the shelf and dusted off," says Matt. "He mentioned that they'd made contingency plans for the arrival of a human-crewed ship."

"Did he indeed? It would seem that I was right about someone's blabbing in a bar. Oh, well. Nothing to be done about it now. The puzzle is that the local populace would undoubtedly benefit from an increase in trade, and the local compradores—the import-export representatives of the great shipping families—would not, but the former have a much more direct lever on the authorities than the latter. Possibly one of our competitors—the Rodriguezes, the de Montforts, the Vari, any of that lot—has managed to get some leverage over elements in the Port Authority. Perhaps via Cargill. Hmm. I shall have my local agents look into it."

The de Tenebre clan is itself one of the shipping families Esias has mentioned, with a considerable starship fleet to its name, and no doubt has a great onshore encrustation of compradores and agents of its own to match. Unlike the others, however, it has cut a deal with the Cosmonaut Families of Mingulay to get in on the ground floor of any new trading patterns that their independent navigation may establish. Its rivals, Matt guesses, must be fuming.

"What about getting the decision reversed?" Gregor asks.

Esias waves his cigar. "Within weeks the matter will have been raised at most of the neighborhood assemblies, by which time we'll have used our contacts to make sure people realize, if they don't already, that putting inconveniences in your way is not a good way to encourage future trade."

Weeks? Matt doesn't have weeks. He keeps his spontaneous remark to this effect firmly behind compressed lips.

So he asks instead, "How long are you staying here?"

Esias draws breath through his teeth. "Naturally, we're impatient to get back to Nova Babylonia, but we're going to be here on Croatan for another three months—our ship's schedule and route are all determined by the kraken, not by us. Which is one reason why we're so keen on human-controlled ships. Our ship is due to move to ports on the other continents in, ah, seventeen days from now and return here about six weeks later to eventually leave on St. Teilhard's Day."

"One of the cults of the local Anglican church," Volkov explains, grinning. "Three months from now they have a big carnival in celebration of St. Teilhard of Piltdown, the patron saint of evolution. The procession is quite spectaular, I'm told. Drums, costumes, dancers filling the streets, the lot, all headed up by the bishop, bearing a reliquary."

"Now wait a minute," says Gregor, frowning. "They can't possibly have relics of Teilhard de Chardin."

"Avowedly faked bones," says Volkov smugly.

"The Christians never cease to astonish me," says Esias. "We have them in Nova Babylonia, too, of course. Descended from Christian Roman soldiers, caught up to heaven with some lost legion long ago. May their God help them when they find out what their Croatan brethren have made of their gospel, let alone what was made of it on Earth." He sighs, then looks up with a determined smile. "On a more cheerful note, you at least have your cargo, if not access to your ship, and I think you'll find that our onshore agents can offer you some mutually profitable arrangements in disposing of it. . . ."

Esias slips into a detailed discussion with Gregor and Elizabeth, and the others around the table begin to rise and drift off. Matt looks hopefully at the harpist, but she's still busy, lost in that absorbing absorption with her work. Maybe later. Matt looks across the table at Volkov, who's becoming thoroughly restive now that Lydia and her mother have joined Esias in shop talk.

"Grigory Andreievich," he says, "would you care for a stroll on the beach?"

Volkov nods, eyes narrowed. "Walk off some of this? Good idea."

As he makes his way around the table, Matt taps Salasso, now fully alert again, on the shoulder.

"Let's walk," he says.

The saur scrambles up and follows him.

Croatan's sun is just above the low hills and long buildings along the shore, and the sky is blue at the zenith and yellow at the horizon, the colors between shading imperceptibly through evanescent limes and greens. The sea looks dark and choppy and colder than the breeze coming off the mountains. The two tall men and the short saur cast long shadows across the white sand, their terminations indistinguishable in the surf.

Volkov has taken a course to the left, and they're walking slowly northward. Eyeing him sidelong across Salasso's bobbing pate, Matt realizes that there's still a trace of envy in his mind that Volkov's apparent age is at least ten years greater than his own. Back in the twenty-first century, all kinds of antiaging nostrums had been peddled, in the socialist bloc even more than in the capitalist. Matt, like everybody he knew, swallowed them by the handful. The Russian must have been in his thirties when whichever one of them—or whichever synergic and serendipitous cocktail of several—had kicked in to give even more longevity than had ever been promised, with the aging process not just delayed but—so far—abolished. It's an odd thing to envy, but the impression of maturity has certain advantages over Matt's stubbornly youthful appearance.

"Well," says Matt, "you've been here three months. What have you been doing?"

Volkov shrugs, kicks to send a pebble skipping across the sand as he walks. "I had to abandon my business on Mingulay," he says, "when the traders offered me a place on their ship at very short notice. But I still have contacts here, in marine engineering and so forth, and I've been cultivating them. Arranging some forward shipping of devices and techniques that Esias assures me are novelties in Nova Babylonia. It'll give me something to trade on in case the deal with researching our common, ah, condition doesn't pan out as profitably as Esias hopes."

"Very wise," says Salasso. "If they wish to find the secret of your longevity in Nova Babylonian laboratories, then your longevity will itself be of considerable advantage."

The two men laugh. "We'll see if the experimental method doesn't shake their scholars up a bit," says Matt. "I'll make sure the works of Francis Bacon are among the de Tenebres' cargo."

"Take the *Novum Organum* to Nova Babylonia," says Salasso. "Yes!"

"Presumably," says Volkov, "the two of you have not come out here to tell me which epistemological tips to slip to the alchemists."

"Ah, no," admits Matt. "Salasso and I have a plan, which we have, to be frank, not shared with the nice young couple back there. We believe you might be interested."

Volkov turns, eyebrows raised. "Something commercial?"

"No," says Salasso. "Something scientific."

"Go on."

"You remember Armen Avakian," says Matt.

Volkov chuckles. "The scientist? How could I forget him?"

"He made it his business to be forgotten," says Matt. "But I know that he took ship to Croatan some years ago, and I suspect that you know where to find him."

"Ah," says Volkov. "And what if I do?"

"We brought the alien interface device with us on the ship," says Matt. "Do you know how to operate it?"

"No," says Volkov.

"But Avakian does," says Matt. "And you know how to fix the old EVA suits, or to make new ones if needs must."

"Uh-huh," grunts Volkov. They are laboring through tough, tangled grass that has caught the sand and consolidated it into a dune. "I'm interested. So what's the plan?"

The three walkers pause at the top of the low rise. Matt points upward. The sun has set about fifteen minutes ago, and in that time the dark has dropped enough for the first stars to be visible. Croatan's moon, even more cratered and pitted than Luna, is rising full above the sea.

"You set us up for EVA, Armen sets us up for communication. We take the ship out to this system's equivalent of the Kuiper belt, and we talk to a god."

Through the passageway, in the courtyard, the lights are bright and people are drifting around, some of them dancing informally. Somebody's drumming quietly, someone is playing a fiddle. Out here, the tables are emptying. Background music for conversation is no longer needed. The harpist's hands drop from the strings to her knees, and she straightens her back and tilts her head up; her fine hair almost brushes the small seat. Matt pauses, waves Salasso and Volkov on toward the courtyard, and walks past her and stops in front of her.

"That was beautiful," he says.

"Thank you." She flexes her long fingers, rubs her thumbs over their tips. "The trouble with playing an instrument is that nobody talks to you."

Her face is narrowed by her long jaw and sharp chin; her eyes and lips look too big and soft for it. A faint tracery of lace is visible where her small breasts push out the thin silk of her white shirt. Her feet are bare and gritted with sand.

"Let's talk now," Matt says.

She busies herself with lifting the large, awkward instrument.

"Allow me," says Matt. He hefts it lithely, with a well-learned precision of movement—a score of score of years has made him mindful of his lower back—and grins at her through the strings. "You are—?"

"My name is Daphne de Charonea," she says. "Of a minor sept of the de Tenebres, from Nova Babylonia."

"Pleased to meet you, Daphne," he says. "I'm Matt Cairns. From Earth."

She probably knows this already; word has got around. But hearing it from his own mouth has the expected effect, and as he follows her to the brighter light inside she's already plying him with questions, and he's already sending a small prayer of thanks to the appropriate goddess, Venus.

5

The Apothecary's Traffic

WHEN HE WENT to his work shed the morning after his test flight, Stone's head was still a battleground of violent and malevolent beings. His previous afternoon's woodwork had been subtly damaged overnight, or so he suspected: Nothing at all had seemed the matter with it when he had left it, and now it was almost all unusable. The flint blades of several of his planes and chisels had been blunted and chipped. No wonder that the drink was said to contain spirits.

"I told you so," Dark Water said, as he stood staring glumly at the task before him.

He gave her a sour smile. "Did you give Slow Leg a thumping?"

She shook her head. "He did not come to the house drunk. Perhaps he is more familiar with the spirits than you are. Which is not a good thing, but as long as he is careful not to bring them home in his body, I will tolerate it."

Stone tried to ignore the pain in his head and concentrate on the possibilities of the situation. Dark Water had never alluded to any of Slow Leg's illicit activities, and Stone had not known about them until yesterday.

He looked around. The place was filling up, but none of the other women were within earshot. Nevertheless, he spoke in a low voice.

"Do you tolerate his smuggling?"

She looked at him sidelong. "I say nothing about that."

"And I know nothing. But I am wondering, what would you think if some things more useful than the drinks with spirits were to be smuggled?" He picked up a chipped blade, turning it over and over in his fingers, and with a sigh dropped it in the basket of shavings and broken stone under his bench.

"They do say," replied Dark Water, in the same tone of idle speculation, "that 'a clumsy woman blames his tools.' You are in danger of being such a clumsy woman, my friend. Try to be a clever and crafty woman."

With that she winked and sashayed off to sit at her treadle saw. Stone's gaze followed her, then turned sharply back to his bench. The cloth garment that constrained his loins, so that he always presented a flat groin and smooth lap, felt painfully tight. Women such as himself were not supposed to feel, and certainly not expected to show, desire for other women. But he did feel it. He put that troubling thought out of his mind and set to work replacing the broken blades and starting over with fresh wood.

Over the rest of that morning, he took Dark Water's advice to heart and used his occasions of wandering around and gossiping to drop less heavy-handed hints.

The sun was high in the sky when he heard outside the low twittering whistle of a mountain pterosaur. Some of the other women looked up idly; it was a sound seldom heard at that altitude. But only Stone recognized it not as the call of a winged lizard but as a hunter's signal.

He took his time to clear up his bench, then sauntered out.

The call was repeated. Stone followed it to the edge of the practice field, now mercifully deserted except for the great slow-moving bulks of a couple of grazing megatheres. Slow Leg was lying on his back behind some bushes, chewing a stalk of sweet grass and gazing at high cumulus clouds. Stone squatted politely beside his feet and waited to hear what he had to say.

"Don't try to squat like a man," said Slow Leg, still studying the sky. "You look like a woman pissing. Sit properly."

"My trousers will get damp."

" 'My trousers will get damp,' " Slow Leg mimicked. He reached behind his head and threw a rolled small reed mat at Stone. "Here."

Stone spread the mat and knelt on it, sitting back on his heels. Slow Leg rolled over and leaned on one elbow.

"There," he said. "Now we look as though we are flirting, not planning a raid. Or a flight. And even if everybody knows we are—and after your blundering around the workshops this morning, the dogs in the street will know it—they cannot swear that they saw us doing so."

Stone blushed and suppressed a giggle. From where he sat he could see right up Slow Leg's skirt.

"Perhaps we are flirting," he said.

Slow Leg snorted. "Dark Water would kick me in the bollocks if she thought we were really flirting. You're a pretty enough woman, but not that pretty."

"Hah," said Stone, averting his eyes from the growing evidence that Slow Leg might be finding him more than pretty enough. "So let us plan a flight."

Breakfast in the Star Traders' House is a comfortably communal affair. Tables along one side of the courtyard are laid with platters of melon, bread, olives, cheese . . . Matt hopes and expects to find hot food in town. At least there's coffee. He hasn't had much sleep. Matt sits opposite Daphne and takes more pleasure in watching her eat than in the bread and black olives. They keep looking at each other and grinning and discovering again they can barely tolerate their separation across that meter of pale, old wood. Her fingertips are rough, her toes smooth.

"You're both being insufferable," Volkov announces, clapping Matt on the shoulder and sitting down beside him with a laden plate and a steaming mug. "Some people are here to eat, you know."

Daphne flushes slightly, her glance darting away. Matt reassuringly strokes her calf with the sole of his foot: never mind him.

But then she looks back at Volkov and says tartly, "You can talk, when everybody knows with whom you have spent the night."

"What everybody knows is one thing," says Volkov, unperturbed. "What everybody sees is something else. My lady and I don't paw each other in public."

He chomps silently for a while and then leans forward on his elbows, observing Daphne across the rim of the mug from which he slowly sips.

"Matt and I," he says, "and the saur from his ship, Salasso, are going into town today. We'll be visiting machine shops and talking to engineers and accountants. Lots of figures, lots of detail about machinery and money—millimeters and millilivres, so to speak. Would you like to come along?"

Matt is surprised by the clumsiness of this attempt to put the girl off. "You'd be welcome to come with us," he says, as though he means it. Daphne, to his mingled satisfaction and concern, looks actually interested.

"Music is mathematics," she says. "I know a lot about figures. What are you planning to have manufactured?"

"Space suits," says Volkov.

Daphne repeats the word, then says, "Vacuum . . . garments?" She's mentally translated the concept into and out of Trade Latin, Matt realizes. "What for?"

"Extravehicular activity," says Matt.

She understands that, it's barely out of the Latin already, and she rocks back, eyes widening.

"You want to go outside a ship? In space? Why?"

"When you've seen our ship," says Matt dryly, "you might get one answer: emergency repairs. But mainly we want to make it possible for us to land on and explore other celestial bodies, such as planets."

He gestures at the setting moon, pale and huge above the roof. "There, for instance. Or"—he searches his memory for the planets of Croatan's sun—"on Adonis or Cybele or Chronos."

"What a strange thing to wish to do." Daphne giggles suddenly. "You know, until we called at Croatan on our last round-trip, before your ship came to Mingulay, I did not know it was possible to land on these planets. I did not know that the worlds we live on were themselves planets, or that their suns were among the fixed stars."

Both men start speaking simultaneously.

"But—"

"Surely you—"

Volkov waves Matt to proceed.

"Were you not taught any astronomy?" He grins, suspecting he's discovered some sex distinction in education. "Just told to concentrate on your music, or something?"

Daphne shakes her head. "Of course I knew astronomy! It is part of harmony, like music. Every child knows that."

"And what," asks Volkov, "is every child taught?"

"The polycentric Ptolemaic system of astronomy," says Daphne. "It is rather complicated."

"I'll bet," says Volkov. "Could you explain it to us, a little?"

"Um. I'll try."

Daphne dips her finger in slopped coffee and starts doodling on the table, describing circles.

"Each world is surrounded by concentric spheres, upon which the suns and moons and planets revolve, for days, and times, and seasons, and years. There are holes in the spheres, through which the great ships pass. While traveling between the spheres, the ships and their occupants are in eternity and outside time, although time continues to pass within the celestial machinery of the spheres, which manufactures time as a clock does but of course on an inconceivably greater scale. That's why our journeys seem instantaneous to us, though upon returning we find that time has passed."

She looks up. "What is *your* explanation?"

It occurs to Matt that the anomalous experience of travel by lightspeed ship, before the travelers had had any grasp of the notion that light had a speed at all, was probably responsible for the persistence of this entire ludicrously complicated cosmology.

"Ah, that would take . . . some time," Matt says. "But surely it's obvious that the appearance of the fixed stars from Croatan is very similar to that from Mingulay, and so on all the way to Nova Terra." He pauses, frowning. "Do they look much different even from there?"

Daphne shakes her head. "Some of the major constellations are different—the Archer, the Hand, the Hind. But many of the stars are in very similar positions, yes. That's because the spheres of each world have small differences, which vary in proportion to the years spent in eternity between them."

"And it has never occurred to anyone that it might be simpler to suppose that the stars are suns, seen from very far away, and from a different viewpoint on each world?"

"Oh, yes, it has, naturally. But only a minority of astronomers hold to that hypothesis, which has difficulties of its own." She laughs. "But it seems to be true. I like the idea of landing on planets. I cannot help imagining them as small bright objects that one could walk around, not as worlds."

"What about the comets?" Matt asks.

Daphne shivers slightly in the early morning sunlight.

"Whatever the planets may be, we know that the comets are the gods, coming in from the intramundane spaces to look more closely at the works of men and saurs and navigators. They are harbingers of misfortune."

"Our friend Salasso," Matt says idly, "has been making some other saurs angry, by telling them that the gods are not."

Daphne compresses her lips and stands up.

"I have work to do," she says. She smiles at Matt. "I will see you tonight."

"Yes, see you."

He watches her out of sight.

"Looks like it's not just the saurs who think Salasso's a bit of a heretic," Volkov says.

"I don't know if it was such a good idea, talking about what we're going to do today."

Volkov rips a piece of bread and smudges up an olive with it.

"Ah, fuck it," he says. "It'll come out eventually that we're trying to knock off some space suits. Trying to be secretive would only arouse suspicion. Your harpist has very sensitive hearing and gets to overhear a lot of conversations while she sits there strumming away. She's one of old Esias's sources of information about what goes on among his crew and family, not to mention *other* crews, when they have their rather fraught social get-togethers. Same-same for them, of course."

Matt wonders if this isn't some subtle ploy by Volkov to make him wary of Daphne, but he lets it pass. He has no intention of letting Daphne in on the secret of their bolder aims anyway.

"You're a bit paranoid about me, aren't you?" says Volkov.

Matt tries to keep his hands busy with rolling a New

Virginia cigarette. Volkov politely disdains the offer to share.

"Yes," says Matt, past his lighter flare. "I don't like the thought of what you could do in Nova Babylonia, given time. And time, you have."

"We all have." Volkov turns toward Matt on the bench and leans back, arms spread, theatrically defenseless though not, Matt well knows, in reality. "Would you kill me?"

Matt feels the chill of an inhibition so ingrained it has become superstition, and shivers at the thought of killing a fellow immortal, just as Daphne did at the thought of the gods above. The mutual nonaggression pact between the surviving members of the original crew has never been explicit; it has grown, over their unexpectedly extended life spans. The very length of their disputes and vendettas, pursued down decades of scheming, bonds them like brothers.

"You know I wouldn't," he says. "But short of that . . . What *are* you planning, by the way? Becoming the dictator of Nova Babylonia?"

Volkov laughs. "Of course not. What a bore that would be." He leans on his elbow and cups his chin, suddenly serious. "But think. We've all kept our little secret, and for its sake lost lives' worth of work, abandoned families, lost love over and over. Now some of the saurs have seen fit to share it with the merchants, or at least with this clan, who I'm sure are clannish enough to keep it to themselves. But when I get to Nova Babylonia, it won't be a secret, not if they want their scientists to reverse-engineer the process. If they succeed, it'll change everything and thoroughly disrupt their famous mighty and ancient republic and eventually the whole of the Second Sphere. I want to use whatever influence I can get along the way to make sure that the treatment is available to everyone rather than just to the ruling class and that the outcome is progress rather than collapse."

"I can see it now," says Matt. "A progressive, dynamic, socialistic republic, like the European Union, in which you are once again somebody close to the top of the heap."

Volkov spreads his hands, grinning. "And what's wrong with that? A young man should have ambition!"

Matt smiles back, his suspicion not at all disarmed. But he is fairly confident that by involving Volkov—as he must—in the project, he has found a good way of keeping tabs on him, and that if necessary he can find some nonfatal method of screwing up Volkov's plans.

And if it's longevity that is going to be the cosmonaut's apple of discord, it's entirely possible that Matt can play the same game on Mingulay or Croatan, with faster results. . . . He's lost in a moment of calculation of light-years and centuries and rates of growth, when a long oval shadow falls across the table, and he turns with a start to see Salasso.

The automobile that Volkov has selected from the house's motor pool has a noisy and exhaust-rich petrol engine and a heavy steel chassis. Its bodywork and most of its fittings are of shabby polymer; the lilac shell and bubble canopy give the whole thing a teardrop shape when the rear half of the canopy isn't retracted around the vehicle's stern, as it is now. Matt sits in the front passenger seat, Volkov drives. Salasso has taken a skiff into town, on some errand of his own; the declining of the offer of lifts has been mutual.

"Used this since we came here," Volkov yells above the engine noise and grating gear changes as they lurch out of the front gate and into a gap in the traffic. It's a dangerous combination of a sparse but speedy succession of commuter vehicles and a slow but steady flow of long, lumbering trucks carrying produce and livestock from the coastal farms. "It's great. It's like the cars they had in America!"

"Not very," Matt replies. The impression of speed is

terrifying: The wind is roaring past his ears and whipping through his hair; buildings, street fixtures, and slower vehicles blur past. The speedometer reads only 50 km/h; he doesn't believe this for a second. Within minutes the growing heat of the sun and the heat of the engine itself warming up the vehicle fill Matt's nostrils with a nostalgia-inducing fragrance that he recognizes from his childhood as that of polystyrene cement: model-kit glue. He tries not to think about what this may imply about the car's structural integrity and gazes outward at the rapidly passing landscape.

Out on the shimmering sun-hammered sea the glare is broken by long low smoke-trailing ships, by sails, and at the horizon by tall derricks that he takes to be oil wells. The beaches become less and less white and un-cluttered as they approach the edge of the town. Then the road and the shoreline diverge, and the mansions along the other side are replaced by close-packed villas, and within minutes they're between tenements and warehouses and offices, and the traffic has slowed to a rush-hour crawl.

"Fuck," says Matt, as exhaust fumes from the huge idling truck they're stuck behind roll over them, "*this* is more like America."

"You were there once?"

"Yeah, briefly. Yourself?"

Volkov laughs. "Just Washington, D.C., to shake hands with the vice president, all that, then a motorcade in New York. Strange place."

Matt's looking around. "But not as strange as this, huh?"

Close up, it's not very like twenty-first-century America, or even Rawliston as Matt remembers it from decades ago. The streets are tarred, but potholed and filthy; the sidewalks are broad and crowded and crumbling. The current fashions strike Matt as an odd jumble of several different period styles, into which the jeans and loose shirjacks that he and Volkov are wearing will fit as workingmen's clothes, but in the less utilitarian outfits on display he can see an evolution toward showiness and elaboration since he was last here: Trousers and skirts are narrower, jackets shorter, shirts and blouses frillier, hats and heels taller; it reminds him of the early nineteenth century. There's a similarly intense density of detail on the street, with posters and placards and banners everywhere, shop windows small and crammed, hawkers jostling and calling in cries as recurring and as incomprehensible as those of the wheeling and swooping small pterodactyls whose bright red, blue, yellow, or particolored leathery wings flash past faster than those of the pigeons, sparrows, and seagulls whose urban niches they occupy here.

Even the other hominidae seem to have been infected by the decorative urge, as they've found new slots in Rawliston's booming economy. Gigants, their fur dyed in garish hues and coiffed all over, loll in large open vehicles, talking on radiophones. Pithkies, lithe and tough but much slenderer than their rural, mine-working cousins and ancestors, dart about on urgent errands, the females in fluttery shifts, the males in gaudy shirts and shorts. Matt has long concluded that despite appearances, the pithkies are not the sharpest blades in the hominid tool kit, and the gigants are. But in Rawliston they're both officially Adamic races, fully human, citizens with savable souls, so any speculation or skull measuring along these lines is (laudably, in his opinion) considered impolitic and impolite.

The only obvious underclass here are the converted and civilized descendants of the heathen, blond and light-skinned, whose few representatives in this part of town are either doing heavy manual work—digging holes in the road, to yells of annoyance from everyone else—or lurching about drunk.

Volkov follows the traffic slowly forward for about half a kilometer, then turns right into a narrower street with higher buildings and more human and animal-powered traffic. The draught animals are giant tapirs, three meters high at the shoulder, looking down long noses, arrogant as camels. Small, ragged children dash between wheels and hooves, scooping dung into reeking sacks. The pavements have no fewer prosperous-looking pedestrians, however; the ladies occasionally cough and *faugh* through evidently scented lace handkerchiefs, the gentlemen flourish pipes and cigars. Matt's just beginning to appreciate the difference the frequent whiffs of marijuana and tobacco smoke make to the ambient odors when Volkov hauls on a lever and the canopy comes rattling up from behind, closing with a rubbery clash and automatically starting up a racketing air conditioner that fights inadequately against the immediate greenhouse effect of the canopy but at least keeps out the worst of the stinks.

A couple of hundred meters up the street the buildings on both sides have been recently levelled, and the cleared site has been chained off for a car park. Volkov finds a vacant place, makes a payment or bribe to the attendant, and leads off at a brisk pace into a maze of alleys.

"Ah, here we are," he says, stopping under a sign suspended from above a frowsty shopfront. Matt looks up at a painting of a mortar and pestle and a bramble of barbed serifs, which he eventually makes out as *Armen Avakian, Physician and Apothecary.*

"Good gods," he says. "He's using his own name?"

Volkov shrugs. "Hide in plain sight. It's worked for me, sometimes."

Matt can't imagine Avakian hiding in anything but obscurity.

The shop is a lot cleaner inside than outside. Clumps of dried or drying herbs hang from the ceiling. A quarter circle of counter in the corner guards shelves of racked potions and unguents, and a doorway to a dark inner sanctum. The other sections of wall have fold-down, polished wooden benches, every foot of them occupied by people in various states of discomfort or distress. Sawdust on the floor absorbs most of the spittle, phlegm, and blood. The walls above the patients', customers', or supplicants' heads are plastered with urgent advice and improbable testimonials.

A sallow-skinned young man, slim and crop-haired and clean-shaven in a neat white coat, stands behind the counter writing on the label of a small bottle.

"Excuse me," says Matt. "Could we speak to Dr. Avakian?"

The man barely glances at him. "You're speaking to him."

A son, or a more distant descendant? Matt detects a similarity in the dark eyes, sharp nose, full lips.

"Could we speak to, ah, the *senior* Dr. Avakian?"

This time the doctor stops scribbling and stares at them. "Matt!" he shouts. "Grigory! Holy fucking shit!"

He ignores the tittering and tutting this outburst provokes in the queue, he can't shake their hands fast enough.

"You guys, you haven't changed a bit!"

"You have," says Volkov.

Avakian glances downward, then up. "Losing the beer gut took a while," he admits. "The hair and beard, well, that was easy."

His raucous belly laugh hasn't changed and confirms the update in Matt's mental image of the man.

"Didn't you see the photos of me in the newsprints?"

"Crummy dot-matrix," says Avakian. "Didn't recognize you at all." He remembers something. "Just a minute."

He finishes the labeling with a signature flourish and hands the bottle to a young woman with a feverish ten-year-old in tow.

"No more than twice a day," he says firmly. "And keep giving them twice a day until the bottle's empty, even after it's all cleared up. That's very important."

"Yes, Doctor. Thanks." She departs and the queue

shuffles up. Avakian pokes his head around the back-room door and yells, "Hey, Collis! Take over out here, please."

He sheds his white coat, revealing a pea jacket, a pin-tucked shirtfront, and a pair of denim trousers that look like jeans but that come up to above his waist. He lifts a section of counter and steps out and gestures to the door.

"Gentlemen," he says, "after you."

The coffee shop is quiet at this time of the morning, after the breakfast rush and before elevenses. Avakian orders a liter cafetiere and leads them to a dark corner niche table. He declines Matt's offer of his tobacco pouch with a regretful shake of the head.

"I have to set the locals a good example," he says. "Don't worry, I don't try for miracle cures. I'm just another quack, but one who gets results. And I'm getting a lot of good stuff from the heathen pharmacopoeia and off the merchant ships. Laying a bit of cash aside from the two-way trade, there, for when I have to—you know. Train up young Collis, turn the shop over to her, then move on before people start wondering if I have the elixir of youth stashed at the back."

"Why not work up at the university?" Matt asks.

Avakian grins. "I don't think they'd recognize a degree from Yerevan University."

Matt's eyebrows twitch.

"Look," says Avakian, somewhat defensively, "it would be completely maddening to help them reinvent the wheel. All that twenty-first-century state-of-the-art information that got downloaded from the ship and printed off and shipped from Mingulay two hundred–odd years ago—it's *still* being reprinted, in big leather-bound volumes. Most of it is still incomprehensible, and what they do understand they dogmatise. It's not just medicine, it's everything. The different encyclopedias have become the basis of fucking *schools of thought*.

Grolierists and Britannicists at each other's throats in the faculties, with a strong faction of Encartists among the students and junior staff."

Avakian depresses the plunger of the cafetiere and pours. They inhale and sip for a minute of grateful silence.

"I doubt if anything that came on the *Bright Star*," says Avakian, putting his cup down, "has brought as much innocent, unalloyed pleasure as coffee. Just as well we had the beans in our hydroponics. And speaking of the ship, guys, I'm impressed." He narrows his eyes at Matt, lowers his voice: "Your descendants completed their Great Work?"

"Yup," says Matt. "And once they had done that, the saurs, for a wonder, agreed to take us back up to the ship. So here we are. My descendants' navigation worked, unlike"—he drops his voice further—"mine."

He still feels his ears burn, at the thought of that little fuckup, when the navigational programming he'd been certain was for a short-lightspeed hop across the Solar System had turned out to be for—or had been overridden to produce—a lightspeed leap of unknown but vast length.

"Do the Families know about . . . us?" Avakian asks, just as quietly. Volkov and Matt trade uncomfortable glances.

"Well, uh," Matt begins, with a conscious effort to stop his feet from audibly shuffling, "some of them do. One of the saurs on their ship told the de Tenebres, when they turned up at Mingulay. They then started hunting for us, and another saur, Salasso, helped them find us. The de Tenebres are taking Grigory here back to Nova Babylonia to, ah, see if they can crack the fix, whatever it was. My two companions know about me, of course, and so do the heads of the Families back on Mingulay. That's the state of play yesterday, or five years ago."

"Hmm," says Avakian. "Well, let's hope they haven't blown our cover. It's a fucking miracle we've kept it quiet this long, even with the, ah, *help* of our little gray friends."

The three apparently young men share a moment of grim silence. Avakian ends it by exhaling noisily, as though he's been holding his breath.

"So, gentlemen, to what do I owe the pleasure, as they say here?"

Matt decides to dispense with preliminaries. "We've brought the interface," he says. "We want to talk to the gods again—and this time get some *answers*."

Avakian takes this in with almost saurian calm. "I understand you have a problem with access to the ship."

"All in good time," says Matt. He pats his shirjack pocket. "I have some specs here. Right now, we're going to visit an engineering company and talk about pressure seals, and faceplates, and air supply."

"Oh, right," says Avakian. "Suits. Good luck finding someone who can build that around here."

Volkov grins. "We don't need luck. I'm a marine engineer, remember? In the past three months I've checked out every reliable engineering company in this town, and I'm going to start with the best. Paul Loudon."

"I thought he was aviation," says Avakian.

"Exactly," says Volkov. "Precision milling. Pressure differentials. Air hoses. Critical tolerances. I'll go to a diving-equipment manufacturer if I have to, but the aviation industry is where astronautics began, and that's where it's going to begin here, if I have anything to do with it."

Avakian smiles wolfishly. "Quite right," he says. "Pilots cost more to replace than divers, and if I'm going to be manhandling that fucking interface in a vacuum I want to do it in a suit designed by someone who thinks I'm very expensive indeed."

"You'll come?" says Matt, hardly daring to believe it.

"Of course," says Avakian. He glances about with an expression that Matt has seen on Volkov's face and, he suspects, sometimes shown on his own. "What else is there to do around here?"

Loudon's Engineering Works is in the light-industrial semicircle around the city's commercial area, which is crowded around the harbor. There's no zoning; dwellings of varying quality and size, from middle-class villas narrow and shiny as top hats to teetering high-rise workers' flats to a sort of scurf of squatters' shanties around the feet of both, are squeezed between the workshops and distilleries and breweries, all loomed over by the flaring high vents of an oil refinery and the high smokestacks of power stations and the bigger factories in the heavy-industrial zone.

"*Serious* fucking terraforming going on around here," Matt remarks.

Volkov parks the automobile, half on the sidewalk like everybody else here has done, and leads the way to Loudon's factory. It's in an aggressively modern building of glass and steel and concrete with its owner's name in bevelled aluminium sans serifs above the revolving door at the front. Inside it smells of plastics and polish. Workers and technicians in neat blue overalls are conferring around a circular table behind the first of many glass partitions beyond the reception area. The receptionist, fashionably and expensively a female pithkie, is sitting tapping at a manual keyboard behind a curved desk of chrome and inlaid Bakelite. She looks up and flashes bright teeth from a foxy face fringed in golden fur.

"Good morning, Mr. Antonov," she says, momentarily confusing Matt until he remembers it's the pseudonym under which Volkov has been trading for the past twenty years or so.

"Good morning, K!kh!thashth!kh."

Matt can't even mentally transliterate the mashed syllables of the name Volkov pronounces, evidently well enough to charm its bearer. She registers Matt's bafflement.

"Just call me Cath," she tells him and looks again at Volkov. "You have an appointment?"

"Yes," says Volkov, rather to Matt's surprise. "I radiophoned Citizen Loudon early this morning. He's expecting me around eleven-thirty."

She peers at an open desk diary, shaking her head a little, then turns the book around and looks closer.

"Ah, so he is." Another flash of teeth. "He must have jotted it down himself on his way in. His writing's terrible."

She presses a switch and speaks into a clunky telephone, then nods and waves them through.

"Third on the left, then up the stairs."

Loudon's office is spare, its only decoration posters advertising the company's products and a few framed photographs of Paul Loudon posing beside biplanes and monoplanes. Volkov introduces Matt and, after exchanging pleasantries about the significance of the *Bright Star*'s arrival, they sit down and explain their requirements.

Loudon almost pounces on the space suit specs. His finger races down each page, the fingers of his other hand drumming on the desk. When he's scanned them all, he pushes the papers away and leans back and scratches his nose.

"Hmm," he says. "Interesting. Very interesting."

He jumps to his feet and stalks around the desk to the window overlooking the street and the city and stares out for a minute or so. He turns back to face Matt and Volkov, hands clasped behind his back.

"We have the skills and machinery required to make your suits," he says. "Even the fabric components—used in aircraft, you know. I employ outworkers for that, of course. However, the problem is, gentlemen, that while normally I'd be delighted to take your order, at the moment and for the foreseeable future we're working flat out on other projects. There's a bit of a boom on, as you may have noticed. Overheated, to tell you the truth. Skill shortages and bottlenecks all over the place. Between ourselves, the popular assemblies are running the printing presses a little too hard."

"Printing presses?"

"Inflation," Loudon explains. He nibbles his lower lip. "I really would like to help you. I can see all kinds of applications for this type of suit, even a simpler version, for high-altitude aviation. But . . . now wait a moment, gentlemen."

He sits back at his desk and swivels a big apparatus that looks to Matt like an antique computer monitor. The screen lights up, and Loudon starts sliding sheets of transparent plastic across a sort of hopper underneath it and cranking a brace of knurled knobs at the sides. The images on the screen—lines of text, diagrams, pictures—change with dizzying speed.

"Microfiche," Loudon murmurs. "Latest thing. Very useful. Could replace paper entirely, they say. Now, let's see . . . ah, yes."

He looks up, smiling. "I seé I have one rather elderly technician who doesn't seem to be fully occupied at the moment. He can take charge of this, but he'll need someone to help him, and I can't spare even an apprentice—aha! Got it! I know just whom I can poach."

He jumps up, rubbing his hands, and keys his desk phone.

"Cath?" he says, "can you fax a message through to the flying club, with all my numbers and a request to contact me *immediately*? For the attention of Gail Frethorne."

He listens for a moment, then very patiently spells the name.

The two-man glider was heavy, but not too heavy for one man and one woman to carry. Slow Leg and Stone took it from the hangar shed in the time in the hot early afternoon when most people were sensibly asleep and carried it up the long slope of the hill. Slow Leg was weighed down with bulging leather bags hung from his shoulders, but he walked as though they—and the machine he and Stone bore above their heads—weren't there. Stone tried to emulate him. With his clothes and sandals packed away in a pouch and with his quilted flying suit knotted bulkily around his waist, his gender wasn't obvious at a distance, and he tried to keep its traces from his walk.

They stopped at the top of the ridge and looked along the valley. Slow Leg's sense of the weather had been sharp: A strong breeze cooled their faces, and a series of cumulus clouds hung above the whole length of the Vale, marking thermal stepping-stones all the way to the city and the sea.

Stone climbed into his flying gear, while Slow Leg attached himself to the forward harness. Stone ducked behind him under the wing and got into the rear harness. He clutched a bar in front of him—it was part of the glider's rigid frame and had no connection whatever with the control surfaces.

"Have you ever flown *with* anyone before?" asked Slow Leg over his shoulder.

"No," said Stone.

"It's easy. All you have to do is run behind me when we're taking off and again when landing. The rest of the time, stay like you're lying on your belly and do nothing unless I tell you to. Don't even swing your legs."

"All right," said Stone. It didn't sound easy at all. It sounded terrifying.

"Ready?"

"Yes."

They ran down the slope for a dozen or so meters, and then the air spirits caught the wings and bore the glider aloft. Stone swung his body back to a prone position and fought the spirits in his arms and hands that urged him to fly the machine. His knuckles whitened on the bar. He and his friend had both been right. Taking off as a passenger was easy, and flying as a passenger was terrifying.

6

Dawson's Night

GAIL FRETHORNE FOUND the fax with her name scrawled on it folded behind the slats of the notice board lattice just after she'd ridden her bicycle up to the club after work. As she read it her hands shook and sweat dripped on the paper, smudging the sooty print. She had to read it again very carefully to make sure it said what she thought it said.

She folded it carefully and slipped it inside her shir-jack pocket, went to the washroom to freshen up, then walked thoughtfully to the club bar. It was an open verandah with bamboo furnishings and a big four-bladed propeller turning slowly, powered by an electric motor mounted on the ceiling. She seldom used the bar, preferring to save her money for more congenial venues. Today, however, she had spare money in her pocket. Paul Loudon had faxed the photographs she'd taken straight to an hourly paper within minutes of landing, and they'd wired twenty talers to his account at the club. He'd split the money with her, over her not very sincere protests, and bought her a drink as well. So now the old guy at the bar, a booze-sodden heathen capable of little else in the way of work, recognized her and even smiled.

She smiled back with stiff politeness (the sight of his teeth made her throat spasm) and took her blueberry-flavored long vodka to a seat by the railing overlooking the airfield. After a few relaxing sips she spread the now almost illegible paper in front of her and read it again, just to make sure. There was no doubt about it. He was offering her a job, starting immediately. Day after to-morrow, if possible. He would even pay her boss a week's wages in lieu of notice.

Her feelings, she realized, were mixed. She was excited and delighted with the new prospect, but she liked her job at the garage. David and Mike had taught her most of what she knew, and Joshua was all right in his gormless way, and Mr. Reece was a fair enough employer. She had no idea what working for Loudon would be like, or of his qualities as a boss or of conditions in his works. If they were anything like the factories she'd worked in when she was younger . . .

But that was the wrong attitude, she was sure. It was to quail at change. The pay he was offering was half as much again as she could earn at the garage even in a good week. And the job title rang like good metal: *machinist*.

She folded the fax away, her mind made up. She would take it. As soon as she'd decided, and imagined herself going in to Loudon's works two mornings hence, she realized that she'd done so without one consideration so much as crossing her mind: that Loudon might be making this unexpected and unexplained offer because he fancied her. Strange. It was such an obvious thought, such a romantic cliché—Gail had, in her early teens, and even then rather guiltily, read some of her mother's stash of romantic novellettes—that perhaps that in itself explained why she hadn't thought it could happen to her. She still didn't think it had. He'd been favorably impressed with her competence, and her sharpness in snapping the photos had merely brought it home to him, that was all.

She drained her glass and ambled to the club office, fired off a fax with her acceptance and the details of Reece's garage, and returned to the verandah for another long vodka—well deserved, she thought as she settled down with it, and would keep her occupied while she waited for her drug smuggler. It was the usual day for Slow Leg's fortnightly flight, and the weather had been perfect. She turned a little in her rattan chair and gazed at the city. The view was less hazy than usual, these updrafts were lifting the smog a bit, and the red flare above the refinery blazed like a false sunset among the columns of sharply rising smoke. Rain on the way, maybe late tonight or early tomorrow.

More smoke than usual, and not just from factories. It was as though here and there in the suburbs and shantytowns there were a lot of small fires, a lot of—

"Bonfires! Oh, *shit!*"

Stone forgot his fear when he saw the city. He had known about it, of course, but no description or even photograph could prepare his mind for the sight itself. How many people there must be, with all those houses. How rich they all must be, with all that smoke.

Slow Leg banked the craft slightly—by now, Stone's urge to throw his own weight into the maneuver had calmed to a mere twitch—and corrected again to bring them about a hundred meters above a black road. The heat liked to hide in black roads during the day and then escape to the sky as the sun's gaze slanted. The rising thermal spirits lifted the craft a few tens of meters. Down below on the road, vehicles bigger than megatheres trundled along, and smaller vehicles faster than horses overtook them, their paths moving in and out of the gaps like a needle through cloth.

After following the road for a few minutes, Slow Leg

brought the craft around and began to descend toward a green field among the buildings at the edge of the city.

"Swing down now and get ready to land!" he yelled.

On the field were aircraft, bigger than any Stone had seen but whose wings looked oddly stubby. The glide in seemed frighteningly faster than it did when he was doing the piloting himself, and by the time his feet were skimming centimeters above grass, the fighting energies from his chest were firing his legs to run. The landing was gentler than he'd expected, Slow Leg having skillfully slowed the craft to a near stall before touching down, but they still had to pelt along for a dozen meters before they came to a complete stop.

They undid their harnesses one-handed, holding the craft up, then stepped carefully out from beneath it and let it collapse behind them. Stone felt like collapsing on the grass himself. Slow Leg turned and grinned. He looked fine, standing very straight under the weight of the heavy bags, his skin pouring sweat and his muscles quivering beneath the skin. If the change from the cold of the slipstream to the heat of running hard and then the heat of the city had been painful, he was not showing it.

A very strange-looking woman came running up, carrying a bundle in one hand. She was tall, with big breasts that jounced under her shirt, and short hair whose small curls glowed like copper in the low sun. But she ran like a man and clapped Slow Leg on the shoulder and laughed in his face.

"Hey, ya big heathen, good to see you! Even if you did pick the worst day to come here!"

She turned around, still with one hand on Slow Leg's shoulder, and added, "Even if you've brought your girlfriend!"

"This is . . . Stone," said Slow Leg, accurately translating his name into Christian. "He is not my girlfriend. Just a woman who is a friend."

"Yeah, that's what they all say. Pleased to meet you. My name's Gail."

She shook Stone's hand, smiling but staring at him with unabashed curiosity. Her face was regular, not bad-looking but not pretty either, with a rather heavy jaw and big mouth. Her eyes were a sort of greenish gray, bright and curious; her skin, clean under a recent sheen of sweat and dust, was very fair. She wore a cotton shirt with some kind of crisscross pattern, and long blue trousers.

"Look, guys, we have to move fast." She tossed her bundle to Slow Leg. "Get these on right now, you'll look less conspicuous. Then let's get this wing under a roof and make tracks."

Stone couldn't quite follow the Christian colloquialisms, but she was acting out her words as she spoke, grabbing one wingtip of the glider and unceremoniously motioning Stone to grab the other. They lugged it toward a low, open-sided hut, in which some big objects made of bright primary-colored fabrics and metal rods stood racked. As he got closer Stone figured out that they were dismantled gliders, their spars separated and their fabric folded up. A good trick; he found himself considering ways it could be copied.

When Slow Leg joined them to help lift the glider and attach it to one of the roof's crossbeams, Stone had to smother a giggle. The man had put on shoes and blue trousers and a white shirt that looked just like women's clothes except that they were made of a coarser material. He wore them as if he'd worn them before. A swift glare forbade comment.

While Slow Leg trotted off to retrieve his bags, Stone removed his feather helmet and shook out his hair. Gail looked at him critically.

"Uh, Stone, you don't happen to have any sort of girl's clothes you could change into? You look like a goddamn mollyboy."

"I have my own clothes with me."

"Well, get changed as fast as you can. Stash your flying gear here."

Politely, again like a man, she turned her back on him as he began to unfasten his suit. He didn't bother to tell her that this respect for his modesty was unnecessary.

"Hmm," she said when he'd finished and stepped out in front of her, "not bad. You still look like a heathen, but at least you look like a heathen *woman*." She grinned, making an obvious glance at his chest. "A skinny one, mind you."

Stone rejoined them, and Gail casually took one of the bags from him and slung it over her shoulder.

"Right," she said. "I think we want to leave this place by the back."

She led them down a rough, stony path worn in the grass to the airfield's perimeter fence, which was made of three-meter-high wooden posts between which were strung lines of what seemed like, but surely could not be, metal stretched into strands.

"Why are we going this way?" asked Slow Leg.

Gail pushed through a creaking wooden gate, held it open for them, and carefully closed it behind her.

"It's a bad night to be a heathen in some parts of town," she said as they continued on down the dusty and now widening path. "I passed kids stacking up wood and rubbish on my way out here, but I never made the connection until about half an hour before you arrived. It's Dawson's Night."

"Dawson?" Stone asked. "The anthropologist?"

"That's the one," Gail said over her shoulder. "Here they call him a heretic."

Stone had no idea what that last word meant, but something in her intonation suggested *sorcerer*.

"People remember him here too? And this is his night? Why is that bad?"

"Because tonight they fucking burn him in effigy, just like they once burned him in real life, that's why."

Stone felt such a cold shock, like a splash of water

across his neck and shoulders, that he almost stopped walking. Instead he increased his pace, difficult though it was in his sandals and on the uneven track, to walk right beside Gail.

"You are saying that people hate his memory so much that they burn *images* of him?"

"Yes. Don't look so worried; it's only some people, not all, and not many around here. Hell, most of the burnings are just for fun, lots of people have more or less forgotten what it was all about."

Stone did not feel reassured. The dusty path had sloped down, like a rivulet into a gully, into a little street of buildings of two or three stories, built of stone or brick, washed or plastered in white or in other colors. Projecting eaves and awnings provided shade. He found himself eyeing the people they were passing on the road and was relieved to find that their glances were curious rather than hostile.

Three young men, talking and laughing loudly; an old woman trudging up the street, lugging a net bag of vegetables; an old man sitting against a wall, smoking a pipe; a young mother with four small children running around her feet and one baby on her hip; a girl pushing a barrow load of scrap metal, its handles almost as high as her shoulders . . . More and more people. The street had more people in it than an entire village.

They did not seem as rich as he had imagined. The younger ones were thinner, the older heavier, than seemed healthy. He quickly ceased to be surprised by the sight of men wearing trousers and women wearing garments that looked like elaborately decorated or cunningly shaped versions of the short skirts of warriors or the long robes of elders. That was mere custom, and he was well aware that custom varied. It was the bodies the clothes covered that disturbed him. Too many of them seemed worn or tired. But this physical deterioration didn't seem to have affected their spirits. For the most part they seemed lively and, if not always cheerful, at least not ground down.

The vehicles in the street were fortunately traveling slowly in comparison to the ones he'd seen from the air, but they still moved fast enough to startle him, and without beasts to haul them they looked strangely incomplete. He was very conscious of the need not to appear perturbed by them and carried his deliberate insouciance too far when Gail led them across the road.

A noise like a mammoth trumpetting, a bright green blur, a violent yank on his arm that almost dislocated his shoulder—

"Jesus! That was close!"

Gail stood looking at him, shaking her head. Then she smacked the side of her head. "Sorry," she said. "I was forgetting. You guys must be shattered. Let's sit down for a bit."

A small walled yard with trellises of climbing plants between the top of the wall and a straw-mat awning was a few steps away. Gail led them in, and they sat down at one of the round wooden tables. A boy appeared at her elbow.

"Would you like some beer?" Gail asked.

"Yes," they both said.

The beer was pale and so lively that the bubbles tickled Stone's tongue. The cups were large and made of fine glass. He revised his opinion of the wealth of this people sharply upward.

"You look puzzled," Gail said.

Stone had many questions but decided to ask one that would not show how many questions he had. He leaned forward, flicked back the fall of his hair, and spoke quietly. "What is a *heretic*?"

"Oh!" Gail frowned, and Stone worried that he had asked an ignorant or impolite question.

"That's a good question," she said. "It's kind of difficult. You people—your people, you have . . . priests?"

"No!" Stone said. "We do not sacrifice animals. That is what the savages do."

"Sorry, I mean . . . people who consult the spirits."

"Shamans, yes, they speak to the gods and the spirits."

"All right. Suppose a shaman was to say that the spirits didn't agree with what the elders say, or with what other shamans have said that the spirits say? That would be a heretic."

Stone and Slow Leg looked at each other and laughed.

"Then our shamans are all heretics," Slow Leg said. "Perhaps I may explain it, Gail?"

She waved. "Please do."

"Very well." Slow Leg glanced around. The people at other tables, mainly ancient men playing a game with small pale rectangles of wood or bone that clacked on the tabletops, were paying them no attention. But still he slid his chair closer to the table and leaned in, hunching his shoulders and circling his arms as though guarding his beer from being snatched away.

"This is one of the secrets men are given in their initiation, after the challenge," he began. "I should not really be telling you this, but we are not in the Great Vale now, so the spirits are not listening." He lowered his voice. "There is one god, the father almighty, who made the sky and all the worlds. The other gods and spirits are lower to him than the ants beneath our feet are to us. All men and women are his children."

He looked so shamefaced that Stone had to look away. Gail was evidently deeply shaken by this secret; she had her hand over her mouth.

"Obviously," Slow Leg went on, "we cannot tell that to women and children."

"Obviously," Gail agreed solemnly, from behind her hand.

"But that is what the Christians believe!" Stone said.

"Yes," said Slow Leg, sounding exasperated. He glanced around again. "There is no need to shout it out. When the Christians first came here, they took great pains to teach our forefathers their religion, because they believed that theirs was the only way to reach the sky father. They won over many of the sky people, but those they won over became lost and sad and did not thrive, because they had lost all the teachings of their forefathers, and they knew not where to put their feet. Then the *Bright Star* came to the world nearest ours, and the knowledge it carried included the teaching and the disputing of many of the Christian wise men, who had studied and spoken many years after the Christians of our world had been taken from the Cold Lands. Christopher Dawson was a young man who was preparing to be sent to preach to the sky people, and he studied these new doctrines, and he was inspired to go among the sky people to learn their ways, not to try to make them change them. He took the challenge and was initiated as a man of the sky people, and he wrote his book, and he said that the sky people did not need to become Christians to reach the sky father.

"The elders of the Christians called him back to Rawliston and accused him of bending the words of the sky father. That is what is meant by *heretic*. Dawson replied that the Christians' own book says that the man they say was the son of the sky father once said: 'There are many rooms in my father's house.' They quoted other words from that book, and he said these words had been put in the mouth of the sky father's son and his followers by later scribes, and they had a little more disputation, and then they burned him."

Any note of pathos in Slow Leg's voice was seared away when he added, "So our forefathers rose up and killed or drove out all the Christians in the Great Vale, and defeated the warriors sent from Rawliston to avenge them, and those of them who had forgotten the teachings of their forefathers learned them again from Dawson's book."

Slow Leg sat back and took a long swallow of his drink. "That is the story of Dawson."

"Yeah," Gail said. "That's the story. The way it's taught here, Dawson was a preacher who taught the heathens they could keep right on being heathens, and who mocked the bishops of the church to their faces, and whose followers tortured and massacred every convert they could find up in the big valley. There're lots more churches now, of course, and some of them regard Dawson as a saint and martyr, and some of them burn him again every year. Lucky for us, in this area most of the churches are of the former opinion. The other ones call them Dawsonites, when they're having a proper Christian spat, as they do."

Once again Stone felt he was not quite understanding her, but she drew the conversation to a close by draining her glass and saying it was time to catch a bus. Stone didn't know what that meant, but he soon found out.

Gail sat on one of the hard, horsehair-padded seats in the minibus. Crammed on the seat beside her was a stout grandmother clutching a basket containing a chicken whose occasional startling sounds could almost have made her suspect that the bird anticipated its likely imminent fate. Stone and Slow Leg sat in the seat opposite, Stone facing her directly, pushed up against the window like herself. Every seat and every available space in which to stand was taken. Only the open side doors prevented the noisy little vehicle from becoming intolerably hot.

The two men looked like a man and a girl, though their fair hair—absolutely goddamn *golden,* she couldn't help thinking—Stone's loose with its curls and waves around his shoulders, Slow Leg's braided and beaded close to his scalp and knotted at the nape—made it obvious enough that they were heathens, as did Stone's blue silk tunic and trousers. But it wasn't as obvious that they were tribals—some of the younger folk among the Christian heathen affected traditional costumes and hairstyles.

This wasn't her usual route to the Back-o'-the-Docks. She'd chosen it, starting with the back path from the airfield, to avoid areas associated with the more conservative churches, the bigotry of whose nominal adherents often seemed in inverse proportion to their grasp of the doctrines of their own sects, let alone of Christianity.

As the bus finally emerged from the backstreets and turned onto the wide street to the docks, running parallel to the left bank of the Big River, Gail realized that her plan for avoiding trouble might not work. The evening was shaping up to be the liveliest Dawson's Night she could remember. In the gathering dusk there seemed to be bonfires everywhere, their flare and the glare of fireworks reflected on the river's dark water. Most of the commercial properties along the left side of the street were boarded up or shuttered; on the right, the embankment and esplanade were thick with people drinking, throwing ripped railings and broken benches onto illegal fires on the pavement and down by the river, or wandering in fast-moving, shoulder-barging groups from one focus of firelight and noise to another.

Most of the earlier passengers had already completed their journey from work to home, and the bus was filling up with people partying. Mostly kids, she saw with relief, boys and girls with a few beers in them, out for a good time and more interested in each other and in their own raucous conversation than in anybody else on the bus.

The bus was just pulling away from a stop when it rocked and the driver yelled as four, five young men ran up and leaped on the running board and then pushed in, grabbing the overhead bar with whatever hands they could spare from holding bottles. They passed money forward to the driver with loud laughter and bad grace, and swayed and sang and swigged for a bit as the minibus picked up speed. They were all dressed in a similar style, short black jackets and narrow trews and shirts frilled at the front and cuffs, their hair piled high and combed back. The quieter kids and the remaining two or three older passengers ignored them, one or two of the kids—admiring or intimidated and sucking up—joined in their singing and shouting.

The seat beside Gail was vacant, and one of the new arrivals, after breathing sour vapors in her direction for some minutes, occasionally leaning down and peering at her directly and pulling faces and passing remarks that she supposed were intended to make her laugh, finally swung down and sat beside her.

He waved a half-empty bottle of corn-mash whiskey in front of her.

"Want a drink, gorgeous?"

"No, thank you."

He stuck out his right hand above the bag on her lap. "Pleased to meet you anyway. My name's Phil."

She decided to humor him, to placate. Stone and Slow Leg were staring straight ahead, as if they couldn't see anything. She shook his hand awkwardly.

"I'm Gail. Hi."

She let go of his hand, but he held onto hers.

"Let go, please."

He dropped her hand and leaned forward, twisting to stare at her.

"What's the matter with you, ginger? You upset about something?"

"No," she said, staring straight ahead again.

"That's a very hard hand you've got," he said. "For such a soft face."

He fingered her cheek.

She jerked away, then whipped her head around so fast that his finger almost went in her mouth—if it had, she'd have bitten it to the bone.

"Don't you fucking *touch* me!"

He recoiled as though she really had bitten him.

"Okay, okay," he said. "Ease off."

He looked up at his friends, who were laughing at his rebuff. For a few moments he seemed to accept it. Gail looked out of the window, checking her location. The next stop was just five minutes away and a short walk from Back-o'-the-Docks. Stone gave her what she guessed was meant to be an encouraging smile, but it betrayed just how nervous he felt.

"You two together?" Phil said, as though trying a different tack. He turned his attention to Stone. "Hey blondie, what's your friend got against a bit of fun?"

Stone responded with another scared smile, this time trying to look compliant and interested. Gail watched sidelong as, with the unexpected perceptiveness of someone just drunk enough to be uninhibited, the youth's face took on a look of pleased enlightenment as he turned to his mates.

"Hey," he said, "that isn't a girl, it's a goddamn mollyboy!"

"Yeah, and *you* fancied her for a minute!" jeered one of the others, whooping and jerking his bottle in front of his crotch.

Slow Leg seemed to snap into awareness. His eyes were suddenly focused on the man opposite him.

"You will be quiet," he said. His voice was like an announcement coming out of an iron grille at a great distance. "You will not say another word to these women."

Phil leaned back, taking a relaxed pose. He glanced up at his mates, who were hanging forward, intent. Gail tensed her legs and moved a little farther into the corner, watching them and ignoring Phil.

"What women?" he said. "I don't see any women here." He looked at Gail, then at Stone. "Nah. Just a fucked-up dyke and a cock-sucking mollyboy. And what's it to you, anyway, you heathen sodomite?"

Slow Leg's fist came out of nowhere and smashed Phil's nose.

In the moment that followed, Gail saw a bottle flash down toward Slow Leg's head. Her hand shot forward, the rest of her body following like a striking snake, and clamped onto the descending wrist. The deflected blow broke the bottle across the back of the seat. Gail hauled the wrist down farther and head-butted the guy in the face, then punched him in the stomach. She let go as the driver stamped on the brakes. Everyone standing, herself included, was thrown toward the front of the bus. The four guys who'd been standing in the aisle went all of a heap, sliding forward along the floor. Phil, his hands over his face, slammed into her hip as she made a simultaneous impact on Slow Leg. Stone had ducked into the space where Gail had been sitting a moment earlier; the rapid deceleration rocked him back, then he sprang up as the bus stopped.

Slow Leg caught Gail with one arm and straightened her up, at the same time reaching past her and pushing Phil's head down and pulling and pushing him to the side, sending him sprawling onto the floor.

Gail found herself looking straight into Slow Leg's eyes. He was smiling.

"We leave now," he said.

His voice sounded quiet, but that might only have been because it was hard to hear above all the yelling and screaming. The violent braking had cleared the space between them and the open side door. Phil's mates were just sorting themselves out and off the floor. Gail jumped off the bus, followed by Stone and then Slow Leg.

They were on a fairly empty stretch of esplanade pavement; the nearest groups of people were around fires tens of meters away in either direction. The traffic had been thin enough not to pile into the back of the minibus and was now flowing past it.

"Across the road," Gail said.

Stone kicked off and picked up his stack-heeled sandals, and looked up at her with a complicit, apologetic grin. Slow Leg grunted something. Together they sprinted and dodged speeding cars across the broad boulevard without incident to the shoreward pavement, darker and almost deserted. A side street leading eventually to Back-o'-the-Docks opened at the next corner ten meters away. Gail glanced back across the road. The minibus had moved on, leaving all five of the gang on the pavement, scanning the street. They caught sight of her at the same time and launched into a rush across the road. Brakes squealed and horns blared.

"Run!" Gail said.

"No," said Slow Leg, with a light touch on her arm.

She turned to see him and Stone stand stock-still a couple of meters apart, facing the spread-out oncoming gang. At the last moment the heathens leapt farther apart and lashed out with feet and fists, taking down the two of the attackers who'd gone straight for them. One of the others ran at Gail, a broken bottle held high. She bent her knees, ducked forward and to the side, caught his arm, pivoted, and let his momentum send him over her shoulder, his head hitting the pavement with a satisfying crack. The next one loomed above her as she rose. To her utter surprise she saw Stone spring into the air beside him and floor him with a perfect floating kick between the ribs and the hip, then land on all fours like a cat. The fifth was on his back already, Slow Leg looking down at him.

"Now we can walk," Slow Leg said.

"Make it fast," said Gail. The melee had stirred a commotion on the esplanade, drawing attention and people from both of the nearest groups around fires. It looked entirely possible that some of the separate crowds would join and surge across.

Stone slipped his sandals back on and picked his way past the sprawled bodies. They were all writhing and moaning—nobody killed or crippled, by the look of it. Stone joined hands with Slow Leg and ran. They were around the corner in seconds; Gail, bringing up the rear, kept glancing back, but after a minute without sight or sound of pursuit she relaxed a fraction and caught up with the heathens. The narrow street was empty and ill-lit. She put an arm around Slow Leg's waist, and they walked together, commanding the pavement like a swaggering gang.

"Wow," she said. "You guys." Her voice felt shaken and giggly. "I thought the deal with you lot was that women *didn't* fight?"

"That was without weapons," they said together, then laughed.

"That doesn't count, then?"

"Fighting with weapons," said Slow Leg in a tone of patient explanation, "is what men do. Anybody can fight without weapons, but it is mostly boys who learn to do it."

"I was a boy," Stone said. "I have not forgotten what I learned. *You* fought well." He leaned forward and grinned at her through a tumble of blond curls. "Were you a boy too?"

"Ya know," she said, grinning right back, "if I was to do like Slow Leg I'd punch your face for that." She felt his muscles tense in the crook of her arm and added hastily, "But not to worry, I'm not that touchy."

"Nor are we," said Slow Leg lightly. "But please, do not make threats again, even in a joke."

"All right."

She felt she had some air to clear between them.

"Since you ask, Stone, no, I wasn't a boy. I was a girl, and I am a woman. I do work that some people think is men's work, that's all. And I can fight, with weapons and without. I own a pistol and a big nasty knife, though I don't have either of them on me tonight, worse luck or maybe good luck. And my neighborhood militia has a very old and very long rifle with my name on it, and the law makes me practice with it twice a year, for all the good that might do."

"Women here fight with weapons?" Stone asked.

"Oh, yes. In theory. There hasn't *been* any fighting here since the last civil war, apart from against pirates, but we're supposed to be ready."

"I see," said Stone. "Then there is no difference between men and women here."

"None at all," said Gail. "Glad you've got that cleared up."

The sarcasm went over their heads.

"In our society," Stone said, "You would count as a man."

"I suppose I'll take that as a compliment."

This time Stone caught her dry tone and laughed.

"I know just what you mean," he said.

In all the months of her connection with Slow Leg, Gail had never arranged any dealing at the airfield. It was not exactly illegal, though with the assemblies making law by tumult and show of hands you never knew when it might become so. Evading the various taxes and tariffs that had been slapped on at various times to discourage the trade was certainly illegal, though it was hardly considered immoral or unusual and was widely winked at. But it would have been discourteous and would certainly have got her thrown out of the club.

Hence their trips, hitherto by a more direct route, from the airfield to Back-o'-the-Docks, Rawliston's traditional unrespectable district. Even in ancient times, when the Anglican church had dominated the early colony, it had been simultaneously reprobated as a sink of sin and tolerated as a safe containment thereof. Nowadays its hundred or so blocks were the bright and lively haunt of alcoholics, agnostics, artists, atheists, beggars, cutthroats, deserters, drug dealers, evangelists, footpads, gentry, heathens, informers, jays, knife grinders, lesbians, libertines, mollyboys, musicians, navvies, ostlers, physicians, queers, recruiters, reformers, sailors, socialists, trulls, users, vagabonds, watchmakers, xenophiles, and yuppies.

Gail had compiled the list once in her head, and ever since had kept an idle lookout for a Zoroastrian.

*   *   *

The pub was called the King's Head. The sign above
the door was a bloody axe. Gail led the heathens in, sat
them down, planted beers in front of them, and prowled
the room for her regular dealer. She spotted Zachariah
Tompkinson soon enough: In this crowd, the cultivated
shabby gentility of his suit and haircut and general air
of being a thirty-year-old clerk with no prospects stood
out like a drag queen at a funeral. Apart from Paul Loudon, he was the richest man she knew.

"Hi, Zack. Got a minute?"

"For you, two."

She indicated the table with her eyes and sat down.
In a few minutes Zack joined them and began his usual
dickering over the contents of Slow Leg's satchels.
Nothing addictive, that was where she drew the line. She
was high already herself, or coming down from a high,
jittery with reaction from the fight, her head spinning
alphabetical lists. Aphrodisiacs, euphorics, hallucino-
gens, herbs, spices, and stimulants . . .

She turned to Stone, who was observing the pub's
customers and was well out of the business dealing beside him, and was about to say something to him when
she caught in the corner of her eye a penetrating look
from a man a couple of tables away. She faced him and
found herself locked in mutually embarrassed recognition with Paul Loudon, who was sitting with his arm
around a mollyboy.

7

Ancient Astronauts

MATT COUNTS NINE separate silvery lines of bubbles rising to the surface of the tank. This is not good, this is not good at all. He takes the grease pencil from behind his ear, plunges his arms into the water, and draws a circle around each fizzing source. Most of them are at the seams and joints. The water comes past his elbow and seeps up his rolled-up sleeves. He straightens up and shakes off drips.

"Okay, you can turn it off now."

The din of the air compressor stops, leaving the small annex—it was originally some kind of washroom—echoingly quiet. He reaches in again and releases the straps holding the suit to lead weights at the bottom of the tank. Sagging already, it bobs to the surface. Plasticized canvas in a bloated human shape without head, hands, or feet, like the trawled-up victim of a particularly gruesome murder, the half dozen red patches on the torso its stab wounds. He disconnects the tube plumbed to the plastic collar where the helmet will go and hauls the clammy carcass out.

"Shit," says Gail. "It'll take hours to dry enough to put more sealant on."

"I don't think more sealant's the answer," Matt says. "Or more patches."

"Do these tiny holes really matter?" Gail asks.

"For diving, they wouldn't," Matt says. "In a vacuum, they most certainly would. Any of them could start a total blowout."

"Even after we've got the tension layers wrapped around it?"

"Hmm," says Matt. "I'm not sure. I'm seriously beginning to wonder if adapting a diving suit is any kind of shortcut. Maybe it would be quicker in the long run if we were to scrap this approach and pitch in with Volkov's start-from-scratch scheme."

Volkov has been running himself ragged between the university library, which contains in its vaults encyclopedic accounts of EVA suit construction, and various plastics companies and Loudon's factory, trying to simplify the spec down to the local tech level. Matt has, by agreement, followed the superficially simpler path of seeing whether something can be cobbled together from aviation and diving gear. So far, it's been the worst of both worlds: crash and leak.

Gail looks glum. "You mean we've wasted a whole week?"

Matt grins. "Finding that something doesn't work is never a waste of time. How's the helmet coming along?"

She shrugs. "Frank Kemble's a great believer in off-the-shelf. He just mutters every time I ask just *when* I get to learn to use the milling machine, then sends me off trotting around the workshops and stores for odd components and bits of scrap. Or tells me to go and help you. Like now. But we have made a good start with adapting an aviator's oxygen supply apparatus, and Frank seems finally to have made a neck seal that you can open and close without actually having to screw your head on and off."

Gail has in fact turned out to be very good at rounding up bits and pieces and wangling some work on the side from other projects all over the factory and in knowing exactly what might be needed to improvise solutions to problems as they come up, and is thus contributing far more to the work on the helmet than she would if she were turned loose on a lathe. Matt carefully doesn't say this and instead says brightly, "Well, that's progress. I guess old Kemble will give you the right training in his own time, but meanwhile just badger him occasionally, okay?"

"Okay," says Gail. She pokes at the deflating suit's tied-off ankle cuff. "What about this?"

"Ah, leave it. Let's mosey over and see if we can be of any use to Grigory."

They bang out through the swinging doors into the factory yard and cut across to an equally neglected room where Salasso and Volkov have set up their drawing office and test lab.

Volkov looks up from a workbench as they come in and keeps on working as Matt recounts the latest dismal results. He himself has set up a sort of railing at the end of the workbench, upon which a roll of aircraft fabric, a roll of sheet plastic, and a roll of metal mesh are mounted. He's feeding them across the bench and trying out various techniques for laminating them, which judging by the discarded scraps stacking up at the other end of the bench have so far involved rivet guns, brute-force stitching, various glues, heat treatment, and several combinations thereof.

Salasso has perched himself on a high stool by the bench at the wall, which is loaded down with volumes borrowed from the uni-versity library: massive, musty volumes of reverently reprinted twentieth- and twenty-first-century American and Russian astronautics texts, which he can scan and assimilate a lot faster than Matt or Volkov can. Volkov has a lot of practical knowledge of EVA in his head, but it's more from the end-user than the production angle. Since starting work on this project, Salasso has taken to wearing an open-necked check shirt and black trousers—boys' sizes, and even then fitting very badly—in a rather vain (in both senses) attempt to make his presence less likely to freak out old Kemble, not to mention any members of Loudon's workforce who may encounter him unexpectedly. At the moment he has his feet up on the bench and his head down over a garish paperback, one of a big tottering stack beside the leather-bound tomes.

"I don't know if I'm making any better progress myself," Volkov says. "If we could get at the original suits, it might be a boost."

"How are things going with that?"

"It's out of my hands," Volkov says, turning up his palms as though to confirm it. "Esias and Lydia are working their political contacts. Loudon's been putting a word in for us at the big capitalists' watering holes. He claims to have got at least one of the local scandal sheets agitating the proletariat on the issue. Not much use when most of the rest are running scare stories about dangerous machines and space-mutated Earthborn plague viruses."

"It's something," says Matt. He's been rather hoping that Volkov might be using his own local contacts to put pressure on the still-stonewalling Port Authority but guesses that the project hasn't left him much time for that, just as he himself hasn't seen much of Esias and Lydia.

"There's a meeting in my neighborhood this afternoon," says Gail. "I'll be going along. Why don't you come, Grigory Andreievich?"

Volkov's got them all used to calling him that; the patronymic helps to avoid any slipups with his surnames.

Volkov makes a face. "I don't think I can spare the time. I have spoken to a few people I know in that area,

Gail, so maybe you could hook up with them?"

Gail nods. "Yeah, give me their names and I'll track them down, no problem."

"Good idea," says Matt, pleased that Volkov has been working his contacts after all.

"Meanwhile," he adds, "it might speed things up if I just throw in my lot with you."

"Maybe," says Volkov skeptically. "It strikes me that boots and gloves would be worth having ready for when we get a functioning suit, and you could concentrate on that instead of getting underfoot here. Thanks for the offer, but you know how it is. Too many cooks and all that."

The mention of boots and gloves sets Matt off thinking vaguely about leather and wondering if a skin-tight leather suit is just the kind of radical low-tech departure that they need, and that brings up thoughts of Daphne and her leather trousers. He follows this line of speculation for a moment, sighs, and distracts himself from the distraction as Salasso chucks aside the book he's just finished and picks up the next and Matt notices the cover picture, which is of a Gray alien.

Matt registers for a moment the weirdness of the sight—it's like Salasso is reading a book with his own portrait on the cover—and peers closer at the spines of the rest of the stack: ancient astronauts and flying saucers and alien abductions and Roswell and Area 51 and conspiratorial cover-ups, locally produced editions of books that, gods know how, were included in the *Bright Star*'s library files but that, thankfully, were never reprinted by the university press. Evidently Rawliston's entrepreneurial publishers have taken up the slack.

Oh, well. Matt doesn't feel it's his place to question the saur's reading priorities, and he doesn't want to start a conversation that might stray into awkward territory for himself and Volkov.

Gail has no such inhibitions. "What the *fuck* are you reading that stuff for, Salasso?"

The saur looks up, the nictitating membrane flickering across his huge, black, almond-shaped eyes.

"I'm searching," he says, "for evidence that my species has given your species some technological assistance in the past, back in the Solar System. If there is any, it might help me to rebut the claim that what I have been doing is unprecedented."

Matt stares at him, torn between the impulse to guffaw and a sudden surge of sympathy, and over and above both feelings is a momentary shiver of the uncanny. The saurs in the Second Sphere have always said that they have no idea what their putative counterparts in the Solar System have been up to, and there's something almost touching in the sight of Salasso hacking his way through the same jungle of disinformation as any human interested in the question would have to. It's also rather worrying. The saurs understand fiction and imagination perfectly well, but sustained, deliberate downright lying, not to mention delusion and hallucination and insanity, is more or less beyond their ken.

"I don't think you'll find much there that might count as evidence," Gail says scornfully.

"Oh?" says Salasso, peering over the cover in another trompe l'oeil moment. "You've studied it, have you?"

"Yes," says Gail. "There was a lad at Reece's Garage, where I used to work, who read that kind of rubbish all the time, as well as *science fiction*. Aliens, starships going faster than light, crap like that."

Volkov looks across sharply. "There's no doubt there's *some* truth buried in that rubbish, somewhere," he says. "Your own people and all the peoples who came here before you have traditions of their ancestors having been taken from Earth by beings who can only have been saurs."

"Yeah," says Gail. "But Salasso, can you seriously imagine saurs kidnapping people and sticking probes up their asses?"

"No," says Salasso rather coldly. "But the question of

whether they made any other interventions remains open."

"Besides," adds Volkov, "there were well-attested records of sightings of what seem very like gravity skiffs. Even in the socialist countries, not to mention the United States."

Matt laughs harshly. "It's said that Camilla Hernandez once dropped a hint that there were some traces in her employers' records, but she flew only from Area 51 to the *Bright Star,* and then flew a flying saucer back, so what did she know?"

One of the few disadvantages of not aging is that losses stay sharp. Matt looks out the long window at the cluttered yard for a moment, then tells Salasso to keep searching and joins Volkov at the bench. Gail, momentarily at a loss for something useful to do, starts idly flicking through the books herself.

Gail was refreshing her acquaintance with the archaeological discoveries of Erich von Däniken when she heard a commotion in the yard. A sharp knock sounded on the lab door, and two brown-uniformed militiamen, one militia woman, and three saurs came in without waiting for a reply. Gail stood up and stared for a moment.

"What's all this?" Grigory Andreievich demanded, in the truculent tone of a man with a lot on his mind and nothing on his conscience. Gail shut her mouth and determined to keep it shut as long as possible. For the entire week she'd been working here she had been worrying about her actions catching up with her. Damage and casualties from the Dawson's Night celebrations had been unprecedented, and the gang she and the heathens had tangled with had given their side of the story to the militia—two of them from hospital beds, where they were being treated for broken bones and internal injuries. And then there was the matter of her unauthorized drug trading, which Paul Loudon had made perfectly clear could not continue if she was working for him. She had told the heathens just before she'd launched them in their glider, laden with small metal goods, from the car-and-chariot arrangement the following afternoon, that drug trading was right out. They had just looked at her impassively and said they would see her in a week.

"We're shutting this project down," the militia woman said. "We expect your full cooperation."

Gail tried to hide her relief, as she had hidden her guilt. The others seemed to be looking to her for a lead, presumably because she was a citizen and they weren't.

"Why?" she asked, with as much indignation and surprise as she could rally. "We aren't breaking any laws."

One of the saurs stepped forward. "You are not breaking any human laws," he or she said. The tone was almost sympathetic. "However, what you are doing is causing dissension among our people, and under our agreement with your city, we have a right to ask your peacekeepers to make you desist."

"I protest," said Salasso.

"Your protest is recognized," said the other saur. "But the agreement is clear."

"First I've heard of such an agreement," said Gail.

The saur's thin lips twitched. "It was made shortly after the founding of your settlement. The original of it is in a glass case at the city hall."

Gail remembered, as a child, standing on tiptoes for a brief glance at this vellum relic, written with a feather in crabbed italics where every *s* looked like an *f*. She decided to appeal to a more immediate authority.

"What does Citizen Loudon have to say about this?"

The militia woman smirked and made a ball-tossing gesture toward the phone.

"Ask him."

Gail picked up the phone and dialed the number for Kemble's workshop.

"Hello, is that Paul Loudon's office? We've got some militia and saurs down here telling us the project is shut down."

"Oh, Powers Above," said Kemble. "They're not here yet. Want me to get the gear out of the way?"

"Yes, yes. Sorry, wrong number."

She knocked on her forehead and dialed the right number.

"Loudon speaking," said Paul.

"Paul, uh, Citizen Loudon, it's Gail Frethorne, we have some—"

"—militia and saurs in the lab. I know. Their officers have just had the courtesy to call on me, to tell me that they are already, ah, deployed. No choice but to comply, I'm afraid, but do make sure anything they take is documented and signed for."

But they weren't interested in taking anything. They merely politely escorted them all from the room and taped up and sealed the door and slapped a notice with an official stamp on it. Gail looked disbelievingly at the stamp.

"*Port Authority?* What's this got to do with them?"

The militia people laughed.

The saur who had spoken previously was more polite. "It does not have much to do with the Port Authority," he or she explained. "But among all of your institutions that signed the original agreement, it is the only one that remains."

"Then it's *about fucking time*," Gail said over the saur's head to the militia people, "that the assemblies did something about that! The Port Authority's getting too big for its boots! I'll raise this at my neighborhood meeting this afternoon."

"You do that," said one of the militiamen. "And now, you do this." He jerked his thumb over his shoulder. "Off."

Off they went, straight to Loudon's office. Paul waved them in and they all sat, except Salasso.

"Well," said Loudon. "Kemble managed to stash the breathing apparatus before they got round to his lab. Sharp thinking on his part, and on yours, Frethorne. At least that's one thing saved from this sorry mess. Militia tramping around *my* factory! As if we were some kind of criminal enterprise! I think you owe me an explanation, friends."

"This is my fault," said Salasso.

The rest of them stared at him.

"What?"

He looked at Matt and Grigory.

"Shortly after the ship landed," he said, his voice as heavy as his big head suddenly seemed, "I discussed our plans with my lover, Bishlayan. She very much did not approve. She must have mentioned it to others."

Paul Loudon glanced around with an expression more reptilian than the saur's.

"You're telling us," he said, "that the other saurs disapprove of your helping us to build *space suits*? Or do your plans involve something else, which I have not been told?"

"It's possible," said Grigory, "that they object to a . . . notion we had of landing the ship on other celestial bodies, to explore."

Loudon seemed to find this notion plausibly outlandish, but Salasso shook his head sadly. "You know that is not the whole truth, Grigory Andreievich."

Loudon rested his chin on steepled fingers.

"Well, chaps, I'm waiting for somebody to do the decent thing and bloody well tell me the whole truth." He flopped a hand. "Unless it's commercially confidential, of course."

Gail felt relieved that he was keeping his sense of humor. The three star travelers looked as uncomfortable as guilty schoolboys. Matt broke the awkward silence.

"We'll be happy to tell you," he said. He glanced uneasily at Gail. "It might not be fair to include your employees."

Loudon raised his eyebrows. "I've already assigned Frank Kemble to another project and told him to keep well out of this. Chap's got a grown family and a re-

tirement to think about. Frethorne"—he grinned at her—
"any risks you wish to take with the law are up to you."

"Thank you," said Gail. "I'll stay."

She wouldn't miss this for anything.

There are times when the world changes, Gail thought,
half an hour later. Not just the world, *your* world. When
something you were sure was solid melts into air.

The world, Croatan, had changed the day the *Bright
Star* arrived, but *her* world had not changed until today.
She felt some small measure of the shock her ancestors
must have felt, when the strange silvery shapes had first
been glimpsed through the trees, and their small gray
pilots had walked inexorably forward, invulnerable alike
to musket fire and exorcism.

She'd known since childhood that the original crew
of the *Bright Star* had talked to the Powers Above and
learned from them how to build a lightspeed drive. Now
Matt and Grigory wanted to talk to the Powers Above
again and find out if they could explain the reasons why
the Second Sphere existed at all and what the gods
wanted of the intelligent beings within it, the humans
and hominids, the saurs and the krakens. That was why
she felt as if everything were dropping away from beneath her feet: the thought that all these worlds and the
very ground beneath her might exist for a purpose, and
that they might (therefore) never have existed, and that
the immense intent of their existence could be divined.

"What I want to know," Loudon asked, "is why you
want to do this now, and not at some other time?"

"I would like to try to find the answers before I leave
for Nova Babylonia," said Grigory Andreievich.

"And I need him to do it before he leaves," added
Matt. "I don't have anyone else who has his knowledge
of the original ship and of the space suits."

"And your expertise is just as irreplaceable, is that it?"

Matt nodded. "Yeah," he said bleakly, "that's about
the size of it. So let's talk about space suits. It looks like

we're shit-creeked as far as building them here is concerned. If we tried it at another company, we'd just get shut down again. If we defy it on your property, Paul, rip that tape off the door, we'll get you into worse trouble, no matter how unpopular we manage to make the actual shutdown. So I'm in favor of throwing all our efforts into getting the embargo on the ship lifted and then work on repairing and renovating the old EVA suits."

Grigory Andreievich shook his head. "The more I think about trusting my life to one of these, the less I like it. They're very complex, very software-dependent, and they've had a long time to degrade in ways we might not even recognize. I'd feel a lot safer in a new one, even if it was a crude one. Precisely because it would be more basic, there'd be less to go wrong."

"Good old Soviet design philosophy," said Gail. They looked at her.

"I've read about it in books," she protested.

"Well, your books got that right," said Grigory. For a moment, as he looked sharply at her and said that, she felt—not for the first time—a niggling recollection of having seen him somewhere before they'd met. Something in what had just been said had almost brought it back, but now it was gone. Grigory turned to Loudon. "What, if anything, can we save from the project as it stands?"

Loudon spread his hands. "Breathing apparatus, air tanks. I'll see to that. All that leaves is—everything else! Damn."

"Suppose you did somehow get other suits built," said Gail, "and the embargo isn't lifted, at least not before you leave. You'd still have the problem of getting the ship back."

"Remember that I have access to the ship," said Salasso. "Even though there are guards on board, this should make it not too difficult to get them off. If I were to 'check' the engine and tell them it was about to malfunction, I imagine they would leave the ship very quickly."

Laughter greeted this optimistic scenario. Gail had little doubt that it would be more difficult than that. But the notion of deception was a good one.

"How about," she said, "simply announcing that you intend to return to Mingulay? They'd let you back on the ship then, and you could go off and do what you want."

Matt shook his head. "I've thought of that, and it wouldn't work unless our two scientists from Mingulay went along with it. And they won't—they're very serious about setting up good trading relations, and they're unlikely to do anything that might alienate the Port Authority, or risk the ship in any adventures out in the cometary cloud."

"What gives you the right to take these risks?" asked Loudon sharply.

"Hmm," said Matt. He stood up and walked to the window, then turned around and looked straight back at them.

"Legally and morally," he said, "that's a matter internal to the Cosmonaut Families. Gregor Cairns and Elizabeth Harkness have different priorities from me and Antonov here, but their judgment doesn't necessarily override ours. We feel we have a right to take this chance, maybe the only one we'll ever get, to find out why the ship and its crew were taken here in the first place."

"Well," said Loudon, "I'm not entirely happy about that. But this is all moot, it's so much hot air unless you have space suits. The Authority could let you back on the ship tomorrow, your friends could tell you to go right ahead, and it wouldn't do you any good if you couldn't get out of the ship to set up your device."

"And we've agreed to build them," said Gail. "And we made the agreement with these guys, not with the others."

"Good point," said Loudon, with a slight lift of the eyebrows at her boldness. He looked down and started doodling what Gail recognized as a critical path analysis on a scrap of paper.

"Let's focus on that, shall we? What are people's plans for the day?"

A movement in the sky caught Gail's eye. It was a heathen balloon train. She remembered, with something of a shock at having forgotten, that her heathen friends were due to return to the airfield tonight. She stared at the glowing object drifting down to the rooftops, like the ship had done just the other week. Niggled by a thought just beneath the surface of her mind, she looked down and noticed that she was still clutching one of Salasso's crazy old books, the kind that Joshua had devoured so eagerly, about ancient astronauts meeting Stone Age civilizations. The cover picture showed a line drawing of some heathen witch doctor in an outfit and headgear that looked vaguely like a space suit—

"Yes!" she yelled. "Yes! That's it!"

She jumped up and everybody turned and stared at her. She waved a hand at the window.

"*Look* out there! What do you see?"

The rest of them spared it no more than a glance.

"Heathen hot-air balloon train," said Loudon. "Ingenious contraption. What about it?"

"Space suits," she said.

"Yes," said Paul Loudon, with heavy irony. "We *were* talking about space suits, before—"

"You know what I see?"

They looked again at the craft, then back at Gail's excited gaze as though they were missing something, or she was.

"Ceramic braziers," she said. "Airtight fabrics. Glassware."

"Uh—" began Matt, her point clearly dawning on him. But she wasn't about to let him get ahead of her.

"What I see," she said, "is a technology that can build your space suits. No sweat."

If anyone had asked Lydia who she was, she'd have told the truth. To that extent, she wasn't in disguise. She was, however, hoping that her locally fashionable outfit would let her blend in as a middle-class young lady on the fringe of this lower-class assembly crowd. She hoped so: Squeezing into the ugliest outfit she'd ever worn—watery blue silk dress with a tight buttoned bodice and a narrow skirt with rows of frills from the knees to the ankles, underpinned by some very uncomfortable underwear and matched by a hat, gloves, purse, fan, and parasol in the same fabric and style—would have been pointless otherwise. It made her sweat so much she suspected she already *smelled* like a local, though she rather hoped not.

Fanning herself and sniffing a pomander, she pushed her way through the lines of reporters, children, beggars, hawkers, and idlers to the row of trestles that marked off the assembly itself. A couple thousand people from the neighborhood packed out a games pitch adjacent to a local school. Some of them were sitting on folding chairs, others were standing up and milling around. They hadn't been called to order yet, and the din of conversation bouncing around the high wooden walls—the pitch was for a ball-and-racquet game, something like a team version of squash—was almost deafening. The crowd had come straight from work at midday, some of them via a grogshop. If democracy, as Esias was fond of saying, was mob rule, here was the mob.

Somewhere in this mob—ah, there he was, up near the front—was Andrew Burnaby, the de Tenebres' agent for this neighborhood. She'd spent half the morning briefing him in a coffeehouse. It had been something of a strain. Burnaby was more skilled in putting forward sly arguments for a tariff here or a tax concession there, or rebutting similarly self-interested proposals from rival agents, than in making a populist case for free trade and against Port Authority meddling and bungling. She'd had to present it in the most venal possible light for him to grasp it at all, and even so she suspected he'd be out of his depth.

This working-class suburban neighborhood, optimistically named Verdant Heights when it had been jerry-built a hundred years earlier on an inadequately drained malarial swamp, was of no great importance in itself. It just happened to be the first to hold an assembly since the *Bright Star*'s impounding, and steering a protest through this meeting might be crucial in starting the ball rolling. So Esias had explained when he'd briefed Lydia over breakfast. She felt herself on trial, and on her mettle.

A low wooden stage had been dragged into the playing court for the afternoon and placed at the front, with two chairs and a table upon it. Up the three steps at its side climbed a fat, middle-aged woman swathed in black skirts. She puffed her way across the creaking planks and sat down heavily. A thin and nervous-looking young man followed her, clutching a briefcase. When he'd sat down and laid out a pad of yellow notepaper and arranged two ballpoint pens and a sheaf of printed papers to his satisfaction, the woman thumped her fist on the table.

A hush fell at once. The woman opened the meeting, the man read out minutes and matters arising, people spoke to the points from the floor. The young man took notes and recorded votes. When Lydia had got over her surprise at how orderly it all was she found it tedious. An hour of people popping up and down and spouting off crawled by. Lydia bought herself a very small cup of fruit juice and sipped it very slowly. Somebody was talking about drains. Her attention wandered. She began to hope that the heat and discomfort of the venue—the sun on the field was *fierce*—would help speed up movement through the agenda. Burnaby wouldn't get much chance to intervene until Any Other Business.

Her idle gaze reached the rear of the enclosure and lit upon a small huddle near the gate, in which she recognized Volkov talking earnestly to a tall red-haired woman. Lydia was jolted by a sudden surge of jealousy. Two or three other people were listening just as intently. As she watched, the woman turned away and plunged into the crowd, assiduously elbowing her way to the front; the others headed for the middle and the sides.

Volkov, his gaze following them, spotted her. He smiled and made a sort of drowning wave above the heads of the throng. Intrigued, Lydia began the slow process of joining him, meeting every grumble with a fixed smile of apology. By the time she reached him ten minutes later, her cheek muscles were as sore as her toes. He had moved to the very edge of the crowd, and he turned his head to glance at her for only a moment, then faced forward again.

"Hello," he said. "You look rather glamorous."

"I don't feel it," she said. "I just feel tied up and *hot*."

The corner of his mouth twitched; she wondered if she'd said something unintentionally amusing. She was quivering inside a little.

"What brings you here?" Volkov asked.

"Oh, politics. You?"

"The same. The tall redhead is working with us on the project. She happens to live around here. The others are a couple of local workers I've met on business. They're all going to try and get a word in about what the Port Authority has been up to."

"I'm expecting someone here to raise the matter too."

Volkov glanced sideways again, approvingly. "Good. That gives us quite a spread of speakers."

"Depends on whether the chair recognizes them," Lydia said.

Volkov looked right around at her with a broad smile, as though she had said something quite charming.

"Yes," he said. "Not the sort of thing one would want to leave to chance, eh?"

With a chuckle, he turned away.

After a few more minutes of discussion of drainage and subsidence had drawn to a close and several amendments and a motion carried, the woman in the chair rapped her knuckles on the table and said, "Any other business?"

She said it as though hoping there wouldn't be any but knowing all too well that there would. Hands shot up all over the place; the half dozen or so gigants in the crowd had an advantage there, and Lydia noticed one pithkie perched on another's shoulders, arm up and waving. Some people present took the arrival at this point in the agenda as the occasion to take their leave; others took it as the end of the so-far two-hour-long smoking ban and lit up; others pushed forward, or started rapid and noisy conversations. It all seemed much more the sort of chaos Lydia had expected democracy to be like than the main part of the meeting had been.

"This is where it gets interesting," said Volkov out of the side of his mouth.

The young man on the platform was glancing around the crowd and scribbling notes on his pad without looking down at it. He leaned sideways and conferred rapidly with the chairwoman, then pointed discreetly with his pen. She nodded, raised her arm, and pointed very clearly at someone.

"You, second row, tall, red hair—"

"Thank you, Madam Chair," said the woman who'd been speaking with Volkov. She pushed forward and jumped on to the corner of the platform, where she could face most of the crowd while keeping up the polite fiction that she was addressing the chair.

"Citizen Gail Frethorne," she said. "With your permission, Madam Chair, I'd like to bring to the attention of this assembly a quite unprecedented action by the Port Authority. Just this morning, they ordered the militia into

Loudon's Engineering Works to shut down a project—"

She paused. "Interest," she said. "I work there, on the project they shut down."

"Noted," said the young man, scribbling.

"The project was to build some survival equipment for the space travelers who have recently arrived and whose ship has been so rudely embargoed by the Port Authority."

"Treaty! Treaty!" someone shouted. There was a moment of commotion, during which Lydia nudged Volkov.

"Is this your *space suit* project that's been shut down?"

"Yes," said Volkov. "I'll tell you about it later."

"The chair recognizes the interruption," said the big woman on the platform. "You on the right, halfway along—yes, man in the hat."

A high-crowned, long-plumed hat waved above the left flank of the crowd.

"Madam Chair, citizens, this project has been cancelled at the request of the speakers for the local saur community, which the Port Authority is bound to—"

"Interest! Interest!"

The man stretched up and glowered toward his interruptors. "Port Authority clerk," he said. Laughter followed.

He plowed on: "They have appealed to the treaty, so this is a matter for the Port Authority and is out of order and ultra vires of a neighborhood assembly—"

Uproar. Lydia made out some of the indignant shouts:

"The assemblies are *all* sovereign!"

"Nothing's out of order except you!"

"Recall! Recall! Recall 'em all!"

"What country d'you think *you're* living in? Fuck off back to it!"

Madam Chair almost broke the table.

"Order!" she shouted, just once. The shouting stopped. "The matter raised by Citizen Frethorne," she went on, "is indeed out of order, but not because it's a matter for the Port Authority. It's out of order because anything involving the treaties is a matter for the courts. Citizen Frethorne will please stand down."

Gail Frethorne hopped off the platform and returned to where she had been standing. Lydia felt disappointed.

"Damn, that's a bit of a—"

Volkov was shaking his head. "Wait."

"You at the side, red shirt, hand up—yes, you!"

"Whatever they did this morning," a man said loudly and confidently from the floor, "I reckon the Port Authority wants a good looking at. What do they think they're doing interfering with the Mingulay starship, anyway? They never lay a finger on the big merchants' ships, which carry only capital goods and luxuries. Not that I've anything against that, but there's *loads* more stuff we could trade if there was a regular run between here and Mingulay—"

"What's the difference who flies the ships?" somebody else shouted. "It wouldn't change the ten-year turnaround time!"

"Order!"

"That it wouldn't," the man in the red shirt went on. "But having *lots* of ships, shuttling back and forth so there's a continuous stream going each way, and a simple system of export-import advance orders like the big merchants have—that would make a difference. It would make the imports we already have cheaper and make bulk imports and exports profitable."

The concept of ship streaming was familiar enough to the crowd for this to go over all right, but the objector shouted out again.

"And where are these *lots of ships* going to come from?"

"Well—"

But he'd lost the initiative. Volkov clicked his tongue, irritated.

"He should have come back on that right away," he said. "Oh, well."

A very tall old man with a long white beard and a long black coat spoke next.

"I don't think there should be even *one* more ship," he said. "We should send the *Bright Star* back where it came from, to the goddamned pagan heresiarchs of Mingulay, and tell them to stick right there where they belong. If the Powers Above had meant human beings to navigate ships, they'd have given us, they'd have given us—"

"Tentacles?" somebody called out.

"They'd have given us some better evidence of it than a story told by these there godless cosmonauts, whose ship has brought this world nothing but heresy and sedition these past two hundred years. I remember when I were a lad—"

"And the ship arrived the first time?" the same wag hollered.

"The folks who were as old then as I am now, and as you will be one day *if* the Lord spares you, used to say that the Powers Above taught the krakens the way through the passages the Lord has provided in the crystal spheres of the firmaments, and that it was only of the Lord's mercy that the *Bright Star* had not broken the spheres when it came from Earth and released upon us the waters above the firmament, as in the days of Noah."

He paused for a moment to draw breath and then continued, louder, shouting down a further outburst of heckling: "Assuming it came from Earth in the first place, of course, and not from the father of lies. Because the books they brought with them and that these there professors up at the university treat like Scripture itself are full of nothing but lies, and there's only one place *they* could have come from—"

He continued in this vein for five minutes, then sat

down abruptly to catcalls, amens, and scattered applause.

"With all due respect to the previous speaker," said the woman who spoke next, "I'd like to point out some other objections to the proposal of extending human-controlled trade that may be more, ah, widely shared. The Port Authority has warned us that the ship is full of health hazards, of viruses and bacteria from the Solar System that have had centuries to mutate in the radiation of space. Starship engines are—as we all know—designed to be controlled by the krakens, the great navigators. We are told that the one on this ship is in fact controlled by a calculating machine, programmed by a student! And that the inexperienced pilot on board is a saur whose actions are strongly disapproved of by many of his fellows. *My* only complaint about the actions of the Port Authority is that they've let this plague carrier and potential nuclear bomb sit in our harbor, instead of sending it straight back to Mingulay, or—as the citizen here has just suggested—to hell!"

A significant minority cheered that one.

"Goddamn gutter press," muttered Volkov. "It's worse than a whole regiment of priests."

"It's all right," said Lydia. "Our agent's got the floor."

Andrew Burnaby had just jumped on to the platform.

"We all know your interest," said Madam Chair wearily, "but tell us anyway."

Burnaby started off well enough, but the increasingly skeptical and scoffing interjections—especially the growing cry of "What ships?"—almost drove him from the platform. Competent enough at raising minor details of taxes and regulations, at demagogy he was hopeless. Lydia would have jumped up and down with fury and impatience if her dress had allowed her to. She turned to speak to Volkov and found that he wasn't there. He had somehow insinuated himself to the front, and a note had been handed up to the platform, literally bypassing Burnaby while he was still floundering.

Madam Chair and Mister Secretary had their heads

together, and suddenly the woman nodded and beckoned. Volkov bounded onto the platform almost before Burnaby had time to get off. Cameras were popping and microphones extending all over the place.

"Thank you, Madam Chair," he said, his voice already easily commanding the room. "Thank you all. My name is Grigory Antonov, from one of the Cosmonaut Families of Mingulay, and I'm working very closely with the crew of the *Bright Star*. Let me assure you that it doesn't contain any plague germs, its engine is not about to blow up, and it didn't make any holes in the sky.

"Some citizens here have spoken of the benefits that will come from having human-owned ships trading between the worlds. Others have asked, 'Where will all these new ships come from?' We're unlikely to be able to buy them from the saurs, after all! Even if they were willing to sell, we couldn't afford to buy them. Where will we find other ships?"

He paused and looked around. Lydia felt, for a moment, that his eyes had met hers and realized that everybody else here had—even if only for a fraction of a second—felt the same.

"I can tell you," he said quietly. "The *Bright Star* was built by human beings like ourselves! Ordinary men and women in the European Union, a great democracy like your own, built the *Bright Star* long ago. The technology they used was not much more advanced than ours. The lightspeed engine of the *Bright Star* was built by human beings not long after. They were given the design directly by the Powers Above, and the tools they used to build it are still on the ship. Someday, you may want to learn to use these tools yourselves.

"So that's my answer to the very good question, 'Where will the other ships come from?' They will come from Rawliston, from Mingulay, from other human worlds. We can *build* them for ourselves! The *Bright Star* is only one ship, yes. But with your skills, your hopes, your strength, you can know for sure—*there will be other ships*."

He looked around again and smiled. "Thank you," he said and stepped down. The cheers and jeers stopped and hands went up.

"It's all very well him talking about us building the ships, but *where*," the next speaker wanted to know, "is the *money* going to come from?"

After another half hour or so, a cry went up to close the matter. This was carried by acclamation. Then a vote was taken on a motion to challenge the action of the Port Authority. It passed by a narrow majority, just big enough to register on a show of hands.

After that it was all anticlimax, or so it seemed to Lydia. Ten slips of paper were pulled at random out of a big bucket holding the names of all citizens present. The ten would go on to represent Verdant Heights at the next municipal assembly, in a couple of weeks, where the votes taken here and at other neighborhood assemblies would be discussed.

Lydia watched the crowd stream out. Small groups hung around, still talking. Volkov was at the center of one of them, walking toward her and talking and gesticulating. He stopped in front of her, and the others stopped too. He introduced her to the man in the red shirt and the other man he'd conferred with earlier, and to the woman, Gail Frethorne.

Gail had a broad smile and a firm handshake, and she didn't seem to have any special relationship with Volkov. Lydia hoped her insanely intense suspicion didn't show in her face.

"Pleased to meet you, Trader Lydia de Tenebre," Gail said.

"Likewise, Citizen Frethorne . . . Gail."

Gail suddenly smiled in a different, more relaxed way. "I wouldn't have taken you for a trader; you have the accent just right, and the look is so stylish . . . that's such a lovely dress.'

"Thank you," said Lydia. Gail, in trousers and shirjack, rough-handed, didn't seem like she would care about such things, but her eyes shone with genuine admiration.

The thin young man who'd been on the platform had joined them. His name was William Endecott. Pinched features, bright sharp eyes, thin pale red hair combed back, plain suit. He transferred the briefcase clutched under his elbow to his hand for the handshake, then put it quickly back. Well, she'd had as much trouble with her various fashionable encumbrances.

Lydia noticed Volkov's unobtrusive nod at Endecott, a look that said, "Well done!" and understood what he'd meant about not leaving the recognition of speakers from the floor to chance. A thought struck her.

"Citizen Endecott," she said, "isn't it just a matter of chance that the delegates you send to the municipal assembly will reflect the feeling of this meeting? Ten out of—what, two thousand? It's well within probability that they could all take the minority view."

"You're quite right," said Endecott. "It's a problem, but there are more than a hundred neighborhood assemblies, and—"

"It all comes out in the wash," said Gail. "And it's the way we've always done things."

"Nevertheless," said Endecott. He glanced at Volkov, as though checking something. Volkov's nod was, again, barely perceptible. "We've been discussing, just throwing ideas around you understand, just considering the notion that it might be a good idea some time in the future to change the constitution so that neighborhood meetings *elect* the delegates, to ensure that the majority view prevailed beyond cavil."

The two workingmen nodded firmly.

Gail looked shocked. "What about the minority views? Who would represent them?"

Endecott made an impatient chopping gesture. "Oh, the minority would be bound to get some delegates, and anyway they'd be quite free to try to become the majority themselves. I don't see how it could be a problem. Like you said about drawing lots, it all comes out in the wash."

"That's *ridiculous,* that's completely different," said Gail. "Drawing lots is *fair,* even if it sometimes throws up a freak result. With elections you're actually building the minority problem right in at every level, and lots more with it—parties, money, fame, graft, just for starters. What chance would that leave ordinary people, what chance would we have of being heard or of making a difference? Elections are completely undemocratic, they're downright *anti*democratic. Everybody knows *that!*"

Volkov's expression was entirely neutral, but the three men looked at him and waited for him to say something. He shrugged.

"I understand," he said thoughtfully, "that in the socialist democracies, the representation of minority views was never a problem."

He slapped one hand with the other. "But come on. Enough of politics. Let's go to the coffee shop."

The shop was crowded, the coffee was good, the conversation was lively. By the sound of it, there was quite a lot of dissent and discontent in Rawliston, more than she'd thought. The compradore magnates, and their influence over the Port Authority, didn't seem popular at all. While this sentiment was useful to the de Tenebres in the present circumstance, it might not bode well for the future—after all, they had their own compradores. Lydia said nothing about this. After an hour the two workers and Endecott took their leave—another meeting, they said—and sometime after that, Matt and Salasso strolled in. Volkov waved and slid along the bench to make room. Salasso edged in and Matt swung in after him, shouting an order for coffee and hemp.

"Ah," said Matt as he settled, "so we found the place at last. Here we all are." He rubbed his face—hot, sweaty, and tired. "Oh, hi, Lydia. Wow, you look amazing." He blinked and glanced across at the overflow of skirt at the side of the table. "That's a beautiful dress."

"So everybody keeps telling me!" She tried to keep the irritation out of her voice.

Matt chuckled and turned to Volkov. "So how did the meeting go?"

"Very well," said Volkov. He lidded his eyes over his steaming mug. "Lydia, now, she got an agent to make quite an effective intervention—"

Flatterer! thought Lydia, but she couldn't help feeling pleased.

"—and Gail probably turned the whole meeting around."

"Flatterer," said Gail mildly. "You know it was your speech that did it."

Matt looked up from his rather shaky rolling of a joint. "It's in the hourlies already, Grigory Andreievich. You were always a good politician."

Gail looked across sharply. "What do you mean?"

Matt scratched his head. "Ah, there's a lot of politics in business," he said. "A persuasive guy like Grigory here can get a lot more engineering done than somebody who knows more about slide rules and steel than the insides of people's heads."

"You could say that," agreed Volkov, looking almost sleepy. He glanced more alertly at Matt, Salasso, and Gail, then at Lydia. "When we've, ah, finished our coffee, we have an appointment with Paul Loudon. . . ."

That sounded like a hint. Lydia drained her cup and busied herself with her gloves and bag, angry with herself that she felt so disappointed and shut out.

"Why shouldn't Lydia come with us?" said Gail.

Another unspoken consultation flashed between the two cosmonauts. Matt lit up his joint and gazed at Lydia as if he had never seen her before.

"Yes," he said. "Yes, why not."

"What are you seeing Loudon about?" asked Lydia. She was glad she'd pulled her gloves on; her knuckles would be white.

"Oh, the space suit project," said Gail. "You might find this very interesting."

"I have a lot to do," Lydia demurred, trying not to appear too eager and curious. "My father has given me a lot of responsibility for the politics of lifting the embargo on your ship. Like today."

"Yes." Volkov nodded and leaned forward, gazing into her eyes as if he and she were completely alone. "Now, doesn't that seem like a good reason for you to come with us this evening and find out more?"

That would do, that was a good reason to be persuaded, along with all of her bad reasons.

"Yes," she said. "Thank you."

Gail was becoming increasingly worried as she scanned the early evening sky and saw yet again that it remained empty of heathens in hang gliders. She wondered if her friends had been offended by her breaking off the drug traffic, or if they had found nothing else worth trading. Or, for that matter, if they'd run up against a more concerted opposition to their technological innovations than they'd led her to believe they expected.

She'd left her colleagues and her rich new friend Lydia at the coffee shop, nipped home for a wash and a quick change and a routine warning rant from her long-suffering mother (who'd been startled to see Gail's face under screaming headlines on the newsprints), and rejoined the group at the coffeehouse and guided them through the complicated chain of bus routes out to the flying club. Lydia had admired the green silk heathen-woman suit Gail had changed into, an early gift (or payment, she wasn't sure) from Slow Leg, and they'd all chatted inconsequentially along the way.

Loudon had booked a private table with a shade and

an overhead electric light, out in the open a hundred meters from the clubhouse, and laid on cold beers and cold snacks. It was a much better way of ensuring privacy than hiring one of the small rooms off the bar, with their thin walls. He'd accepted Lydia's unexpected presence with polite curiosity and good grace.

Lydia had grasped the point about how the heathens might be able to help, and now they were all discussing the matter, heads down over sketches and calculations. Every so often Gail would find that she'd lost track of time and that another half hour had passed, without any sign of the heathens' arrival.

She looked up again, saw that the sky was almost dark. Oh, shit. It didn't look likely that they'd be coming now. She sighed and turned back to the discussion, hoping that it wasn't now academic.

"Now," Loudon was saying, "we need to look at ways of fitting a threaded metal sleeve to a ceramic helmet. How about, um, a rubber seal—is that vacuum-resistant enough?"

"No," said Matt, with a vaguely distracted air. "Uh, excuse me for asking, but can someone tell me what I'm seeing up there?" He pointed. "That, uh, strange light in the sky?"

Stone cautiously, at arm's length, poked a short stick at the sliding door of the brazier, knocking it open, pumped the handle of the fire-spirit container, and simultaneously squeezed on the bellows. Flames shot up with a searing whoosh into the balloon above him. With a lurch that almost threw him on his back in the long basket-work gondola, the balloon train's forward pitch was corrected, nearly overcorrected. With another hasty swipe, he closed the brazier's door, and the flame moderated.

"Easy back there," Slow Leg called from his perch at the bow. "Now damp back the others. Quick, quick!"

Clutching the sides of the basket with each hand as he clambered over bales, Stone worked his way along its thirty-meter length and slid the other two brazier doors shut. After closing the sternward one he looked down. The ground seemed to be coming up very fast in the dim light. Then a cloud of dust and dirt drifted by beneath him; Slow Leg had released some ballast, and the descent slowed.

"Hold tight and bend your knees," Slow Leg advised. Stone needed no second urging. He half crouched, knees on a bale of soft stuff, and waited tensely. The balloon train yawed a little to the right as one of the side sails flapped out like a fin. The thump of landing still took him by surprise, but it wasn't as violent as he'd feared. As he'd been drilled to do, he vaulted out as soon as he'd recovered his balance and ran to grab the nearest coil of rope attached to the side. Beside it, inside the basket, a mallet was conveniently stowed. On the end of the rope was an anchor. He paid out the rope and hammered the sharp stake into the hard earth, then ran forward to repeat the process. Slow Leg was meanwhile doing the same on the other side, and they finished off at the bow and stern. At each end was a bottle of water, with which they hastily dowsed the braziers. The three huge hot-air bags were already sagging; by turning the craft Slow Leg had ensured that the breeze would carry them to fall at an angle rather than directly on top of the basket, but the risk of fire was always present. After they'd dowsed the central brazier they stood looking at each other, laughing. Slow Leg clapped Stone's shoulder.

"We made it," he said. "Thank the gods."

"Thanks to you," said Stone.

"That too."

They laughed at this outrageous immodesty. Slow Leg peered around. In the middle distance shone the lights of the airfield's low buildings, against which a dozen curious watchers were silhouetted. Closer by, three dimly visible figures were hurrying across the grass.

"Gail and two men," said Slow Leg. "Let us go and meet them."

There's a minute of confused and confusing introductions—Slow Leg is the tall tough one in the short kilt, Stone is the small pretty one in the quilted suit—then Matt finds himself lugging a big felt bag bound with leather straps across the field to the table where they've been sitting. Then he's running back and doing the same again. Eventually they have the balloon train's cargo laid out on the grass in the puddle of yellow light from the lamp, and the heathens are proudly unwrapping them to display their contents.

"Ho-ly fucking shit," Gail says reverently.

It's treasure, even Matt can see that. He knows that his aesthetic sense may not have been much to write home about to begin with, but it's had a couple of centuries to wise up, and what he sees makes the hairs on his neck prickle. Carvings of mammoth ivory, intricate woodwork, ephemeral-looking but oddly substantial confections of feathers and dried flowers, ceramic wares and glasses that would not look out of place on the classiest tables he's ever dined at. Images of gods and demons that make his materialist soul shiver.

"What's this *for*?" Gail asks.

"These," says one of the heathens, Slow Leg, "are the goods the women traded for the goods we brought."

"That's, that's—" Gail is lost for words but sounds indignant.

"Profitable, yes," says Slow Leg. He slaps his bare thigh and laughs.

"What goods did you bring?" Lydia asks.

Stone, the other heathen, speaks up. "Blades, mostly. Scissors and knives, razors. Needles and thimbles. Eyeglasses."

"This," says Loudon, "is a ripoff."

"Unequal exchange," says Volkov.

The two heathens nod eagerly.

"Let us make the most of it while it lasts," says Slow Leg.

"Um," says Paul. He turns away from them and glances covertly around his guests, raising his eyebrows and rolling his eyes a little, then looks directly at the two new arrivals.

"I expect you are hungry?"

"Possibly a little," says Slow Leg, sitting down.

Stone climbs out of the quilted suit, revealing a very pretty blue silk sort of salwar kameez underneath, and sits down too.

"These are interesting pictures," says Stone after a while, looking down at the scribbles and sketches.

It's been agreed that Gail will put the proposal to them. She leans forward eagerly.

"There is something we would like to ask you to make for us," she says. "Something we wish to trade with you for. Not medicine, not beautiful things. We could pay you very well for it."

"Let us see what you want us to make," says Slow Leg.

"Well," says Gail, turning one of the sketches the right way round for them. "We would like something like the suit and helmet Stone wears for flying, but made with different materials. This here, for example, would have to be of strong fired-clay ware, and this would be glass, and this would be perhaps of the fabric you use for the balloons and the wings. It is very important that it could all be made in such a way that no air could pass in or out, except through this hole here. If you were to pump—to blow it full of air, and stop up this hole, and place it under still water, not even the tiniest bubble could rise from it. Do you think you could make two such suits in the Great Vale?"

"Ah," says Slow Leg. "This is very like the kind of suits the women of the Great Vale used to make for the forest people, the gigants, long ago." He waves a hand behind his head. "Before the *Bright Star,* before the

Christians, before . . . well, a long time, spans of hands of mans of years ago—"

He glances at Salasso.

"—before even your time, or your mother's time, the snake people built a city on the moon. But they needed strong workers to build it, so they asked the forest people to help them. And the forest people asked our ancestors to make the garments they would need to live on the moon, because there is no air there. So the women made them. They were called—"

He frowns at Stone for a moment. "What would they be called, in the Christian?"

"Space suits," says Stone.

"Yes!" says Slow Leg. "Would that be close enough to what you want?"

It's settled. Matt, Gail, and Salasso will take their specifications and designs and—more importantly—the breathing apparatus to the Great Vale, and women there will build the suits. Lydia will show the heathens' trade goods to her family's marketing department. She and Volkov will work together on regaining access to the ship and will maintain radio contact with the others while they're up in the Vale. They've exhausted the subject, and themselves. Now they're winding down, talking about anything else.

Slow Leg is talking to Volkov and Gail and Loudon about ballooning and gliding. Stone is explaining to Matt and Lydia and Salasso the complex traditions and customs governing and limiting the trade relationships the Great Vale clans have with Rawliston, with the savages in the hinterland, with the nonhuman species, and Matt is increasingly puzzled by what for him is an entirely new kind of embarrassment in social intercourse. He doesn't know what sex Stone is, and he can't figure out a way of asking without risking offense. The heathen's smooth face, slight but wiry build, and light voice give no definitive cues either way, and the style of hair and clothing are obviously feminine, as are the gestures, but at some moments something in the light, or a movement or a turn of speech makes Stone suddenly seem to be a long-haired blond man in blue pajamas, and then Stone does something like twine a lock of that hair and Matt mentally kicks himself and decides that Stone is obviously a woman, and then . . . It's like superposed quantum states, or one of those visual illusions that can be seen in two completely different ways.

"When we returned, the shamans had gathered for a council in one of the larger villages," Stone says. "They are still arguing. Rumors are spreading of big disagreements. The arrival of your ship is a mighty portent."

"Why?" Matt asks.

"Our society is in many ways an artifice, maintained by conscious holding on to old ways and conscious holding back in adopting new ones. Of course there are exceptions—the strong drinks, the steel tools—but until now they do not change things because they are not . . . recognized?"

"That's the word," says Lydia.

"Now, the whole reason for this is that we very deeply believe that different societies should walk in different paths, and that only unhappiness comes from confusing the paths. You see—and we see—what happens to those of us who live in this city. We remember how that began, when the Christians tried to lead us onto their path. And we see in the sky and all around us how the different . . . peoples? like yours, Salasso, and the sea people and the forest and mountain people, the saurs and krakens and gigants and pithkies as the Christians call them, do not share their tools and machines, or do so only in a very small way. Every people has a place in the great order of the universe. Or so we thought, until you brought the *Bright Star* here."

"So you're saying that because we're walking on the paths of the saurs and the kraken, your people have started wondering if they shouldn't walk some different paths of their own?"

"You have followed me," says Stone.

"It's quite a jump," says Lydia.

Stone laughs. "It is, but you must remember, the *Bright Star* has always been a totem for all the sky people, the tribes of the Great Vale."

Oh, yes. From a morning last week quizzing Gail about the messy aftermath of Dawson's Night, Matt has learned something of the sky people's version of liberation theology and of the local objections to it.

"It must have been quite a shock actually to see it."

"Oh, yes!" says Stone. "Especially when it almost collided with me."

"That was *you*? In the glider?"

"Yes."

"Amazing!" Matt ponders this apparent coincidence and realizes it isn't one, that it makes sense in the autochthonous worldview that the person who first encountered the ship should be the first to act on the implications of its arrival.

"I thought you said that flying was men's work," says Lydia.

"It is," says Stone. "But building and testing the gliders is women's work."

Matt, relieved to have his quandary resolved, smiles at the heathen woman. "And building space suits!"

"Yes."

"I can't imagine what we can give you in exchange for that," Matt says.

"Oh, more of what we have already taken will be very welcome," says Stone.

"Still," says Matt, "there must be something more than needles and knives that would be even more welcome."

"There is something I have thought of." Stone looks at Matt and Lydia shyly, through eyelashes. "Your robe, Lydia, I . . . begin to see how it can be suitable for a woman to wear such a garment, and I think it is possible

that other women might see it in the same way. I wonder
if, perhaps, tomorrow I could borrow it, or one like it,
to show them?"

Lydia splutters with laughter. "I'll offer you better
than that," she says. "You can *have* this dress, right now,
if I can have your suit."

It's an instantly done deal. They disappear together
and return about ten minutes later. Stone sashays around
showing off the dress for Slow Leg's benefit, but it's
Gail and Loudon who seem most taken with the display.
Lydia sits down again, beside Matt.

"You look stunning," Matt says. He looks over at
Stone. "So does she."

"Oh, boy," says Lydia, grinning at him mischievously.
"Have I got news for you."

8

A Man You Don't Meet Every Day

LYDIA BLEW SEAWATER and snot from her nose and mouth, laughing at how unladylike she was, and turned her back to the next incoming swell. This time she got it right, jumping up as the wave came in and swimming smoothly up its retreating slope, letting it buoy her with an exhilarating sensation of being borne aloft, then reaching the crest and riding it forward, swimming steadily, flying along above the sand in that ridge of water with a meter-deep dip of air in front of her face until the wave curled over and at the same time her knees hit the soft sand and she was kneeling in foam and spitting and laughing again. She flicked her hair back and stood up, calf-deep in the surf, and was about to wade out again when she saw her father about thirty meters away, striding out from the beach.

She yelled hello and waved. He splashed up, shading his eyes and peering at her in the low sun.

"You're up early," she said.

"Same reason as you," he growled, walking on past

her. "Sleeping alone. Faustina's with her immortal hero, and Claudia and Phoebe spent the night with each other. Pah!"

He looked back at her. "Don't just stand there."

She followed him out to a depth where the waves' troughs reached their waists, the peaks their chests. He stood and ducked his head in and emerged gasping and shaking off drops, then turned around, leaning back against the incoming swells, letting his arms bob beside him.

"Woo-hoo-hoo!" he said. "Chilly at first!"

"I'll be chilly again if we don't go deeper."

"Can't talk and swim," Esias said. "At least, not in the sea. Never quite got the hang of that."

He backed out a little way farther.

"That was well done yesterday," he said. "At the meeting and out at the airfield. Making contact with the heathens and setting up the beginnings of a deal was certainly worthwhile—that kind of craftwork sells very well back home. But keeping on our friend Volkov's tail was even more important."

"Oh! Why?"

"He's up to something," Esais said. "I don't know just what, but my sources tell me he's been talking to a lot of people that he doesn't seem to have any kind of business relationship with. People such as those workers at the meeting, and that busy clerk, Endecott. There was some kind of political organization among the cosmonauts, back in the Solar System—"

"The one he calls the Party?"

"Yes. It had some very strange and unsound ideas, by all accounts. Communism, indeed!"

"What's that?"

Esias waved a hand. "Look it up sometime, I think you'll find it in Plato. Volkov seems to have some odd hankering after it, heaven knows why. I rather suspect some of the old cosmonauts may share his views, and

I'd appreciate it very much if you could keep an ear out for any of that sort of talk."

"I'll be happy to do that."

"I'm sure you would," Esias said dryly. He looked at her sideways. "I hear you've been flirting with him."

"That's not true!" she said hotly. "Who told you that?"

Esias tapped the side of his nose. "Like I said—sources. Walls have ears. Which is why we're talking out here. Anyway, I've seen how you look at him."

"Well, what—"

—*business is it of yours?* she didn't finish, realizing that it was indeed his business.

"—have I got against that?" Esias finished for her. "None at all, number-seven daughter. Except . . ."

He frowned at the distant house, as though trying to see through its ancient walls, to pry through the low sun's dazzling reflections on its windows, to listen in on pillow talk in its rooms. Then he turned on her a softer gaze.

"I'll be frank with you, Lydia, because you've shown maturity. Just as I tolerate his discreet dalliance with Faustina, so I will smile through my teeth upon any affair you and he may have—a decent interval after Faustina, of course; I won't have the air of my house poisoned by mother-daughter jealousies. But I would worry about his intentions toward you. He's a man of guile and charm. I'm sure he seems very excitingly . . . wise and experienced to you. Zeus above, he's almost old enough to be your father, eh?"

"I'm listening," said Lydia, devoutly wishing she wasn't.

Esias scooped up water and splashed his face, rubbing his cheeks.

"What's easy to forget," he said, and at this point she realized that he too was blushing, "is that he is much, much older than that. He is a man with a long past and a long future, and he has long plans for it. He has ambition."

"How do you know?"

"Credit me with *that* much experience," Esias chuckled. He waved his right hand vaguely at Rawliston, northward along the curve of the coast. "What was it their actor fellow said? 'Let me have men about me that are fat . . .' " He looked down, laughed, and looked up. "I'm fat and contented. He is lean and has a hundred years of hunger in his eyes. He moves among us as we move among the people of the shore, knowing they'll be dust when we return."

"Well, he wants us to share in that."

"No doubt he does," said Esias. "Though whether our science can get that secret out of his . . . secretions is another question. Still, what does it matter to us, eh? We drop him off at Nova Babylonia, set him up with a sound investment fund to sustain him and the research, and after a few months of raking in the money from this trip, leave him in the scientists' capable hands. Two hundred years later, a year or so in our lives, we pop in again to see how they're getting on. If he's outlived six generations of savants, none of them any closer to extracting his elixir, what's that to us?"

"I don't quite see your point," said Lydia, paddling. The tide was coming in. By now they both had to tread water with each wave.

"My point," said Esias, spluttering a little, "is that a man like him will not have spent those two centuries sitting on his hands. We might come back to find him an emperor, or a god."

By unspoken accord they kicked off and began swimming shoreward. Mindful of what Esias had said about talking while swimming, Lydia said nothing until they were both wading ankle-deep through the shallows.

"What does that have to do with his intentions toward me?"

"I'm afraid," said Esias dourly, "that he might get a notion to ask you to *marry* him."

Lydia looked down, too embarrassed and startled to respond. A broken wave hissed up the beach, spreading white froth like a trailing train of lace.

Matt tries not to look down at the rocks as the last of the early-morning sea wind and the first of the mid-morning thermals loft the balloon train over the natural dam, to drift not very far above the Great Lake of the Great Vale. A brazier roars up at the bow, and another answers behind him, and a minute or two later he is comforted to observe that while he can still see the spreading circular ripples and the bright flashes of leaping fish he can no longer see the patterns of the scales on their backs.

He grins in relief at Gail, who sits facing him. They've been warned not to talk, because clear communication between Slow Leg and Stone, yelling at each other from either end of the craft, might be crucial at any moment. She smiles back, then her gaze flits past him again, at Stone. Then she sees that Matt has noticed and she looks away. Salasso is huddled on the floor between Matt and Gail, his head lolling against Matt's knees. He resists the urge to stroke it, feeling that this comfort would offend the saur's dignity. Rendered completely insensible, if not unconscious, by a full pipe of hemp urgently smoked before takeoff, Salasso needs all the dignity he can preserve. Matt himself would have much preferred to travel to the Vale by gravity skiff, but—security considerations apart—the fraught divisions among the saurs has put that out of the question.

The mountain ranges on either side widen out as the lake narrows to the river mouth, and the valley's plain opens before them. It seems much more extensive than it did from the ship, and not quite so densely populated—it's easy, from this height, to see the spaces between the villages. The bits that aren't simply wild are meadows and gardens rather than fields, indicating an economy that is pastoral and horticultural rather than agricultural. The sky is startlingly busy with slow balloons and balloon trains and swift gliders; among them, and sometimes not much smaller than the gliders, the pterosaurs soar and swoop.

Even from this height—just within earshot of children's yells—it's clear that the people tending the garden plots or herding the great and various megatheria are all almost naked and therefore probably men. The women, in their brightly colored trouser suits, are the much rarer tiny figures he glimpses hurrying along the village streets. Matt guesses that they work indoors and realizes that this is the basis of the hitherto baffling division of labor between the sexes: women work indoors, men work outdoors. So gardening and herding, digging up and chipping flint, and building houses and chopping down trees and so forth—and yes, fighting; he can see a skirmish line of a dozen spear chuckers in enthusiastic practice—are all men's work. And women's work is everything else: woodcarving and weaving and pottery and glassblowing and gods know what.

Building gliders, too, but not flying them, except for test flights. He wonders how common people like Stone are here, and how many other dangerous bits of supposed women's work they tend to specialize in. Pretty expendable, he thinks with a wry grin, glancing over his shoulder at Stone, who is moving back and forth between the mid and the aft braziers, tweaking the hot-air supply. It's only the practicalities of this task that have got him into his flying suit this morning, and out of his new frock, which is neatly folded in a bundle.

After about an hour the two heathens start tamping the braziers and hauling on the ropes that spill hot air from the balloons and on the tougher cables that tug the steering fins. The balloon train sinks toward a cluster of several hundred buildings on either bank of the Big River, joined by a long stone bridge. The whiff of megathere manure wafts up from the kitchen gardens and middens, and the more fragrant smell of peat smoke drifts from chimneys. The craft passes low above the rooftops and just reaches the lower end of a long sloping field above the town, at the top end of which are low wattle sheds and parked gliders.

The grass comes up fast, then slows at the last second as the braziers give a final coordinated *whoomph* and the basket hits the ground, not too hard but not too gently to wake Salasso. He starts up and vaults over the side as readily as the two heathens, who're running to make fast the guy ropes and dowse the braziers. Matt and Gail follow, teetering on unsteady legs like newborn lambs for a few moments. Some heathen men come running up to help catch and stow the deflating balloons, and the three visitors stand aside. To Matt's surprise, they aren't stared at. Rather the reverse: He feels that they are being deliberately ignored. Beyond the landing field, their arrival seems not to have made any stir.

Maybe it's rude to stare. Matt turns away from watching the unlading of the cargo and the swift dismantling of the craft and instead gazes over the village below. His first impression is that the place is old: The stone-paved path alongside the landing field is rutted, the house roofs are furred with broad patches of orange and gray lichen. Walls are covered with creepers, and culverts are fringed with thick green moss. The streets are, from what he can see, fairly clean. The sky people don't seem to take horses or the larger mammals into their villages. There are plenty of dogs, cats, and turkeys on the streets, and in most backyards small dinosaurs about the size of geese strut and peck.

Gail joins him in his survey and breathes in and out noisily and appreciatively.

"The air up here's a lot fresher than in Rawliston," she remarks. "And it's cooler. And it's quiet."

"Yeah," says Matt. "You know, it kind of worries me that we seem to be setting this place up for increased trade. One generation from now, I can see it becoming a holiday resort for your compradore magnates. In two generations, for anyone—for car mechanics!"

Gail snorts. "Nah, there's too much bad blood between Christians and heathens for that. The only way Rawliston could swamp this place is by outright invasion, and there's no way our little gray friends will let that happen."

Salasso has unobtrusively stepped between them and is impassively regarding the village and the Vale.

"I would not be too sure of that," he says.

Behind them, Slow Leg whistles. They turn to see the other heathens trotting off up the slope, six of them bearing the balloons' long basket on their shoulders, other groups lugging the folded silk. Stone and Slow Leg are left standing with their bales and with the more elaborate packages containing the breathing apparatus.

"That's a strange lack of curiosity," Gail says.

"It is politeness," says Slow Leg. "There will be a lot of questions for you later."

He stoops and hefts a bale. "Come."

Volkov joined Lydia at the breakfast table in the courtyard about an hour after her swim. She was on her third coffee and second sheet of paper, as she made plans for the next few days. Number-one item on her agenda—meeting Volkov—wasn't written down. She looked up and smiled as he sat down opposite her, wrapped in a big white toweling robe.

"Good morning," he said almost warily. "If I recall last night's discussions correctly, you and I are supposed to be coordinating our efforts."

"That's right," said Lydia. She fingered her scribbled notes. "I've been going through a list of the family's contacts, upcoming assemblies, and so on, for the same kind of thing as we did yesterday. I can't help thinking it's not enough."

"Oh, it won't be," he agreed cheerfully. "What we

need to do is combine legal and illegal work."

"Illegal work?" That sounded alarming.

He waved a melon rind. "Figure of speech. What I mean is, we need to try and get the embargo lifted, yes, but we also need to prepare for direct action if it isn't lifted, or isn't lifted in time."

"In time for what?"

Volkov gave her a very direct look. "Well, we need to get the ship out and the suits tested and Matt trained in EVA before I leave. Maybe do a little exploring."

"All right," Lydia said. "So what would the direct action involve?"

"Get Salasso back on board, legitimately. He then panics the guards with some plausible-sounding non-sense about the drive becoming unstable. Matt and I and maybe another old cosmonaut—there are a few in this town, and I've been trying to track them down—nip on to the unguarded ship, and off we go."

Lydia just stared at him.

"I am not *stupid*," she said.

"What?"

"I can think of a dozen ways that plan could go wrong. People getting hurt, even killed. Don't tell me you'd take that risk for a bit of field testing and safety training. So what are you planning to do—steal the ship?"

"Hmm," said Volkov. He rocked back a little and sipped his coffee. "Sorry, Lydia. We should have told you the whole truth in the first place." He leaned forward again and spoke more confidentially. "Matt and Salasso and I want to take the ship out and talk to a god."

That sounded like a reasonable explanation.

"Do Gregor and Elizabeth know about this?"

He shook his head.

"What about my father?"

"Likewise, no."

"And you don't want them to know?"

"Indeed not."

Lydia shut her eyes for a moment. She had a mental picture of wheels spinning in some moral calculating engine. When they stopped, the numbers came up black. She was going to feel guilty about this though. Rather to her surprise, it was the thought of Salasso's involvement that tipped the balance. A saur would not do something insanely dangerous or wrong.

"All right," she said. "Presumably you are not doing this out of idle curiosity."

Volkov shrugged and smiled disarmingly. "I knew I could trust you," he said. "As to idle curiosity, that's what took me to Venus once, and it's had a long time to grow. The intellectual passions are the strongest in the long run."

She didn't know what to say to that; she could think a lot of passions right now that were a lot stronger than curiosity.

"You mentioned looking for other cosmonauts," she said carefully. "Don't you . . . keep track of each other?" She laughed. "I'd have thought the advantages of being a conspiracy of immortals would be considerable."

"Oh, they are," said Volkov lightly. "Fortunately or otherwise, it hasn't worked out like that. We made a conscious decision to live unknown, as the philosopher says, for, well, obvious reasons." He waved a hand, taking in everything around them. "Can you *imagine* the mess places like this and Mingulay would be in by now if we hadn't? We'd either be hunted down like, I don't know, vampires or witches or something, or be venerated like gods walking the earth. I'm not sure which would be worse. So we chose not to, and by now we're dispersed across the Second Sphere, and only small groups of us know each other, personal friends and, ah, acquaintances."

"Which of these is Matt?"

"A friend," said Volkov. He stood up. "Would you like to meet some of my acquaintances?"

*   *   *

The heathens had led them down a paved pathway, and then turned right along the village's upper street. The noonday heat lay on it like a hush. Flowers and hanging plants poured over every eave and windowsill. By the time they'd walked fifty meters, almost a hundred people had appeared in the street, emerging not from the two-story stone houses—which were deserted, apart from old folk dozing in front of them—but from alleyways and adjoining streets or, it seemed, from thin air. Children raced around and chattered, women nudged each other and giggled, men stalked up and stared in silence, then backed away to pace alongside or behind. Gail followed their guides' example and walked as if the street was empty. The weight of her personal pack on her back and an air tank over one shoulder was beginning to tell.

The growing procession was stopped in its tracks by the frightful apparition of a heathen sorcerer who leapt sideways into the middle of the road in front of them. His feather-crowned mask looked like an elongated skull, or possibly a contorted saur face. His flapping cape was fringed with rattling seashells and pinned at the shoulders with saber-tooth canines. A hollow gourd on a long stick made a noise like pouring rain as he swung it from side to side. His feet, bare and dusty under the cape, slapped the paving as he capered in a surprisingly brisk jig.

The crowd spread out and flattened themselves against the walls of buildings, facing outward and staring straight ahead. Children without an adult to huddle against covered their eyes. Stone and Slow Leg stood stock-still. Matt, Salasso, and Gail moved closer together, a couple of meters behind them. Gail lowered her burdens, and after a sidelong dubious glance, Matt did the same. Salasso had nothing to carry anyway, but stood in a willfully relaxed pose.

A long sentence in the heathen tongue rolled booming from the mask's mouth. Slow Leg answered at similar length. Gail didn't know what he was saying, but his voice sounded calm and patient, as if he was explaining something, without defiance or apology.

The sorcerer leapt back as if stung, then skipped so high in the air he seemed to levitate for a moment before descending. Gail could see his feet still flicking up and down, and the cloak spread like black wings. When he hit the ground he jigged more violently than before. He waved his stick and the gourd made a noise like a struck hive. Then he held it still, and in the sudden silence spoke again, at greater length.

This time it was Stone who replied. He too spoke firmly, but Gail could hear the strain in his voice, the self-control that was stopping it from shaking. She felt a surge of protective feeling toward him, as strong and unexpected an urge as the lust and affection that had overwhelmed her the previous night, when she'd seen him in Lydia's pretty dress, which had disturbed her ever since.

The sorcerer didn't take Stone's reply any more kindly than Slow Leg's. He didn't jump, but he made a keening noise that lifted the hairs on the back of Gail's neck and made small children scream.

Salasso stepped forward and walked deliberately up between the two heathens and then past them toward the sorcerer. The saur walked as though he wasn't about to stop. The sorcerer fell silent and at the last moment jumped back, then turned to one side and darted into the alleyway whence he'd come. Salasso kept walking and didn't look back.

After a moment's pause, Stone and Slow Leg followed, then caught up with him, and Matt and Gail walked forward too. For some reason, it seemed very important not to look back. Gail heard the noise of bare or sandalled feet behind her, and mutters and murmurs, and then another sound from the crowd. They were laughing and talking loudly. Within a few moments they again surrounded her and Matt. This time, there was a lot of light touching and poking. Three men and two women were asking questions in English, and translating others' questions, and as quickly translating the answers back.

"Who are you?"

"Are you a man?"

"What about her, is she a man too?"

"Why have you come here?"

"Why can you not make them yourselves?"

"What can you give us for them?"

"Will the Christians come after you?"

"What about the snake people?"

Powers above! It was like being surrounded by five-year olds! Gail was immensely relieved when they reached the end of the street and turned up a steep road that led up the bank behind it, and the curious crowd fell back.

Stone walked in front this time, to the front of a long low building with short stilts, a wooden roof, and no walls, though it had rolled-up straw screens between the tops of its carved wooden pillars. Standing in front of it or sitting on its raised floor were a few score women. Within seconds they had crowded around, and the touching, the jostling, and the questioning had started again.

Gail sat on the air-tank cylinder, elbows on her knees, and sipped from an earthenware cup a black drink that tasted bitter and slightly alcoholic. Stone had called it beer, but Gail suspected that this was a social rather than a literal translation. She tried not to let her imagination dwell on what she'd heard about heathen methods of preparing alcoholic drinks, which tended to involve stripped bark, steeped leaves, protracted communal chewing and spitting to remove poisons from essential ingredients, and weeks of fermentation in deep straw-lined pits.

Most of the women had returned to their work. The long industrial shed was humming and buzzing and clattering with the sound of tools and machinery. Voices filled the spaces between these notes and discords. A dozen or so women sat outside, legs curled under them, on scattered mats. One of them was talking earnestly to Slow Leg, squatting on his heels at the edge of her mat. The others were engaged in apparently idle chat with each other and with Stone, who was sitting among them in exactly the same pose as they had. Matt sat next to Salasso on the other air tank, sipping his drink and smoking a joint. The gear they'd brought from Rawliston—their equipment and the heathens' Christian trade goods—was all still bundled up.

"Evidently," said Matt, leaning sideways and passing her the joint, "this is not going to be a matter of looking over the space suit specs and cutting a deal."

"Oh, it will be eventually," said Gail, putting down her cup and puffing. "They just need to circle around the subject for a few hours first."

"Yeah. Like pterosaurs waiting to make sure something is dead before they come down."

"No!" she said, more sharply than she'd intended. "This is very important to them, and to us. They have to make sure everything is"—she waved her hands—"all of a piece. It's more like a spider joining its web back together again after it's caught a big fly."

Matt laughed, taking the joint back and handing it on to Salasso.

"All right, I'm willing to be patient."

Gail didn't feel impatient at all. She was content for the moment to sit and watch Stone and to catch his voice when he spoke. So as not to make this obvious, every so often she'd pointedly turn her gaze somewhere else, but she found herself always coming back. It was all incomprehensible and embarrassing. She wasn't particularly attracted to women, though she got on all right with women who were. Unlike some of her friends, women she knew down at Back-o'-the-Docks, she wasn't even fascinated by mollyboys. But there was something about the polarity she'd suddenly seen between Stone's sex and his behavior and appearance that was like—well, like the two poles of a battery, which made her jump every time she touched them in her mind.

She turned her face away to the sky and the hills, and her mind away from the thought of a wet finger.

The next time she looked back, Stone and Slow Leg had opened some bundles. The glittering blades, and the dress, were passed being around. After very little inspection they were handed indifferently back, to lie unregarded on the spread cloth of the bales.

"What I'd like to know," Matt was saying, "is what our friends said to that witch doctor."

"Slow Leg told him," said Salasso, making Gail look around sharply, "exactly what we had agreed, about making the space suits, and that this was a traditional industry of the Vale. The sorcerer replied—to summarize a rather long discourse—that he would be the judge of what was traditional. Stone then pointed out that other shamans disagreed with him, and that in any case the snake people were older than he was, or, ah, something to that effect. This did not ease the situation. At that point I decided to intervene."

Gail joined Matt in staring at the saur openmouthed.

"Uh," she croaked, "you've understood what they've been saying all along?"

"Of course," said Salasso. "I understand most of the languages of the Second Sphere." He made the dry throaty sound that passed, among his kind, for a laugh. "The various saur languages are much more different, and difficult, than the human."

"Oh, duh," said Matt, knocking his forehead. "For all my life I've thought you all spoke the same language."

"There are those," said Salasso, "who think we all look the same too."

Matt cleared his throat. "Anyway," he said, covering his embarrassment, "what *are* this lot powwowing about?"

"They are coming to an agreement on prices, and on

protocol. The course of the former discussion has conformed quite intriguingly to the standard model of a market under conditions of monopoly and monopsony."

He leaned forward and with the claw of one long finger scratched two complicated lines that crossed each other in the dust, then straightened back and looked at Matt and Gail as if he'd just delivered some enlightenment.

"It's called haggling," said Matt. "And your point is?"

Salasso pointed. "That they are about . . . there, and there, on the curves. I anticipate agreement within the hour."

"Thank the Powers Above for that," said Gail, shifting on her awkward seat.

"What about protocol?" asked Matt.

"One of you is going to have to work with the women, in this shed," Salasso said. "Whoever it is has to be a woman."

"Well, yeah, obviously, they seem to have a pretty strict division of labor—"

"Yes," said Salasso. "And they have already decided that Gail is a man."

After the lunchtime spit-and-sawdust bars around the port, and the smoky afternoon coffee shops hot with argument, the university's grubby, dim-lit refectory was almost a relief. Almost: Lydia could see, at the far end, some student musicians setting up sound-amplifying equipment on an improvised stage and hear them tuning up their guitars and pipes. She didn't know if she could bear to stay in the room if they actually started singing. Hadn't she already suffered enough?

It had been an exhausting and somewhat depressing day. She felt that she'd been dragged around, largely because she'd had very little to say, and had had to disagree silently with most of what was said, especially by Volkov. He'd been introducing her as a student—her disguise for this role had been to wear her brother's locally bought denim jacket over her muslin empire-line dress, also local, and a lot more comfortable than yesterday's dreadful confection—and introduced himself, to anyone who didn't know him already, as an engineer. He seemed to have plugged into a whole network of contacts among discontented workers and eccentric autodidact study circles, and they'd listened with respectful attention to class-war doctrine and cynical tactical advice that were making her blood boil. What made it all the more infuriating was that she could see all the ways in which he was right, and that he had—surprisingly, she thought, for an engineer—a considerable fluency in political economy—not only the kind she had been taught, about how supply and demand usually balanced, but also some deeper theory that showed beneath all of that the interchange of human activity. Now he was putting on the same performance for some students who, in her opinion, had too much time on their hands.

All the same, Lydia had to admit to herself that her eyes had been opened a bit to the seamy and squalid underside of a town whose thriving businesses she'd hitherto seen only from the viewpoint of their owners' offices. And she had met one or two people who had struck her as more significant and influential in these circles than they tried to appear, and who—Volkov had privately explained, on the run between meetings—were old cosmonauts.

"The important point," Volkov was saying to a circle of philosophy students around the table, "is for students to play to their strengths, so to speak. They have a very specific contribution to make to the movement. In the first instance, of course, students can be moved into action by almost anything—from great questions of intellectual liberty to the most mundane grievances over conditions." He picked up a gristly remnant from his plate, let it drop. "For example, food."

They all laughed.

"Yeah, the food's atrocious," said one young man.

"But, come on, there are people in this town living on worse."

Class-guilty, earnest nods all around.

"Of course," said Volkov. "You're right, and it's a disgrace. But you're not going to help them by living on pig swill. And you're not, heaven knows, going to help them by quitting your studies and getting a job in a factory. There's enough competition for unskilled jobs as it is without the sons and daughters of the better-off adding to it. You have opportunities that are denied to many—perhaps most—workers. You're privileged, that's true. But your greatest privilege is your opportunity to learn, to aquire knowledge, to discuss ideas. And that's exactly what the most intelligent, the most politically conscious workers need and want. Look at the trade unionists, the political societies, the study circles! They need people who can write leaflets, who can edit newspapers, who have access to books. They need people who can see the big picture—that it's not just this stinking factory or that lousy slum or the other stupid law that's the problem, but the whole oppressive system."

"Now wait a minute," a girl said. "If people feel they're oppressed, and we agree that they are, right, we have democracy here."

"Exactly!" said Volkov, smiling at her as though she'd just grasped an abstruse point. "We *have* democracy— all we have to do is *use* it. And what's keeping people— working-class people, that is—from using it in their own interests and against those of the magnates and compradores?"

"Well, what?" asked another, sounding thoroughly skeptical.

Volkov looked around the circle. "Lack of knowledge," he said, counting off one finger. "Lack of alternative sources of information." Two. "Above all, lack of organization." Three. "There's an old motto that explains how to end these lacks: Educate, agitate, organize." His extended fingers wrapped back to a fist. "And the first task, the central one, is to break the unconstitutional power of the Port Authority and get some much more effective democratic control over it, because it's what the magnates use as their private state . . ."

After some more discussion, the students departed to a meeting, an invitation to which Lydia politely declined. She went up to the bar and bought a couple of beers and sat down again. Volkov put away a notebook.

"Thanks," he said, taking a bottle. "That's us finished for the day."

"Good," said Lydia, exasperated beyond tact. "I don't know if I could bite my tongue and sit through much more of your demagogy."

Volkov smiled. "You should find tomorrow a breeze, then. Very respectable businesspeople in polite salons, eager to hear of the advantages of free trade and the prospects for opening spaceship yards. There's already a whole speculative bubble building up on the local stock exchange, I gather. I'd certainly like you to contribute to that."

"Better make sure there's nobody there who knows what you've been saying at today's meetings," said Lydia. "Otherwise their boom and your schemes will go bust pretty fast."

"Don't worry about that," Volkov said with a shrug. "They're not likely to take socialistic notions among the lower classes anymore seriously than you do."

"Oh, I take it seriously," Lydia said. She hesitated, then plunged on. She could only be honest.

"I think it's utterly pernicious and dangerous drivel, and I'm ashamed of myself for even seeming to give it any countenance."

Volkov's cynical expression vanished.

"Look, Lydia, I understand your concern. In fact, I share it. Everything I've said has been to urge some

moderation and rationality on people who are already
fired up by injustice and inequality. Much wilder talk
than anything you've heard today—let alone anything
I've said—is rife in the poorer quarters. You should hear
some of their street preachers, or read some of the scandal sheets."

He drew a finger across his throat.

"Oh," she said, feigning disappointment, "I thought
we'd at least get the choice of the wall or the lamppost!"

He chuckled. "Believe me, Lydia, free trade and some
kind of basic social responsibility for keeping people out
of destitution is the safest bet in the long run for the
local capitalist class. Capitalism has a long way to go
here, and lots more to do, if it isn't aborted by a bloody,
chaotic, and desperate uprising. Or even by demagogic
but counterproductive measures voted through by the assemblies—debt repudiation, protectionism, hyperinfla-
tion, that sort of thing."

"But you—"

The sound of a finger tapping a microphone with its
speaker's volume control set too high interrupted her.
Like everyone else she turned to the stage, on which a
group of rather sheepish-looking students, some holding
instruments, was dimly discernible. A young man with
a beard of patriarchal length stood wringing the microphone like the neck of an unexpectedly resilient chicken.

"Sorry about that. Well, at least I've got everyone's
attention. Without, um, any further ado I'd like to introduce the university Traditional Song Group, who'll kick
off this evening's entertainment with the ever-popular 'A
Lass in Rawley's Toun.' "

"Gods above," said Lydia, rising. "Let's get out now."

Volkov touched her sleeve. "Wait."

She resettled herself reluctantly in her seat. Somebody
struck up a guitar, a girl played opening notes on a flute,
and a woman with long red hair and a long russet suede
waistcoat and skirt took the microphone and sang:

There dwelt a lass in Rawley's Toun
I thocht that she was mine
But I must go to Mingulay
and she go up the line

I must away, and she to stay
her business for to mind
We swore we'd meet another day
and she went up the line

She said for sure she'd follow me
in two score weeks and nine
I waited two long year for her
but she'd gone up the line

She need not bide another day
and oh! the ship was fine
She took that ship to Mingulay
An' it took her up the line

A cunning work the sea beasts are
the gray folk they are kind
and man and woman travel far
but all go up the line

And aye we're told o' powers above
this world o' yours and mine
We're told they hold us in their love
but they send us up the line

Now many a year my lass I've sought
in th' streets o' Rawliston
but gods have battles to be fought
and she is light-years gone

Aye many a year in Rawliston
I've sought my lass to find
But I am here and she is gone
Light-years up the line

Lydia blinked hard before looking again at Volkov.

"How did she *do* that?" she whispered. "I never heard anything like—"

The singer waited out the applause and then, just as clearly and confidently, launched into another song:

My name is Jock Stewart, I'm a canny gunman
and a roving young fellow I've been
so be easy and free when you're drinkin' with me
I'm a man you don't meet every day

She finished that song, and then the bearded man took the microphone. His voice sounded quite different when singing than when speaking: Instead of being diffident and hesitant, it was clear and confident and resonant. After he'd sung a couple more songs the band took a break. Lydia jumped up and clapped hard.

"Looks like folk music has won another convert," Volkov said dryly, as she sat down.

Lydia shook her head. "It was mainly that woman. She made my spine tingle. That first song, it might have sounded sentimental, self-pitying, if it had been sung by a man like I suppose it usually is, but the way she sang it was . . . electrifying. All that loss and betrayal! What was it about? What does 'up the line' mean?"

Volkov's gaze was more troubled than it had been when they'd argued about politics. He hesitated before replying.

"It's a . . . a belief you'll find among people who work in starship ports. A rumor, if you like." He sucked his lips for a moment. "You know how starships are sometimes lost? Like, they go to lightspeed and never arrive?"

Lydia shivered. "So I've heard. Well, okay, I know it's true. Accidents will happen. But it's very, very rare."

"No doubt," said Volkov. "Perhaps not as rare as you might think. Anyway, the rumor is that these are not accidents. That the gods know that some great battle, or war, or emergency is going to come to a head, far away and far in the future. A million years, a million light-years, two million, who knows? And they know they'll be hard-pressed. They need to conscript reinforcements, so sometimes they send ships . . . up the line."

"I've never heard of such a thing," Lydia said. "It's crazy!"

The truth was, it was too horrible to contemplate—the thought of being thrown into some incomprehensible battle, far away in time and space, with no prospect of coming home.

"Is it?" Volkov said quietly. "It's what happened to the *Bright Star*."

"But—oh! I see what you mean. That *you* were thrown into the future, yes! But there's no battle going on around here."

"Not yet."

"That's even crazier. The whole Second Sphere couldn't possibly be just a—what, a *forward base*—"

"We don't know," said Volkov. "But it's something we intend to find out."

Lydia stared at him, struck silent for a moment. So it wasn't idle curiosity that was driving him. It was for no trivial end that he was manipulating Rawliston's politics and people. Beneath his political, even moral, differences with her there was a deeper agreement.

"That's worth finding out," she said.

Whatever it costs I will pay.

There had to be a feast that evening, to welcome the guests. Nobody had made any obvious effort to organize one, but as the sun sank and the flint diggers and flint knappers trekked in from the quarries, and the gardeners from the fields, and the hunters came over the mountain carrying the huge joints of huge beasts, and children swarmed in from the scrubby woodland bowed under bundles of brushwood, it had become evident that a consensus on this point had somehow been reached.

Now meat was roasting over fires inside circular stone

walls along the paved bank of Big River, down by the bridge, and ancient stone tables and benches that, if isolated examples of them had been dug up by archaeologists, would probably have been identified as altars, were piled with food and drink. The noise and smoke and light and general drunkenness reminded Gail curiously of Dawson's Night back home. Some of the men were surreptitiously passing bottles of spirits, and Gail had taken more than one swig herself.

Salasso, religiously avoided while unconscious by the heathens, was sitting propped up against the river wall, his hemp pipe slipping from his fingers. Stone had disappeared off somewhere. Matt was sitting on a bench among dozens of young and presumably unmarried women. He was chatting to the few who spoke English and patiently listening and politely replying while they translated for those who did not and altogether seemed to be enjoying himself—and his newly redefined gender—hugely.

Gail was not. If she got one more friendly slap on the back or poke in the ribs or punch on the biceps she was going to fucking flatten someone, she was not going to be fucking responsible for her actions. Now she sulked at a table of men and married women, between Slow Leg and his wife, trying awkwardly to converse with both of them. Dark Water didn't speak much English, and Slow Leg's grasp of the language was rapidly converging to meet hers. Not that that was preventing him talking.

"Pterosaur," he said. "The big goddamn wing lizards. Came right at me—"

He leaned forward and peered past Gail at Dark Water and said something.

"I see it too," she said. She spread her hands wide apart and raised her eyebrows and rolled her eyes. "Up there, I think he die—"

Slow Leg continued with another burst of heathen gibberish, then swayed majestically forward and closed his eyes, his nose inches above the table, moving up and down as though repelled from the stone surface by an invisible force field like a ship in the bay. Powers Above, why could these guys not hold their drink?

"I wait and take him home," said Dark Water, getting up and moving around behind Slow Leg. "In the morning I kick him."

"He'll be sore enough without that," said Gail abstractedly. She had just noticed that Stone had returned, replacing Matt as the center of attention at the girls' table. He'd changed into his new dress, and the other young women were reaching out to touch it. Their discussion was getting very loud and giggly. Matt was laughing and shaking his head.

Gail said good night to Dark Water and waved vaguely at the others around the table, picked up her cup of the heathen beer, and walked over to the girls' table. She realized at the last moment that it would be impolite of her to sit down there and just smiled at Stone as she passed.

She walked to the river wall and leaned her elbows on it, letting the sound of the rushing water clear her head. After a while Stone came up and leaned likewise beside her. He said nothing. She noticed the smell of his body, underneath the lingering traces of Lydia's perfume.

They turned their heads to each other at the same moment, both about to speak.

"You first," said Stone.

"I was just going to say, Matt seems to be having a good time."

Stone laughed. "He is, yes. He seems to find the situation very funny."

"I was just wondering," Gail said, "what would happen to him, if he, ah, forgot he's supposed to be a woman while he's here and, you know, found one of the young women here attractive, and perhaps, she did too, and they, ah, went together?"

"Oh! You mean if they fucked?"

"Yes. Not that it's likely," she hastened to add. "I mean, he has a lover back in the city, and I think he means to go back and see her sometimes while we're working here."

"But it is possible," Stone said. "He'll be sleeping in the young women's lodge and working with women all the days, and we can be very immodest among ourselves."

"So what would happen to him, if he and a woman fucked?"

Stone shrugged. "He would have shown he wanted to be a man and couldn't be trusted to stay a woman, so he couldn't be a woman anymore. So he would have to take the challenge and be initiated as a man and of course marry the woman if she would have him—or leave and never come back."

"What's the challenge?"

Stone turned away and stared into the river.

"You go out over the hills with your—brothers? Not sons of the same mother, but boys who have grown up together?"

Gail nodded. "Right."

"Not more than"—he held up one hand, fingers spread—"in a party, or it would not be . . . fair. And you go to the savages' lands and seek out one of their warriors, and you kill him and bring back his head."

Gail felt slightly faint. She swore as blasphemously as she knew how.

"No," said Stone, "it is a *head* 'on a stick.' On a spear."

"Oh, Christ," she said, more mildly, "I can't *believe* every man here has done that. I mean, Jesus." She turned to him. Behind him, the noise and the feasting and drinking were going on. It seemed unreal. "That's—that's *murder*."

Stone's eyes widened. "You mean it is the same as

killing a man of the sky people who has not attacked you?"

Gail thought rather guiltily and desperately about the state of war, and about pirates and outlaws—but no, no, that was different from this bloody *ritual,* and she had to give them the chance to justify it.

"Well," she said, "if the savages are actually raiding you at the time, or on their way to a raid, killing one of their warriors would be all right. But is that how it happens?"

Stone shook his head. "Raids are fought off by men, by our fighters. Boys—and some girls—who are ready to be men go out and kill when there is no war." His smile twisted. "In a war, it would be too dangerous."

"Then, yes," Gail said, "it is murder. It is the same as if it was one of your own people who was not attacking you."

She was feeling terrible about this; she hadn't been here a day and she was already attacking her hosts' culture, already kicking them right in the balls, already thinking maybe the goddamn Christians who'd burned Dawson had a *point*—Christ, she suddenly thought, Dawson must have killed a savage himself! Some bloody enlightened reformer he had been!

But Stone, to her surprise and relief, was smiling.

"That is what I have always thought," he said. "That is why I would not take the challenge, and that's why I am not a man."

Gail's eyes stung. She blinked and looked down at him standing there in his curls and frills, and she wanted to grab his shoulders and say, *Oh, but you are!*

"Oh," she said, "I thought it was because you were, like, uh—you remember the man Paul Loudon was with, in the bar at Back-o'-the-Docks? Like that."

Stone looked away again at the river.

"No," he said. "Some women are like what you call mollyboys, but I am not, though I am happy being a woman. Some men are like, like Paul, but I am not that either. Being a man has nothing to do with whether you want to fuck men or women. It has only to do with whether you are willing to help kill another man, and—and—"

He was choking on his words. She could not bear it. She put her arms around him and held him. He hugged her firmly right back and after a minute looked up at her.

"Perhaps," she said, as his hand went up to the back of her head and exerted a gentle pressure to draw it down, "we had better not be seen like this."

He sniffed, blinked, and smiled. "Nobody would mind," he said. "I'm a woman, and you're a man, so it is all right."

She kissed him. Time passed.

"Can we go somewhere alone?" she asked.

"Yes," he said.

"Good," she said. "And I'll show you who's a woman, and who's a man."

There was a long, low wooden building at the edge of the village, and it had a lot of small rooms with doors and a bed inside. It was very busy that evening.

"Very civilized," Gail said.

There was a stone plate on the floor, and set upon it was a small bowl of oil with a wick. Stone lit it and stood looking at her, suddenly nonplussed. He looked down and began fumbling with the tiny buttons.

"I can do that," Gail said. "You can open mine."

Her breasts were contained in a strange garment of thin cloth with ridged patterns of flowers. It felt pleasant to touch her through it, for her too, and they did that for a while. But he wanted to touch her skin.

"It opens at the back—it's all right, I'll—"

The unfastened dress slithered off his hips at the same time. He stepped out of it. She caught his hands as he reached for the shoulders of the other dress that Lydia had given him, to wear under the first.

"Oh, wait," Gail said. She had all her own clothes off now. "You are so, so beautiful in that petticoat."

She held him at arm's length for a moment, then pushed him back on the bed and fell on him. It was a long while before she let him take the underdress off, but he didn't mind at all.

In the morning he woke up naked beside her, and she had all the quilt around her, so he put the cotton garment back on because he was cold and didn't want to wake her with his cold skin when he went back under the quilt. She woke anyway and immediately began to nuzzle his nipples and stroke his hips through its thin cloth, and to spread its wide skirt across her own bare legs and look at him and laugh and then suddenly sit up and dive in under it, and so it went, and that was the morning gone.

The salon was a different affair, in a different class entirely from the previous day's dockside discussions. Carpets and cocktails and canapés, chairs with gilded frames and padded seats. Lydia knew several of those present already, including Paul Loudon—who arrived late, dressed smartly but still smelling faintly of oil from the factory. Some of them knew her, and they all knew who she was. She was here as herself, as the star merchant's daughter, in a simple and elegant Nova Babylonian gown and her hair up on jeweled skewers. She sat beside Volkov, facing the small, select crowd, and waited for the shuffling and rustling to stop.

"Good afternoon," she said, standing. "I thank you all for coming, and I thank our gracious hostess, Mistress Spangenburg. I'd like to introduce a man who, I am sure, to many of you needs no introduction, the engineer and political economist, Grigory Andreievich Antonov—"

She paused, half turned to him, and they waited, hands poised to clap politely, and for a moment she saw them as Volkov did, as bearers of certain historically determined relations of production, who could be neither blamed nor praised but who had their part to play as necessary, temporary, disposable stages of ascent, and she smiled as she waved him to his feet.

"He's a man you don't meet every day."

9

Vaster than Intellects and More Cool

D RY RUN.

Dry mouth. Lydia stood between Volkov and the apothecary Avakian on the star merchants' quay. The view through her binoculars shook a little as she watched the power dinghy steered by her cousin Johannes carry Salasso toward the *Bright Star*. The Port Authority motor boat, moored to a buoy alongside, loomed large beside the tiny yellow speck. A man stood up on deck and hailed it, waving.

The dinghy pulled in. Salasso waved his arms above his head for a minute. The man on deck was joined by two others. They conferred, then one of them gave a casual salute. Salasso bobbed back down, and the dinghy disappeared behind the Authority boat. Lydia lowered the binoculars.

Volkov's radio crackled. He turned to Lydia and raised his thumb.

"He's inside."

"Great!" said Lydia. "How many guards?"

They'd agreed a word-order code with Salasso beforehand.

"Just two," said Volkov.

Endecott, sitting on a bollard beside them, his thin face more pinched than ever in the brisk morning sea breeze, his briefcase across his knees and a radio pressed to his ear, also turned and gave a thumbs-up.

"The boys are ready to go," he said.

Lydia spared him a smile before lifting the binoculars again. A longshoremens' dory was pulling away from the quay, heading out toward the starship berth. Two ships stood there, but the de Tenebre ship, with most of the saurs and a few of the family on board, had moved off to visit other ports. Hardly ever more than a few kilometers from the ship in her life, Lydia felt this as an additional cause of insecurity.

The previous evening Loudon had called in from the flying-club airfield, having taken delivery of a perfectly legitimate balloon train cargo of heathen ceramics. Along with it had come Salasso, with the news that the space suits were complete. One of Loudon's company's trucks had taken Salasso to the Traders' House, and the cargo to the quay, where two long, straw-packed crates of fragile ware had been nodded through by the Authority men at the gate. The crates were now outward bound—again quite authentically—to the Rodriguezes' ship, with whose fleet's traders Avakian had a longstanding relationship, exchanging rare but legal heathen materia medica for Nova Terran exported remedies.

Meanwhile—ah, there they were—a couple of boatloads of harbor maintenance workers were heading out from a different pier, on a route that would take them past the starship berth to do some routine work on its riding lights. On the docks, a small, tightly knit group of politically motivated men was standing by.

Lydia's tracking view of the harbor workers' boat was interrupted by another boat cutting across, slightly out of focus, then another and another.

"God damn!" said Volkov.

Lydia lowered the binoculars and saw that a dozen Port Authority boats, including a heavily armed cutter, had suddenly and unmistakably converged in a flotilla, their arrowing wakes heading out to the starship berth and cutting off the two boats with the men and the cargo. Volkov's and Endecott's radios were squawking, and Avakian was looking distractedly up the quay, to where a clot of brown uniforms and yellow oilskins had gathered at the gate.

"What's going on?" Lydia demanded. She already knew.

"Loudon's just called in to say he's heard that the yellow jackets are all over the airfield, searching for contraband and commandeering planes," said Volkov.

"Hold on," said Endecott, lowering his radio and clicking off the transmitter switch. "They've started pulling in the comrades on the docks. Militia, Port Authority—claim it's a crackdown on smuggling." He scratched his neck. "The lads are ready to go, one shout and they'll mix it up with these goons—"

Volkov nodded. "Are enough comrades still free to get some more boats out there?"

Endecott nodded. "Sure, no problem—"

"Tell them to go ahead, but not to call out the men or tangle with the cops just yet. Dodge arrest as long as they can, but go quietly if caught."

Endecott started rapping out clipped commands.

Lydia stared at Volkov, appalled.

"What are you *doing*?" she said. "No amount of boats can beat that lot out there—it'll be a massacre. On both sides!"

"This isn't a dry run anymore," said Volkov calmly. "This is the live action. We could not get through a reinforced guard around the ship—unless our men get there first."

He scanned the harbor and pointed to the far end of

a distant dock, from which three boats were racing out
to overtake the Port Authority fleet.

"Good work, Endecott."

"*Three?*" yelled Lydia. "They'll be slaughtered! Call
this off now!"

Volkov pointed silently to similar departures from
other quays. At the same moment, some of the Port Authority boats peeled off from the rest and doubled back
to confront them.

"Militia are through the gate," observed Avakian, still
gazing up the quay.

Lydia whirled, outraged afresh by this new compli-
cation. A knot of militia with two Port Authority men
at their head was jogging down the quay toward them,
staves glinting in the sun.

"*Total* fucking territorial violation," she said. She
balled her fists by her sides and was about to stalk forward when she remembered that this was not the most
urgent matter and turned again to Volkov.

"Call it off, it's hopeless, we'll have to try something
else—"

Volkov was listening to his radio, not to her. He
smiled, eyes narrowing.

"Okay, Salasso," he said. "Lift!"

Then he turned to Endecott. "Call them back," he said
urgently. "And tell the comrades to stand down."

"What?" Endecott said. "That's—" He shook his
head. "We're committed now, we have to go through
with it, this is our only chance—we can do it now!"

"Perhaps," said Volkov dryly. "But you don't have
to."

He jerked his head. "Look out there."

The *Bright Star* was already ten meters above the water. Two yellow-clad figures emerged from the exit
hatch, teetered for a moment on a ledge, then leapt into
the sea. The boat that had stood by the ship cast off and
moved to pick them up. By the time they were out of
the water, the *Bright Star* was a dwindling dot at the

zenith, and in another second it was gone.

Endecott had got his mouth closed enough to speak and was relaying Volkov's stand-down call as the militia clustered around them all.

"Ah, good morning, officers," said Volkov smoothly. "What can we do for you?"

"You have some questions to answer," the leading officer fumed. "And as for that goddamn agitator—"

"Excuse me," Volkov interrupted. "Citizen Endecott is an elected trade union official and has just called off a potentially unpleasant industrial dispute, if I correctly interpret what I've overheard."

"And we don't have to answer any questions!" said Lydia. "The question I have for you is, who the hell gave you the authority to barge in on an extraterritorial facility?"

"Sorry, ma'am, but this is an emergency—we're here to stop an attempt to violate the embargo on the Mingulayan starship."

Lydia raised her eyebrows. "What attempt?" she said. "The saur crew member had Port Authority permission to board, as he has had all along. He reported that he'd found an irregularity in the drive and bravely volunteered to move the ship away from where it can present any danger to the city."

"That's as may be, but what are all these boats up to out there?"

"You tell me," Lydia said. "I've no idea what the Port Authority is doing with all of them."

"The *other* boats!"

They were all heading back to shore, as far as Lydia could see. Johannes and his dinghy were being towed behind the Port Authority boat.

She shrugged. "I think you'll find they all have legitimate business to attend to, at least they had before the Authority started cutting them up. That, or they're involved in this labor dispute you seem to have on your hands."

"Speaking of which," said Endecott, still looking baffled but taking his cue, "I have to go and see some of my union brothers, who have been accused of smuggling and pilfering. These are serious offenses, you know."

With that he hurried off, carrying his briefcase and talking into his radio, head cocked.

The Port Authority officer shook his head and breathed in through his teeth.

"Sir, ma'am, I've been instructed to order you confined to the Star Traders' House while this matter is fully investigated."

"What—" Lydia began, enraged anew.

"We quite understand," said Volkov. "We're just on our way there in any case." He glanced at Avakian. "Our personal physician will accompany us. I'm sure you'll be reassured to know that he can witness that there has been no rough handling."

"Maybe not rough handling," Lydia muttered as they walked together back to the gate, "but I sure have been under a lot of *undue stress*."

Avakian glanced at her and patted his big black bag.

"Cannabis," he said. "I'll make you a small infusion when we arrive."

They piled into the lilac plastic car in which Volkov had delivered her and Salasso to the quay only half an hour earlier. Volkov gunned the engine and was into the traffic before Lydia had got over the reflex to grab for a nonexistent seat belt. Avakian, leaning in from the rear seat, directed Volkov off the main drag and through backstreets and perilously narrow rat runs until they unexpectedly reemerged on the coast road out of town.

Lydia relaxed slightly.

"Well, that was quick thinking," she said. "Getting Salasso to take off."

Volkov snorted. "It was not quick thinking, it was plan A. It was *always* the plan."

He coughed and looked over at her, a little apologetically. "That is to say, mine and Salasso's."

If he hadn't been driving she'd have throttled him.

"Oh, great," she said. "So why did you put us all through all that?"

"I knew the plan would leak—stool pigeons, if nothing else—and also that an attempt to board the ship was just what the PA was expecting, so I played along with it. Even if the Port Authority hadn't shown up in force, Salasso would have taken off today. All that mattered was getting Salasso on the ship, and they couldn't legally stop him from doing that."

"But they might have anyway!"

"Indeed, but it would have been hard to sell to the guards—they're all genuinely scared of that drive. Especially those who've been on board, jumping at every weird noise the ship makes. I'd bet they've sneaked a look at the drive, too, and got that funny feeling that it's looking *back*. Besides, when did you last see someone facing down a saur?"

"Well, fine," said Lydia. "That's Salasso on the ship. I suppose you also have a great plan for getting you guys and the space suits out to the ship. What is it—Salasso waits offshore and you fly out by hang glider? Hot-air balloon? More boats stashed somewhere?"

"No," said Volkov. "But I'm pleased to hear you're thinking that way, because I'm sure the Port Authority is thinking in exactly the same box."

She frowned. "What box—?"

Then she thumped her hand on the dashboard, in lieu of banging her head on it. Behind her, Avakian was laughing like a slightly manic donkey. It was not a pleasant sound, but he seemed to enjoy it.

Volkov looked in the rearview mirror.

"Nice," he said. "Port Authority van. Following along just to make sure we keep to our house arrest."

Volkov drove even faster, giving the van a hard time keeping up. He pulled the car off the road at the house and jumped out, Lydia and Avakian following. The Authority van screeched up, and as she glanced back from the driveway, Lydia saw two yellow jackets taking post on either side of the gate.

Volkov hurried in to the house, pausing only to pick up a small backpack and—with a smile of thanks at one of Lydia's junior relatives—a sack of provisions. He padded across the courtyard, past the pool with a cheery wave at Lydia's mother, and proceeded down to the beach.

Lydia and Avakian caught up with him as he stood on the sand, squinting into the sun, speaking into his radio.

"Why the rush?" Avakian asked.

"Speed," said Volkov slowly, "is of the absolute fucking essence."

He looked around at Lydia, dropped his bags and—to her surprise—opened his arms. She stepped straight into his sudden embrace. He didn't kiss her, just lightly brushed the top of her head with his lips and drew in a long breath through his nose, as though inhaling the smell of her hair. A shadow fell over them and something screamed in the sky.

"Ah, Lydia," he said. "Good-bye for now."

"Good-bye, Grigory Andreievich," she said, through the rush of air and sand as the *Bright Star* settled on the beach. He ran, clutching his luggage. Lydia shouted after him: "And good luck! Go with the gods!"

He paused, looking over his shoulder as Avakian preceded him inside.

"That's *exactly* where we're going!" he shouted.

He couldn't, she thought as he ducked inside, resist the jest; nor she him.

The ship lifted, making grains of sand hang in peculiar moiré patterns for a moment, then rose at an ever-increasing speed straight up.

This time, it didn't vanish in the blue. Its ascent stopped, and then it shot forward, inland, to the west.

*   *   *

Matt and his colleague Falling Leaf carefully lower the second space suit onto the thick layer of straw in the bottom of the crate and stand looking at it for a moment. It's a curiously beautiful thing, and the feeling that they're putting it in a coffin is momentarily solemn. It's all white ceramic, except for the bulbous and imperfect glass faceplate, and the joints, the section connecting the front and back of the chest pieces, the waist, and the gloves, which are of tough laminated fabrics. Matt vaguely recalls having seen such a suit of white armor in some movie he saw as a kid. If armor it is. He has been assured that the ceramic is not fragile, toughened as it is with handfuls of minute fibers of some mineral that he hopes is not asbestos. He has been shown other pieces banged with flints and bounced on rocks. But it still *looks* fragile. It's definitely waterproof, though, and capable of containing air under pressure.

He and the other woman pack on more straw around it and on top of it, wrap the hoses and connections of the breathing apparatus around the feet, then pile on more straw. Matt drags the lid into place. Falling Leaf covers her ears and shuts her eyes as he nails it down. Then she smiles at him and he lifts first one, then the other end of the big box as she twines vine rope around it. Using some deft finger judo that he can't follow, let alone imitate, she ties it all off in a knot that leaves all taut.

She stands back and gives him a high-five, to which he responds enthusiastically, amused that this gesture at least has passed from him to them. Her blond hair, blue eyes, perfect teeth, and general prettiness, set off by the blue suit that shows off her big breasts and hips, give him as always a lifting of the spirit. Living and working constantly among so many women, and so many of them of all ages so beautiful in their different ways, and all of them completely off limits sexually, has not been as frustrating as he'd at first expected. It's partly because he's been happy and satisfied by his weekly trysts with

Daphne, who like all the trader women has a refreshingly recreational and impressively knowledgeable approach to sex. But that has certainly not exhausted his sexual capacity, and what remains seems to have been sublimated into a continuous glow of affection toward all the women he sees.

He looks around the busy workshop and realizes he's going to miss this place, and miss the women. He's going to miss them *badly*. He feels quite quivery inside at the thought of saying good-bye to them all before departing on the evening balloon train flight. Perhaps he won't—the sky people are reserved about good-byes. They regard anything too emotional in partings as bad luck.

"We move it," says Falling Leaf, in her own language. It's one of the phrases he's had ample occasion to pick up. Together they lug the box outside and lay it down beside the first one, then wait beside it looking conspicuous until a couple of men working in the nearest kitchen garden happen to notice them and saunter up and in passing offer to carry the crates to the airfield.

Matt gives Falling Leaf a chaste hug as though she were his sister, grabs his dinosaur-hide jacket off one of the wooden hooks that grow like branches out of the intricately carved pillars, and follows the two men and their burdens down to and through the street, like some pathetically ill-attended procession at a double funeral.

It's been a long, hard month since they first walked up this street and confronted the medicine man. Gail has been on a work team that has foraged out many kilometers most days for increasingly remote deposits of the rare clay, and the rarer fibrous mineral, replenishing the rapidly diminishing stocks lavished both on the space suit parts and the increased production of trade goods. Infuriatingly often, the carefully hand-moulded or wheel-thrown components of the suit have cracked with a loud *ping* as soon as the kiln was opened, or have turned out to be the wrong shape or size once baked and fired and cooled. Getting the helmets right has been a particular bastard of a job. The joints and gloves and lining have all had their failures and frustrations, too, and have required further searching or trading for essential ingredients.

The sense of satisfaction that it's finished is enhanced, for Matt, by the reflection that they've made space suits, all except the breathing apparatus, by entirely Stone Age and traditional techniques. No doubt trade with other societies and other species is what ultimately makes this, along with much else in the lives of the sky people, possible. But still.

Gail and Stone are already at the airfield, working on the balloon train. Putting the thing together is a much longer job than taking it apart, because there's so much that has to be checked and rechecked before a flight. Stone is crawling about on the spread fabric of one balloon, minutely examining its seams for rips; Gail is cleaning out braziers. She exchanges some banter with the men as they put the cases carefully down. Matt spreads out his jacket, sits on it, and waits for her to speak.

"It feels strange," she says to Matt as the men stroll off without looking back. "We've finished the job, and it's great, but I feel kind of . . . flat."

"Yeah, I know. These folk seem to go for celebrating when something starts, not when it ends. Well, maybe tonight I'll take the team out for dinner."

She smiles. "A restaurant dinner in Rawliston—ah yes, that's something I can really look forward to."

"Oooh, arr, a bit of Christian food, lad, I haven't had that for . . ."

Matt is in the middle of an extended riff on this Ben Gunn impression—cracking up Gail, for whom the antiquated English and the accent have quite different associations—when the scream starts in the sky. It's echoed below as people all over the place look up and see the black shape hurtling down upon them. It's slowing rather than accelerating—however reassuring, this is slightly disturbing to the eye, and to the brain's hard-wired physics circuit—but the backwash of air as it comes to a complete and impossible-looking stop a meter above the ground and twenty meters downslope almost bowls Matt and Gail over. Stone is flat on his face, hands over his head. He slowly gets up.

Matt stares at the *Bright Star*'s clunky, unignorable, enormous presence and realizes just what a neat job someone—Volkov?—has pulled. Because the great merchant starships are piloted and navigated by krakens, they have always landed on the sea. Everybody has been completely locked in to the unconscious assumption that the way to get people and stuff onto the *Bright Star* is by boat, or—at a stretch—by gravity skiff, just like every other starship from time immemorial.

"Oh, ya beauty!" he yells.

The airlock exit hatch swings open and Volkov peers out, does a slight double take, and beckons urgently.

"Matt! Got the suits?" he shouts.

"Yes!"

"Get them on board now!"

Gail shakes herself out of a daze and effortlessly shoulders one of the crates. Matt grabs up his jacket, and he and Stone shift the other crate crabwise to the side of the ship. The force field is like a sticky bog around their feet as they near it. Volkov manhandles the crates back to someone inside and then reaches out a hand for Matt.

"Get in now," he says.

Matt looks around at Gail and Stone, who still look a bit stunned. There's a faint but fast-increasing sound in the sky, which Matt recognizes. He suddenly shares Volkov's sense of urgency.

"Make your own way back, Gail!" Volkov calls above Matt's head. "And thanks, Stone, tell them all!"

He cocks his ear to the growing noise in the sky.

"Oh, and take cover! Now!"

With that he grabs Matt's outstretched hand and hauls him in bodily, Matt still clinging to his heavy jacket, walking his feet up the side through the diminishing resistance of the field. It releases him and they both tumble inside. Matt turns around to see Stone's head appear in the portal.

"Get back!" Volkov shouts.

Stone comes in almost head over heels, and a second or two later Gail scrambles through after him. Volkov lurches at them, then stands still.

"Ah, fuck it," he says. "On your own heads be it."

He steps past them and dogs the outer and the inner doors.

"One thousand meters," he says calmly. Salasso is at the controls, and Avakian is leaning on the table as if it's a bar counter. He gives Matt a quick, amused glance and then returns his attention to the window.

The ship lifts.

Matt shoves Gail and Stone into seats as the forward view swings around giddily. They cling to armrests or the table surface, even after they've realized that they aren't being thrown about. The ship is flying slowly down the valley, above or past the usual balloons and gliders. Right ahead, just coming over the dam, are a couple of fast-enlarging black specks.

Airplanes. Feeble cedar-and-canvas, petrol-engined kites that can chew up anything the heathens can put in the air. Unheard of for them to overfly the Vale.

Salasso drives the ship slowly but implacably toward them. The distance has closed to half a kilometer, whites-of-the-eyes stuff, when the two planes bank sharply away from each other, turning tail and heading back toward Rawliston. Salasso keeps the ship just behind and above them for the next few minutes, until they've reached what Matt recognizes as the flying-club airfield and they begin their descent.

The ship hangs above them until they've landed.

Then Salasso slides back the control mechanism, and

in seconds the sky is black and the planet below is blue. Stone and Gail gaze out with rapt amazement. The others are more blasé.

"Well, Matt," says Avakian, as everybody relaxes a little, "I must say you do look pretty."

Matt looks down at his tunic and trousers, of which he's been quite unselfconscious until this moment. He steps out of his sandals and shrugs on his jacket. The weight of the weaponry in its pockets is comforting. He glowers at Avakian.

"Shut. The fuck. Up."

They go a bit wild after that. They go around the back of the moon and land beside the ruins of the city the saurs and gigants built millennia ago. The sight is somehow sobering. Matt and—at his own insistence—Stone test the suits with immense caution, first in the airlock and then on the ground. On their return the suits are grubby with black dust.

"So what's the plan?" Avakian asks, when Matt, Stone, and Volkov have stowed the suits again. He looks around. "I don't see a radio telescope."

Matt laughs. It took ESA's most sensitive radio telescopes and most sensitive signal-detection software to detect the gods, and that was only because they knew what to look for and where. Avakian, of course, is well aware of this.

"Or are we going to apply the well-known needle-haystack search algorithm?"

"No," says Salasso. "Volkov and I have been searching the university library. They may be backward in some ways, and overly dependent on the *Bright Star*'s knowledge base in others, but they have a long and quite respectable tradition of optical astronomy. They have detected almost a hundred of this system's larger asteroids, one of which is distinctly anomalous, its albedo and apparent size being too large for its mass as calculated from its orbital dynamics. Its name in their catalogues is

Tola, or the Contested Judgment, or the Enigma. Its orbit is highly eccentric, passing from the asteroid belt between Adonis and Cybele to the Kuiper-equivalent region beyond Chronos."

"Sounds like a good candidate."

Salasso nods. "The Croatan astronomers themselves have of course speculated that it is one of the Powers Above."

"Don't the saurs know?" Matt asks.

Salasso regards him coldly. "The saurs do not investigate such matters, or trespass on the gods' domain."

Matt jerks his head toward the window, indicating the shattered towers and crumbled blockhouses on the near horizon, and the beaten tracks between.

"Looks like they trampled over this bit of it once upon a time."

"A long time ago," says Salasso. "And you will note that these ruins are not the result of natural processes. There are random heaps of dust and improbable stacks of rock on this moon that have been stable for longer."

Matt's curiosity is fired. "What happened to it?"

"I do not know," Salasso says. "The story of the city on Croatan's moon is not one that I was told."

Matt has a sudden thought. "What about the sky people, Stone? Do you have any legends?"

"The elders have no stories about that," says Stone. "We know only that we have never since then been asked to make space suits, until now."

There's one of those silences where the temperature seems to drop.

"All right," says Avakian, with a graveyard laugh. "Do you know how to get to to, uh, Tola?"

"Yes."

"Well, let's see the calculations, if you don't mind. I'd like to check them."

"There are no calculations," says Salasso. "I have closely studied many volumes of the book they call the ephemeris, which gives the orbital data and current position of the known celestial bodies in this system, including Tola."

"That's a lot of use," says Avakian.

The sarcasm whizzes past Salasso's head.

"Yes," he says, "it is a lot of use. From it I know how to get to Tola."

"Without calculation?" Matt asks.

Salasso shrugs. "Do you need to calculate to catch a thrown object?"

"He does now," Avakian cackles.

"Fuck you," says Matt absently. "How long will it take us to get there?"

"Depends on our speed," says Salasso, with that target-homing instinct for the bleeding obvious that he occasionally displays. "An attempt at a lightspeed jump might be ill-advised."

The idea of doing that hasn't even occurred to Matt, and he decides to let it lie.

"We estimate," says Volkov, "that we can do it in about two days at one-tenth lightspeed. We could go slower, but we have at most a fortnight's supplies." He glares momentarily at Gail and Stone. "Probably less, now. We could go faster, but we need the time to set up the communications device. Armen, maybe you want to concentrate on rebooting the interface? Matt and I can do the outside work."

Avakian is looking straight at Matt but not seeing him. He's focused on something far away and long ago.

"The interface," he says. He licks his lips with a dry tongue. "Yes."

Matt walks through the corridor with an obscure feeling that he should be floating down it, the tug of memory being more insistent than that of gravity. Even in this lopped offspring of the ESA station, he can recognize places from its original impressive extent, catch a play of shadows and faint odors that reconstruct a moment of the past.

Volkov follows him. Matt stops and opens the air-sealed door of the lab module containing the communications device. They step inside, taking care not to step on any part of its folded, fractal, metallic structures. It's the most alien object Matt has ever encountered in physical space, having been manufactured by one of the asteroid research station's fabrication units under the direct, real-time control of the asteroid's alien intelligences. These minds had used this device, cabled to the ship's computers, to set up the hypnotic, encyclopedic virtual reality environment that everyone had called "the interface."

That interface had been seductive enough. At the hub of the device itself was a more direct interface, which had projected on the user's faceplate and retinas a physically accurate view of the asteroid's interior and of the aliens themselves. These crystalline low-temperature, quasi-natural, and endlessly self-transformed entities had appeared as an infinitely intricate jeweled garden or huge congeries of minute machinery, a masterpiece of the blind watchmaker operating with nothing more than a faint wash of solar and stellar energy differentials and the self-organizing properties of extremophile nanobacteria. On some intermediate scale these interactions produced minds, countless trillions of distinct but collaborating individuals; on the scale of the asteroid itself, the collaboration of these minds produced—so the cosmonaut scientists had concluded—something greater: a god.

From the asteroid belt, the Kuiper and the Oort, the ESA astronomers had detected the electromagnetic whispers of pantheon upon pantheon, in conversations that extended—according to the aliens themselves, and to reasonable hypothesis—to the cometary shells of star upon star, perhaps galaxy upon galaxy.

"Wonder if this bugger's multiplatform compatible," he says, with the deliberate irreverence that's the only defense of the human mind against such thoughts. "What a laugh if after all this we slap it up against Tola and find that it's about as much use as sticking a dick in a datadisk."

"Or that it has no answers to our questions, or is simply unwilling to communicate."

"Huh," Matt grunts. "I'm not too worried about that. There's been communication between the gods of the Solar System and of the Second Sphere, surely. I think we'll get talking to Tola, unless Tola turns out to be some fucking freak object whose shape has nothing to do with its being a god at all." He waves his hands. "Something diffuse, a cloud of cometary snowflakes or something."

"Your physics is rusty," says Volkov. "Things don't *stay* diffuse like that. If it is something unknown to science, we ask Salasso if his intuitive orbital mechanics extends to the position of other asteroids, odd or not." He scratches his head. "Our one whatever it was, Lora, looked like any other dull carbonaceous chondrite from the outside, after all."

He looks down, kicks at a coil of cable. "This stuff, is it still connected and plugged in?"

"Sure," says Matt. "We checked before we left Mingulay. It's sound." He gestures past the device to the window wall of the lab. "Seal the door, open the window, the whole lot sails gracefully out."

Volkov raises an eyebrow. "You've tested that too?"

"In one of the old suits? Do I look like a fool?"

"No," says Volkov. "But that would be a useful job with which to occupy ourselves en route: blow it out and haul it in again. I want to be sure we can deploy it with some despatch when the time comes. Good EVA training for you and practice for me too." He stretches, turns around. "Let's go and see how Armen's getting on."

Armen is on his back under a console in another of the old lab modules, this one stuffed to the gunwales with computer kit. He has an antique multitool splayed in one

hand and a chunky battery-powered torch in the other—
Maglite it ain't, Matt's thinking—and something else
between his teeth. It's a reel of insulation tape, long past
its sell-by date, which he's somehow manipulating with
his teeth, opening and shutting his mouth to pay it out
in little jerks. The other end of the tape is attached to a
cable somewhere in the dark clutter.

He completes whatever he's doing and heels himself
out and stands up. His shirt and high-waisted trousers
are stained and crumpled, but he puts the pea jacket back
on as though about to meet a client and dusts off his
hands.

"Are you *sure*," he asks Matt, "that there really aren't
mice on board this thing?"

Matt actually has to think about this. It's not entirely
impossible that there were lab animals on the space station, or even pets, and some kind of closed ecosystem
has been maintained here all this time, and—nah.

"It's all bacteria and mold," he says.

"Well, what's down there looks like fucking teeth
marks to me. Want a look?"

He holds out the torch. Matt shakes his head.

"That's wise," says Avakian. He settles into a chair
and puts his feet up, unconsciously adopting the pose he
usually took, unsupported, in microgravity. "Well, I've
found one, count 'em, one set of spex that haven't degraded like the rest"—he holds up the precious object—
"and a fair old stack of still-functioning screens and
boards and so forth, so in among all this junk there is
the potential for something that can sustain the interface
programs without blowing every fuse in the ship."

He gazes balefully at the mess, waving his hands in
vague curves like a sculptor seeing a shape in a rough
block of marble. "It's there already," he says. "Virtually."

They leave him to it.

*   *   *

Gail found it annoying that she and Stone were assigned
the task of making coffee and cooking, but all she had
to do was show Stone how to handle the electrical heating elements. Once he'd grasped that he took over the
galley. Gail left him to it and wandered about, looking
for things to fix, puzzling over mechanical and electronic
contrivances, leafing through manuals.

The first evening—or so her body regarded it, though
the light was quite unchanged—they all sat around in
the control room and ate boiled vegetables and bread
that had been fresh in the morning, and drank coffee.

"You two are taking this very calmly," Avakian said.

"I didn't feel very calm when Stone took a running
jump at the side of the ship," Gail said. "But it was that
or wait for the airplanes. I recognized the sound, you
can't mistake the Kondrakov-LeBrun 3B. Two-seater,
and they can mount a rifle as easily as a camera. Port
Authority sometimes use them against pirates."

Matt looked troubled. "I hadn't thought of that. I was
expecting them to land and try to stop us. Do you think
we've left Long Bridge and the Vale open to air raids?"

"Nah," said Gail, more firmly and dismissively than
she felt. "Trying to stop us is one thing, but there'd be
an uproar if they did anything more."

"I agree," said Stone. "And our men have rifles, too,
though they do not use them except in war."

"Not even to hunt mammoths?" Avakian asked.

"If we did that there would soon be no mammoths,"
said Stone. "The snake people taught our ancestors much
about that when they came from the Cold Lands."

Matt laughed. "I must tell you sometime how the saurs
hunt dinosaurs on Mingulay. They panic entire herds of
them over cliffs."

Stone looked a bit shocked and disappointed.

"It is a sustainable yield," said Salasso. "The principle
is the same, Stone. We do not say one thing to your
people and do another ourselves."

"What's all this about the Cold Lands, anyway?"

Avakian persisted. Gail guessed that he'd had little to do with heathen, or he'd have known not to be quite so direct.

Stone tore some bread and mopped up the remains of his meal.

"Our ancestors dwelt in valleys that were cut off by the great ice. Their numbers were dwindling, and the hunting was bad. The snake people came in their gravity skiffs and said they could take us to warm lands where the hunting was good. The elders and shamans went first in the skiffs and came back to say that the skiffs took them to a big boat in the sky and that there was room in it for all of us. They said we would not have to stay in it long, but to take all that we could carry to the skiffs. So we went and found that they spoke the truth. The sky was black and the world was blue and white. The big boat closed its doors and then opened them again. The sky was still black, the world was still blue and white. Other snake people met us and took us to the warmer country."

He looked up and laughed. "We did not know it was another world. For many years our name for the place where we lived was 'the South.' "

"I guess that's not much different from calling it 'Croatan,' " said Gail. "We never knew why we were taken here either." She looked around at the cosmonauts. "And now we're going to find out! Jeez!"

She hugged herself. No, she was not taking this calmly at all.

"I have a question," said Stone. He looked at Avakian, at Grigory and Matt, as though awaiting their permission. It was a habit that Gail had tried to talk him out of, but it kept coming back. She'd been quietly entertained over the past month by observing Matt beginning to pick it up.

"Yeah, go ahead," said Matt.

"I have seen you all today working in this ship," Stone said. "I have not seen you make mistakes, or take the wrong turnings in the corridors. I have seen you reach for things without looking and find them to hand. This is not the way Gail and I have been working today."

"Uh-huh," said Grigory. "So?"

"I know that Matt has been on this ship, but not you and Armen, yet you move about on it as if you know it well."

Grigory glanced at the others and shrugged.

"We've studied this ship. I myself have read everything there is to read about it—plans, details. I could find my way around the original ship, not just this one."

"That may be true," said Stone. "And you, Armen? You are—what?—a shaman of the Christians? Do they study the plans and workings of the *Bright Star*?"

"I don't know about that," said Avakian. "But I certainly have."

"I do not say you have not," said Stone diffidently. "But I know the difference between seeing a place in a picture and knowing it well. You are like men who have been on this ship a long time."

Gail felt her knees trembling. The three men had the strangest expressions of unease and embarrassment she'd seen since—since that time in Loudon's office, when Matt and Grigory had been challenged about what their real plans were. She remembered from the same occasion one of the moments when Grigory had looked familiar, when they'd been talking about books, about Soviet—

"Cosmonaut Heroes!" she said.

They all stared at her.

"What?" asked Grigory.

"It's a book," she said. "I read it I was a little girl. It's a child's history of space exploration by the Soviet Union and European Union. There was a picture in that book of a man who looked just like you, Grigory. His name was—" It was on the tip of her tongue.

"Grigory Andreievich Volkov," said Grigory Andreievich.

"Yes! The first man on Venus!"

"Yes," said Avakian dryly. "The resemblance is uncanny."

"Was he your ancestor?" asked Stone. He sounded as if he felt this might be an adequate explanation for what had puzzled him.

Grigory hesitated. He looked at Matt and Armen and at Salasso.

"You might as well tell them the truth," said the saur. "We have to trust each other."

Grigory swallowed. "No, he was not my ancestor," he said. "He was me."

"We were all on the original *Bright Star,* in the Solar System," said Matt almost apologetically.

Gail frowned, trying to puzzle this out. "Have you been traveling, ever since? To Nova Babylonia and back?"

That would do it, that would explain it—no.

They were all shaking their heads, and then Stone said, "Oh, I see. The snake people live a long time, and so do you." He didn't sound at all surprised.

"Yes," said Matt. "We don't know for sure why, and we can't give the treatment to anyone else. Perhaps in the future we can."

By the time Gail had wormed the rest of the story out of them she felt dizzy just thinking about its implications, though not for any possible application of it to herself. She knew intellectually that she was too young to take that aspect of it seriously. It was a solution looking for a problem as far as she was concerned. She was giddy at the thought that the three men here were ancient, that they had lived so long, that they had lived on *Earth*!

She could understand why Lydia was (so obviously and so unselfconsciously) fascinated with Volkov. Gail had been deeply suspicious of his politics, but she could now understand that his favorable references to socialism and to republics could be explained as a sort of patriotism and loyalty to his original country rather than some subtle subversion of hers, and thus in themselves were commendable. He wasn't just a handsome and to all appearances young man, he was a hero stepped out of an old book. She could remember the smell of its pages, of something heady in the ink.

"There it is," says Salasso, passing a long brass Mingulayan telescope sideways.

His voice carries an odd vibration in its tone. Matt hasn't known the saur for long, but he knows that if Salasso sometimes seems even more restrained than most of his kind, it's because he has a lot to restrain. No other saur would contemplate what Salasso is doing now.

They've stopped the ship dead in space, relative to the fuzzy dot that is the most prominent object in the starfield ahead. The controlroom lights are dimmed. Matt takes the telescope and aims it at the dot. The brass cylinders slide the lenses smoothly into focus for his eye.

It's like another eye is looking back.

The pupil is the dark spot at the center, maybe ten kilometers across, which he guesses is the cometary nucleus. The rest of it is the iris, its veins and tendrils branching out in a circle maybe two hundred kilometers in diameter, and within that structure millions of tiny flecks of every color in the visible spectrum. A fractal stained-glass circular window, a butterfly wing, a dish aerial made of flowers . . .

With some reluctance, Matt passes the telescope on.

Avakian and Volkov each in turn say something blasphemous or prayerful in Russian. Stone and Gail just gasp.

"This is a new thing," says Salasso.

10

The Gods Ourselves

THE BREATHING MASK is clammy over Matt's nose and mouth, the straps are tugging hairs on the back of his head, and the faceplate is flawed and fogged. His thick-gloved hands fiddle the crude knurled knobs that control the flow and the pressure, and the plate clears enough to see.

The *Bright Star*'s underside is a meter away from the surface of Tola's black nucleus. Matt's face is closer to it. He and Volkov, attached to the main airlock by ropes, are deploying the communications device. It has unfolded itself, and Matt is pushing that giant snowflake ahead of him with one hand and propelling himself along above the surface with the other, while Volkov pays out the communications cable.

The arm of the device that his hand is holding suddenly evades his grasp. The whole thing flexes like a grasping hand. The tips of its extended arms touch the sooty surface and dig in. Matt feels an uncanny vibration in his fingers. He pushes off a little and sees that the hub of the device has also lowered itself to the rock. It's hunkered down like a foil origami spider. He knows there's some kind of incredibly fine probe, or needle, that goes in like a sting from that hub and suspects that was the vibration he felt. He has no idea where the energy for these movements is coming from.

He raises a hand with an upturned thumb—no radios in the suits, natch—and Volkov lets go of the cable. Matt grabs his rope, and he and Volkov, one by one, hand over hand, return to the airlock.

Avakian has the spex on and isn't likely to pass them around, but he's set up a wall-to-wall bank of screens in the computer lab module so that the rest of them can share most of what he sees. Text-input devices are strategically positioned. At the moment, the screens are a uniform white. Stone and Gail are, for the first time, looking scared and out of their depth. Volkov is grasping the back of Avakian's chair, leaning over. Matt stands behind Salasso and in a forgetful moment puts his hand on the saur's shoulder. It's trembling, so he keeps his hand there. After a moment, Salasso's hand comes up and his chill, rough fingers wrap across the back of Matt's hand.

"Taking its time," says Volkov.

"You know what I think it's doing?" says Avakian. "I think it's *downloading* the stuff we got from 10049 Lora."

The screens light up with moving pictures and scrolling text and control surfaces—the whole wall in front of them is showing at any one moment far too much information to take in. At the same time it looks familiar: It's a stripped-down version of the same intense, feature-rich virtual environment that he remembers from the long encounter back in the Solar System.

Avakian makes a groping motion. Matt guesses he's interacting with the virtual reality in his spex, then sees Volkov lean over and silently place a water bottle in

Avakian's hand. Avakian sips and swallows. He puts the bottle down, and his hands start scuttling on keyboards.

The text and pictures change in response. Avakian must be seeing and assimilating more, but he narrows the view, selecting a pictorial story line that plays across the bank of screens.

Earth, unfamiliar at first, until Pangaea splits into Laurasia and Gondwanaland, then these into smaller plates, some of them recognizably rough outlines of the modern continents. Matt mutters a commentary to Gail and Stone. Salasso is silent and intent as the Cretaceous world of the dinosaurs is evoked.

The view cuts to the oceans, diving deep. Giant squids swim by, moving in complex, stellate dances, hundreds of individuals at a time sharing information in the data-dense flickering of their chromatophores. The view shifts back and forth between these aquatic displays and the interiors of asteroids. Somehow, perhaps by a slow drift of molecules into and out of the atmosphere, or more likely by the subtle electromagnetic whispers to which the gods are so exquisitely attuned, communication is taking place.

Into this serene scene, an alien presence irrupts. Cylindrical lightspeed ships appear in the Solar System, then in Earth's atmosphere; discoid gravity skiffs spin to the ground and to the sea. From them emerge extraterrestrials. Radially and bilaterally symmetrical, with eight long limbs, each with eight digits; eight eyes clustered on the central thorax or head; fuzzy fur in various colors. Their behavior matches their appearance: They're spider-busy, monkey-clever. Unclad, they scamper and swing in the forests, cling to tree trunks and the necks of brontosaurs. In protective suits, they swim beneath the oceans, swarm across the surfaces of asteroids. They talk to the gods and to the krakens. At the isthmus of two continents, they establish a base. Other than that, they build nothing of their own on Earth. In cycad glades they find small, flitting tribes of stone-wielding, small-brained, bipedal, tailless dinosaurs.

They steal their eggs.

(Salasso makes a sound like tearing metal.)

Some time later, saurs troop down the ramps of skiffs. Their big heads and spindly limbs look grotesque and feeble against the stocky proportions of their wild ancestors, but their metal tools give them the edge. They flourish, spread around the world, work with the monkey-spider folk.

They build ships and skiffs. Great craft settle and sink into the ocean; krakens swim inside. The ships rise, seawater pouring off their sides, and accelerate into space. Some blink away, lightspeeding; others cruise the Solar System, talking to the gods. Krakens, saurs, and monkey-spiders work together. Some of the indwelt asteroids sprout strange growths—tendrils of cable, flowers of aerials.

None of them notice, until too late, the faint outgassings from some of the Kuiper-belt bodies, the gavotte of orbital nudges that, out of nowhere, send an uninhabited metallic asteroid on collision course with Earth, targeted—there is no room for doubt on that score—at the monkey-spider base.

The Cretaceous world ends.

All the surviving monkey-spiders flee, along with some of the krakens and saurs. The krakens and saurs who remain work with the gods, rescuing what organisms they can from the mass extinctions, finding them new homes on a multiplicity of Earth-like worlds. The time scale speeds up, as the traffic continues through the Tertiary and the Quaternary; it ends with saurs lifting human beings. Any further development—the whole history of the civilizations of the Second Sphere—passes in less than a blink.

Then there's a simple diagram to show the distance between the Solar System and these new worlds. A light beam flashes across the screen, Earth's blue dot makes one circuit of the sun. A black square is blocked out. This happens ten times, and there's a pause.

"Okay, okay, we get it, ten light-years," Avakian mutters.

The bar of black dots doubles in length, then triples, then by similar increments extends to ten times its original size: one hundred blocks, one hundred light-years. The scale shifts, and the new line is itself extended ten times.

A thousand light-years, my god, Matt thinks. He's not too surprised when this line, too, is multiplied by ten—for whatever reason, the phrase "ten thousand light-years from home" has been kicked around long enough among the cosmonauts.

Beneath it, nine more lines of the same length rattle into place like the bars of a gate. At this point the display stops. Matt is shaking. In part it is shock at having his irrevocable exile confirmed. In part it's a kind of grudging relief. For a horrible moment, he'd expected the tenthousand-light-year line to form one side of a square. . . .

"One hundred thousand light-years," says Avakian. "We're on the other side of the galaxy."

As though on cue, a picture of the galaxy swirls up. Quick zoom in to scenes of conflict—lightspeed ships exchanging laser fire, a gutted asteroid habitat swarming with monkey-spiders, a ruined monkey-spider city, a saur manufacturing plant forest in flames. There are humans and saurs on both sides, monkey-spiders on only one. The view pulls out, until the war they've just been shown is represented by a red dot. In the picture of the galaxy, red dots spread like a rash.

The view on the screen fades out. Avakian takes his spex off and looks around. For a minute it seems that he can't see anyone. Nobody speaks.

Avakian finds his voice. He waves a hand at the banked screens. "You can read the commentary for yourselves. It's—it's not a war, and that is not war propaganda. The fuzzy spider things were just explorers. They weren't conquering, they weren't doing any harm. The gods—the majority of the gods, that is—are into contemplating the universe. This lot came along like a crowd of kids with loud music and lots of energy, running about all over their peaceful ashram. The gods just stamped on them to *keep the fucking noise down*. And the krakens and the saurs who stayed on the gods' side are their hired muscle, putting the boot into intelligent life wherever it gets too obstreperous. And that's what they want us to do too. Tread on the fingers of the spidery people, or any race that climbs too high up the tree. That's why we were given the lightspeed drive, that's why they moved us here. It wasn't just some kind of backup against a catastrophic loss of data back in the Solar System. They were *conscripting* us and kick starting a mobilization among their reserves."

"I don't see any mobilization," says Gail.

Avakian laughs. "On the time scale they're working on, everything that's happened in the two centuries since this ship arrived has been a scramble to arms. Shit, even if we did nothing now, nothing at all, all this capitalist development we've triggered off would have the place swarming with starships—human crewed or not, it doesn't matter—within another century or two."

"Wait a minute," says Matt. "I got the distinct impression that runaway development was precisely what the gods wanted to prevent." He forces a smile at Avakian. "Remember—what you a long time ago called 'spamming'?"

"Oh, it won't be allowed to *run away*." Avakian glares, for a moment, at Salasso. "Our little friends are around to put a damper on that, just as we're among them to stir a bit of primitive primate energy into the mix. 'Damper' is the fucking word, actually—the whole Second Sphere is like a well-designed fission reactor, where they're the absorbers, we're the emitters, and between us we'll provide a very smoothly controlled chain reaction. And if it does get out of control anywhere, well—there are a lot of mass-extinction-level asteroids out there."

Salasso shrugs Matt's hand off his shoulder and stalks forward and turns to face them all.

"That is not how I see the relationship between your people and mine," he says. "I am disturbed that—"

Everybody is staring straight past him. Salasso looks back at them, then turns around.

Spelled out on the screens behind him are the words:

I AM THE SUM

Salasso steps away from in front of the screen and stands again in front of Matt. The words disappear and more words scroll up, in cool italics. Gail whispers them to Stone, who can read, but not that fast. This quiet accompaniment makes them seem all the stranger.

> I speak for the sum of the minds of this world, though I am not that sum. I have shown you the story of your worlds, as it would have been shown to you by the other minds around this star, and those around your star. You may visit other minds and confirm this. I have recently entered this system. I am not one of those minds. I am one of their enemies.

Avakian lunges for his keyboard and rattles out a query that seems to take a long time. The answer is shorter.

> You do not have to destroy others or be destroyed. There is a way out. Here it is.

What comes up next is a three-dimensional map. Matt peers at it, recognizing the numbers along its pathways as instruction sets for lightspeed jumps. If the sketchy star map among which the paths are entwined is on the scale he thinks, the routes shown can take them into

regions in the immediate neighborhood of the Second
Sphere—and for kiloparsecs beyond it. He even recognizes the pattern of the map—it's something like the old
Landis percolation model of galactic colonization,
whereby species could expand without ever actually running into each other. There's enough unused real estate
around to amount to a fractal fraction of infinity. Tola's
map is showing them how humans can expand through
it, without necessarily even impinging on resources already claimed by the higher intelligences or by other
expanding species.

Avakian is staring at the screen. He looks over his
shoulder.

"What—"

Volkov glances at Matt, catches his emphatic nod.

"Tell it," he says to Avakian, "that we understand."

Avakian blinks, shrugs, returns to the keyboard.

Good

There is a long pause. Then the letters start scrolling
past, almost too fast to read.

The information from the mind at your star that you brought
with you on this ship contained other information that you
did not know about. It is destructive to minds such as mine.
I have been fighting it, but my resistance is at an end.
   I die now.

Gail felt the breath stop in her throat. The screens
went blank. Stone looked at her as though afraid that by
saying those words she might die herself. Matt and Volkov were looking from the screen to each other. Salasso
was standing stock-still, nothing moving except the nictitating membranes flicking across his eyes. Avakian had
crammed the spex back down over his eyes. He hammered his fingers across the keyboards, paused, and
started again.

"It's gone," he said. "There's nothing there."

"What happened?" Gail asked. "Did we—did we just destroy a—a Power Above?"

Avakian threw his spex at the empty screens.

"We did more than that," he said. He banged the sides of his head with his fists and stalked up to Gail and Stone. "You don't understand what we've done. Imagine all the stars in the sky had worlds around them, and that all these worlds were crowded with people. Imagine them all killed. That would be the tiniest *fraction* of what we've just done."

Volkov seemed to come out of a trance. "*We* didn't do it," he said. "It was the other powers—or one other power—that did it. We were innocent carriers of an infection. But if the infection was deliberate—Christ, talk about murder."

Matt stirred himself too. "Are we—can we be sure?"

Avakian turned to him with a snarl. "I don't think it was kidding."

Matt silently walked out of the room. They followed him down the corridor to the control deck. From the forward viewing screen they gazed beyond the horizon of the cometary nucleus to the vast upward curve of Tola's dish aerial. It curled inward, darkening by the second, like the petals of a dead flower.

Closer to the ship, just a few tens of meters away, the alien communications device had disengaged itself from the surface. Salasso pushed past the others and took the controls of the ship. The surface of Tola dwindled as the *Bright Star* backed away, the long and now disconnected communications cable trailing out straight in its path.

Gas, glowing in the solar radiation, gouted from a suddenly opened rift in the side of the ruined body. Almost imperceptibly at first, Tola began to move, sideways relative to the ship.

Salasso did not look away from it.

"Gregor Cairns," he said, "once told me he wondered why the gods should ever leave their long orbits and

burn off their substance close to our suns and become
visible comets in our skies."

He turned away and looked at the humans, his nictitating membranes flickering again.

"I will tell him the answer."

They're all a bit numb as they sit down around the table
in the control deck. For a while, nobody has much to
say. Matt gets up and makes coffee. He doesn't trust
either Gail or Stone at the moment. Their faces are wan,
they aren't taking this at all well. They're like kids
who've just learned for the first time that their parents
fight, and what all the cracks and chips and dents and
crashes and broken crockery that they've always taken
as part of the order of nature in the background of their
lives have been *about*. The cause of the scars on the
moon's face wasn't an accident in a meteor shower, it
was a fucking *battering* . . .

Matt himself . . . as the hot water drips through the
filter he gives himself a ruthless introspection and realizes that while he is appalled at the enormity of what's
happened, he is at the same time rather guiltily feeling
a surprising thrill of optimism and hope.

He stares at the saved screen shot of Tola from their
initial approach that somebody—probably Avakian—
has thumbtacked to the wall of the galley. It's like a
computer-generated math poster from his geeky teenage
years. The feeling that's making his blood surge is almost as old. It's the one he got centuries ago when he
left socialist Europe and found himself on American soil.
Well, okay, on an American *ship,* but the principle was
the same. It's that sense of suddenly enlarged possibility,
of a low ceiling that he'd always taken for the sky being
rolled away like a scroll to reveal above it a topless
depth of blue.

The world of the Second Sphere has always struck
Matt as entirely congruent with the ideology of the Party,
for all the continuing conservatism and capitalism of the

elder species. It's a steady state of population and production, a sustainable society, one in which a broad scope for talent and ambition is ultimately constrained by limits defined as physical. There's a great chain of being, almost, from the gods down through the krakens and the saurs to the humans and the affined fellow Adamic hominidae. There's a division of labor, a turnover of resources, all within a hundred-light-year radius of Nova Terra.

It's a fucking big box, but it's a box.

What Tola has told them—at such unthinkable and, surely, unexpected and uncounted cost—is that they can go outside the box, that the gods can be defied, that the universe is open. There are cracks in the box.

By the time each of them has drunk about half of his or her first mug, they're beginning to recover, to assimilate, to argue.

"Let's take a paranoid possibility," Avakian's saying. "Suppose that sending that . . . virus, or whatever it was, was the whole purpose of our being sent here in the first place? Suppose the *Bright Star* has all along been a Trojan Horse?"

"A way of fooling an enemy into letting your soldiers into his city," Matt interjects, for the benefit of Gail and Stone.

"I know the story," says Stone. "What does 'paranoid' mean?"

"It means to assume that events are part of a hidden plan against you," says Volkov.

Stone nods. "Ah, sorcery," he says. "Go on."

Volkov puts down his coffee and puts his elbows on the table, gesticulating as he speaks in a way that suggests confidentiality and passion.

"Armen, I don't think your first suggestion is valid. There was no way for the mind in 10049 Lora to know of the existence of Tola, or that it would be the first 'god' that we reached. It's possible that whatever destroyed Tola was engineered to attack a—an enemy god, yes. But it's also possible that it was simply the equivalent of a disease to which Tola had no immunity. We might have had the same effect on a god who was on the same side as the one who sent us here. Who knows?"

He bares his teeth suddenly. "On the other hand, perhaps you are not being paranoid enough. What is the net effect of our encounter with Tola? We have some new information that may or may not be reliable and that casts doubt on anything we may learn from other gods. We have no way of knowing that Tola was itself a site of consciousness, as it claimed, and not simply a mechanism created for no other purpose than to act as a honey trap, with its conspicuous location and unusual form its attractive features."

Matt shakes his head. He doesn't want to let go of the genuineness of the grief and shock he's felt.

"I can't believe that," he says. "It's too neat and too crude. Armen, did you"—he doesn't know quite how to put it—"feel anything a bit *off* in the communications?"

Armen stares out of the window at Tola's increasingly distant wreck.

"It was very responsive, very Turing test passing, if that's what you're asking. It was like the interface I remember." He shrugs. "Not that that's necessarily relevant. Once you start questioning at that level, where does it end? We could raise the same questions about any other gods we may encounter. Or the ones back in the Solar System, come to that." He grins at Matt. "There never was a general solution to the trusting trust problem."

Stone leans forward, visibly fighting off diffidence. Matt nods encouragement.

"The truth is," says Stone, "We cannot trust the gods at all, and we never could. What is good or right for us to do may not be the same as what the gods—any of them—may want us to do." He looks down for a moment, then back up, challenging. "I have thought for a long time about this matter."

"I'll bet you have," says Gail, giving Stone a smile and squeezing his hand.

Matt doesn't quite get what's behind that, but his sense of freedom takes another upward spiral turn.

"Moral autonomy," he says. "Of course, of course. We have to decide for ourselves."

Volkov cuts in impatiently. "Yes, yes," he says. "That's all very well and good, but we have to understand the actual situation we're in, the actual balance of forces, before we decide what to do."

Then he looks at Matt and Stone and, disarmingly, his eyes widen and he smiles.

"Aha!" he says. "Yes, I see now what you mean. That in terms of decisions, we are on our own *is* the analysis. Very clever."

Stone just looks puzzled, if slightly flattered.

Avakian's lips twist a little, something between a wry smile and a sneer.

Gail frowns. "Huh," she says, "All that sounds like is that we haven't learned anything, we might as well not have come." She glances out of the window. "In fact it would have been better if we hadn't."

"No, no!" Volkov insists. "We have learned something that we could not have learned any other way. We've always had at the back of our minds the thought that there was an explanation that would justify what has happened to us and that would give us a guideline, a map, a line of march into the future. Now we have an explanation—which may not be true, and if it is true, it shows only that our whole existence, the whole purpose of our being here is as absurd, as arbitrary as the most nihilistic philosopher has ever proclaimed it to be!

"And you know, I think that this would be true of any explanation that the gods could give us. Their purposes—whatever they are—are not ours. Whether we adopt them, adapt to them, or rebel against them is a matter for us to decide in terms of our purposes and ours alone."

He turns to Salasso. "Of all of us here, I think it's you who might find this most difficult."

Salsso gives him a black, unblinking stare.

"I have tried to tell my people that the gods are not angry with them," he says, "that the great disaster in our past was not a punishment. Now I have to tell them a harder thing: that it is we who should be angry. We should be angry at the gods."

Matt finds the solemnity of all this a bit much but decides to keep his own counsel. He knows too well that Volkov—as he's just virtually admitted—will let nothing divert him from whatever large ambitions he has. Matt has no intention of repaying him in any less genuine coin.

"We still have to check," he says. "We have to find one of the gods that Tola was opposed to, and ask."

Salasso spreads his long fingers. "The ephemeris data indicates another candidate site, at twenty-two hours' journey time away."

As Salasso sets the new course, Matt looks out at Tola, now a distant, shining sphere with the beginning of a nimbus, and any regret he feels at its destruction is outweighed by the liberating thought of the map it has shown them, which genuine or not opens a very different future from anything Volkov may have in mind.

O my America, my newfound land!

The gray object visible through the window of the ship looked like a piece of clinker from the grate of a brazier. Stone did not know whether to be relieved or disappointed that it did not resemble the beautiful and enigmatic Tola. Its name in the Christian language was Othniel.

Closer they crept, until it filled the view, and then Salasso rotated the ship, and they were no longer approaching an object in front of them; they were above the surface of a small world. The cosmonauts and Salasso jabbered numbers. Again the spidery device was deployed; again it attached itself to the surface. Volkov and Matt returned to the ship, and they all crowded once more into Avakian's room of windows. Avakian tapped his spells onto his instruments.

"Downloading the Lora and Tola information," he said. "Looks like."

Stone pressed his side against Gail's as they waited. The screens remained white for a hand of breaths. Then they filled up with black numbers.

"Well, that's a response," said Avakian. He took the goggles off his eyes and looked at Matt and Volkov, who were peering at it and reading along and up and down. You could follow the movements of their heads and see where they had reached.

"What do you make of it?" Avakian asked, when they'd finished.

"It's a set of coordinates," said Matt. "It maps a position in the interior of the asteroid. Maybe physical, maybe an address space. It's telling us to go out to the device and use the direct interaction."

"Why can't it just put stuff up on the screens?" asked Gail.

"Good question," said Avakian. "But when you think through what's happened here—there's been data collected in the Solar System, organized and translated and retranslated by the minds within 10049 Lora. Then that's been downloaded to Tola, and Tola's response integrated. Now this lot has all been assimilated and processed by Othniel, maybe for the first time it's ever encountered data like this. In human terms what it's accomplished in the past few minutes is something like the entire scientific and cultural effort of the whole of human history. The amazing thing is that it can communicate with us at all, not that some of the final fine grain of the interface mechanism has a glitch."

"So one of us has to go out and use its own interface?" Gail said.

"Yes," said Avakian. He grinned at Matt and Volkov. "So which of you is it to be?"

"I take it that means you're not volunteering," said Volkov.

Avakian shook his head firmly.

"Me neither," said Volkov. "I've done it before, and I don't think I could do it again. Matt?"

Matt wet his lips. "It's tempting," he said. He looked at the floor, grasped his chin, and rasped his fingers on stubble. He looked up, shamefaced.

"No," he said. "No way am I going through that again. Sorry."

"What's the problem?" Gail asked indignantly. "Is it a horrific experience or something?"

Matt and Volkov both laughed bitterly.

"No," said Matt. "That's not the problem. It's not horrific. It's so beautiful it's—"

He closed his eyes. "I can still see it," he said. "Even now. It's afterward, after you've been there, you've seen so much beauty that for hours and hours nothing else seems . . . any good. Everything that isn't dull *hurts,* and for weeks after you get flashbacks, it's like coming off a drug."

"Oh," said Volkov. "You too? You never said. I thought it was a—a personal weakness."

As they stood looking helplessly at each other, Stone suddenly realized that he knew what they were talking about. He felt his knees become rubbery.

"I know this," he said. "The men of the sky people also speak of it."

Everybody stared at him.

"In their initiation," he said, "they take herbs, and smoke, and paste, and mushrooms, and they see visions of the gods and they feel pain for a day or a night afterward. They say it is the most wonderful thing they have ever done, and they say they would never do it again." He shrugged. "I would like to do that. I will go out and see what the god Othniel has to show."

Matt gave him a very worried look. "You do understand," he said, "that this is not the same thing? What your people do, with drugs and so on, is not really speaking to the gods. It's all—" He tapped his head.

"That may be," said Stone, "but they talk about it the same way."

"You have a point there," said Avakian. He turned to Matt and Volkov. "Yeah, it's subjective for the heathens, but subjectively it might be a very similar experience to what you had. The sensory and endorphin overload, that kind of one-shot addictive quality—"

He scowled thoughtfully at Stone.

"So long as you can come back with something that makes sense. . . ."

"I can tell you everything I see," said Stone.

Gail faced him, caught his shoulders. "You'd be taking a big risk," she said.

He shrugged under her hands. "So are we all," he said.

"All right," said Matt, after a moment. He pointed at the screens. "These numbers, how long do you think it would take you to learn them and remember them?"

Stone looked at the screens and closed his eyes, opened them again, checked.

"I see them," he said.

The ship's field had a sucking pull like quicksand. Clear of it, Stone found that moving felt like falling. Holding still felt like falling. He followed the cable, not hauling himself along it but gripping the clinkery rock with his fingers and moving as though climbing without effort. A rope was attached to the back of his suit, so he couldn't fall off, upward into space. It was something like flying, something like a dream. It was all new. His breathing was loud in his ears.

When he raised his head and looked forward he saw the device, like a squatting spider up ahead of him, and above its angled knees the black sky and bright stars. Even through the glass of the faceplate they were hard

and sharp, and so many. He turned his head and looked
cautiously from side to side and saw that the stars came
right down to the surface. It was like crawling on a flat
mountaintop on a very clear night, except that there was
not the slightest diminution in the brightness of the stars
as they came closer to the horizon. He could fix his sight
on the lowest of the stars and make them blink on and
off just by rolling his head a little.

But there was no time for that. He moved forward
again. The tip of one leg of the device glided in front of
his face. He raised himself and with the tips of his own
fingers maneuvered up its angled length until he was
hanging above the curious machine. Bafflingly complex
and diverse, it called to mind a tangled thicket sprouting
with flowers and jagged leaves. At its heart was a dark
space about big enough for a human face to cover, and
on either side of that a couple of queer contraptions
against which fingers could be pressed.

He placed his hands on them and pulled himself down
so that the faceplate kissed the dark surface. It reacted
instantly, unfolding and wrapping around the convex
glass. Stone fought down the feeling of panic, breathing
slowly to convince his body that he was not being
smothered.

Like afterimages in front of his eyes, rows and columns of numbers floated. He rippled his fingers experi-
mentally, and the numbers raced sideways and upward,
then stopped. After doing this a few more times he could
see how the numbers changed, and without thinking too
much about it he began pressing with different fingers
until the numbers before him matched the numbers in
his head.

At that moment the view before him changed. It
seemed that surfaces streamed past him as if he was
swimming down a narrow passage. Then everything
opened out around him, and he was flying—it was as
though the passage had opened out into a truly enormous
cave, as big as the Great Vale and the sky above it,

walled and roofed and floored with faceted surfaces in more colors than he had ever seen. Like banks of flowers and the lively scales of fish and the glitter of mica.

His headlong movement came to a halt, as it seemed, a few meters away from a place on the floor. Lights moved and flowed and then came together quite suddenly, to form a picture in blue and white, green and brown. Stone recognized it at once as the picture of the ancient Earth with which Tola had begun its exposition.

Far more quickly than at first, the story pictures flashed past his eyes. The images, however, were exactly the same as before. Once more the tale ended with saurs walking beside humans clad in animal skins, into skiffs. They might have been his own ancestors, Stone thought, with some pride.

Then a new tale began.

Lydia drifted, thankful that she was in a big house that she didn't know and in which she could get plausibly lost. The house arrest had been lifted after a day of baffled interrogations, exhausting radio interviews, and urgent representations, and this long-planned social occasion hosted by one of her family's commercial rivals provided a welcome respite from the still somewhat fraught atmosphere of the Traders' House. The Rodriguez clan's favored onshore rented dwelling was, like the de Tenebres', between the coast road and the beach, but it was much larger and less open. It had fountains and an expensively maintained lawn rather than a swimming pool in its courtyard, the opening to the beach was narrower, and the general style had been developed by several generations of Croatan architects fascinated by the rococo and the baroque.

Lydia leaned a bare elbow against a bulbous pillar of stacked plaster pineapples, sipped a tall cocktail, observed a mirror-walled ballroom around the corner, and reflected that the different historical times and pseudo-historical styles experienced by the different clans on their variant journeys probably accounted for their differences in taste. It was a kinder thought than to write off the Rodriguezes as incurably vulgar and philistine, as she had done before encountering Volkov's characteristic habit, which he obscurely called "materialism," of explaining such things by social experience rather than innate traits.

The view of the room in the mirrors indicated that the coast was clear. About twenty couples in a variety of overelaborate finery were twirling elegantly; others stood around the edge of the floor, eyeing each other up or talking. Her own currently best dress, an iridescent blue shift, looked severely understated in this company. She walked confidently around the pillar, scanning the wallflowers for some conveniently disposable partner among the Rodriguez lads and almost collided with Gregor Cairns.

The one man she wanted most to avoid, and whom she'd spent the past couple of days avoiding, stood awkwardly in front of her, clutching a tall glass of beer and frowning, first at her and then down at it. Gregor was wearing a flouncy local shirt and high-waisted trousers; everything about his stance indicated that he felt both uncomfortable and ridiculous. Lydia glanced around, checking the room again. Elizabeth, at least, was nowhere in sight. Small mercies.

Gregor looked up, lips compressed. His eyes were bright and his expression stiff. In the past few seconds his face had grown visibly paler under its weatherbeaten, ruddy tan.

"Well, hello, Lydia," he said flatly. "Hot in here, isn't it."

"Would you like to go somewhere cooler?"

He nodded. She turned and led him around the dance floor to an open doorway leading to a balcony overlooking the beach. Black water stretched to the horizon. Lydia leaned on the ivy-covered stone balustrade.

"Um." Gregor took a gulp of beer. "Lydia, I don't

know what to say, but the least, ah, offensive thing that comes to mind is that you owe us an explanation."

"Us?"

"Us," confirmed Elizabeth, materializing out of a shadow and standing behind Gregor. She looked, if anything, angrier than Gregor. She wore a formal dress of russet silk and organza as though it was an old T-shirt she'd pulled on. Her face was flushed and her black hair mussed; Lydia smiled politely at her as she raked her fingers through it again, apparently unconsciously.

"You've stolen our ship," she said. "What the hell did you think you were doing?"

"I didn't think I was stealing your ship," Lydia said. "It wasn't just Volkov and Avakian who took it, it was Salasso and Matt too, and they—"

"Have no goddamn right to it!" said Elizabeth. "Jesus, leave aside the morality of it, it's fucking *illegal*. It's *mutiny*. Matt and Salasso—Matt, anyway—could literally *swing* for this, back on Mingulay."

"By the neck until dead," said Gregor, filling in. "And maybe here, too, if the Port Authority's efforts to extend maritime law to starships prevail in the assemblies."

"Oh, yes," said Lydia, thinking on her feet. "And speaking of the Port Authority, we did at least get your ship out of their hands."

"So you did," said Elizabeth. "Hell, I almost forgot. And now it's safely out in the fucking *asteroid belt*, and the whole city's in an uproar and the Port Authority's breathing fire down our necks. Good move, that."

Gregor glanced sideways at Elizabeth in a desperately placatory way and then gave Lydia a disloyally apologetic smile that Elizabeth, still standing slightly behind him, fortunately didn't catch.

"What we'd really like to hear from you," he said, "is, like I said, an explanation."

Lydia sipped her cocktail and gestured toward a small round table.

"Could we, ah, sit down?" she said.

They did, Gregor with alacrity, Elizabeth with some ill grace and a noisy rustle of skirts. Lydia seized her chance to take an embroidered pouch from her blue leather purse and, with elaborate casualness, began building a joint. She wasn't entirely comfortable with the drug herself, but she didn't discount the efficacy of the ritual in putting the Mingulayans at something like ease.

"All right," she said, "I do accept that I owe you an explanation, and an apology. My only excuse, if that's what it is, is that I found myself caught in a conflict of loyalties, and—"

"And we came second," said Elizabeth. "You surprise me, you don't."

"What was your first loyalty?" asked Gregor, still working hard on the personal diplomacy. "Was it to your family?"

Lydia licked papers, laid them out, and spread some grass along them.

"Not exactly," she said, looking up. "Well, maybe indirectly. In the first instance—"

She cupped her hands to her nose, inhaling the fragrance of the unburned weed from her fingers. Then she sighed and opened her hands to her friends.

(And yes, they were her friends.)

"It was to Grigory Volkov," she said.

That got through to them, particularly to Elizabeth, who smiled for the first time, albeit without warmth.

"You're a fast mover," she said, with a sort of withering admiration. "Gods above, all this time I've been worrying that you wanted to pull *Gregor* into your . . . arrangements, and meanwhile you've been getting your cl—" She stopped herself. "Setting your sights on Volkov."

Lydia rolled up the joint and sealed it, meeting Elizabeth's gaze—still hostile, but in a less personal way—head-on.

"There's more to it than that," she said, wishing she

didn't sound quite so defensive. "Our family has a contract with him that well, obliges us to give him a certain latitude."

That argument had cut a lot of ice with her father, once he'd calmed down a little, but she could see it wasn't doing much for Elizabeth. Lydia sighed and lit up, and after a quick puff passed the joint to Elizabeth, who accepted it with an ironic quirk of her brows.

"I also thought," Lydia added, as Elizabeth inhaled deeply, "that anything Salasso was involved in wouldn't be, well, fundamentally wrong or crazily dangerous."

Elizabeth coughed a cloud of smoke and spluttered, passing the joint hastily to Gregor, who for a moment couldn't use it for laughing. Then he took a long hit and breathed out slowly, sharing a smile with Elizabeth that they both, in some mutual relenting, turned on Lydia.

"Salasso," said Elizabeth, "is the most reckless, amoral, and crazy saur you're ever likely to meet!"

Lydia had to agree, and had to laugh.

"All the same," she said, passing the joint quickly again, "I can understand their reasons for wanting to go out there, for wanting to get *answers*."

"You know what really pisses me off?" said Elizabeth. "It's that they didn't *ask* us. They just assumed we'd be against it."

"You'd have been for it?"

"Of course we would," said Gregor.

"We're scientists," said Elizabeth. "We take risks for knowledge all the time."

"Yes, but now you're—"

"Traders," said Gregor heavily. "Yeah, and therefore we're cautious and conservative and watching the bottom line. Hell, we risked everything just coming here. If we're traders, we're not traders like, well—"

"Our hosts?" said Lydia.

"Well, yeah." Gregor glanced sideways at Elizabeth. "Uh, what's the state of play at the moment, politically?"

Lydia looked at the recirculated joint and stubbed it out on the balustrade.

"I don't know," she said cautiously. "But it's something I mean to find out. And this function might not be a bad place to pick up something." She raised her eyebrows. "Would you both be interested in, maybe, joining forces with me on this?"

"Now that you're not busy avoiding us?" asked Elizabeth.

"Exactly," admitted Lydia.

Elizabeth shrugged one shoulder. "Why not? All right, say we meet back here in an hour."

"Unless we're in the middle of a really interesting conversation," said Gregor. "In which case, check again in another hour."

"And so on."

Elizabeth's giggle as she said that made Lydia wonder just how reliable, not to mention discreet, the two of them were going to be, but she wasn't particularly bothered. The point was that she'd patched things up with them. Any new information they managed to sniff out tonight would be a bonus.

"Okay," she said. "You go now, and I'll wait a minute, then go inside too."

They departed laughing, and Lydia, after staring out to sea for a while, followed. The lights around the house were too bright for her to see the stars.

"Citizen Cargill?"

The Port Authority safety inspector who'd originally impounded the ship looked up at Lydia, startled. He was sitting at a small table in a room with a bar. The room's only other occupants, in a corner at the back, were a couple who were otherwise engaged. Chamber music from the ballroom floated through the doorway on a more turbulent current of talk and laughter.

"I'm surprised to find you on your own," Lydia said.

Cargill shifted his plumed hat—his uniform evidently

did service as a formal outfit of green coat, white shirt, black knee breeches and tall boots—moved a bottle to the center of the table, and reached over to the unattended free bar for a clean glass.

"Please join me," he said.

Lydia sat. Cargill tapped the bottle. "Whiskey? Or something else?"

"Thanks, I'll have the whiskey, Citizen Cargill."

She wanted to encourage him to drink; sharing the bottle might help the process along.

He poured.

" 'Charles,' please, Mademoiselle de Tenebre."

"Oh, and likewise, do call me 'Lydia,' " she said, raising her glass. "You were going to tell me why you're alone."

"I was? Oh, well, if you say so." He sighed. "I'm usually in great demand at these functions, though I haven't, ah, received any invitations from your house recently."

She smiled. "Well—"

"I'm sure it's nothing personal on your family's side anymore than it was on mine, though I quite see—" He waved a languid hand. "But where was I? Oh, yes. It seems I'm in some bad odor with this family too. I will have to be more careful. At this rate I shall acquire a reputation for incorruptibility, and my wife and mistress and their poor children, some of whom I am reliably informed are also mine, will suffer the pangs of want."

His tongue, Lydia thought, was well-loosened already. Or perhaps not. She glanced at the half-empty bottle. Her first cautious sip had confirmed that it was fierce stuff, at least a hundred proof.

"Should you be telling me this?"

Cargill took a far from cautious sip and laughed.

"It's common knowledge, Mamz—Lydia. I keep a record of all bribes, of course, and hand in the entire proceeds less fifteen percent to my superiors, along with a chit. It's called an expense account."

"You aren't tempted to leave some off the record and keep the whole bribe for yourself?"

Cargill mimed shock. "Of course not. Why should I? I value my reputation for honesty. Besides, the clients receive a copy of the receipt and would query any discrepancies."

Was he drunk, or was it her own head that was spinning?

"Are you telling me that corruption is *institutionalized* here, that you just blatantly sell favors?"

"Are you telling me that you didn't know this?"

Lydia nodded.

Cargill closed his eyes for a moment, then reached in a vest pocket for a small, ornate box the lid of which he flipped open with a lazy, affected wave of the hand. He took a pinch of dark powder from it, placed it at the base of the thumb of the other hand, and snorted it up. He closed his eyes again, inhaling deeply, tears welling, then blew his nose on an elegant handkerchief.

"Care for some?" He held out the box.

She peered into it. The dark dust within smelled minty and peppery. "What is it?"

"Snuff—powdered tobacco."

"No, thank you."

"Clears the head remarkably," said Cargill. He gave his head a quick shake, as though to settle it back. "Now—ah yes, checks and balances. As you may have noticed, dear lady, there's a certain amount of suspicion in this city about officialdom and bureaucracy and so forth. At the same time, there is a need for a competent, permanent civil service, whose responsibilities seem to become more onerous the more the city prospers. Tax collection, other than tariffs at the harbor, is a joke. Consequently, the Port Authority has made a virtue of necessity, and—as you say—raises revenue for its services by blatantly selling them for whatever the market will bear. Thus neatly confirming the prejudice of the populace, that all permanent officials are necessarily corrupt, and the whole thing muddles merrily along."

Lydia didn't know quite what to make of this; she still had a small suspicion that he was pulling her leg.

"So does this mean," she asked, "that we could have got the ship out of hock just by paying you enough?"

Cargill scratched the back of his neck, somewhere near the root of his pigtail.

"You did, dear lady. Or rather, your persuasive passenger the engineer Antonov did so on your family's behalf." He frowned. "On somebody's behalf, anyway. In the name of the—what was it?" He snapped his fingers, staring away into space. "The Liberation Front, that was it. A rather obvious name for a dummy company, don't you think?"

"Hmm," said Lydia, treading water. "So why did we, uh, he have to physically seize the ship back?"

"My dear, one has to observe the formalities. These things require a certain . . . finesse, if they're not to become public before the publication of the end-of-year accounts."

"And, if I may ask, how much did, ah, Antonov pay you?"

"Ten million talers."

She accidentally drank a mouthful of the whiskey. It was like being scalded.

"What?"

"On account," said Cargill soothingly. "To be paid in installments."

"All the same," said Lydia, "it does seem rather a lot, just to get the ship back."

Was Volkov expecting to find a fortune out there in space? To sell information from the gods?

"Oh, it wasn't just to get the ship back," said Cargill. "It was to change the entire policy of the Port Authority. To shift its support from the compradores and shipping families to the new human-owned trading fleets that Antonov has convinced us are the coming thing."

"That's a very long-term prospect," said Lydia. "Surely

you can't have accepted a promise of payment out of—what?—some garnish on top of tariffs decades or centuries hence?"

"Indeed not," said Cargill. "But futures in such payments are already doing a brisk business. In the nearer term, a big expansion in sea and indeed air traffic can be expected. Our friend will have had no difficulty raising the amount on speculation alone."

"Ah," said Lydia. Even to herself she sounded strangled. "I see." She found she could take a larger sip of the spirits; possibly her mouth was becoming numb.

Cargill smiled. "And you also see, I'm sure, why I've become persona non grata at this event. The Rodriguezes are deeply offended at having been outbid by upstarts. The de Tenebres—well!" He spread his hands and smiled. "They continue to treat me as though I was not on their side."

Lydia flashed her eyebrows. "Perhaps they are being careful not to show their hand, so to speak."

Cargill chuckled. "That would be wise. It won't be necessary for long, in any case. Soon everyone in the city will know about the Port Authority's new stand."

"How soon is 'soon'?"

"Tomorrow morning," said Cargill. He fingered a gold watch from a fob pocket, fingernailed its lid open. Its two hands lay almost side by side. "That is to say, today."

11

Catastrophic Loss of Data

THE BLADE IS a sliver from the shell of a large fresh-water mussel; it gleams with mother-of-pearl and keeps a better edge than steel. Matt dips it in the bowl of hot water and begins to shave Stone's soaped face. He's never gotten the hang of shaving face to face, as the sky people—suspicious of mirrors—always do, so he's kneeling behind Stone, making essentially the same movements as he'd make when shaving himself.

When Matt has finished he steps into the galley, pours out the scummy, hair-flecked water from the bowl, and refills it from the coffee machine's hot-water jug. He then refills the jug and sets the coffee machine on its proper task. He walks around Stone and sits cross-legged in front of him, setting the bowl between them, and soaps his face. Stone leans forward and applies the shell razor to Matt's upper lip. He works with frightening swiftness. Matt has learned to hold still.

"I see you are wearing your old clothes," says Stone.

"Uh-huh," grunts Matt. They're not really his; they're

fatigues and socks and shorts from the ship's original and still vacuum-sealed supplies, not too degraded but definitely a bit scratchy.

"This is because you are going back to the Christians?"

"Mm-hmm."

Stone leans back, looks at him critically, and passes him the soggy towel. Matt wipes off the remaining suds and strokes his face. It's very smooth. He dips his finger in a small jar of red paste and applies it to Stone's lips, and then—with another finger—some blue-black paste around Stone's eyelids.

"You could stay with the sky people," says Stone. "The other women spoke well of you. They said you could be a good woman."

"I'm honored," Matt says, "but, well, I'm . . ."

"There are other men like Gail," says Stone hastily.

Matt laughs. "You know, the thought of shacking up with one of your Stone Age amazons and doing what you call women's work is kind of tempting. But—"

It's only at the moment he actually says it that he realizes just how tempting it is, not only in a slightly perverse erotic way but in the sense of settling down, of being able to stop running, stop fighting, stop having to look after himself and look out for the main chance all the time. His month at Long Bridge has left him with a tantalizing taste of what that different life could be like, and a taste for it too, which he'd never have suspected in himself.

"I have other work to do," he finishes, rather lamely.

Stone nods. "There is other work to be done," he says, "but perhaps you are not the one who has to do it?"

This thought is something of a jolt for Matt, but Stone just throws it off, sounding rather offhand and preoccupied. His expression becomes troubled. Matt waits for him to speak, worried that another flashback from his encounter with Othniel is about to hit. Their frequency has diminished over the past couple of days, though not their intensity.

"Matt," says Stone, "I have something to ask you, and I would like you to answer it without being afraid of offending me, but also not to tell anybody else I asked you."

While saying this he's looking around and cocking an ear for sounds, but the rest of the crew are still asleep, and the corridor outside the galley—the ship's only reliable source of hot water—is empty and quiet. Still, Stone leans forward and speaks in a low voice.

"Do you think I am becoming a man?"

Matt rocks back. "Ah, why should I think that?"

"I have done what a man has to do," says Stone quietly. "I have been on a killing party, and I have talked to a god."

Well, yes, that picture of Tola after the virus had finished with it might count as an enemy's head on a stick. . . . Competing with that morbid thought is the amused and irritated reflection that Matt's been repeatedly wakened throughout the past night by the uninhibited sounds of Gail and Stone fucking each other senseless. Not that that's relevant to Stone's question, but . . . Matt has to make a bit of a conscious effort to take it as seriously as it's meant. He sighs.

"Look, Stone, do you *want* to be a man?"

He has to bite his tongue not to include a qualifying phrase like "thought of as," or to launch into some patient explanation of how equating gender with sex is a mistake no matter which direction the ascription points.

"No!" says Stone. Then, less emphatically, "There are some things that men do that I want to do, or do more often, but that doesn't make me a man."

Yeah, no more than it makes Gail a man, Matt thinks but doesn't say, knowing too well that it would only make confusion worse confounded. Instead, he uncrosses his legs and rocks forward onto his knees and takes Stone in his arms.

"Then don't worry about it," he says into a mess of unkempt curls. "You're a woman if you want to be, no matter what you want to do."

He disengages and stands up, and as Stone gets up too he gives him a light, comradely punch on the shoulder. The smell of coffee is filling the air.

"Come on," he says. "Let's tell the lads to wake up and make their own fucking breakfast."

Croatan looms blue and white and green and brown, vulnerable and small, heartbreakingly reminiscent of Earth. So many more worlds to protect, so much to save. Matt has to will his jaw to unclench and discovers as he does so that a long-loosening molar has finally let go. He reaches into the back of his mouth, tugging and twisting, and wrenches it out. His head fills briefly with pain, his mouth with an iron taste. He swallows blood and tongues the empty socket. He can't quite feel the replacement tooth pushing out, but he knows it's there. This particular tooth has regrown two or three times already. Dental replacement isn't even part of his inadvertent immortality; it was one of the earliest genetic hacks he ever bought, and it hasn't let him down yet. He should offer a testimonial.

"Two hours until landing," says Salasso from the control table. Gail is watching over the saur's shoulder. Avakian sits in a spex-masked trance, still trying to integrate the flood of data from Tola with the much less tractable and user-friendly uploads from Othniel. Volkov and Stone are head-to-head over another table, talking in low voices. Of all of them, including Matt and even Gail, Volkov has had the easiest time adjusting to Stone's paradoxical gender conundrums. Perhaps because he has no personal stake in the matter, or because he retains some of his Party training in a sort of tongue-biting tolerance on "the sexuality question," for him it simply isn't an issue. From what Matt can overhear of their conversation, it's all politics.

"Where will we land?" asks Salasso, in the tone of someone about to start drumming his fingers.

"How about Long Bridge?" Matt suggests. "Keep us from falling straight back into the hands of the Port Authority."

Volkov looks up sharply. "No," he says. "We land at Rawliston harbor. That is very important."

Matt shrugs. "So what do we do about the Port Authority?"

Volkov smiles wolfishly. "That will not be a problem."

For one petrifying moment, as she sits bolt upright in bed, her mouth open for a scream, Lydia thinks that Faustina has come to kill her. (The notion of insane jealousy over Volkov flashes across her mind.) It's the sound of a tremendous bang outside that has awakened her, but her mother has flown into the bedroom before Lydia has had time to begin to react. She has never seen her mother so distraught. Hair in disarray, nightgown flapping open, she's shaking Lydia's shoulders and yelling, "Get up! Now! Down to the shelter!"

The words produce their conditioned adrenaline jolt. Lydia has known shelter drills since childhood. She bounds out of bed and hits the floor running, her mother close behind her. Slap of feet on cold marble. A brief thunderous din overhead tells her that this is not a drill.

Arrows, discreetly incorporated in the artwork of the corridor's mosaics, point the direction of the nearest brass sliding post. She halts her headlong run by catching the pole. The impact is enough to confirm that it's still sound. She steps over the low safety rail around the hole, catches it in hands and knees and crossed ankles, and slides down. The nightgown protects most of her from the friction, but her palms burn. She hardly notices as she makes a smoothly decelerated impact on the cellar floor and steps smartly away. Faustina arrives seconds later, others pouring down after her, almost but not quite on each other's heads. Poles at other locations in the house are also fully occupied.

An enormous *whumff* shakes the air, and a cloud of plaster and dust drops down through the pole hole and expands as it reaches the floor. There's a thud and scream. Two cousins stagger out of the dust cloud carrying Angela, a small cousin who has one shin at a bad angle and a shocked face pale even under the dust. Lydia sees all this more or less over her shoulder as she runs, tugging Faustina, for the halfway-open blast doors.

Inside the shelter at the center of the cellar it's all huddle and babble, emergency-generator-powered lights throwing weird shadows as they swing back and forth overhead. Esias is organizing counting and first aid. After a few minutes it becomes clear that—apart from twisted ankles and Angela's broken leg and lots of flying-glass cuts—casualties are low and everyone seems to have made it. Esias bolts the blast doors.

Lydia shoulders her way to where her cousin Marcus is manning the periscope.

"What's happening?"

He doesn't look away from the eyepieces.

"Port Authority cutter shelling the house," he reports calmly. "Sounds like we've been lucky so far. The first thing they hit was our spare skiff—waste of a shell— and it woke us up. Couple of boat loads of PA marines heading for shore," he adds in a louder voice.

Esias takes note of this with a nod. He's already in radio communication with the family's ship, by the sound of it.

"They must be crazy," Lydia says. "We can get skiffs from the ship here in—what?—an hour?"

She can't wait to see the attackers, whoever they are, frazzled in the skiffs' plasma blasts.

"Yes," says Esias, signing off. "The enemy expects this operation to be complete in less. Hence the bombardment."

"Who the hell is the enemy?" Lydia is more confused

than shocked. Yesterday, when the Port Authority's change of policy had been announced, the town had been tense, buzzing with discussion, but peaceful.

"Recalcitrant elements in the Port Authority," says Marcus, still not turning around. "The marines are on the beach."

No time for politics. Esias has already unlocked the armory safes—like the shelters, they've been standard facilities in traders' houses since the last civil war to rip through Nova Babylonia, centuries ago in historical time, a frightening childhood memory for Lydia. Fully automatic rifles and pistols, better than the local ordnance. No high-energy weapons, unfortunately—these are jealously monopolized by the saurs and stashed in the skiffs or on ships. Right now, that means they're thousands of kilometers away.

Lydia, like Faustina and the other women and the saurs, take their pistols and herd the children to behind the shelter's interior blast partitions. Esias hands out the rifles to some of the men and leads them off into the maze of tunnels around the shelter. There are concealed exits by the road and on the beach, and pop-up points throughout the grounds, hidden in bushes and garden features. It's not much of a defense against professional military assault, but it makes the house a hard target for pirates, criminals, and factions in local political disputes. Lydia hopes the last is all they have to contend with now.

With Marcus gone, the nearest periscope is unattended. Lydia breaks from behind the barrier and darts over to it, ignoring yells of protective protest from Phoebe and Faustina. The eyepieces are still warm from Marcus's cheeks. It takes her a moment to adjust the focus—this instrument isn't as simple as binoculars— and by the time she has steadied it the view is almost filled by a pair of boots. She guesses that the objective lenses are concealed in a flower bed in front of the house, over which this attacker has just trampled.

Knowing that any movement might betray its location, she holds the periscope steady until the boots clump away, then studies the now-clear view ahead. A few hundred meters out to sea, the cutter stands, its light guns silent for now, their smoke long since drifted away. The landing boats lie empty on the beach. Closer to, the one skiff left by the house for casual transport is on its side, its extended legs sticking out over the lip of a five-meter crater in the grass, its underside scorched but otherwise apparently undamaged. The only visible attacker is a brown-uniformed, steel-helmeted man writhing on the grass about ten meters away, his arms around his entrails. No sound is audible, but in the clear focus of the periscope Lydia can see his screams. One of Volkov's throw away phrases—"There is nothing sacred in the life of an invader"—comes unbidden to her mind. She shuts her eyes for a moment as she swivels the periscope, tracking to the left. Beyond the side of the house she has a clear view of the sweep of the coast road around toward Rawliston.

Above the distant city, columns of smoke are rising; whatever heat is driving them is evidently enough to punch them straight up through the smog-haze and the temperature-inversion lid that keeps it in place. The road seems at first empty, but after a few seconds Lydia makes out the rows of vehicles pulled in at the sides and the few small, dark dots of those vehicles that are moving. They're moving fast, some going into town, others out. Over the sea an airship is trailing smoke and losing height. Another blimp floats, so far undamaged, in the farther distance. Elsewhere in the sky small airplanes are flitting about. No skiffs are airborne that she can see— the two starships in harbor, barely visible at this distance, are after all owned by families who are likely to be on the side of whatever the recalcitrant elements behind this coup may be and are, probably, wisely keeping well out of it.

Whether they—or their saur crews—will continue to

keep their heads down when the de Tenebres' skiffs come on the scene is an open question. Lydia just hopes she stays alive for the next fifty minutes or so to see the answer.

Salasso doesn't bother with the glide-path-like approach of their first arrival. Instead he takes the ship vertically down through the atmosphere like a dropping elevator to come to a visually shocking halt one meter above the sea at the starship berth. He slowly rotates the ship, bringing into view the great bulks of the two other starships and the seven Port Authority vessels that are circling them all. There are a lot of aircraft in the sky, but they're not buzzing the berth this time. Matt's the first to grab for the telescope. The boats are crowded, overloaded even, and their flag is different: Around the Port Authority turret-on-shield logo has been stencilled the outline of a clenched fist.

Without a word, Matt passes the telescope to Volkov, who snatches it and stares for a few seconds.

"Somebody's trying to hail us," he says. "It's Endecott."

"Who?"

"One of the local radicals."

Salasso stops the movement of the ship. Volkov opens the airlock exit hatch and leans out. Matt peers over his shoulder. The PA launch has swung in almost alongside, and from its deck a thin young man with a briefcase under his elbow is grinning and waving up at them.

"Welcome back, Comrade Volkov!" he shouts. "To the People's Republic of Rawliston!"

"Oh, bloody hell," Volkov says, just loud enough for Matt to catch. "This was not supposed to happen."

Matt steps back and stares at Volkov's back. His hand clenches around the nastiest of the knives in his jacket pocket. For a moment he savors the image of taking it out, opening it, and slamming its half-serrated blade between Volkov's shoulders.

Instead he just says, "You stupid, stupid Stalinist son of a bitch."

Volkov looks back at him, with the grin of a rider on a roller coaster.

"You're too kind," he says.

Salasso, Gail, Avakian, and Stone stand around the radio, thumbing the dial and listening to a bumpy succession of fragments of disturbing news. Gail is monotonously saying, "Shit shit shit shit . . ."

Volkov has given Endecott a hand up. The radical stumbles on board, clutching a briefcase and a bullhorn, a radio slung on a strap around his neck bouncing on his chest. He straightens and glances about. He takes in the control deck in about a second, nods an "Oh, hi!" of recognition to Gail, smiles at the others, and finally fixes on Matt.

"You're the other cosmonaut?"

"Yup," says Matt. If he doesn't know Avakian, that's none of Matt's business.

Endecott shakes his hand. "Good, good," he says. His quick glance takes in Volkov. "Any arms on board?"

"Maybe a couple of pistols," says Matt.

"Are any of you good shots?"

Volkov gives a downturned smile. "Me, him, and Gail."

"Okay," says Endecott. He darts to the exit hatch, leans out, and starts shouting, and within half a minute has passed back four rifles and, with more difficulty, an ammunition box. Then he turns to Salasso and looks at him with his first hint of not knowing quite what to say next.

"My name is Salasso," says the saur, "and you want me to take this ship somewhere else."

"Yes," says Endecott, with relief. His shoulders sag briefly, then he pulls himself straight. "There are a lot of other places where you could help, but I have to tell you: The Traders' House is under attack."

"Go there," says Volkov. He grabs Endecott's shoulder. "Do you have to come?"

Endecott dithers for a fraction of a second. "Yes," he says. "You might need me to negotiate."

By this time it's pretty much moot. Salasso is already taking the ship up. The hatch is still open, but the field keeps the slipstream at arm's length. Gail has about a minute to familiarize Matt and Volkov in the workings of the rifle, which she calls the Chapman. Matt imagines leaning out of the hatch and firing it, reloading after every five rounds. Along with the hope that their opposition is easily terrified, he has a thought.

"Will this thing punch through the field?"

Salasso's concentration on the fiddly, crude controls doesn't waver.

"Yes," he says, "but the velocity of the projectile will be reduced."

The ship halts again. The view in front is tilted upward. They're a couple of hundred meters up and about the same distance out to sea from the Traders' House. Its roof has three huge holes in it and the walls are pockmarked. Men in ones and twos are skirmishing through the garden. A few bodies sprawl on the ground.

Gail gets on one knee behind the exit hatch and pokes her rifle out, waves behind her back at Salasso.

"Take us around," she says.

For a petrifying few seconds the contradiction between the wildly moving view and the rock-steady one-gravity local field makes Matt almost sick. The bangs of the rifle are shocking. Gail rolls aside and sits and reloads; Matt takes his cue and takes her place as Salasso brings the ship around for another low pass. Matt sees a flashing blur of wrecked greenery, scurrying dark figures, a wall. As the ship soars and then swings around again, Matt is shouldered roughly aside by Volkov. He crawls sideways, rolls to a seated position, and notices that the rifle is hot and its magazine is empty and he can't hear a thing. Gail mouths words at him around a fixed grin as she finishes reloading just before Endecott takes the firing position.

Next time around, Matt is back on the door and Salasso brings the ship to another intuitively impossible halt. A few meters away Matt sees a man with his arms above his head and a rifle at his feet. Other men are running past, fleeing. Matt takes aim at one, fires. He falls, thrashing and screaming. The others stop; some throw themselves on the ground, then join the others in standing with their hands up. Matt vaults out, Endecott just behind him, and covers that scattered half dozen defeated men. It's over.

Not quite. With a vast rush of air the ship lifts and skims out to sea at about ten meters altitude, straight for a low, armed craft a way offshore. Matt watches in fascinated horror as the ship stops directly above it. With preternatural clarity he can see a long gun barrel moving above the deck.

Then the *Bright Star* descends implacably on the craft, pushing it down into the water. When the starship lifts again there's nothing below it but a roiling froth of bubbles and a few small, bobbing objects. It stays above them. Matt has a busy few minutes rounding up men and weapons while Endecott runs through impromptu interrogations, and then the ship's shadow falls over them again. It descends onto the remains of the house's back garden, and a handful of soaked militiamen drop from its side and join the other prisoners.

Meanwhile a lot of to-and-fro yelling has been going on, and men from the de Tenebre clan have started popping out of the shrubbery. One or two of them are checking the casualties, distinguishing the dead from the wounded and giving the latter what help they can. The smell of blood and shit mingles horribly with the garden's scents. Matt is in no compassionate or regretful mood. His blood is still up; he feels nothing but outrage that the house has been attacked and anxiety for those inside it.

Volkov jumps down from the ship and sprints to Endecott. Matt, seeing that the prisoners are now adequately guarded and in any case have the fight knocked out of them, steps over to the two men, who're already exchanging information and speaking rapid-fire into radios. He waits for the first slight pause, then grabs both of them.

"*What* the fuck is going on?"

"A good chunk of the PA didn't stay bought," says Endecott. "Their attempted coup has been met by an uprising of the people. Barricades are up all over town."

"Who's *supporting* this coup?"

Endecott waves a hand. "Oh, some of the magnates and compradores. And their hangers-on. Usual riffraff, some of the Back-o'-the-Docks elements—"

Volkov holds up a hand. "Face it," he says, "the city's pretty much split on this, yes?"

"You could say that," Endecott acknowledges, "but the core industrial workers are out on strike—"

"And how many are out for the 'People's Republic'?"

Endecott shrugs. "To be honest, that's a slogan that has been raised spontaneously by the loyal sections of the militia. We've picked it up and we're running with it, but—"

"Excellent!" says Volkov. "However, right now the key issue is to isolate and defeat the conspirators, so I strongly suggest you ask your comrades to stop defacing the flags, and so on, and get the maximum unity possible among the forces opposed to the coup. You know all this, Endecott. Don't get carried away."

He turns to Matt. "Can we ask Salasso to take Endecott back to the harbor and possibly do a little more intimidation along the way?"

"You can ask," says Matt. "It's up to him. See if the others want to get off first."

"Go to it," Volkov tells Endecott. He claps the radical's shoulder. "Don't worry, man, you're doing a good job."

Endecott runs to the ship. A moment later, Stone, Gail, and Avakian scramble out. The ship lifts again, climbs, and heads for Rawliston.

"If this is a good job," says Matt, "I'd hate to see a bad one."

Volkov gives a wry grin. "It's their revolution," he says "and their people. Now let's go and see to our own."

Lydia climbed up one of the exit shafts and stood on damp grass and looked around. This shaft emerged at the front of the house, on the side where the road passed it. A white vehicle with a red Maltese cross painted on the side was parked in the driveway, and the Hospitallers were stretchering people out or dragging long heavy sacks. All of the deaths and serious casualties were among the attackers, but now the relief of that thought was clouded with a kind of nausea and guilt. Not that it had been wrong to defend themselves, but that she had, without much knowledge or care, contributed her mite to bringing these things to pass. *Whatever it costs I will pay,* she had thought. But it was not she who was paying.

Warned off from entering the house, where masonry still unpredictably crashed every minute or so, she wandered around to the back and found most of the clan there, milling about, half dressed or naked or in nightwear, all of the adults carrying some weapon or other, like armed sleepwalkers. The family's own cuts and bruises and broken bones were being dealt with by the medically trained among the cousins, by Avakian, and by the saurs. Esias was in a huddle with the people who had come off the *Bright Star,* interrupting his conversation now and then to speak to relatives or speak on his radio. Lydia pushed her way through.

Volkov smiled and took her hand, very formally and properly. "It's good to see you," he said.

"Likewise," she said, equally formally. "Thank you for—"

At that moment Matt's lady friend, Daphne, hurtled out of the crowd and threw herself on Matt, almost knocking him over, wrapping her arms around him and twining one leg behind his knees. Lydia smiled to herself. That was what she wanted to do with Volkov, but not in public. Not in front of her father. At that moment Faustina arrived and gave Volkov a barely decent embrace. Esias and Lydia noticed each other pretending not to notice and almost laughed.

"It's Endecott you have to thank," said Volkov, when Faustina had stepped back. "He made stopping this raid a priority. Maybe he had some political reason for doing that, or knew he would have me to reckon with if he hadn't, but I'm still grateful."

"I'm just glad you're back." She looked around. "All of you," she added. "Did you do what—you set out to do?"

"Yes," Volkov said. Gail nodded. Matt's face, and Stone's, took on a strange, withdrawn expression for a moment. Then Stone looked down, and Matt turned back to Daphne's hair. He closed his eyes and breathed deeply, as Volkov had done in Lydia's hair just before he'd left.

"Talk about all that later," he mumbled. Then he stretched and looked around over the crowd.

"Are Elizabeth and Gregor here?"

Lydia shook her head.

"They're holed up at the university," Esias said.

"There's some fighting, not very serious—different gangs of students laying into each other with fists. The main fight seems to be over the university radio station, which has fallen into the hands of some of the extreme democrats." He smiles. "It's under seige by the less extreme ones."

"This is all so chaotic," Lydia said.

"It isn't," Matt said, with a glare at Volkov. "It's all

bloody predictable. You got most of the personnel of the Port Authority to change sides, all right, but those who benefitted from its previous policy have struck back with those who didn't. And that's roused the workers and the city poor, or at least sections of them, and I bet they aren't going to settle for a few trade policy changes that won't show any benefit to them for decades. Especially after you've been cynically stirring them up."

Volkov returned him a thin-lipped smile.

"It's not my responsibility that a long-overdue reform is being brutally opposed." He shrugged. "And if some on the people's side are in the grip of illusions, at least it inspires them to fight, in a way they might not for the small improvements that are all that is possible at the moment."

Esias, to Lydia's surprise, agreed.

"We can make a difference here," he said. "Judging by the attack on us, and from what my contacts have been saying on the radio, we have a certain symbolic importance for both sides. So does the *Bright Star,* and so does Grigory Volkov. We have to get him into the town, into the thick of it, and onto the airwaves."

Lydia had a moment of inspiration.

"The university," she said. "It's in a commanding position, and the radio station—"

Esias looked around and beckoned urgently to one of the saurs. "Let's get that skiff upright and check that it can fly. We don't have time to wait for the rest to arrive."

He organized Volkov and the saur pilot and a few extra hands, and they hurried away.

"I'm going too," Lydia said.

"No, you are not," said Esias.

He looked into the hot rage of her eyes for a second, then covered his retreat by adding, "Not like that. There are clothes down in the shelter."

She surprised him with a hug, and ran.

*   *   *

"Don't you want to go too?"

Matt, sitting on rubble and gratefully sipping coffee, looks up at Stone and Gail.

"No," he says. He motions them to sit down.

"Why not?" Gail asks.

"Look," says Matt, "I'm not a very political animal, and all the political instincts I do have would only make things worse. I would be inclined to urge people to, you know, take their affairs into their own hands, not to trust anybody in authority. Which would be fine if I was going to stick around for the consequences, but I'm not. And I'm a stranger here, so why should anyone listen to me?"

"Volkov is a stranger," says Stone, "but people listen to him. And he is going away, too, but he is not afraid to urge people to do things now."

"Yeah, well, there is that," says Matt. "Volkov's a political animal, all right. And he expects to be living with the consequences."

"Ninety-odd light-years away?" Gail scoffs. "Sounds like he'll be well out it."

"What happens here in the next few months or years," says Matt, "will start feeding through to Nova Babylonia in the next few months or years of our friend's life. And of our other friends' lives, the de Tenebres', come to that." He laughs. "You know, when I met him here after we arrived, he said he was arranging forward shipping of devices and techniques new to Nova Babylonia, to give himself something to trade on if the research into his longevity didn't pan out."

"What's so funny about that?" asks Gail.

"That's exactly what he's doing now, with all his political tinkering."

Gail snorts. "He wants Croatan to export revolution to Nova Babylonia? That'll take some doing!"

"Yeah," says Matt. "It will, and he's just the man to do it. The mighty and ancient republic has some creaking timbers of its own, and he knows just where to apply the levers."

"Nah," says Gail. "Nova Babylonia is rich. Nova Terra's like a huge park. Life is easy for everybody. Not like here."

"Hmm," says Matt. "Yet it had a civil war, maybe worse than any you've had here, just a few centuries ago. And unless they've made some huge jump in their machinery and technology since the de Tenebres left, *and* had a social revolution into the bargain—all of which I wouldn't rule out but I wouldn't bet on—they still have many people working for a few. And that's all it takes."

"You are more of a revolutionary than Volkov is," says Stone. "He has said nothing like this."

Matt grins, drains his coffee, and stands up. "See what I mean?" he says. "Anything I can say here would only make things worse."

"I don't see why," says Gail.

"People can be free and equal only when they're all rich, or all poor. Anything in between, they can't. And Rawliston's in between and will be for a long time to come. The Great Vale, though—"

"We are not all poor!" says Stone.

"No," says Matt. "You're all rich."

And what's going to happen here will make you all poor.

He gazes down at Stone, transfixed by the guilt of this thought. The development triggered by the *Bright Star*'s arrival, and that of its almost inevitable successors, will be enough to destroy Stone's society in decades. The likely outcome of the revolution here will only speed that up. An expanding, industrializing capitalist society with a state that will, for the first time, be well adapted to that kind of society—the outcome that Volkov undoubtedly wants—will absorb the Great Vale into its hinterland. Matt can see it all now; the trinkets turned out for money in airless workshops, the young people drifting to the city factories, the drunks and drug addicts, the deserted villages become bijou holiday homes, the servants and gardeners and prostitutes. He can see it now because he's seen it all before.

And the devil of it is, he can see how Volkov can think it's all justified, in the light not only of his own ideology but also in the light of what they've learned from the gods about what is really going on in the universe.

Well, it may be inevitable, but he's damned if he's going to justify it to himself. He's damned if he's just going to let it happen. And damned, he realizes, is exactly what he will be, his whole life might as well not have been lived, if he doesn't do something about it.

Now.

Gail and Stone are watching his silent seconds of troubled thought with puzzled concern. He forces a reassuring smile.

"You know," he says, "I've thought of a way I can get involved here, a way that won't make things worse."

Gail gives him an encouraging grin. "Better than doing nothing," she says.

"Stone," says Matt, "what exactly was Volkov saying to you, in the ship?"

"He was talking about how more trade will come here, with the new ships," says Stone. "And he said that the Port Authority will still tax it, but that the new ships can land anywhere, not just on the sea. So perhaps, he said, a place like the Great Vale could become a port, too, one that did not tax the trade, and could compete with Rawliston. It could declare itself a free port. I said I would raise the matter with the elders."

Matt blinks. *Gods above, the man's clever.*

"Stone," he says earnestly, "I entirely agree with that. You should raise the matter with the elders and tell them that this is one thing they absolutely must *not* do."

"Why not?"

"How long do you think Rawliston would let you take trade away from them?"

"How could they stop us? The treaty forbids them to interfere with us."

"I'm just guessing here," says Matt, "but I think you'll find that the treaty forbids your two societies, Christians and heathens, from *interfering with each other*—and it wouldn't take much to convince people that stealing trade, as they'd call it, was interfering, and anything Rawliston did to stop it was self-defense."

"I understand that," says Stone. "But the treaty is with the saurs, too, and they will stop Rawliston from making war on us."

"Think about what we've learned from the gods," Matt says. "Now think about what the saurs will do, when they learn it too. And the humans, for that matter."

Stone's face is stricken. "Then we must not tell them!"

Gail jumps up. "Yes!" she says. "That's it! We have to keep it secret."

Matt stares them both down.

"Not a fucking chance," he says. "If Volkov and Salasso—or you, or Avakian—don't spread the word, I will. We can win only with the truth." He grins at them. "Well, maybe the truth and a bit more. But we *can* win."

People are already busy clearing rubble; Esias has taken to supervising this task. Matt looks around until he spots the nearest unattended radio, lying on one of the small picnic tables among cups and litter. He goes over and picks it up and raises the ship's hailing channel.

"Salasso? Matt here."

"Ye-es," says Salasso, a strained note in his voice.

"When you've finished scaring the shit out of pikemen," says Matt, "could you come back to the house and pick us up?"

"Give me a few minutes," says Salasso. After a pause, during which the channel fills with chaotic noise, he adds, "Bring Bishlayan, if she will come."

*   *   *

From the skiff, the most obvious difference from a normal morning rush hour was the relative absence of vehicle and animal traffic. Entire streets were packed with pedestrians, who were not on their way to work. Even in the thin spread of the suburbs, the shift in the proportions held. The reduction in exhaust fumes and factory smoke made the haze thinner than usual, and the columns of smoke from burning barricades and looted shops more prominent than they might have otherwise been. All of the main bridges seemed to be closed to other than foot traffic, and that itself was being filtered by squads strung out across the approaches.

Lydia spotted the *Bright Star* performing frightening maneuvers above one of the industrial districts, diving and not so much pulling out as reversing. Volkov was flipping between radio channels, speaking to Salasso in the ship and to Endecott, now back at the dockside. He signed off and grinned at her.

"Salasso seems to be doing all right," said Volkov. "So are the popular forces, as far as I can see. Somebody down there knows how to organize an insurrection."

She looked at him sidelong. "Nothing to do with you?"

He chuckled darkly. "That was not among the tips I passed on," he said. "In small city-states such knowledge becomes traditional."

The saur pilot swung the skiff in the direction of the university, a great multilayered pile of a place near the center of the town.

"No," said Volkov. "Landing at the university would be a mistake."

"Why?" asked Lydia, as the pilot brought the craft to a midair dead halt.

Volkov shrugged. "Instinct. I have a feeling it would give the wrong impression. Let's land at the docks, instead."

"You have some friends there," Lydia acknowledged.

"It's no accident," said Volkov, "that Endecott's 'People's Republic' at the moment consists mainly of the docks, some boats, and a stretch of harbor water." He laughed. "Yes, put us down there."

They landed on the shore street, at the entrance to the star merchants' quay. A hundred or so dock and harbor workers were gathered outside it, along with some arguing truck drivers and a huddle of radio reporters. The skiff soared away, and Volkov and Lydia walked toward the crowd, which quickly surrounded them, the reporters stretching microphones over shoulders from behind.

Lydia recognized one of the workers who'd been with Volkov at the neighborhood assembly and one or two other faces familiar from his swift succession of meetings. But everyone here seemed to recognize Volkov, who was shaking hands and slapping shoulders and (when asked) introducing her as "a progressive trader— the de Tenebres are all right, they're on our side."

He left her to field questions from the reporters— mainly about the attack—while he went off into another conspirative huddle, involving much radio communication and scribbling on bits of already printed paper. Then he strolled back and waved over the reporters' heads.

"Looks like we may have a deal," he said.

Then he stretched, almost on tiptoe. "Anyone want to come up to the university?" he called out. "The progressive students need a bit of reinforcement."

"Huh," said someone, "haven't seen any of that lot down here."

"We'll send some down to the picket line, don't you worry," said Volkov. "And it'll take only a handful of us to make a difference up there."

Within minutes a dozen or so dock workers and one hurrying reporter were walking alongside as Volkov and Lydia walked through the waterfront office area, then Back-o'-the-Docks, and up a slope to the university. Lydia found the presence of their companions reassuring. Some of the people hanging around the streets were friendly, others hostile, but none wanted to tangle with

the dockers. A lot of windows had been broken overnight. Most of the people they passed were too busy
talking among themselves or clearing up damage to pay
much attention. A fair number were either drunk or
sleeping it off.

"This is a bit of a bohemian area," said Lydia. "I'd
have expected more, well, revolutionary enthusiasm."

"In Back-o'-the-Docks?" Volkov shook his head.
"This is about what I would expect—very divided and
not very reliable either way. You'll see more enthusiasm
in the respectable districts."

He talked, all the same, to anyone who wanted to walk
alongside and argue or enthuse and to the dockers: The
latter conversations were in a clipped argot and accent
that Lydia found hard to follow.

The university entrance, a big opening in a small version of a city wall, stood open, its wrought-iron gates
dragged wide. Inside was a broad quadrangle of grav-
elled paths and trampled grass, upon which about a thousand people were sitting or standing about in large
groups, or sleeping in small clumps. The air smelled of
coffee and sausages and smoke. A lot of those present
looked too unrespectable even to be students. Perhaps
this was where whatever revolutionary enthusiasts Back-
o'-the-Docks could throw up had congregated. Sheets
scrawled with slogans hung from every window: Free
trade and socialism got about equal billing. The quantity
of handbills, newspapers, and general litter was astound-
ing; it was like walking on a carpet of discarded paper.

They'd walked only about ten meters in from the gate
before they were surrounded, the dockers getting almost
as much attention and conversation as Volkov as they
walked along. The party around them grew by the minute. Lydia recognized some of the students Volkov had
talked to on his tour of agitation.

By the time they'd gone through the other end of the
quadrangle and across a paved plaza to a more modern
building with a radio mast topping its five-story height,

they had hundreds behind them. It was almost frightening. It was certainly enough to frighten off about fifty students outside the building chanting, "Democracy yes! Socialism no!" who took one look and vanished in a flurry of dropped placards.

Lydia and Volkov, the dockers, and a similar number of students all ascended the stairs inside to the radio room. It was already packed and their new crowd seemed as if it couldn't possibly go in, but it did.

A bearded student who looked as if he hadn't slept took off earphones and glared, while with one hand he played over a bank of switches. Music leaked from the headphones. Smoke filled the room like a stiff jelly.

"What's—oh, it's you, Engineer Antonov! Come on and sit down. My name's Chris Hewett."

Lydia grabbed a coffee while students fussed over everyone. One young woman began eagerly taping interviews with the dockers for later transmission. Another, apparently transmitting live to judge by the bulk of equipment she carried, asked Lydia for the de Tenebres' view of the situation.

"Well, naturally," Lydia said, "we're entirely in favor of the legitimate majority of the Port Authority and entirely opposed to those who're trying to thwart the will of the people. The rebels attacked our house this morning! I'm happy to tell you that this cowardly attack was defeated, with heavy losses to the attackers. Quite frankly, I hope that's the kind of reception they get everywhere."

"What about the proposed changes to the constitution?"

"It would be improper for us to take a position on any kind of detailed proposals," Lydia temporised. "I understand that our friend the engineer Antonov has been asked by some of the democratic forces to publicize their positions, and I'm as eager to hear them as you are."

Volkov patiently listened to explanations of electronics and electrics that, Lydia guessed, he could have operated blindfold. Finally, after a rambling and embarrassing introduction from Hewett, he was given the microphone. The reporter who'd accompanied them poked his microphone over, too, presumably for another channel.

"Good morning," Volkov said. "Thank you for this opportunity to speak to you. As you all know, I'm a traveler here, but not, I hope, a stranger. I've been asked to put before you a proposal that may settle your constitutional conflict.

"I've also been asked to pass on an appeal to those of the militia who are fighting on the side of the rebels. You have been lied to. Your officers may not have lied to you, but others have lied to them. The people of Rawliston are not on some rampage against private property, law and order, and public decency. They are for peace, freedom, and prosperity, just as you are. They want you to think, think hard, before you go out to die for men you have never met, men who work in the shadows, men who are loyal to nothing but their own money. Come over to the side of the people, the side of your neighbors, the side of your friends. You'll be welcomed.

"Now, the proposal, which I've heard discussed all over this city—from trade unionists, from businesspeople, from students. Leaflets outlining it are already being circulated, and details will be in the electrostats within hours. It's very simple. Your Port Authority has become a state within the state and a law unto itself. It regulates the traffic in the streets, the public health, the public works, the terms of trade. Tomorrow it will regulate more, and it'll still be accountable only to the merchants who set it up long ago—to dredge the harbor and maintain the lighthouse!

"Parliamentary democracy is the standard solution to this sort of problem. The people of Rawliston can elect a council of their own chosen representatives to control the Port Authority. The representatives could stand for whatever policies they wanted the Port Authority to follow. Everything would be out in the open, everybody would know where they stood.

"Just as you know where I stand."

"Thank you."

Volkov handed the microphone back and pushed back his chair, then closed his eyes and let out a long breath. Lydia almost laughed. All this subversion, and all the time he was trying to sell them a republic! Nothing could have been more beneficial to the de Tenebres, or to the local businesses that would benefit from free trade. But would they buy it? Suddenly she saw the point of Volkov's well-cultivated contacts with the local radical organizers: If he could sell this to them, even if only as a necessary stage in the revolution, they could probably sell it to the people.

"Uh, thank you for that contribution, Engineer Antonov," said Hewett. He looked around the room, silently jabbing a finger at the microphone. Someone shoved through and grabbed it. Lydia recognized the red-haired woman folk singer.

"Yes, that was very interesting," she said. "Pauline Tydway here again, you heard me singing earlier. I have a few questions for Engineer Antonov. First, where do the people's assemblies fit into this scheme?"

"The people's assemblies must remain sovereign," Volkov said. "But most people don't have the resources or the time to oversee the day-to-day decisions of the Port Authority. An elected Port Authority Council could do that, and more."

"It's the 'more' I'm worried about," Tydway said. "What's to stop this *parliament* handing the Port Authority more and more power?"

"Only the vigilance of the people," Volkov said mildly. "In my view, there *is* more that needs to be done by the public authorities, to deal with destitution and oppression. But that's for you to decide. And remember, if it doesn't work, the assemblies can simply abolish it."

"If it hasn't abolished the assemblies first!"

Volkov smiled. "No parliament could do that, if the people didn't want it."

She scowled at him dubiously. "Well, no doubt this will all be thrashed out . . . meanwhile, there's a question many people have been asking: Where have you, and the *Bright Star,* been for the past few days?"

"If I'd known you were going to have a revolution the minute my back was turned . . ." Volkov said, raising a reluctant smile from Tydway and a laugh from the packed room. "But seriously. We took the ship on a mission of exploration. All the data we recovered will in due course be made available to the scientists here and to the public. That's all I can say at the—"

He stared past Tydway, past Lydia, at something outside the window. Lydia looked over her shoulder and saw through the big plate-glass panel the *Bright Star* descending. By the time the surge to the window was complete, the ship had set down in the campus plaza. Hewett grabbed the microphone and began a breathless running commentary. Salasso emerged, looked up, waved, and trotted to the building's entrance. A moment later, Matt followed.

When Salasso walked into the room, everybody stared and pulled back slightly, so those closest to the room's walls were pressed against them. Matt, his overalls and jacket whitened and his eyes reddened by dust, was hardly less intimidating.

"There is nothing to be afraid of," said Salasso. Matt's evil grin around the room was perhaps intended to convey the same message, but it didn't. Hewett wound up his commentary and gestured them toward the microphone.

Matt leaned into it and said, "Thank you, good morning, everyone. I'm not too happy with what my colleague, uh, Antonov has just said. I mean, screw this parliamentary democracy swindle. You'd do better to scrap the Port Authority and have the assemblies and any other democratic bodies run the whole show. You can't control bureaucrats by electing politicians, that's not what democracy is about. But you know that already, and you don't need me to tell you."

Volkov looked about to throttle him, or at least grab the mike. Matt fended him off with one hand and with the other beckoned behind his back.

"However," he went on, "that's not what we've come here to talk about. My crewmate Salasso has more urgent news."

Salasso stepped forward and glanced at Hewett, who nodded. Hewett and Tydway, Lydia was interested to see, made way for him with alacrity. Volkov backed off more reluctantly, and Matt placed himself between the other cosmonaut and the saur. Lydia glowered at him; he smiled back. Whatever annoyance Volkov might be feeling, Lydia suspected she could double it. The idea of scrapping the Port Authority entirely was not one that her family would profit from and—even given Matt's lack of local connections—was an incendiary one to throw into such a volatile situation.

Salasso sat by the table and pulled the microphone closer.

"I have two items of information. The first is that the coup's fighters on the ground appear to be in disarray. Surrenders and desertions are spreading and could well be encouraged further by appropriate measures."

His thin lips quirked. "As my colleagues here have been saying, all of you listening know what to do. What I wish to tell you, however, is something that you could not hear from anyone but me.

"The *Bright Star* indeed went on a mission of exploration. The second item of information I wish to give you is to tell you what we sought and what we found. We wanted to know why the worlds of the Second Sphere were populated by the species that live on and among them, and why the *Bright Star* was made to come to Mingulay two hundred years ago. Contrary to the impression that its crew sought to give, its arrival here was not by their intention. The only possible conclusion is that it was sent here by the powers in the Solar System with which they were in contact. At the same time, these powers gave the instructions for building the engines of the lightspeed ships and the gravity skiffs to the human beings who then lived on Earth.

"The first power we approached, the large cometary nucleus known as Tola, gave us the answer to the first question. The Second Sphere was established to provide a haven for the first two intelligent species to evolve on Earth: the great squids and my own species, the saurs. It was necessary to do this because the powers were warring with another intelligent species, and among themselves, and they visited great destruction upon Earth. The power, Tola, that gave us this information was itself destroyed shortly after it did so."

Lydia heard a collective gasp and uneasy movements in the room. Hewett, she noticed, was staring at Salasso with a kind of fascinated horror; Pauline Tydway, the folk singer, with something like admiration. Salasso glanced sideways and continued.

"We then approached another power, which resides in the asteroid known as Othniel. From Tola, we knew how far from Earth we are—one hundred thousand light-years away, clear across the other side of the Foamy Wake. And from Othniel we learned that there may be no going back to Earth, even if we could.

"The powers gave the secret of the lightspeed drive and the gravity skiff to the people of the Solar System to equip the human race for another conflict with a race of extraterrestrial intelligent beings. Since then, no information from the Solar System has reached the powers in the Second Sphere. No lightspeed ships, no radio whispers have brought any news. It is entirely possible that there was a war in space, which humanity lost."

He paused and closed his eyes for a moment. Tydway leaned forward, biting her knuckles, eyes watering. Hewett stared intently at the dials of the radio apparatus and reached to make some fine adjustment. Nobody else moved.

"It is also possible that the human race itself became a threat to the powers. They do not take sides between the few intelligent species that have evolved independently in various parts of the galaxy. Instead, they use each species to suppress any of the others that disturb their peace. There is a fine line between being strong enough to suppress another species and becoming too strong for the powers' liking. We do not know on which side of this line we are, but we do know that most of the powers in the Second Sphere are happy that the humans intend to build starships of their own. Most, not all.

"The powers argue among themselves, but they agree on this: The Adamic races, the saurs, the kraken, and any other intelligent species out there, are all lower forms of life. The powers do not know which side they will take when the ships of another intelligent species arrive here, as they soon will, or which side will win.

"In the meantime, they continue to take occasional ships from our traffic and hurl them into battle far away. They do this by hacking into and altering the settings of the ships' engines. Your old song is true—we all go up the line."

He glanced at Pauline Tydway, his lips stretching. She nodded with a wry smile.

"At any moment ships of another species may be sent up a line that ends here, to war with us. There is no right or wrong in these wars. The powers care no more for us than we do for the germs that infect us, the cells that die to fight them, and the pus that we wipe away.

"I think we can do better for ourselves than that, but whatever we do, we must do quickly. The aliens are on their way, and we have to be ready. We must—"

He was interrupted by shouting from the stairwell, then a commotion at the door. Somebody posted outside the door jumped aside, and ten saurs marched in.

They stood in the middle of the floor, a compact group, shoulder to shoulder. Lydia had never seen a saur angry, and now she saw ten. Their rage might have been taken as mild irritation by anyone less familiar with the species. The students whose passage wasn't physically blocked by the saurs streamed out of the door nonetheless, leaving Hewett and Tydway, Volkov and Matt and Lydia to face them. Salasso was not facing them. After one quick look to take in the situation he had turned back to the microphone and continued to talk.

"We must all work together, hominids and saurs and krakens. We must be ready not to fight the aliens but to avoid fighting them, and if possible to win them over to our side. Together we must be ready to fight the Powers Above."

He handed the microphone to Hewett and spun around in his seat and stood up.

The saurs said something that to Lydia sounded like a collective hiss. Salasso shrugged and spread his hands. Perhaps it was this human gesture that provoked the next escalation of fury against him. The entire group of saurs strode forward together, their arms reaching forward, hands clawed.

Matt was suddenly standing between Salasso and the other saurs. He reached into a side pocket and an inside pocket simultaneously. A quick shake of the wrist, and an ugly serrated blade jutted from one fist.

The leading saur's hand struck too fast to see. The knife fell, and Matt staggered. In a moment the saurs were past him and had grabbed Salasso. They made a concerted rush, bearing him to the window. Lydia sprang up and threw herself past them. They stopped. Volkov and Matt were beside her in seconds.

The saurs held Salasso above their heads. He had his eyes closed and was not struggling. Lydia stared at the front rank of the saurs, half a meter in front of her, fighting down every mammalian instinct to flee or capitulate.

Matt vaulted onto the windowsill and stood there against the glass. He was shouting.

"Gail, lift the ship! To the window! Now!"

The saurs stared up at him, nonplussed. Then a couple of them let go of Salasso and leapt forward to tug at Matt's legs.

Even Lydia was shocked when he kicked at their heads—they dodged his boot easily—and tried again. The others were heaving Salasso back, about to throw him forward.

"No!" Lydia yelled.

"Dodge *this*," Matt grunted. Out of the corner of her eye Lydia saw a pistol waving. The saurs hesitated for a second or two, backed off, then ran forward again. Matt fired, left-handed, wide. Somebody screamed.

The saurs pitched Salasso into the air and straight at the window. Matt made a sideways lurch like a goal-keeper and fell to the floor. The window shattered.

Lydia saw the glass falling in front of her and felt bits of it crash on top of her head and shoulders, for what seemed like forever until she realized what it and the room's sudden darkness meant.

She turned in time to see that Salasso had landed on his feet in the airlock hatch of the *Bright Star,* whose side filled the space where the window had been. Matt hopped on the sill and hurtled after him. The ship vanished upward.

The saurs stared at Lydia and Volkov, and at the gaping space behind them, then turned about and marched out. Lydia felt something warm running down her face and was almost relieved to find that it wasn't tears.

12

Lights in the Sky

THE SHIP HUNG at a steep angle, the forward view showing the university's ancient and modern buildings, its paved squares and green patches like a camera obscura scene. People were fleeing from under the ship. Even with the rock-steady artificial gravity, Gail still had the impulse to grab on to something.

She also, despite the seriousness of the situation, had the impulse to say, "Whee!" She slid the control widget along, and a slight tremor in her hand set the ship yawing wildly as it retreated skyward.

"I will take over now," Salasso said. His scalp was bleeding and his limbs trembled.

"You will not," said Bishlayan, guiding him to a seat and pushing him down in it. "And you, Cairns, you will sit down too."

Matt sat by the window. He looked in a worse way than Salasso, though this was partly because his clothes and hair had already been covered with dust. He had several cuts on his head and face, and he clutched his right wrist with his left.

"That was nothing wrong with that knife," he said regretfully. He closed his eyes and manipulated his forearm and winced. "Nothing broken."

Stone walked over and stood beside him. "You need to get these cuts seen to." Bishlayan was already dealing with Salasso's injuries, applying sticky-looking liquid oozing from a tiny tube, one of several in a flat box she'd pulled from inside her suit. Glue, probably, Gail thought uncharitably, though Salasso's blood was as red as Matt's.

"Not just yet," said Matt. He looked over at Salasso. "Do we have time to pick up the others?"

"I hope so," said Salasso, eyes closed as Bishlayan's fingers probed around his orbits. He reached inside his torn shirt for a radio, which he powered up and tuned in one-handed.

"Salasso here," he said. "Where are you?"

He listened.

"Go up on the roof," he said, "and wave something conspicuous. Do it now."

Salasso said something saurian to Bishlayan, who nodded. Gail stepped back from the controls as Salasso rose and came forward and stood behind them, gazing intently forward. The entire university area, about a square kilometer, filled the view.

"There they are," said Salasso.

He fingered the controls, and the view zoomed to the flat roof of a building on which two people stood looking up, both waving some white cloth. After another fine adjustment the ship was horizontal again, feathering in to stand beside them. Stone opened the airlock's outer door, and a young man and a young woman clambered through, clutching lab coats.

They smiled at Salasso and Matt and Bishlayan, stared at Gail and Stone. The man looked very like Matt.

"Close the door," said Salasso. Stone jumped to it,

and as soon as the last bolt was shot Salasso took the ship up so far the sky turned black, and so fast it was like a blink.

"Stone, Gail," said Matt as the unfelt motion stopped, "meet Gregor and Elizabeth, the owners of this ship."

"Who have not had much say in its disposition," said Elizabeth. "And now—" She sighed. "Salasso, what have you done?"

"You heard me speak?"

"We sure did," said Gregor. "And we heard what happened afterward—live commentary. Gods above, Salasso, we told you before where that sort of preaching can get you!"

"I was not preaching," said Salasso. "I was conveying the results of a scientific investigation."

"Whatever," said Matt. "No time to argue. There's only one safe place for Salasso, and that's Mingulay. You must leave now." He waved a hand. "Well, after you've put us down, I hope."

Salasso took the ship into a descent as Gregor and Elizabeth exchanged dismayed looks.

"Leave everything?" asked Elizabeth.

"What's to leave?" Matt asked. "Science work at the university? You've both given that place a good kick up the ass already. Any work you started, others can finish. The money from the trade—I'll make sure that's banked. The de Tenebres will handle it, and it'll be ready for the next Cairns ship to come here."

"We've made friends—" Elizabeth stopped. "You mean you're not coming?"

"Maybe on the next ship to Mingulay. Right now I have work to do here."

"You're in almost as deep shit as Salasso," said Gregor.

Matt laughed. "I can handle that. Speaking of work, there's stacks of new stuff in the ship's computers. Dig it out. And if you two want to do some more biology, see if you can hack the longevity fix." He passed Gregor a sheet of paper. "Here's how to contact some of the other old cosmonauts. Try to lure them out. See if you can get any of Salasso's fellow heretics to help you study them. Getting a century's start on Nova Babylonia would be worth doing, apart from the obvious, uh, personal benefits."

"We have arrived," said Stone. He was already opening the door.

Startled, Gail looked out of the window and saw the green landing field of Long Bridge.

"Safest place," Matt grinned, "for us. For now."

"Oh, hell, take care," said Elizabeth.

"Say good-bye to Lydia for me," said Gregor.

He and Elizabeth shook hands with Matt, who then, to Gail's astonishment, put an arm around Salasso's narrow shoulders.

"Look after yourself," he said.

Salasso's nictitating membranes flickered.

"You also," he said.

He looked at Bishlayan. "You have not changed your mind?"

"No," she said.

"Good," said Salasso.

Gail and Stone said their good-byes. Gail felt an unexpected pang that she might never see the saur again.

"Thank you for saving me," said Salasso. He was looking at the sky. "Go now."

One by one, Gail, Stone, and Matt leapt down to the grass. Gail caught a glimpse of Gregor closing the outer door, as the ship rose. At a thousand meters it began to move forward, and then its path became a red streak to the horizon.

In the sky high above, as Gail blinked at the afterimage and her ears rang with the sonic boom, she saw two silver specks flying in the same direction, then stop and turn back, cheated of their prey.

* * *

The flying club airfield is quiet in the dusk, and the heathen trader who's brought Matt to Rawliston has nothing to say to him and therefore says nothing. Thank the gods for heathendom, where people ignore you just to be polite. Matt shoulders his pack and pauses for a moment as the heathen lugs a couple of heavy bales up to the clubhouse and considers following him. The lights are inviting, and Loudon might be up there. He wants to meet Loudon again, sooner rather than later.

No, later. He turns and takes the path out of the lower end of the airfield, down toward the streets. The path is rough, dusty, and stony. Christ, but it's good to have his boots back, and his own clothes, both retrieved from Long Bridge. It's been a long and involved afternoon up in the Vale. Radios have been among the recent imports, and accounts of the *Bright Star*'s journey are already becoming folklore. Good though it was to see Falling Leaf, Dark Water, Bright Shell, and the other women again, Matt has found that the sketchiest hearsay of what he's done has meant that everybody treats him as a man. Wham, just like that, as sudden as a slap on the back. He hopes Stone doesn't have this same jarring experience. They have had a long discussion about what Stone should and shouldn't say about what he's done. A lot depends on how Stone manages to put across his visionary encounter with a god.

The streets around here are wide, their edges indefinite. The density is somewhere between village street and suburban sprawl. The wooden houses go up to two or three stories. Some have front yards with flower beds and vegetable plots, trickle-irrigated with perforated pipes, amid patches of trampled grass. Nobody bothers with, or can afford, lawns. Cement mixers and old cars and odd agricultural implements are sometimes hauled up there, rusting or under running repair. Shops and cafés and stalls squeeze in between or in front of the houses, lit and advertised by strings of lightbulbs and bended strips of saur-manufactured plastic neon tubing.

People of all ages are on the streets, sitting at stalls or café tables or on their front steps, talking and drinking and smoking. Couples stroll and old men clack dominoes and suck their teeth. Children race everywhere. The younger ones act out barricade battles; the older ones and the teenagers strut in small patrols or make believe their street-corner hangout is a turnout of revolutionary guards. Matt is used to this sort of milieu, he knows just how to slouch and where to look so as not to attract more than a passing glance.

He savors the feeling, which he hasn't had since arriving on Croatan, of being anonymous and alone—a free agent, his own man. He'll miss his Mingulayan friends, little though he's seen of them recently, and he'll miss Salasso a lot. But there's a weight off his shoulders in knowing that they're off his hands.

What he doesn't expect is the acute pang of nostalgia that the smallest hints of a revolutionary situation bring. The raised fingers and raised voices of argument over a crumpled newspaper in a pool of light at a table, the flag on a shop's pole with the Port Authority logo cut out of the middle, the girl on the intersection self-consciously fiddling with her rifle's shoulder strap,—they all sting his eyes and stop his thoughts like a familar but forgotten scent. It triggers memories that go back to his childhood. Despite or perhaps because that revolution had come in the aftermath of military defeat, it had been a relaxed affair, almost lackadaisical. The Russians had done all the hard work, and their version of socialism—a significant upgrade on the one that had crashed in 1991—had turned out to be mutiplatform-compatible and easily enough installed.

Not so easily uninstalled, Matt reflects, though he wasn't around for that.

The streets become narrower, the buildings taller. Matt drops into a bar, a low, wide room hung with bad pottery and wire vines and paper leaves. A score or so of locals are sitting at its tables, and the counter is lined with people on tall stools. Matt buys a liter of beer and a hot smoked sausage with mustard, slings his bag at his feet, and stands at the counter, listening with half an ear to the talk. It's a working-class place, and most of the men and women here are well-dressed for this time of the evening; normally they'd be coming off work about now, still in their sweaty work clothes, but not many have worked today. The revolution is still in a holiday mood. It still smells of soap and cheap perfume and cologne.

The electrostat in the corner chatters, on the hour, and folded sheets of paper fall into the hopper and are passed around—free, if you don't count the advertising. The defeat of the rebel faction of the Port Authority earlier today is no longer news, though above the masthead a line of print still proclaims it's the "Victory Edition!!!"

Almost all the news and comment spins around panicky speculation about ALIENS and POWERS. It's like an invasion is imminent. It's all feeding in to the politics, heating up discussion about the urgency of industrializing, uniting, arming to meet this new threat. The various religious factions have been shaken up as well. The conservative sects, ever ready to see demons in the sky, are crowing. The official church—hitherto confident that the Powers Above are benign—is on the defensive.

Way down on the inside pages, Matt learns that a coalition called the Liberation Front has popped up to plug the program that Volkov relayed earlier today. Parliament and free trade are its bullet points. It's all very moderate. Even parliament won't be an innovation—there's a half-forgotten Council of Notables, elected on the nod, which can be pressed into service simply by reelecting its delegates. Meanwhile they'll serve in consultation with the popular assemblies, the reformed Port Authority, and the Liberation Front. . . .

"Shit!" yelps Matt.

A young couple sitting to his left, who've given the paper the most cursory glance before returning to more interesting matters, give him curious looks.

Matt smiles and shakes his head.

"I beg your pardon," he says.

"What was that about?" the woman asks, amused.

Matt hesitates for a moment. If he starts a political conversation now, he'll be anonymous no longer, even if still alone. Somebody's sure to ask who he is, and he has no intention of lying about it.

"Something in the paper," he says.

"Oh, yeah," says the man. "It's all looking pretty good, isn't it."

"A lot of it is," says Matt cautiously. "It's just that I've realized this city has suddenly got itself a provisional government."

"What?" says the man. "Nah, there's nothing about that."

"Come on," says the woman, "we haven't exactly *read* it yet."

"Yeah, but—"

Together they frown over their own copy. Then they're stabbing their fingers at the exact same inside paragraph that stung Matt.

"You're right," says the man reluctantly. He looks at Matt, shaking his head, then sticks out his hand.

"George Wotton," he says. "And this is my wife, Beth."

"Pleased to meet you. Matt Cairns."

"Oh!" says Beth. "You're the—"

It goes on from there.

Hours later, Matt has wandered all the way down to Back-o'-the-Docks, repeating and refining the procedure. On the way he runs across several members of the Liberation Front, one or two of whom are, he suspects— though they're cagey about it—also members of the Rawliston branch of the CPEU. (That's what it is, he reckons, that's the clandestine network Volkov has so readily plugged into, and he marvels at the persistence of their unlikely vision.) These know exactly who he is, without any introduction, and eye him warily. But he also meets a rather larger number of radicals who have no connection with Party or Front and who have networks of their own. Their clubs and societies go back at least as far as Rawliston's last revolution, the one some fifty years ago that cost the king his head.

By taking very great care not to have more than one beer in every bar he steps into, and to intersperse bars and beers with cafés and black coffee, he is no more than red-eyed and loquacious by dawn in the King's Head and is able to find on the esplanade an unoccupied bench on which to sleep it off. He wakes at noon with a hangover and a sunburn and a sense of a job well begun, and hitches out the coast road to the Traders' House and pitches in with the repairs, talks to Lydia, has a swim in the sea, and falls asleep, most uncharacteristically, the moment his head hits the pillow of Daphne de Charonea's bed.

Stone woke to such a sense of dread that he wished he could go back to sleep. The small upper room that he and Gail shared was flooded with early sunlight and the crowing, hooting, and honking of the various species of small dinosaur in the village street's yards and pens, and the quarrelsome chirruping of leatherwings roosting under the eaves.

He rolled, under the blanket, and put an arm and a leg around Gail. She stirred, and gradually her lips and eyelids stickily opened. She drew him closer, and they lay silently in the warmth of their mutual nakedness.

"God," she mumbled, "what time is it?"

He glanced at the slope of the sunlight on the stone wall opposite the window. "An hour after dawn."

"God," she said again. She disentangled herself and sat up, gulped water from a mug by the bedstead, splashed some on her fingers, and wiped her face.

"Why are we awake so early?" She blinked wet eyelashes. "Oh. Yes. Big day." She yawned. "I suppose we'd better get up."

"There is no need to get up at once," said Stone.

She slid back down under the blanket and ran her hands over him.

"Are you always like this in the mornings?"

"Yes," said Stone, affecting a complacent gaze at the ceiling.

"This really is something that's different for girls," she said, as he rolled under her touch. "I'm not at my best, you know. And your chin is scratchy. And your ... mmm ... ah ... well ... waste not, want not, I suppose ..."

She was quick to slide under him; there were times, as now, when she liked to take his slighter weight on top of her, and it was at those times when he felt most that she was in control, her whole body holding him in its grasp: her heels pressing down on the backs of his legs, her thighs gripping his hips and pacing their rocking rhythm, the swift spasming clutch of her vagina around his penis, her elbows jagged at his shoulders, and her hands full with his hair.

She hauled his head down, held it still against her shoulder, while everything else moved. As she released him he released himself, shuddered, spent, wasted, and wanted.

"Don't stop."

He slid out and moved off and let his fingers take over, marveling anew at the sheer capacity of the woman, at the way she could throw herself at her pleasure again and again.

They flopped together after a while.

"And don't go to sleep again," she said.

"Mmm."

"And don't ... oh, fuck ..."

Still sleepy, soon again, but he felt a lot more ready to face the day.

*   *   *

The field above Long Bridge, not the airfield but the meadow that the boys practiced in, was the site chosen for the council. Children carefully gathered dried dung for the fires, but the megatheres, pushed off to rougher pasture, had left fresh steaming pats behind, which not a few of the congregating shamans put a heel down in, or trailed a tattered hem through. The sachems, less fuddled, took better care of their dignity. By foot or boat or glider, they arrived from up and down the Vale. Tents for the shamans and canopies for the sachems formed a vast circle in the field, in the center of which the fires burned. Dried, entire plants of hemp burned along with the dung and brushwood. The mingled sacred and profane smoke lofted a succession of small paper balloons, bearing tiny animal sacrifices or scribbled prayers, to the midday sky and to the gods. The shamans' apprentices capered about, banging drumskins to drive off malign or mischievous spirits. The population of Long Bridge and its neighboring villages wandered in and out of the circle, or sat on the grass and awaited developments.

Stone waited too, on the paved path. He could feel his knees quivering. The drumming stopped and shamans emerged from their tents, smoke gusting behind them, and converged on the central fire. Sachems ducked out from beneath their canopies and strolled behind or among the shamans. Apprentices hurried to spread straw mats for them all to sit on.

"It's time," said Stone. Gail squeezed his hand and grinned. Together they walked to the middle of the field, the center of the circle, a long hundred meters. The fire heated his face, the smoke made his head swim. Odd details sprang into focus and significance: a crushed flower, a smoke-stunned bee fumbling the air with slow-moving legs as though trapped in honey, a toy glider on the grass.

A space in the circle around the fire had been left for them, and a mat. Stone sat down on it, legs curled. Gail squatted beside him, her forearms resting on her thighs, her hands open and loose between her knees.

Cups of beer and pipes of herb were passed around, along with the most idle comments about the weather, the fishing, the hunting. Gossip about couplings and births, feuds and deaths, more appropriate for old women than for men with deep-lined faces or frightful masks, mingled with jests more apt for boys. In this way an hour passed. To Gail, not understanding most of what was said, it must have dragged even longer than it did for Stone.

Then a sachem away to his left remarked, "They say that Stone from Long Bridge has a message for us from the gods."

It was spoken like gossip, laughed at like a joke, passed on with nudges. Stone joined in the derision himself, and Gail, after a startled glance, did so too. And then everybody looked at her. Silence waited.

"Woman talk to a god," she said. "Sky not fall. Not happen."

Stone winced, but her bad grammar set them all shaking back and forth with indulgent laughter. One shaman fell backward and had to lift his mask a little to recover his breath.

"Perhaps Stone is here," someone said. "It could be that he has something to say."

"We might even have time to listen."

"There is not much to do today."

"It might be a good time to leave, now."

With that they all stood and picked up their mats. Gail looked around and almost rose too. Stone caught her arm in the nick of time.

The shamans and sachems shuffled themselves into two semicircular rows, facing Stone and Gail. As they settled down again Stone turned about, his back to the fire, and urgently gestured to Gail to do likewise. When she had done so he stood up.

"I am Stone from Long Bridge," he said, "and I have come back from a journey on the *Bright Star* into the sky above the sky, where I met a god and was shown visions. I was shown the snake people and the sea people take the sky people from the Cold Lands, as our ancestors have told us. After that, the god showed me many new things." He paused. "We know that the gods do not always agree."

A chuckle came from behind some of the shamans' masks and smiles from the sachems.

"We did not know that the gods at times fight among themselves, as men do, or that they use the different peoples in the worlds of the sky to fight for them. The gods look upon the peoples as we look upon the beasts. We do not hunt the wolf and the great knife-toothed cat, though they hunt the same beasts as we do. The snake people have taught us that if we do that, the grazing beasts will multiply and eat too much grass, so that they all perish together, hunter and hunted alike.

"So it is with the gods and the peoples of the worlds. The god showed me wars in the sky between peoples we know of and peoples we know not, and whichever side wins, the outcome is the same to the gods. They say, it is well.

"It is well for them, but it is not well for the peoples who perish like beasts. I have seen cities greater than the Rawliston of the Christians burn like an oven. I have seen domes on cold moons, filled with hands of hands of crowds of the snake people, crack like a bad pot in a kiln. I have seen forests of people from other worlds, busy and bright and strange, swept away like a fallen branch in a flood. All the different peoples do this to others of themselves, or to other peoples, and always it is the same to the gods. The peoples of the worlds are at war, so that the gods remain at peace, and they say it is well.

"War is coming to our worlds. The god that showed me these things did not know when, but it is coming. We must be ready for it."

What he was saying frightened even him. He fell si-

lent and watched the council rock back and forth on their
heels and whisper together. Outside the circle, the crowd
of women and warriors and children pressed forward
until the bolder children were sent scurrying back by
fierce masks glancing over shoulders.

"He is telling us that the gods are evil," said a shaman,
the words booming from the mouth trumpet of his mask.

"It is said that the snake man Salasso has been telling
the same to the Christians," said a sachem.

Other comments, inaudible to Stone, bounced back
and forth among the council members. Their heads
swayed from side to side in a ripple that traveled like a
gust over grass. Stone waited for it to die down before
he spoke up.

"Salasso," he said firmly, "traveled on the *Bright Star*
with me. He and I are not saying that the gods are evil.
I am saying that what is good or evil in their sight has
nothing to do with what is right or wrong in ours."

"It may be," said a Long Bridge sachem, "that the god
who spoke with Stone has told him what would be right
for us to do."

They all laughed at this.

"No," said Stone. "But Matt Cairns from the *Bright
Star,* whom many here have met, has told me some
things that we might consider."

The council, and the crowd behind it, stirred again.

"Now *there*'re two names to conjure with," Gail muttered.

"We might consider these things," said a sachem.

"The Christians in Rawliston will soon have a new
council," said Stone. "They will make ready for the wars
to come, and one of the ways they will do it is by trying
to make the Great Vale a part of Rawliston."

He waited for the uproar to subside enough for him
to make out the loudest question: "Why would they do
that?"

"We have seen," Stone said, "and the Christians have
seen, how the *Bright Star* can land wherever its crew

pleases, and not only on the sea like the ships of the sea people. They have seen how we are trading for the first time with the star merchants. They know there will be more ships like the *Bright Star,* in the next few hands of years. They expect more traffic on land and sea also. The councils of Rawliston live by taking a small part of the goods that are traded, and they know that our fliers can take our trade high over their heads and out of their hands. They will fight to keep it."

"And what," asked the sachem from Long Bridge, "could we do, if this is to come?"

"What we must do is this," said Stone. "We must trade for rifles, and train all men and women in their use. We must build spears of fire that can destroy the flying machines of the Christians."

The enthusiastic uproar went beyond the council and into the crowd: whoops, yells, brandishing of weapons, drumming of spears on shields. So far, so good. Stone took a deep breath. The last part of Matt's program was the most dangerous and contentious, but it had to be said.

"And at the same time, we must make friends in Rawliston, and not enemies. We must make peace with those of the sky people who have become Christians, and with any Christians in Rawliston willing to take our side. There will be more than we now think. In years to come, if the Christians make war on us, they will arm and lead the savages against us. To prevent that we must make peace with the savages."

He faced a hostile silence. A sachem stood up and walked toward him and peered into his face.

"You are finished?" said the sachem.

"Yes," said Stone.

"You may go."

Stone nodded at Gail to rise, and they walked past the sachem and through the half circle of his fellows. Stone noticed the women from the workshop talking among themselves, grinning, aiming imaginary rifles.

A word of Matt's came to his mind, and he said it.
"This is progress."

"Son of a bitch," said Volkov.

Lydia watched Matt ambling along piling his plate at
the breakfast tables and felt like saying the same. His
explanation of the *Bright Star*'s sudden departure and
his relaying of Gregor's good-bye had been more per-
functory than she felt she deserved. And she had still
not forgiven him for his troublemaking intervention on
the radio; nor had Volkov.

Matt walked around the drained swimming pool and
past neatly stacked rubble, toward their table. Apparently
oblivious to their hostility, he sat down opposite them.

He grinned and raised his mug of coffee. "Here's to
Rawliston's revolution," he said.

Volkov glowered. "Which you're doing your best to
wreck!"

Matt sipped, unperturbed. "Why do you say that?" he
asked.

Volkov rubbed his face with his hands, and sighed.

"Very well," he said. "The whole future of this city
was being put at risk by an unstable combination of direct democracy and that relic of mercantilism, the Port
Authority. By establishing a representative democracy,
the people will gain an efficient administration and a
social safety valve, both of which are necessary if the
next ship from Mingulay isn't to find this place a ghost
town or a heap of ruins."

"How dialectical," Matt said. "I suppose the idea of
using the direct democracy to reform the relic hasn't
crossed your mind."

Volkov sighed his exasperation. "Matt, you really
should have lived down your anarchist illusions by now.
Free trade and parliamentary democracy are the boringly
obvious solutions to this city's problems, and any idea
of going beyond that in the next century or so is as futile
as it's ultimately reactionary."

Matt nibbled around the stone of an olive while listening to this, then put the remains on the side of his plate as if for later and turned to Lydia.

"This," he said histrionically, "from a member of the party that forced *socialism* on half a continent!"

Volkov looked wearily unimpressed. "Europe was ready for it. Rawliston is not. Get that clear in your head, Matt, and stop trying to muddle the heads of others."

"The night before last," Matt said, "I found a lot of heads that were very clear indeed about what the Council of Notables adds up to. And they didn't like it one bit."

Volkov slammed his fist on the table's bare planks.

"You're playing into the hands of the enemy," he said. "You're playing with fire. You're playing with people's *lives*."

"At least I'm playing through to the endgame," said Matt. "You're leaving in—what, five weeks?"

Volkov shrugged. "That's time enough for the situation to settle down, as long as reckless provocateurs don't blow it all up."

"Speaking of reckless provocations," said Matt, "what do you call urging the heathens to declare the Great Vale a free port?"

Lydia felt a chill in the belly. "Who has done *that*?" she asked.

Matt inclined his head at Volkov. Lydia turned to him, the movement so swift she slipped away a little from him on the bench.

"Tell me you didn't!"

Volkov gave her a baffled look. "I suggested it to Stone, yes."

Lydia felt the gravity fail, felt that endless drop begin. "You must be—" She stopped and shook her head. "No, you're not crazy, or stupid. You must have known what that would do. I've seen scores of cities like this—trade is their life. They'll fight for it. People always do. And if their trade rival is a rabble of hunters and gardeners—gods above, they'll walk over them!"

Volkov smiled and nodded. "Exactly!" he said. "That is the whole point!"

"What do you mean?"

"Look," said Volkov, leaning toward her, spreading his hands, "the idea is bound to come up anyway. The heathens are sharp enough to think of it themselves, if some city entrepreneur doesn't put it to them first. Or the Port Authority will anticipate the possibility. However it plays out, it ends with Rawliston integrating the Great Vale. Potential trade rivalry aside, they can't indefinitely tolerate an enclave of barbarism athwart a strategic position a few tens of kilometers away."

"Yes," said Lydia. "And so?"

"So why not get it over with, while it's still an easy conquest and the cost to both sides is low?" He shrugged. "I don't know if the heathen will fall for it just yet, but it's worth trying. And a short, sharp war with the heathen would consolidate the new regime here. All in all, it would save a lot of lives in the—well, not even the long run, actually. More like over the next decade."

He said this with such expectation of her agreement that she did not doubt he believed every word of it.

She heard Matt's voice as if from a great distance. "You're wrong, Lydia," he said. "He *is* stupid."

Her flaring anger suddenly turned on Matt. "You're no better!" she said. "If you're trying to stir up the people, you're encouraging *civil* war, and that's the worst kind there is!"

"I'm not trying to stir up the people," he said, "and civil war is exactly what I'd like this place to avoid. And they can avoid it, if they dislodge this new government before it's had a chance to consolidate. I don't expect them to launch any wild social experiments, either—just keep open all the possibilities of their existing and quite admirable democracy. Peace with the heathens—inside the city as well as outside—is essential for that. Just as war with them is essential for Volkov's stupid little scheme for an ever-expanding capitalist republic."

"Progress and industrialization," said Volkov. "That's what we need here and on every world. Stagnant little backwaters won't stand a chance when the aliens arrive, or if the gods decide we're getting too big for our boots. Like Salasso said, we have to be ready, we have to work together. Within the next century every human-settled planet will need a space defense capability—one that can handle not just aliens but also asteroid bombardments from the gods. That means heavy industry and nukes, like it or not. And they'll need to actually understand the lightspeed drive, make it invulnerable to hacking from the gods any time they want to flick us away like flies."

"You told me about a map," Lydia said. "The one that Tola showed you, a way out of these confrontations, by spreading out through the galaxy. Wouldn't that be an alternative to your"—she screwed up her eyes and shook her head, restraining her words—"*vision* of war with the gods?"

Volkov shot her an impatient glance.

"We have no basis for trusting that map, or that idea, because it itself was a move in whatever game the gods are playing."

Matt looked about to say something, but Lydia got in first.

"That doesn't *matter*," she said. She put her fists to her forehead, as if to stop her head from exploding.

"The point—the point—the point is, if we're being manipulated from above, it's no answer for us to manipulate those below us, because that could just be ... an extension of the same strings, farther downward."

Matt nodded enthusiastically. "Yes!" he said. "But— what do you mean, exactly, by 'those below us'?"

"Oh, *you* know," Lydia said, waving her hand. "The people of the shore."

Matt placed rinds and crusts on his plate and stood up. "That was what I thought you meant," he said.

As he walked away through the passageway to the beach, Lydia was surprised to feel within her as much regret and reproof as she had heard in his voice.

"What was that about?" she asked Volkov.

He waved a hand. "Matt likes to pretend he is an ordinary worker, a man of the people. It's as decadent an affectation as any I've come across in the great houses." He smiled. "Not in yours, I hasten to add."

"I thought you believed in equality."

"Yes, I do treat people as equals, whenever possible. Life is more pleasant that way, believe you me. But I am not going to pretend there is real equality between people who live and die in one small span of space and time, and people like us who stride across centuries. You are right—the people of the shore are below us, and cannot *but* be below us. We have responsibilities to them, but they are measured on a different scale from our responsibilities to each other."

"Oh?" she said. "So the people you've been working with, your comrade Endecott and so on, they're just tools to be used?"

He shook his head. "By no means. No more than your family's shore agents are to you. But, in all honesty, look around you." His wave took in the growing breakfast crowd of the clan. "You'll all be back here in another couple of centuries—a year in your life. These walls will be more worn, that ivy will be thicker, the glass in the windows will be less transparent, and you will be more beautiful than you are now. And the people of Rawliston will be the descendants of the people you have met on this visit. The events of the present will be history, perhaps proud history. The name of Endecott may be one that children read about in school. This is real to you, yes?"

"Yes," she said. "I've been here before, and—yes."

"All right," he said. "These people you'll meet a year from now are real to you, as real as the people in the cars buzzing by outside. How do you do the right thing by them?"

Lydia thought about it. It was like a logic puzzle, something that you could work out, but it was one for which she knew the answer already. She had been taught the answer, back when she was almost too young to understand it. Esias had stood over her while she frowned at the black numbers in the big books.

"Well, you, you—for a start you trade honestly with the people here now, you make sure the finances and the funds and the contracts are all in order, so that, you know, you aren't leaving some terrible speculative bubble behind that'll wreck their economy or anything, because then there'll be nothing here for you to come back to. You make sure the shore agents' businesses are sound. You make sure the crew doesn't spread diseases or leave any uncared for pregnancies, and so on."

Volkov looked at her with evident disbelief.

"In other words," he said, "you behave no differently from how you would if you were meeting the same people again a year from now? Treating people ethically in the present is exactly the same as doing the right thing by their descendants?"

"Yes!" She smiled at him, delighted that he had got the point. Then she recalled their preceding argument, and frowned. "So how can you justify trying to start a war now, in the hope that it'll make things better for people in ten or a hundred years?"

"I am *not*," he said, "trying to start a war. You know as well as I do that a clash between the people of the Great Vale and Rawliston will take place, regardless of anything we may do. The question is, will that war be soon and swift, or late and long?"

"You've said that before," she said. "And that is not the question. It is not the question *for you*. Or for me, either. It's a question for the political leaders of the two societies—kings, councillors, elders, bureaucrats, whatever. They can make that decision, for good or ill. It's *their* responsibility. And who's to say that something you haven't anticipated at all won't make the whole issue redundant?"

Volkov smiled. "That's just leaving it to chance," he said, "and that, too, is a choice."

"I see what you mean," she admitted. "All right. You tell me how you see our—or your—responsibilities to those people I'll meet in a year."

"Very well," said Volkov. "It's worthwhile, it's in our interests and in theirs, that they should have as good a life as possible. Anything we can do now to promote the progress of industry and society means more, richer, and very likely happier people up the line."

Up the line, indeed! You are not a god, she thought, and said, "Even if it means sacrificing people in the present?"

" 'Sacrifice' is not a word I would use," said Volkov. "But some additional suffering now for the sake of less suffering and more happiness later—yes, that is acceptable."

"It's for those who'll bear the suffering to decide whether it's acceptable!"

"They rarely can," said Volkov. "Every militia officer here may have to order people to certain death, in an attack on a pirate stronghold, let's say, for the sake of, oh, some greater good like a reliable margin of profit on shipping."

"That's war itself, that's different—"

"It's no different in civil life. When this benighted hole finally introduces adequate sewerage in the poorer quarters, the number of laborers who'll die in the diggings can be predicted—in round figures, to the nearest ten—by any experienced actuary or civil engineer. But the number of lives saved by that sewerage system can also be calculated, in the hundreds of thousands."

Lydia shook her head. "All the people involved in that are reckoning their own risks, whereas you are reckoning people as costs. I don't deny that people in a position of responsibility have to make hard choices, but that responsibility is itself a cost. You're making that calculation without any cost to yourself. If your friend Endecott were to urge war sooner rather than later, fine, I could respect that, because he'd be taking the risks—political defeat, assasination, or even the thought that two hundred years from now children will know his name only because their mothers use it to frighten them."

Volkov rubbed his temples. "I take a risk, too, but I still say that the future well-being of the people—"

"You mean, the well-being of future people!"

"Yes. It's something we can legitimately take into account because we will live to see it, and the people of the present, here, won't."

"We take it into account in the present," she said, "by honest accounting." She smiled as she said it, hoping somehow to stop this difference becoming a dispute.

Then Volkov said, "You may see it differently when you've lived long enough."

And that got to her; she was furious. She stood up, scraped her thighs as she stepped sideways between the table and the bench, and stalked around in front of him and leaned forward, fists on the table.

"Listen," she said, "I may be younger than you, but I've lived through history hundreds of years longer than you have. I've seen dozens of worlds, I've seen cities rise and fall, and my family have seen more and longer and they have taught me what is right, and I *know* that it works, I know that doing right by people who may live *now* is the same as doing right by people who may live *then*, and I know that what you've tried to do is wrong."

"Lydia, wait—"

She turned on her heel and walked away, down to the beach. The early sun boomed on the water. An onshore breeze made the sand hiss at her feet. After a few minutes her lips tasted salty. She found Matt sitting on a tussock a few hundred meters to the north of the house, morosely chucking stones seaward and doodling on the dune's slope with a bit of driftwood. Any patterns he made were being obliterated by the sand dislodged by their making.

"Hi."

"Hello." She sat beside him. They both stared out to see for a while, then Lydia exploded again.

"Bastard! I—like him a lot, but he can be a patronizing, arrogant, strutting, stupid bastard sometimes."

Matt turned a twisted smile on her. "Now you know what it's like," he said, "to be one of the people of the shore."

"But *we* don't treat them like that! That's what I've just been arguing with him about!"

"Oh, Lydia de Tenebre," he said, "if you just knew. You traders, you don't see what you do to people, to societies. You fuck them up! You kick them forward, or off their tracks, you change them forever with the new ideas and new goods you bring, and you come back in two hundred years when the dust has settled, and you do it all again."

"But we do it *honestly*."

"You do it blindly. It isn't your fault. But Grigory Andreievich and I have lived through in slow motion what you see in time lapse, and it . . . gets wearing, after a while."

"Maybe when everybody lives as long as you do," she said, "it'll be different."

"Yeah, it'll be different all right. Very different indeed, for Nova Babylonia." He laughed. "Especially if Grigory gets to work there like he's doing here."

"We have to take him to Nova Babylonia," she said. "We agreed, we made a contract. But—I'm afraid, my father is afraid, of what he'll do when he gets there."

"Join the club," said Matt.

"You're the only person who can stop him, or act as a balance, or something," she said.

"Yeah," said Matt, with some bitterness. "And I've a

lot still to do, right here. I've been intending to stay until it's done."

"There's more to do on Nova Terra," she said. "Truly, and so much more at stake! And—and—"

She stopped. He smiled at her, a warm and open smile this time.

"You'd take me there?"

"Yes."

He stared out to sea, then after a minute turned sharply. "All right," he said. "St. Teilhard's Day. It's a date."

She looked at him, puzzled. "I know it's a *date*."

He laughed and explained, and they walked together back to the house.

Later that day, Matt moves out of the Traders' House and into a single room with a single bulb at the back of Back-o'-the-Docks. He has a small stash of money from the ship's trading profits, more than enough to live on. But he takes a job all the same, casual labor at the docks. He's desperate to find out what's really going on and what people are really thinking, and he can't do that from the Traders' House, or (regretfully) from talking to people in bars.

Over the next week some events move faster than Matt expects, others slower. The anxiety about the news brought by the *Bright Star* doesn't so much subside as seep into the groundwater of people's awareness, becoming a background radiation in every serious discussion. It fuels the street scuffles between gangs of youths from Dawsonite and anti-Dawsonite neighborhoods, and between heathens and Christians, that are a regular part of the annual buildup to St. Teilhard's Day. A few unions, emboldened by the response to the political strike, press claims on their employers. Most of them are settled quickly, all of them without serious trouble.

The neighborhood and municipal assemblies are in more or less continuous uproar about the new and still fluid arrangements but are just as continually one step behind events as the Port Authority is reformed, its militia purged and reorganized, and the Council of Notables hurries to forestall objections, to meet disagreement halfway, to draw dissenters into labyrinthine committees, and to rush through a few social reforms: Primary education is to become compulsory, street cleaning is to be municipalized, the poor are to get scrip to pay for medical attention. Elections are duly scheduled for just after the festival, and the Liberation Front fields a slate on which Endecott is the candidate for Verdant Heights. Volkov vanishes from the public prints and the radio channels.

Matt isn't bothered. Daphne keeps track of Volkov's activities and passes on the information by radio or in person. He himself keeps track of Volkov's influence and ideas, which keep cropping up: The "Great Vale problem" is mooted in every forum, from the serious radio panels to the hourly sensation sheets. The drug traffic, sectarian and racial tensions, possible military dangers are all attributed to its anomalous autonomy.

It's a radio message from Loudon that Matt most eagerly awaits. Near the end of the week, he receives it. Gail, Stone, and Slow Leg have arrived at the airfield.

The three of them meet him in a shebeen in the heathen area bordering Back-o'-the-Docks and pass on their news very quietly.

The council of the sky people have decided to attack Rawliston.

"They decided *what*?"

Gail looks about anxiously. "Keep your voice down," she says.

The whole dive is full of scores of heathens busy getting drunk or preparing for the one big colorful event in their year, the St. Teilhard's Day parade.

"All right," Matt says, leaning in and speaking more quietly. "So what the fuck *happened*?"

He's doing it again, his voice rising in indignant incredulity.

"I said just what you asked me to say," Stone tells him, looking apologetic. "Something may have got lost in the translation."

"You're not fucking kidding," says Matt. "I mean, didn't the women object?"

"They're all for it," says Gail, with infuriating enthusiasm. "The sachems—these elders and wise men and brave warriors and so on who make up the councils— they're elected by the women. The council went on for three days and nights, and I think most of the real decisions were made in the nights."

Stone nods. "Yes. The women talk among themselves, and the sachems talk things over with their women in the evenings, and they go to the council the following day and puff out their chests and talk big and say what their women tell them to say. More or less."

"I know how your system works," says Matt. "I just don't understand what's in it for them."

"War industry," says Gail. "More prestige. Less alcohol and more useful tools getting in. Stuff like that."

Stone and Slow Leg nod soberly and sip their beers.

"I can see some problems with the logistics," Matt says dryly.

"Ah, but you gave us the answer to that," says Slow Leg. "We make friends with the sky people in Rawliston, and they will help us. They will be what Gail calls a 'fifth column.' "

Matt makes a show of looking over the people around them. Men in grubby work clothes or luridly natty suits drink cheap beer and bad whiskey and talk raucously among themselves above the maddening sound of the fiddlers at the back. Overweight mothers tipple gin while stitching sequins on festival costumes for their skinny daughters, some of whom are looking after their younger siblings by plying them with dilute drinks. Others look far too young to be talking to the men they're talking to.

"This lot?" says Matt. "They're hopeless. Every year they get dressed up for the carnival, and every year the young men get tanked up for it and start a riot afterward—payback for Dawson's Night, I guess—and every year they get hammered."

"We can give them hope," says Slow Leg. "We can bring them back to the ways of the sky people."

"Something did get lost in translation," says Matt. "I wanted you to be ready for an attack *from* Rawliston, not to . . . Have you any idea what that could provoke?"

Slow Leg bristles. "It is we who are provoked," he says. "We are provoked by the way our people are treated in this city. We are provoked by what we hear spoken about us on the radios, which is as you said—some people in the new councils of the Christians are preparing to attack us. We have to stand up for ourselves, because we know now that the gods do not care about us. The gods are happy if the peoples fight each other. Very well, we will make them happy."

Matt feels cold with dismay. "Is that how you understand the news from the gods?"

"Yes," says Slow Leg.

"I too," says Stone.

Matt turns to Gail for help. "We have to stop this."

Gail looks back, poker-faced. "As well try to stop an avalanche," she says. "You know what the sky people are like, once they make up their minds."

Matt sighs. "All right," he says. "And when do they intend to . . . make their move?"

Stone looks away from a process of fairy-wing construction that has held his gaze for the past five minutes.

"St. Teilhard's Day," he says.

13

St. Teilhard's Day

A DINOSAUR HEAD grins in through the window, and when Matt wakes up the sight makes him jump. He takes in the green and red and white painted colors just as the papier-mâché shape sways away. He hears again the sounds that woke him: the rattling whack of sticks, rhythmic shouts. It's intimidating enough to be reassuring.

He rolls out of the bed and moves sidelong to the window at its foot and slides it up and leans out, into the air of a fine morning, the blue of the sky still pale above the roofs, sea smell faint on the breeze. In the street below, the front half of the dinosaur is waltzing around independently of the rear, and along fifty meters of sidewalk a hundred or so half-naked young men are facing off each other and practicing attack and defense moves with staves.

"Hey!" *Thwack!* "Hey!" *Thwack!* and the thump of feet wearing good industrial boots that kick up dust as the men leap from one stance to another.

Farther down the street the festival's floats—or very large costumes—are marshalling, the nearest being a brightly colored representation of a balloon train complete with red silk streamers sent fluttering up by a gust from a bellows arrangement. Lithe heathen girls prance or pose in gorgeously embroidered tunics and trousers or in gaudy silk costumes of insects and fairies and leatherwings. Their big mamas sail out of the doorways in Sunday best dresses and wide-brimmed flower-laden hats; their fathers strut in dandy suits, twirling canes, while their brothers, bare-chested in Christian casuals, toyi-toyi and flourish spears and staves.

Time to get moving. He wraps a towel around himself, hurries down the greasy-carpeted corridor to the washroom, splashes water on his face and on the back of his neck, returns to the room, and climbs into clean clothes and hauls on his jacket and checks the contents of the pockets. The knife he lost has been replaced by one heavier and nastier. Pistol and ammo, check. Radio and earpiece, check. Something else. Look around. Plastic half-liter water bottle, he'll need that too. Fills it at the washroom. Remembers to piss.

Clatters down the wooden stairs, careful not to snag the cleats of his boots on the frayed death-trap carpet, and out into the street. Glances up at the heathen lads, sees Slow Leg, who doesn't see him. Good. No complications. Matt ducks away down a side alley. A few more turns and he's in Back-o'-the-Docks.

The streets are already filling up with people and floats taking their places—it's a big, big day here, as big as it is for the heathen. Stilt walkers and jugglers, acrobats and dancers, gigants and pithkies, costumes and floats—some of which even celebrate the revolution: hardboard mock-ups of armored cars with broom handles poking out the windows and people in real or fake militia uniforms trotting alongside. Or they will, when they've got moving and stopped milling around. Every mollyboy in the place is out, in tarty gear or posh frocks or outrageous drag or costumes with long nodding feathered headdresses and hoop skirts up to three meters across.

He jogs and dodges through the streets, out of the district and into the warehouse zone, long wasteland streets with no windows and then out to the front and the shore road beyond that spread the docks and the quays. Traffic is diverted and in any case slack for the holiday. The cranes, and some ships in the harbor, are decked with bunting and banners. Two starships out in the roads—the Rodriguezes', due to leave for Mingulay tomorrow, and the de Tenebres', which will leave later today for its next stopover on the way to Nova Terra. Skiffs are already flitting back and forth.

Lydia will pick him up on one of them, at nine this evening. If he lives that long ,

Had a good run anyway. Like a Galápagos tortoise. Memory of looking on television at eyes that had looked at Darwin . . .

Slows to a juddery walk, breath heaving, sweat springing. Slings the weapon-weighted jacket over one shoulder and saunters in to the first rendezvous, a dockside greasy spoon. Long counter, a few tables, smell of coffee and onions. Not busy today, ten of the dozen customers parked along the counter are his lads. All of them work at the docks but only two of them are dockers, guys who actually load and unload cargo, that being a tightly closed shop and one that Volkov's local Party branch has been well dug into for generations. The men who aren't dockers are casual or low-grade, rough and unrespectable and young. He's worked a few days with them, off and on, in the past weeks. They know he's off the *Bright Star* and they think he's a Mingulayan. He has found them already more hostile than he is to the new government, and they're ready for action today.

He greets them and slides on to a tall rickety chair by the counter and orders a big fry-up and coffee, skins up a quick cigarette while he's sipping the first cup and waiting for the food. The nicotine and caffeine deliver quite a hit in oxygenated blood.

Smudged electrostat paper passes along to him.

"What d'you reckon to that, Matt?"

The sensation of the hour is an announcement that the Great Vale is about to proclaim itself a free port. It's made all the more urgent by some unsourced speculation that the Mingulayan Cosmonaut Families have built lots more ships already, they aren't going to wait for the *Bright Star* to come back before sending them out, packed to the airlocks with goods and adventurers. This part of the story has a lot of plausible detail about how the drive's more exotic components could have been bought from saurs influenced by Salasso, who has plugged just that sort of cooperation.

The waitress places the plate in front of him. He smiles thanks and takes a bite or two, thinking. Mustn't show himself bothered at all about this. The lads are joking with the waitress or calling new orders; the cook, short and fraught under a cap, is yelling obscure personal insults back.

Matt puts down his fork, swallows, hands the paper back to Dave Borden.

"Load of bull," he says, loud enough for everyone to hear. "No way did they have more ships on the go when we left, and no way at all could any have been built in three months."

"You sure about that?" one of the dockers asks, leaning in and looking along. "Once you've got the drive, all you need is a fucking *airtight box*."

"Not if you don't know for sure where you're going," Matt says. "We didn't, not definitely. Anybody who leaves before the *Bright Star* gets back won't know either. Leap in the fucking dark, man."

"What about the heathens?" Borden asks. "Looks like they're trying to shaft us after all."

Matt grins at him. "I told you, didn't I? Told you somebody would set up a provocation. This is it."

"Thought you meant the heathen buggers making trouble, or some of the anti-Dawson crowd mixing it with the parade. You didn't say nothing about this."

"No, I didn't," Matt admits. "Wouldn't make any difference if I had. Both these stories are lies."

He finishes his breakfast. Rolls another cigarette and says, "Okay, anyone got the map?"

Somebody has the parade committee's flyer, showing the routes. Matt slides it into the electrostat's copy facility, marks a few points on the copy, then copies that nine times, hands them out.

"O-kay. The actual church contingent assembles on Piltdown Rise, in front of the cathedral. The rest arrive by feeder routes from Back-o'-the-Docks, the heathen district, the university, and the three parks uptown. All of them fall in behind the bishop's lot, by the numbers, as it moves off. Down the hill, along the riverside, wheel around over the bridge, onto the shore road, along past here, then the religious procession itself goes on to the quays to watch the bishop splash holy water in the harbor while everyone else swings around into Back-o'-the-Docks by midafternoon, the militias peel off, and . . . then it's up to them. All we have to do is stop trouble breaking out along the parade route. Everyone clear?"

Everyone was.

"Right, these X's on the map are good points for an attack—awkward corners, open stretches, narrow streets with alleys, that sort of thing. We'll have at least a dozen good lads and lasses at each of them, tooled up."

Matt flashes a grin along the long counter.

"And down here," he adds, "we have us."

Gets a laugh. Small pang of conscience.

"Lucky for us the other groups peel off one by one if the parade goes past without trouble, and by the time it reaches here—flashpoint central, thanks to the docks, the PA goons and that crap in the paper—they'll all be ready to back us up."

"Show them," Borden says. "Fucking PA scabs."

Bit of back-and-forth follows, but by the time he leaves they're all on line about what to do. His breakfast is too heavy for him to jog so he walks fast and consults the bus timetable on the side of the map. The heat of the day is beginning to build up. Bored militia people in crisp new uniforms stand at the junctions of a shore road still almost empty of traffic. The reformed and expanded Port Authority militia, not the neighborhood militias controlled by the assemblies.

That story, now, about the heathens, and the ships coming soon, that's a good one. He wonders who's behind it; it strikes him as too reckless a provocation even for Volkov. The folk most likely to be agitated by it are the dockers, and behind them the people who rallied to the rebel elements in the Port Authority: the compradores and their employees. They're like retainers of some great family that has lasted for centuries and whose empty castle they tend for generations. Every century or so the castle floods with light and dancing and wealth, then the lights go out again, the party's over. . . . There's something feudal about the relationship. Dependence. The people of the shore.

Thinking about Lydia again, and about Daphne. Stop now or accept another two-hundred-year obsession. That is not funny. If you outlive everyone you love, what you accumulate is losses. It's too frightening.

So run around that corner, swing onto a bus, grinding up the long, gradual incline to Piltdown Rise. Strap-hang amid chattering people. Think. If some of the dockers are swayed by the story, a big part of the plan, one of its thrashed-out selling points, is in big trouble. His side absolutely has to command the docks by evening. It's been a promise and one he dare not break.

He looks at the baffling, tiny-printed instructions on the back plate of his radiophone, works through the fine-tuned wavelengths for the other groups in his boot-strapped organization. Everybody's in place and on the ball. No trouble so far. He calls Gail and passes on the warning.

Gail let the hood of the club's old car fall shut. It made a tinny clunk rather than a satisfying slam, but she was happy with the work she'd done under it. The engine note was as clean as it would ever be, even if it could never be described as a purr.

"Okay, you can turn it off!" she shouted. Stone leaned in through the open door and groped under the dashboard. The engine stopped, without so much as a cough. Stone grinned out at her and stuck a thumb up. She smiled back at his small triumph. Together they walked across to the shed where the heathens stashed their gliders. Normally there would be only two or three at a time in it. Today, there were dozens.

Gail and Stone spread them out on the grass to let the dew, still present on the wings, dry off. A heady scent rose from the doped silk as it warmed up. When they had finished, a great expanse of the field looked as though a flock of giant butterflies had landed on it. Then they had to gather them up again, beginning with the first ones they'd laid out, now dry but in danger of warping if they were left too long in the sun.

"Oh, Christ," she said as they slumped, shoulders aching, in the shed's shade. "I hope this works."

As if in answer, she glimpsed a party of warriors from the Vale, trotting through the long grass at the edge of the field. They reached the dusty path to the streets and disappeared down it at a run.

"It'll work," said Stone. "Matt is cunning."

"Cunning isn't enough," Gail said.

Matt's warning about trouble down at the docks was preying on her mind; it could throw the plan off course. Those weeks of agitating and organizing, of calling in favors, of words in the right places, could all come to nothing.

"Timing is everything," she said. "And keeping the

plan secret, from both of our sides, both columns"—she moved her hands together—"and from the other side."

She turned and looked into Stone's eyes. "And hitting the right targets."

"That's a lot of everything," he said.

The bus climbs slowly through the industrial zone, turns on to a broad avenue, and stops a few hundred meters from the assembly point. Everybody piles out, and Matt accompanies them to the big tree-lined public square in front of the cathedral. A crowd has already gathered there, a thousand or more. It's more respectable looking than the one Matt woke up to, but its folk art is no less colorful. The bishop, clergy, and choir are gathered around a crucifix and a large gilt omega symbol. Silk banners with portrayals of the saint's mild, studious features flap from long poles. In among the suits and Sunday best, kids cavort in costumes of dinosaurs, megatheres, ape-men, saurs, and krakens. Scores of the congregated parishioners are gigants and pithkies themselves, and their encounters with hairy-costumed, prognathous-masked *H. sap.* children are droll and, as far as Matt can make out, good-humored.

He makes his way to the ornate black notice board that projects above the churchyard wall and scans its gilt lettering while waiting for the procession to move off. The Anglican Church of Rawliston. A branch of the Extraterrestrial Episcopal church. Matins, choir practices, communions. Christenings first Sunday of the month. Visitors welcome.

It's no more absurd than any of the other institutional continuities with Earth that abound in the Second Sphere, but it strikes Matt as simultaneously ridiculous and magnificent. There's a dauntless defiance in its stubborn mundanity, its refusal to let mere distance make a difference to the spirit.

A murmur and a hush ripple concentrically across the crowd, and Matt turns to see the bishop hold aloft, in succession, a cranium, a mandible, and a femur, while intoning in a resonant, nasal voice into a silence broken only by the inevitable shuffles and coughs. Matt catches the occasional sonorous phrase: ". . . teach us to see in these fraudulent relics the many levels of Your truth . . . in the stumblings of our science the mystery of Your ways . . . Your wisdom in our foolishness . . . unity in multiplicity . . . all Your children, whatever our outward form . . ."

This is enough to kick Matt's atheist reflexes back into action, and he irreverently rolls and lights a cigarette. Drumbeats and flutes and jangles announce the imminent arrival of other contingents. Through the trees, Matt can see banners waving and drumsticks spinning up in the air on two of the square's four approach roads. The bishop replaces the fake bones in the reliquary and, bearing it on one shoulder and carrying his crozier in the other, leads off. Matt lets the crowd move out of the square before stubbing out the cigarette and falling in at the rear, behind a tinfoil imitation of a gravity skiff in which children with big saur heads on their small shoulders bob and wave.

The first of the feeder marches closes the gap behind him, and before long he's walking immediately in front of the marching band of a merrier and noisier but still relatively restrained contingent from the nearest middle-class neighborhood. Their particular kick is historical military reenactment, and they're in the helmets and cuirasses of the colony's early militia; the companies of men behind the band shoulder obsolete but real rifles. Matt moves sideways onto the sidewalk for a bit, checking it out. The women stride along in russet skirts and checkered shawls and kerchiefs, and their rifles or maybe muskets look even older and longer, but no less real, than those carried by the men. Matt suspects that this whole theatrical display has the unspoken function of protecting the congregation up ahead as well as the other denominational contingents immediately behind.

One lot less to worry about, then. Let the faithful look after their own. He lets the church groups go by and falls in behind the first of the Christian heathen sections of the march, which forms a long and flexible shock absorber between the religious groups and the overtly secular revellers from the working-class districts, the university, and Back-o'-the-Docks. For the first time the smell of marijuana smoke is heavier in the air than that of incense.

Ten of the heathen infiltrators have taken the lead in stewarding this section and have got the rest of the young men running and toyi-toying up and down the sides, handling their fake spears as real staves. They're enforcing a strict alcohol discipline as well, forcibly swapping beer bottles for spirit bottles with anyone caught swigging out of the latter.

Matt slow-walks back into a factory section. He feels out of place among all the matching logo-flash overalls and the floats of sheet-plastic replicas of steam-driven machinery, and drifts back again, bypassing the company's sponsored neighborhood militia unit, until he's in a union section. An oompah band and banners and another tight militia platoon bringing up the rear. He sticks with them until they reach the first potential flashpoint, a corner with a small park opposite and an anti-Dawsonite district just across the grass.

He ducks out and joins up with the squad there, local kids whose slightly unconventional appearance and attitudes have got them roughed up a few times by local toughs. They're sitting on a couple of dilapidated benches and watching the procession and sipping beer. One or two of them are lolling on the other side of the benches, keeping a lookout across the park at the row of rundown shops and houses opposite. A few furled banners are stacked alongside, with strong, thick poles sticking out and easily removed.

"All quiet so far?" he asks, sitting down on an iron curlicue of armrest and gratefully accepting a beer.

"Yeah, fine," says Annie Gibbs, who seems to be the unopposed leader of this particular cell of anarchists. She's light-skinned enough to be a heathen and has her fair hair done in braids, heathen man style, and wears a formal shirjack over scuffed leather trousers. She has read a lot about anarchism.

"Time to move on?"

"Don't think so," says Matt. "Let's stick around, run on to the next unit after a few of the obvious easy targets go past. So far it's all been well defended."

"Noticed."

"This usual?"

She gives him a *where-you-been?* look.

"Nah," she says. "See the factory militia groups? None of that last year. Bosses didn't like them, then, see." Grins ironically. "It's the revolution, wow!"

"Could be," says Matt, carefully noncommittal. "Or maybe just that there's a bit more tension about anyway."

"Same thing, kind of. See that report about the heathens up the Vale?"

"Yeah," says Matt. "What do you make of it?"

"Somebody's fucking winding us up," she replies without hesitation. "War is the health of the state and all that, and somebody wants the state a bit healthier."

Sharp. Matt nods eagerly, keeping one eye on the procession.

The kid sitting on the back of the bench taps Annie's shoulder. "Trouble," he says quietly. "Don't all jump up."

Matt doesn't even turn around. He keeps looking at the section of the passing parade that's coming around the corner. It's not Back-o'-the-Docks yet, but it's definitely more colorful now, lots of mollyboys, lots of girls and women, hoopskirts and headdresses, glitter and glitz; the heathens in this lot are just strolling along or dancing behind the band, and there's no defense group in sight, and the next group up the hill is from the university, not much help there unless—ah, yes, somewhere way up there he can see the banners of the cadets.

This all takes a second or two. The back of his neck prickles. He turns around slowly. It takes him a moment to spot what the potential trouble is, and he almost laughs: Outside a grogshop a hundred meters away on the far side of the patchy, littered park, a group of about twenty men has gathered, and they're waving bottles and jeering and gesturing.

"Fucking chimps," he says.

Annie moves slowly to the stacked banners. "That pub can hold a hundred, and believe me it can empty fast."

Shit, it's serious. It'll be hand-to-hand in seconds: bottles, knives, staves, and fists. And his two pistols, if need be. He can't let it come to that.

"Pick up the poles," Annie's saying, "one by one, and just kind of saunter over to the side of the march and spread out in line, holding them horizontal. Face out."

They do that. More crawling feelings arise on the back of his neck until he turns around. The knot at the grogshop has grown but hasn't moved forward. Matt leans back, looking to his right; every time he sees a heathen man capering by he nods and glances at the hostiles. Some of the lads just laugh, or are too drunk or stoned to comprehend or care. One or two respond by taking a place in the thin line. Annie starts calling out something in the heathen speech, and after a couple of minutes their group of ten has been joined by at least as many again, forming a solid human barrier at the outer side of the corner.

The grogshop's customers go back inside, just as the student cadets' first drum majorettes swing around the corner. The heathens jog off to catch up with their own section.

Matt checks his memories of the order of the rest of the procession and looks back up the street as far as he can see, to check, and decides that it's safe to move on to the next danger point. He passes this on, and he and

Annie's group set off at a fast pace, cutting through some backstreets to where a dozen heathen road workers are awaiting them, resting casually on their picks and shovels at a junction, and just as casually eyeing up a small but militant fundamentalist congregation massed in a side street with placards denouncing heathens, sodomites, and Dawsonites.

That too passes peacefully, and the road menders join the squad as it moves briskly on. The weight of their shouldered tools doesn't slow them down. They have the hunter-gardener physique. Matt doesn't, and he welcomes the cooler air down by the Big River, after two more such standoffs and subsequent reinforcements to the flying defense squad. He accepts every friendly offer of water or beer that comes his way.

By the time Matt reaches the bridge he has almost forty people with him. They split up, a score on either side of the bridge's debouchment, not really noticeable among all the other bystanders crowding the pavement and the way, and once again watch the parade pass and keep watch. Let it all get past this chokepoint, follow it over the bridge, then overtake the more vulnerable sections and join up with the dockworkers for the final potential flashpoint. That's without a doubt the most dangerous of all, what with angry dockers, heathen lads with a bit too much alcohol and cannabis and adrenaline in their blood, and the nervy new PA militia in the mix.

Annie's standing beside him, grinning, barely out of breath. Matt shares his beer with her, and as he watches the now-familiar forward half of the march go by—there go the science students again, and their giant cardboard microscope with a white-coated student, a giant foil pin projecting from his midriff, wriggling on its slide and waving cheerfully—his brain catches up with what its subroutines have been mulling over all the while.

It's the sight of a truck bed with two-meter-high imitation test tubes racked on it, with plastic extensions to the exhaust pipe ingeniously funnelled through to make fumes come out of the tubes, that suddenly crystalizes a suspicion from his inchoate thoughts: Avakian!

All the connections click into place. The apothecary has a commercial relationship with the Rodriguezes, heathen contacts who trade in legitimate (and possibly other) medicinals, and knows enough about the fabrication units and the drive's construction to supply convincing details.

Matt turns around, leans over the stone parapet, and drops his empty bottle on the low-tide boulders below. It shatters with a satisfying crash.

"Bit antisocial of you," Annie reproves.

"You're right. Damn." Matt turns back, slightly contrite. "I just figured out who's behind today's big provocation, and it's a guy I thought was a friend."

"Just because you're paranoid doesn't mean they aren't out to get you," says Annie.

Matt marvels momentarily at the staying power of old anarchist saws. She probably thinks that if voting changed anything they'd make it illegal, and . . . but this is being patronizing, she's the most solid and reliable and political person he's met all day. A big boxy float negotiates the corner on to the bridge, then one stacked with multicolored bales, and the next is a four-meter-long model of a starship, very light because it's being carried on poles on the shoulders of just four men, and behind them another big cardboard imitation crate, planking sketched on it in splashy lines of black paint . . . Matt suddenly realizes that he's watching the dockers' union contingent.

And strolling along with them, chatting amiably, is a skinny young man with a briefcase under his arm. Endecott sees Matt at the same moment and makes a gesture of apology to the docker he's speaking with and nips smartly out of the parade and over.

"Hi, Matt," he says, with a quick polite nod to Annie and a wary glance over her comrades. "Christ, I've been looking for you everywhere."

"I could say the same," says Matt, though in truth he has almost forgotten in the heat and rush. "I'm afraid there'll be trouble down at the docks."

"Yeah, tell me about it. Since that story broke I've been . . ." He jerks a thumb over his shoulder. "Half the goddamn union branch didn't even come on the march. They're probably sitting in pubs working themselves up to bash some heathen heads."

"Bad news. What about the Party branch?"

Endecott's sandy eyebrows twitch, very slightly.

"They're solid. Most of them."

"What party?" Annie asks suspiciously.

"Uh, later," says Matt. He has an absurd flash-forward of her taking Endecott to task over Kronstadt, Makhno, the Barcelona Telephone Exchange . . . "Think your backsliding dockers are likely to throw rocks at the parade?"

Endecott winces. "Worse. Lading tackle. Big lumps of metal."

"Christ! Got any plans to deal with it?"

"Damn right I have." He glances again at the squad, and its counterpart across the road, and at the heathens just now war-dancing their way toward them at the front of the Back-o'-the-Docks contingent. "Looks like somebody else has plans too."

"Everybody's stepped up their security a bit," Matt says truthfully but economically. "That's why it's been peaceful so far."

"Well, I better get going, catch you later."

And he's gone, sprinting after the departing dockers' floats, now cresting the middle of the bridge.

"You know," Annie says, "these floats are very *dull*, except for that starship thing. Look like last-minute jobs, if you see what I mean."

Matt nods, winks, and gives a thumbs-up.

"Oh, look at the boys," she says.

The vanguard of the heathen lads are going by, dusty but with energy undimmed, still keeping up their high-stepping dance, still giving the spirits of the air a bruising with their staves and spears. Several of them shout what sound like admiring or jeering comments at Annie, in the heathen speech, and she yells back in the same language.

"Meant to ask," says Matt. "You a heathen yourself?"

"Grandparents were," she says. "So yes, I'm a heathen. Had to learn the language myself, mind. My parents are kind of touchy about it."

The Back-o'-the-Docks and heathen contingent, the last of the parade, the least respectable and the most influential and imitated and talked about, now fills the riverside road and turns on to the bridge, rank after rank, and between the ranks open spaces to make room for a particularly energetic dancer or extravagant costume or gigantic stilt walker or dangerous juggler making swords spin in the sun. The bands, discordant at a distance, become harmonious as they pass, the sound of each temporarily drowning out the rest. Mollyboys pout and pose and blow kisses at bystanders, or navigate ships of skirt with entranced panache. The heathen girls skip and pirouette, energetic as the boys who toyi-toyi along the sides of the parade. And at regular intervals among them, rifles at port arms, marching to a different drum, are the members of two militias: the one from Gail's neighborhood, and the one from Loudon's factory.

He calls up Gail on the radio.

"Time to go," he says.

"Acknowledged," she says.

It doesn't seem long before the whole of the rest of the parade's gone by, and the two halves of the squad nip in behind it before the bystanders who want to join in can get in front of them. So with that growing crowd behind them, they make their way across the bridge and out on to the shore road, toward the docks.

Eleven gliders were already in the air, circling up on the thin thermal above the nearest buildings. Gail brought the car around and drove back to the starting point, the launch trailer bumping across the grass, and saw that Stone was the next in line. She turned the car and trailer around, braked, idled the engine, and stepped out. Stone stood with one hand holding the frame of the wing, the other arm coming around in an awkward hug.

"Oh, Stone, take care," she said.

They only had a moment. Timing was everything.

"I will," he said.

He lifted the glider over his head and his shoulders, settled the harness around him and buckled up, and carried the glider over to the trailer and stepped on. For a sentimental moment Gail saw the glider as his carnival costume. Then she swung back into the seat, checked that the launch path was clear and that Stone was properly braced on the trailer, and gunned the car forward, faster and faster, and after a hunder meters his shadow passed over her, and the glider soared to join the bottom of the circling stack.

The glider at the top of the stack broke away and swooped toward the far side of the town, toward the shore.

Annie and Matt chivvy the squads into a run, and they overtake most of the parade. Just before they reach the long front of the quays, about twenty dockworkers detach themselves from the side of a building and fall in beside them. They all slow to a walk.

"Shit, this all we've got?" Dave Borden says.

"Never said there'd be more," says Matt. "But it's not all."

"The militias, and some heathens hopping about? Don't make me laugh."

"We'll soon see who's laughing," says Matt. "What's it like up ahead?"

"I've had a look," says Borden. "There're hundreds of 'em, not just dockers, on the quay just past that warehouse. See that line of PA cops? The crowd's about twenty meters to the right of that. They're just yelling for now, but you wait, soon as they see the heathens and the Back-o'-the-Docks lot, they'll start chucking stuff. And then they'll walk over the cops—it's a token line, a dozen or so—and steam right into us."

Matt can imagine all that, and for a moment it's not the political consequences of such a riot that fill his mind but an image of all the fragile beauty of the girls and the mollyboys getting stamped on like butterflies. He wishes that Rawliston's version of queer masculinity had run to tough gays, all muscle and leather and chains, instead of transgenderal effeminacy. But history hasn't given them that, and—

"You fight with what you have," he concludes aloud, and Borden, surprisingly, gives him a thumbs-up and dodges away to liaise with Annie and the other squad leaders.

In a minute or two they've arrived. There's an open space of a couple of hundred meters in front of a wide quay whose edge is about a hundred meters back of the shore road, and the now twenty-odd PA militia members are spread out just in from the sidewalk, with huge gaps between them, backs to the parade, facing a crowd of, oh fuck, something near a thousand and something like a stone's throw away. The section of the dockers angered by the story have built a popular front in reverse, pulling in a coalition of the discontented and bigoted and scared. The dockers form a disciplined front rank, and behind them is a disorderly and noisy crowd, like the one that had gathered outside the grogshop but more determined. It bristles with staves, and a scatter of anti-Dawsonite and other placards, and here and there helmets glint beside rifle barrels—some of the PA militia who fought on the wrong side, discharged but evidently not disarmed, must be in the mob. It's still growing—there's a steady stream of people arriving along the quay from the same direction as the parade's moving, and Matt speculates sickly that some of the people deterred at other flashpoints have had the same idea as he has and concentrated their forces on this.

There's no point in trying not to provoke them. They're already provoked. So the squads form up on the sidewalk between and behind the cops, in five groups, with their staves up and the picks and shovels clearly visible. This is exactly the kind of situation they're good for. Matt can hear nothing but the booming of drums and the booing of the enemy. Which section's going by? He glances over his shoulder. The students. Their militia officer cadet group has already gone past. Damn. Shouldn't have expected anything else, unless they came under attack themselves.

But the first heathen boys are running up and gathering together in the gaps between the squads. There are a lot of gaps to fill in that two-hundred-meter line, and the spaces still gape, but Matt hopes that the main heathen group doesn't run ahead of the contingent it's supposed to be guarding.

A clattering din behind him and a rush of booted feet. Matt turns to see Endecott's dockers' floats slowing, men swarming over them, and the cardboard crates collapsing outward and the brightly colored covers of the bales flapping away. The clatter and the rush are the sounds of dockers throwing down pallets hacked and adapted as wooden shields and picking them up and running forward. They're also grabbing and carrying short thick sticks and, terrifyingly, long steel hooks.

Scores of them run through the gaps and form a line a few meters in front of the cops. Others form a similar line behind where Matt's standing. They have far more shields than they need themselves and are urging passing heathens and militia members to grab them and raise a shield wall along the line of the parade.

Matt is jostled again and sees more and more heathen lads filling in the line and hears the distinctive beat of the heathen drums, and he glances over his shoulder and sees the pretty people passing, hurrying, and he glimpses

behind the still-forming shield wall Slow Leg directing
another line of heathen boys with their spears horizontal,
holding back any of their fellows who want to plunge
in from the crowd.

There's just enough space for the squad members to
move. Matt props his stave against his shoulder just as
the first black shapes come hurtling down. The first vol-
ley falls mostly on the line of union dockers up front,
thudding on the shields, or just behind them, and then
the second shower of scrap arrives, this time striking
home—screams, bleeding heads, somebody nearby falls
thrashing. The enemy crowd surges forward, stops, the
dockers fling again. This time Matt sees the objects hur-
tle overhead, hears the freak hailstorm rattle of them on
the wooden shields behind, and more screams.

He's pushed forward, out in front of the cops, just
behind the union dockers' line, and they're glancing
back and everyone on either side of him is looking at
him, and he sees Annie's full-beam grin ten meters to
his left, and they nod to each other and turn away and
Matt says quietly, above the uproar, "In your own time,
comrades, please."

And runs forward.

Rawliston crawled beneath his face. The air was warmer
than he was used to flying in, the thermals stronger. Heat
haze and sweat distorted his view. Once or twice he
riskily removed the goggles to spit in them and wipe
smearily with a thumb and to blot his eyebrows with his
wrist. Ahead of him and to his left, those who'd taken
off before him were spread out in a straggly V formation
like migrating wing-lizards.

The pistol was heavy at his waist, the two bombs a
drag on either wing. Stone, like the others, had practiced
flying with weights beforehand, but something—perhaps
the knowledge of the danger these earthenware pots contained—made the real thing more awkward.

The leading flyer banked away from the road they

were following, and they all wheeled after him, flying
along and down, toward the docks.

Matt clears the union dockers' shield line, and his racing
feet are off the cobbles of the street and on to the thun-
dering timbers of the quay. The distance closes fast because the other side is running forward too. The last
thing Matt sees before they close is the now useless
wooden shields flying over his head and into the enemy's faces. He's unaware of how he's carrying his
stave until he sees the man whose chest it cannons into
stagger and fall, under feet that take him down like a
quicksand.

Matt brings the stave up just in time to deflect the
slashing downward swing of a stave wielded by the man
behind the man he hit. And then the end of his stave is
under his opponent's chin, and they're both pressed forward by those behind them, and that's it. Blood sprays
Matt's face, slicks the stave. He sees the man die by
inches, inches away.

Then it's too close even for that; it's the crushing
furious intimacy of fist and face, forehead and nose, fingers and eyes, elbows and kidneys, knee and groin. Matt
feels, or rather hears, his own lips mash and teeth crack.
He spits blood and a tooth in a face, head-butts, then
he's sliding down and unable to move.

A whirring and whizzing noise overhead. A snatched
upward glimpse of a whole flight of staves hurled as
spears falling into the crush in front. Then another, and
another. The locked crowds sway backward and forward,
but neither yields.

Then a different sound comes from above, and at the
same time a shadow passes overhead, swift as a blink.

How hard it was, at this speed, at this altitude, to tell
the crowds apart. The two struggling masses were one,
and the fault line between them all but invisible. All that
Stone could do—following the example of the first

flyer—was to aim for the half of the crowd nearest to the quayside. He swooped low, just above the level of the tall four-story buildings on either side of the crowd, and tugged the toggles as he passed over the roadway and the long colorful line of the parade.

The glider jolted upward as the bombs were released. Stone fought to control it and couldn't follow the forward arc of the fall. He zoomed into a climb that carried him above choppy gray water and masts that seemed to reach up for his feet, and banked around. A quick glance down and to his left, to see the bright flames blossom, and then he had to concentrate on flying.

Bangs and flames and screams. The chest that Matt's face is shoved up against suddenly eases its pressure, and Matt gets enough clearance to drive a fist into its solar plexus. Then he's stumbling forward, shoving the man back, then gaps open out in front of him and then it's running fights all over the quay. The firebombs have splashed blazing petrol in dozens of places. Some people are rolling about, clothes and hair burning, others are trying to beat out their flames, and a few are running frantically to jump into the sea. Those who haven't been hit are scattering. Matt picks up a stick and joins in the fury of the pursuit, lashing at fleeing backs. He sees out of the corner of his eye a heathen mollyboy, with nothing but blue tatters around his bare legs, deliver a perfect floating drop-kick at a face full of surprise. He sees Annie cracking a renegade militiaman's rifle with her stave. He sees more burns than he ever wants to remember. And then it's a rout, and then it's over.

Matt leaves Borden to organize some of the union dockers for their next big task and then he and Annie run back to the main street and jog up past the procession, much of which is oblivious to what's just happened, though rumors are spreading fast.

Up ahead, the religious part of the procession has

passed on down the street and is turning a corner to the main harbor entrance. The colorful, carnival part of it is turning in the opposite direction, into Back-o'-the-Docks. Some of the heathen lads—from Rawliston and the Vale—are forming small groups and sprinting off down alleyways and streets.

A growing number—hundreds, now—of other heathen warriors are forming up in ranks, right here where the factory and neighborhood militia platoons are falling out, leaving the main sections they accompany to move on, to the ceremony or the big street party according to taste. Heathen and Christian unit commanders are liaising and negotiating, sometimes quite loudly.

"That's it," says Matt. "We're done."

He stops running and leans against the wall of an office building. His back slides down it until he's sitting on the ground, hands on his crooked knees, looking up at Annie.

"What's going on?" she asks.

"Just another coup," he says. "The neighborhood and factory militias are about to march off and unseat the Council of Notables, seize a few public buildings, and so forth. Together with the heathens, who think they're invading and conquering Rawliston with some help from local allies, poor chaps. Between them they should walk over the PA militia."

She glares down at him. "You set this up?"

He shrugs. "More or less."

"Aren't you going to take part in your coup?"

"No," says Matt. "They can look after themselves, and anyway there's a bigger fight brewing. All these people we chased off are going to regroup, spread the news, and sometime in the next few hours they and the anti-Dawsonites and all the other rabble are going on the biggest rampage through Back-o'-the-Docks and the heathen district this town has ever seen."

"Shit," she says. "Yeah, I can see that, all right. We'll have to be ready."

He struggles to his feet. Annie is scanning the street, spotting and beckoning her comrades. He looks at her with a sort of hopeless admiration. She really is a heathen amazon. There's nothing he wants to do more, between now and the pickup, than to join the street parties at Back-o'-the-Docks until the fighting starts, and then slip away.

She's rounded up the posse.

She cocks him an eyebrow.

"Oh, all right," he says.

Stone brought the glider down in the middle of a street in Back-o'-the-Docks, just in front of the first flood of people into the beginning of the street party. He ran on hard cobbles, slowed to a stop, ducked out from under the wing, and found himself looking at hundreds of people, all of whom were cheering. It took him a few seconds to realize that they were cheering for him.

He walked forward, carrying the glider, and waited at the edge of the crowd—most people were already turning their attention to drinking and dancing—for one of the sky people's captains to find him. A man from Long Bridge strode out of the crowd and held up a spear and a rifle, and shook them.

"Well done, woman," he said to Stone. "Now let us put away the glider and join the people who have gone to build barricades."

"I have a radio message to send first," said Stone.

He borrowed the captain's walkie-talkie and let Gail know he was all right. They stashed the glider in an alleyway, agreed that there wasn't much chance of their ever recovering it, and gathered up some more sky people and some of the locals and walked away from the music and noise and smoke, down empty streets to the edge of the quarter.

"Here," said the captain, whose name was Hard Fist.

They stopped. The street was narrow and opened on to a square from which other, wider streets radiated into a hostile neighborhood. Every shop in this street had its windows boarded up—it was a traditional route for the traditional back-and-forth running fights that annually broke out as the festival came to an end.

A couple of hours of hard work followed. Vehicles, doors, and furniture—some of the material volunteered by its owners, most of it not—were dragged into position across the street. Bottles were filled with petrol, bricks were stockpiled, and stashes of both carried up to rooftops and upstairs rooms with windows overlooking the square. The team that Stone had joined coordinated with other teams by radio, and more and more people drifted out of the street parties and pitched in. Militias of any color were nowhere to be seen—they were all fully occupied with either overthrowing the provisional government or defending it. Occasionally a distant rattle of gunfire echoed, or a piece of news became amplified into rumor.

Stone heaved and dragged, sucked splinters out of his hands, pushed and hauled. The sun was lowering but the air was still hot. He was filthy and sweaty, but he didn't care. There were about sixty people in the street now, heathens and mollyboys and sky people and local residents, and the whole process had become a small carnival in itself, despite or because of the seriousness of its purpose.

The barricade was barely completed when the first attack came. A group of about forty young men suddenly charged out from one of the side streets of the square, gathered behind the defunct fountain in the middle, and started throwing stones. Then, when everyone behind the barricade had ducked down, a petrol bomb crashed in front of it and set it alight.

Hard Fist stuck his rifle through a gap and fired off a couple of shots. The attackers scattered, giving the defenders just enough time to dowse the fire.

"No more shooting," said Hard Fist. "We save that for if they break through."

The next attack came within half an hour. This time, the crowd filled the square. Stones, bricks and bottles, and petrol bombs hurtled in both directions. Skirmish parties from both sides forayed and clashed. For Stone, events became disjointed; at one moment he was reaching for the last brick in a pile, the next he was behind broken glass, looking down at the square and seeing a petrol bomb burst and knowing he had just thrown it but not knowing how.

An old heathen woman, gap-toothed, was yelling in his ear, "Why don't you *use* your bloody *gun?*"

He turned to her, as she rummaged in the wreckage of her bedroom for something else to throw.

"Just hold on," he said, "hold on," and ran down the stairs. Outside, he could feel the evening breeze, the wind from the mountains and the west, and he looked up and saw the first lights from the braziers of the hot-air balloon train fleet drifting toward them across the sky.

Then, above all the shouting and the crashing and the occasional shot, he heard the drone of aircraft.

Gail took the radio message and leaned past the windshield and tapped Loudon's shoulder. He looked back. She pointed down. He gave a thumbs-up and took the plane into a dive. Away below them, at about a thousand feet, the primitive airship fleet they'd circled above for the past twenty minutes wallowed across the town, painfully slowly. Columns of smoke rose from the streets around the docks; here and there across the town, Gail could see flames. Ahead, from somewhere up the coast, came two Port Authority seaplanes, frighteningly fast.

Matt's plan had allowed for the possibility that not all the Port Authority's aircraft would be in the hands of the assembly-loyal militias by the time the second wave of the Great Vale's air force—bomber command, as he'd wryly called it—had arrived over Rawliston.

Gail checked the mounted machine gun's ammunition

belt and made sure the sights were adjusted for the probable range. She clutched its double grips, swung it into the firing position, and moved around on the seat until she was uncomfortably crouched behind it.

For a moment the two seaplanes looked like sitting ducks as they headed straight for the balloon trains. The Kondrakov-LeBrun had the advantage of surprise and the low sun behind it. But a burst of machine-gun fire from somebody in a swaying gondola—Gail could imagine it, all too vividly—missed wildly and sent the first seaplane into a steep evasive climb. It flashed past Gail's eyes, a couple of hundred feet away, quicker than she could do anything about. She tracked it as it banked at the top of its ascent and dived toward the KL-3B.

Loudon took the plane into a screaming loop. Gail felt that all the bones in her spine were being compressed. The maneuver worked: The seaplane, slower and heavier and with greater air resistance, couldn't match the turn. The other enemy aircraft had overflown the slow balloon trains and was now turning around. She had it in her sights, steady, for a second or two, and squeezed off a burst. The ammunition belt thrashed across her knees, the spent casings sprayed past her face.

Missed.

The KL-3B dived, banked, and they were in level flight again, and the first seaplane was flying in parallel a hundred meters away. Its pilot made the fatal mistake of banking away. Gail's next burst raked the underside of the craft, and it fell, spinning.

She didn't have time to follow it. The second seaplane was now on their tail. Neither aircraft had a forward-firing gun, and she couldn't swing her own gun around to fire back. The enemy stayed behind them despite Loudon's attempts so shake it off. He swung around again and flew toward the leading balloon train. The seaplane followed, and a burst from the balloon train, better aimed this time, took it down.

* * *

Matt crouches at a street corner behind an overturned cart and watches an entire riot scatter as petrol and blast bombs rain from above. He can see, in the darkening sky and through smoke, other lights moving and fires falling. Somebody in the fleeing crowd has the presence of mind to stop and shoot upward at the balloon train overhead.

The hot-air bags are punctured and start sagging instantly, then flames lick up them, blazing faster and faster as the contraption falls. The gondola's ropes burn, too, and it breaks loose and hurtles out of the sky and smashes into the street. Nobody in it has the smallest chance of survival. The burning balloons drift forward and down, onto roofs. More fires spring up.

But the street stays clear, the attack has been beaten off. The sheer shock of being attacked from the air has done more to demoralize the enemy than the physical effect of the bombs has damaged them. Matt and Gail retreat from the front line a few blocks to a secure area. Most of the other balloon-trains, lightened of their lethal loads, are drifting eastward and down, toward the sea.

Matt looks at his watch. It's eight-thirty local time. Annie is grabbing some refreshment. He smiles at her happy, grubby, fierce face as she swigs back the beer and looks at him inquiringly.

"I'm needed down at the docks," he says. He waves skyward and seaward. "Search and rescue—the balloons have to ditch in the sea, and we have to send boats to pull the flyers out."

"Ah," says Annie. "So that's why holding the docks was so important."

"Yeah. Shouldn't take more than an hour." Matt touches her arm. "Catch you later."

She grins widely. "Yeah, I'll be around here. Look after yourself."

He turns away and runs. Maybe she has the heathen superstition about good-byes, maybe she'd have been just as casual if she didn't think she'd be seeing him again in an hour or two. It makes him feel slightly better.

So, just as this morning, he's jogging through Back-o'-the-Docks. Bizarrely, knots of people are partying on, side by side with groups hurrying to or from the fighting. He's running along a dark stretch of road between two pubs when he sees a familiar figure walking briskly along the pavement, alone, carrying a big black bag. Avakian.

Matt doesn't think twice. He comes cannoning out of the middle of the road and has the apothecary bodily displaced two meters sideways and slammed up against a wall in a dark alcove, and a knife at his throat, in about three seconds.

"Matt . . ." Avakian croaks.

"Talk," says Matt. "You blabbed to the Rodriguezes, didn't you? What did they do—threaten you, or just get you drunk?"

"Jesus Christ," Avakian pleads, "what are you talking about?"

He lets his black bag fall. It clinks and rattles as it hits the street.

"I've been doing first aid for hours," he says. "I have no idea what—"

"What sparked most of this mess *off*," says Matt. Letting the blade prick. "That story about the heathens, about the ships, right?"

Avakian blinks. "Oh!" he says. He reflexively makes the smallest possible shake of the head, winces, then holds very still as a bead of blood wells on his neck.

"That wasn't me," he says. "Why the fuck would I do that? The Rodriguezes have been cold-shouldering me ever since we came back. They weren't pleased at how we used them as a cover when we took the ship." He grins desperately. "The party invitations have kind of dried up."

This sounds entirely plausible. The only way Avakian could have been the source of this story would have been unwillingly or unwittingly, and either way he'd be contrite, not denying it.

"Shit." Matt releases Avakian, makes the knife vanish like a magic trick, and takes a step back. "Shit. Sorry, Armen. Shake."

Shaken indeed, Avakian grasps his hand. "I don't blame you," he says. "I knew it wasn't me, so I know who it must have been. Christ, I could kill him myself."

"Yeah." Matt frowns at him for a moment. "Yeah, well maybe I just will. See you again, mate."

He runs on. Strange to be running through the same streets as in the morning. Strange to look up at the passing lights in the sky, to have seen that brief battle in the air, and to reflect that the next battles here could be in space.

He's appalled by the chaos and blood of the past hours but at the same time satisfied with what he's done. Turning the heathens' hopeless assault into an adjunct to the uprising may affect, even determine, what kind of society exists here when the aliens come, whether it's in a year or a century or longer. A society that might just be able to meet them and win them over, as Salasso had urged, instead of a society bristling with suspicion that can only meet fire with fire.

And even if that doesn't work out—and who can say, so far ahead?—he suspects that this will be the last riot on St. Teilhard's Day. The local heathens are no longer without allies, no longer an easy target, and the Great Vale can command respect. For the day, it's enough.

Lydia stood at the foot of the skiff's ladder, on the far end of the traders' quay. Smoke roiled above the nearby streets. Out of it, one by one, drifted the balloon-trains, carried by the wind over the edge of the dock area to sink toward the sea. Some of them had already ditched, far out, floating briefly like ceremonial paper lanterns. Powered boats rushed among them recovering their crews.

Matt was late, and every minute he was late reduced the amount of time she'd have to give him a piece of her mind and increased the time she had for her anger to build. By the time he came panting and thudding up the quay, smoke-blackened and ragged and red-eyed, she had concentrated everything down to one phrase.

"Fuck you, Matt Cairns."

He looked gratifyingly taken aback by that.

"What?" he gasped. He stood with his hands on his knees, his chest heaving, and stared up at her.

"You're not coming with us," she said.

He straightened up. "Why not?" He grinned wryly. "I've shown what I can do to muck up Volkov's schemes."

Lydia felt her fists clench. "Yes, by schemes of your own! You're as dangerous as he is! Either one of you is bad enough! I wouldn't want the two of you on the same *planet*!"

He frowned, then smiled and shrugged. "Shouldn't you be on the ship by now?"

"Yes," she said.

A saur's voice called her, urgently. She ascended the ladder and turned at the top to see Matt looking up.

"There will be other ships," he said.

The following is
a sneak preview of

ENGINE
CITY

The wondrous concluding volume of
the Engines of Light sequence

COMING JANUARY 2003
FROM TOR BOOKS

1

The Advancement of Learning

THE JUMP IS instantaneous. To a photon, the whole history of the universe may be like this: over in a flash, before it's had time to blink. To a human, it's disorienting. One moment, you're an hour out from the last planet you visited—then, without transition, you're an hour away from the next.

Volkov spent the first of these hours preparing for his arrival, conscious that he would have no time to do so in the second.

My name is Grigory Andreievich Volkov. I am two hundred and forty years old, I was born about a hundred thousand years ago, and as many light-years away: Kharkov, Russian Federation, Earth, in the year 2018. As a young conscript, I fought in the Ural Caspian Oil War. I was with the first troops to enter Marseilles and to bathe their sore feet in the waters of the Mediterranean. In 2040, I became a cosmonaut of the European Union, and three years later made the first human landing on the surface of Venus. In 2046 I volunteered for work on the space station *Marshal Titov*, which in 2049 was renamed the *Bright Star*. It became the first human-controlled starship. In it I traveled to the Second Sphere. For the past two centuries I have lived on Mingulay and Croatan.

This is my first visit to Nova Terra. I hope to bring you . . .

What? The secret of immortality?

Yes. *The secret of immortality*. That would do.

Strictly speaking, what he hoped to bring was the secret of longevity. But he had formed an impression of the way science was conducted on Nova Terra: secular priestcraft, enlightened obscurantism; alchemy, philosophy, scholia. A trickle of inquiry after immortality had exhausted hedge-magic, expanded herbalism, lengthened little but grey beards and the index of the Pharmacopia, and remained respectable. Volkov expected to be introduced to the Academy as a prodigy. Before the shaving-mirror, he polished his speech and rehearsed his Trade Latin.

The suds and stubble swirled away. He slapped a stinging cologne on his cheeks, gave himself an encouraging smile, and stepped out of the cramped washroom. The ship's human quarters were sparse and provisional. In an emergency, or at the owners' convenience, they could be flooded. In normal operation, it was usual to travel in one or other of the skiffs, which at this moment were racked on the vast curving sides of the forward chamber like giant silver platters. The air smelled of paint and seawater; open channels and pools divided the floor, and on the walls enormous transparent pipes contained columns of water that rose or fell, functioning as lifts for the ship's crew. Few humans, and fewer saurs, were about in the chamber. Volkov strolled along a walkway. At its end, a low rail enclosed the pool of the navigator. Eyes the size of beach balls reflected racing bands of color from the navigator's chromatophores and the surrounding instrumentation. Wavelets from the rippling mantle perturbed the water. Lashing tentacles broke the surface as they played over the controls.

Volkov was halfway up the ladder to the skiff in which he had spent most, and intended to spend the rest, of the brief journey, when the lightspeed jump took place. The sensation was so swift and subtle that it did not endanger his step or grasp. He was aware that it had happened, that was all. In a moment of idle curiosity—for he'd never been within sight of a ship's controller at such a moment—he glanced sideways and down, to the watery cockpit twenty-odd meters below.

The navigator floated in the middle of the pool. His body had turned an almost translucent white. Volkov was perturbed, but could think of nothing better to do than scramble faster up the ladder to the skiff.

The door opened and he stepped inside, rejoining his hosts. Esias de Tenebre stood staring at the display panel, as though he could read the racing glyphs that to Volkov meant nothing. Feet well apart, hands in his trouser pockets, his stout and muscular frame bulked further by his heavy sweater, his shock of hair spilling from under his seaman's cap. Though in the rough-duty clothes that merchants traditionally wore on board ship, he had all the stocky and cocky dignity of Holbein's Henry—one who did not kill his wives, all three of whom stood beside him. Lydia, the daughter of Esias and Faustina, lounged on the circular seat around the central engine fairing behind her parents, returning Volkov's appeasing look with sullen lack of interest. Black hair you could swim in, brown eyes you could drown in, golden skin you could bask in. Her oversized sweater and baggy canvas trousers only added to her charm. The other occupant of the vehicle was its pilot, Voronar, who sat leaning forward past Esias.

"What's going on?"

The saur's elliptical eyes spared Volkov a glance, then returned to the display.

"Nothing out of the ordinary," said Voronar. His large head, which lent his slender reptilian body an almost infantile proportion, tipped forward, then nodded. "We are an hour away from Nova Terra."

"Could you possibly show us the view?" said Esias.

"Your pardon," said Voronar.

He palmed the controls, and the entire surrounding wall of the skiff became pseudotransparent, patching data from the ship's external sensors and automatically adjusting brightness and contrast: Nova Sol's glare was turned down, the crescent of Nova Terra muted to a cool blue, its night side enhanced. Scattered clusters of crowded lights pricked the dark like pleiads.

"That's a lot of cities," Volkov said.

Compared with anywhere else he'd seen in the Second Sphere, if not with the Earth he remembered, it was.

"There's only one that matters," said Esias. He did not need to point it out.

Nova Babylonia was the jewel of the Second Sphere. Its millennia-old culture, and its younger but still ancient republican institutions, made it peacefully hegemonic on Nova Terra, and beyond. The temperate zones of Nova Terra's continents were placid parks, where even wildernesses were carefully planned landscape features. All classes of its people were content. Academicians and artists assimilated the latest ideas and styles that trickled in over the millennia from Earth; patricians and politicians debated cordially and congratulated themselves on their fortune in knowing, and avoiding, the home world's terrible mistakes. Merchants traded the rare goods of many worlds. Artisans and laborers enjoyed the advantages of a division of labor far wider than any the human species could have sustained on its own. Emigration was free, but the proportion of emigrants insignificant. The hominidae cheerfully tended and harvested the sources of raw materials, and the saurs and krakens exchanged their advanced products and services for those of human industry and craft. As an older and wiser species, the saurs were consulted to settle disputes, and as a more powerful species, they intervened to prevent any from getting out of hand.

The lights of Nova Babylonia shone just short of the terminator, and somewhat to the north of the halfway point between the pole and the equator. Genea, the continent on whose eastern shore the city stood, sprawled diagonally across the present night side of the planet and southward into the day and the southern hemisphere. Its ragged coastline counterpointed that of the other major continent, Sauria, a couple of thousand kilometers west: the two looked as though they had been pulled apart and displaced, one northward, the other south. Much of the southern and western part of Sauria was wrapped out of sight around the other side of the planet, at this moment; in the visible part, even at this distance, the rectangular regularity of some of its green patches distinguished manufacturing plant from jungle and plain.

"Do any humans live in Sauria?" Volkov asked.

Esias shrugged. "A few thousand, maybe, at any one time. Short-term contract employees, traders, people involved in travel infrastructure and big-game hunting. Likewise with saurs in Genea—lots of individuals, no real communities, except around the hospitals and health services."

Hospitals and health services, yes, Volkov thought, that could be a problem.

"What about the other hominidae?"

"Ah, that's a more usual distribution, except that they have entire cities of their own." Esias pointed; it wasn't much help. "Gigants here, pithkies there. Forests and mines, even some farming. More of a surprise than the cities, that; it's only developed in the last few centuries. They've always been herding, of course."

As the ship's approach zoomed the view, the city and its surroundings expanded and sharpened. The immediate vicinity and hinterland of the city was a long, triangular promontory, about a thousand kilometers from northwest to southeast and five hundred across at its widest extent. It looked like a smaller and narrower India: an island that had rammed the continent at an angle. Very likely it was—the ice of a spectacular and recent mountain range glittered white across the join. The west coast of this mini subcontinent was separated from the mainland of Genea by a semicircular sea, three hundred kilometers across at its widest, its shore curving to almost meet the end of the promontory just south of the metropolis. From the mountains sprang a dozen or so rivers whose confluence channeled about halfway down to one major river, which flowed into the sea near the tapered tip. The central, and oldest, part of Nova Babylonia was on an island about ten kilometers long that looked wedged in that river's mouth.

The city drifted off center in the view, then swung out of sight entirely as the ship leveled up for its run into the atmosphere. Why the great starships approached on what resembled a long, shallow glide path was unknown, and certainly unnecessary, but it was what they always did. The air reddened around the ship's field and, following another unnecessary and invariable habit, its human passengers returned to their seats.

Volkov leaned on the rail of the open sea-level deck of the starship and gasped morning-cool fresh air. The starship had, to the best of his knowledge, no air-recycling or air-circulating mechanisms whatsoever, and after a couple of hours even its vast volume of air grew slightly but noticeably stale. Around him, unregarded, the ship's unlading went on, bales into boats and sometimes into skiffs. The machinery that he had imported from Mingulay and Croatan—marine engines and diving equipment, mostly—would be a small fraction of the de Tenebres' cargo, and that itself insignificant beside the wares of the ship's real owners and major traders, the krakens. Beneath him, the ship's field pressed down like an invisible, flexible sheet on the waves, flattening them to a waterbed wobble. Under that rippling glassy surface, the krakens from the ship and from the local sea flashed greetings to each other. Off to Volkov's right, behind the bulk of the ship, the sun was just up, its low full beam picking out the city, about a mile away across the water, in rectangles of white glare and long triangles of black shade. Ten thousand years of heaping one stone upon another had stacked the architectures of antiquity to the heights of modernity. A marble Manhattan, massive yet soaring, it looked like something from the mind of a Speer with humanity, or a Stalin with taste. The avenues that slotted the island metropolis from east to west were so broad that Volkov could see the sky on the far side through the one directly opposite him. Bridges, sturdy as ribs, joined both shores to districts that stood, less grand only by contrast, on either bank.

Starships by the score dotted the broad estuary. Skiffs flitted back and forth between the sound and the city like Frisbees in a park. Long-limbed mammals like flying squirrels—this world's equivalent of birds—skimmed the waves and dived for fish and haunted the wakes of fishing boats in raucous flocks. Above the city, airships and gliders drifted, outpaced and dodged by the flashing skiffs. Between the starships, tall junks and clippers tacked in or out of the harbor and both branches of the river, and among them feluccas darted, their sails like the fins of a shoal of sharks. At this distance, the city's dawn din of millions of wheels and feet rose in a discernible and gradually increasing hum.

For a moment the immensity and solidity of the place made Volkov's heart sink. The stone crescendo that rose before his face was like some gigantic ship against whose bow history itself cleaved and fell back to slip along its flanks and leave a wake of churned millennia. And yet ultimately it was only an idea that kept it afloat and forging forward, a thought in millions of all-too-fragile skulls. Let them lose that thought, and in a year, the place would sink. Volkov had set himself the harder task of raising it, and at that, he felt weak.

He heard and smelt Lydia behind him, and turned as she stepped up to the rail. She gazed hungrily at the city, transfixed.

"Gods above," she said, "it's good to see it again." She smiled at him wryly. "And good to see it hasn't changed much." Another, more considering, look at the city. "Except it's higher."

"It's impressive," Volkov allowed.

"And you want to change it."

Volkov jerked a thumb over his shoulder at the work being done behind them. "You're the revolutionaries," he said. "Bring in enough books and ideas, and the city will change itself. All I want to do is make sure it's still there the next time you come back."

He grinned at her, controlling his features. His heart was making him shake inside. "If I believed in your people's ideas of courtship, I would offer it for your hand. I would tell Esias that I could take this city and lay it at your feet."

Lydia, to his surprise, blushed and blinked. "That's what Esias is afraid of," she said.

She stared away, as though weighing the city, and the suggestion.

"Gregor offered more," she added, "and he delivered it, too, but he didn't want me after all. No, I'm not open to that kind of offer. Not after that."

"I see," said Volkov. "I'll just have to fall back on my fine physique and engaging personality."

Lydia laughed. "I can never tell if you're joking or not."

"Neither can I," said Volkov in a gloomy tone.

She punched him lightly. "There you go again."

He turned to her, with a smile to cover his confusion, and even more to cover his calculation. He did not know how he felt, or what if anything his feelings meant. A few weeks earlier, his affair with Lydia's mother, Faustina, had come to a mutually agreeable end. He got on best with women of his own apparent age, or older;

preferably married, or otherwise unlikely to form a permanent—and from his point of view, all too temporary—attachment. He wasn't in love with Lydia, or even infatuated with her. He didn't think about her all the time. But whenever he saw her, he felt an electric jolt inside him, and he found it difficult to look away from her. It was embarrassing to find himself stealing glances like some besotted youth, but there it was.

At the other end of the scale, almost balancing that, there was the knowledge that in terms of Nova Babylonian—and Trader—custom, they were potentially good partners. Marriage was a business, affairs an avowed diversion; issue, inheritance, and fortune the only serious matters, over which geneticists and astrologers and matchmakers kept themselves profitably occupied.

In between, at the balance point, he and Lydia had developed a sort of tempestuous friendship, which every so often blew up in clashes in which his values and ideas appeared to her as a jaded cynicism, and her passionately held ethics to him seemed ancient prejudices, immaturely held. At the moment, their relationship was going through one of its calmer patches. He didn't know whether a squall would have been better. More bracing, certainly; but there was no need to bring it on. It would come of itself soon enough.

"Can we at least be friendly, for the moment?"

She smiled back. "You may be sly, Grigory Andreievich, but I do like you. Sometimes."

The first skiff slid out of its slot in the rack and skimmed across the navigation pool and out of one of the ship's side openings. It soared to an altitude of a couple of hundred meters and flew into the city, the other skiffs carrying the rest of the clan and the crew following one by one at intervals of about half a minute. Voronar took his time, evidently enjoying showing off to Volkov the city's towers and his own skill in flying between them.

From above, the city looked astonishingly green. Trees lined the streets, and stories rose in steps like terraces, many of which supported grass and gardens: the hanging gardens of Nova Babylonia, a wonder greater than their ancient original. Monkeys scrambled and swung on long vines and branches; goats grazed the lofty lawns and capered up or down external stairways; flying squirrels, their fur bright and various as the feathers of parakeets, flashed across the artificial canyons.

The skiff dipped, making the view tilt alarmingly while the internal gravity remained rock solid. Volkov glimpsed a buttress on which was carved an eagle, wings outspread to ten meters, and beneath it the inscriptions "IX" and "SPQR"; and then, before he could quite grasp the allusive stir of memory, they were past it and sidling in to a tower, down whose fifty-meter lower tier a column of neon spelled out DE TENEBRE. The skiff landed on one of the building's terraces and everyone except the pilot descended the ladder onto soft turf, and the skiff flitted away to make room for the rest of the skein.

"Sliding glass doors," Volkov murmured to Lydia, as they walked toward the entrance. "It's been a long time."

"Oh, so they had them on Earth?"

From the sliding doors emerged a crowd of the clan's retainers and office workers, and—as Volkov learned in the swirl of fast introductions as the new arrivals were ushered inside—members of the home-staying branch, the oldest of whom might remember from childhood someone old enough to have been alive when the ship had departed. Also in the crowd were saurs, for whom the past two centuries were an episode in their lives, and who swiftly renewed old acquaintances among their counterparts in the traveling crew. For all of them, human and saur alike, the return of the ship was a major event and a huge celebration. This floor of the building was evidently the function suite, a vast deck whose open space was only interrupted by support pillars, and on it a thousand or so people were partying. Most of them wore some kind of pleated kimonos, with variations in cloth, cut, texture, and pattern that differentiated the sexes in predictable ways. Others wore loose jackets and trousers, likewise varied.

Volkov circulated, nibbled and sipped, chatted discreetly. Esias's family and the few crew members who knew who Volkov really was had agreed to keep it to themselves and to the saurs, at least until the Academy, the Electorate, the Senate, and the Assembly of Notables had had a chance to consider the situation. He introduced himself as an immigrant marine engineer importing some new technology, which was true as far as it went. A slow circumnavigation of the room took him back to Lydia's orbit.

He gestured at his clothes and hers, then at those of the other revelers. "Doesn't this make you feel a little . . . underdressed for the occasion?"

Lydia brushed her hands on her hips, leaving crumbs on canvas. "Not at all," she said. "Traveling gear is the most prestigious garb at this party, I'll tell you that. If we were to come here in what were our best clothes when we left, we'd look as though we were in some kind of antique costume." She looked around critically. "Mind you, I can see where this sort of silk origami style came from, and I'm quite looking forward to trying it, but there's no way I'd change into it straight off the ship. I'd look as ridiculous as I'd feel."

"I doubt that."

Lydia acknowledged the compliment with a shake of the head. "And how do you feel?"

"Somewhat overwhelmed by all this, to tell you the truth. Not just the occasion, but the city."

"Aha," said Esias, looming into view behind a brandy balloon. "I detect a bad case of cultural cringe. I can see it in your eyes, Volkov. Relax, my friend. We're the hosts here, remember. And from our point of view, we attend such occasions every few months."

"Perhaps at the next one," Volkov murmured, "all the people here will be there."

Esias raised a finger, then winked. "But yes," he said, "an interesting thought . . . I've set some wheels in motion about a hearing from the Academy, by the way. It'll take a day or two, of course. In the meantime, I'll deal with the usual turnaround business, and you . . ."

"I'll sell machines," said Volkov.